NOT THAT I COULD TELL

ALSO BY JESSICA STRAWSER

Almost Missed You

NOT THAT I COULD TELL

JESSICA STRAWSER

St. Martin's Press
New York

NOT THAT I COULD TELL. Copyright © 2018 by Jessica Strawser. All rights reserved. Printed in the United States of America. For information, address St. Martin's Press, 175 Fifth Avenue, New York, N.Y. 10010.

www.stmartins.com

Designed by Donna Sinisgalli Noetzel

The Library of Congress Cataloging-in-Publication Data is available upon request.

ISBN 978-1-250-10788-6 (hardcover)
ISBN 978-1-250-10790-9 (ebook)

Our books may be purchased in bulk for promotional, educational, or business use. Please contact your local bookseller or the Macmillan Corporate and Premium Sales Department at 1-800-221-7945, extension 5442, or by email at MacmillanSpecialMarkets@macmillan.com.

First Edition: March 2018

10 9 8 7 6 5 4 3

For Skuk, and all the other strong women who
have touched my life

NOT THAT I COULD TELL

1

Ever wonder what your friends really think of you?

I take a lot of care in my appearance, for instance. I'm a small-town doctor's wife, so I need to look the part—even if I don't feel the part. And I have twins enrolled in pre-K at a charter school so obsessed with freethinking it will shove free thoughts down your throat. So I make sure it's obvious to everyone there what happy, healthy, cherished little people my kids are. I never forget to dress them in their pajamas for pajama day. I always sign up to bring the most elaborate snacks to the class parties. I help other moms in the parking lot when their pumpkin seats jam or their strollers collapse. I make a point of knowing all their names.

You probably think I care a lot about what my friends think.

I don't.

None of this charade is for them.

It's no great accomplishment to get someone to believe a lie. It's not that hard, really. Look at me: doctor's wife, working mom, good neighbor. You've already summed me up, haven't you? You're already filling in the blanks.

But whatever you're writing there, it's not the truth. And that's fine by me. It's easier, knowing you don't know me at all. Because as long as you believe that what you see is what you get, I get to stay this way. Poised. Devoted. Alive.

2

Everyone's Favorite Place!

—*Tagline of the Yellow Springs Chamber of Commerce*

Izzy awoke to a deafening downpour beating on the roof of her little Cape Cod. It reached through the dense fog of heavy sleep, through the punishing pain of the previous night's overindulgence, and tugged at the corner of her conscious mind just enough to pull it aside and reveal the too-familiar memory of Josh hovering there. In an instant, she regretted it all—the last glasses of wine that had brought on this ache and this haze, the humiliation of having told her new neighbors all they never needed to know about Josh, even the purchase of this house that placed the pounding rain just on the other side of the ceiling that sloped down to meet her bed.

How bad had it been? She squinted into the gray morning light, trying to remember exactly what she'd told them. The details of the later hours of the night were murky. She wasn't sure she even recalled the short walk home, come to think of it—alarming, though it was just across the street, and Yellow Springs was about as safe as small Ohio towns came. Funny how the brain could hold on to emotions—the warmth of shared laughter and the happy reckless sense of *oh, what the hell, why not* were still clear to her now—so much more tightly than the precise words or actions behind them. She usually wasn't one to overdo it on alcohol. But the other women, all moms with young kids, had been so ecstatic to have a night free, even though it was just a gathering around a backyard fire pit, baby monitors in hand—their enthusiasm had been contagious. She remembered Clara, the gracious hostess, leaning forward to refill her glass every time it fell below the halfway point. She must have lost track of how much she was having.

Coffee. She needed coffee. If only there were someone to bring her some.

She pulled a pillow over her head, trying to muffle the rain. It might as well have been pounding directly on her skull.

Normally, she would have chastised herself for wasting a day with a hangover of this caliber, but the downpour ruined her plans anyway. In a phase of her life that had somehow become defined by putting on a good face, Sunday mornings were reserved for slipping away. Her weekly hike was no ordinary trek. She'd discovered the most miraculous convergence of nature and faith in a nearby ravine, and it drew her like a magnet—the need to find peace. But in rain like this, the steep inclines of the trail would be too muddy, too hazardous. One wrong step, and she could be in the river. And no one would know she'd been swept away.

She could think of absolutely no reason to get out of bed.

Residual sadness—that's all this was. Up until last night's unfortunate slip, she'd been doing much better about *not* thinking of Josh. Really. She had. She was here, wasn't she? Starting over, on her own.

She would allow herself a day—one day only—to recover, in the physical sense *and* the emotional. Given the ruined-before-they-started plans and the should-have-known-better remnants of last night churning in her stomach, she would consider the rain lucky.

She would make some coffee and climb back under the covers and nurse the throbbing in her head and revel in the luxury of doing it alone. No—*undisturbed*. That sounded more appealing.

And under no circumstances would she allow herself to imagine how her sister might be spending her own rainy Sunday back home, a twenty-minute drive away in Springfield. How Penny and Josh would awaken lazily in their bed, with the quiet confidence of newlyweds, in the master bedroom of the house where Izzy and Penny had spent their childhoods. How the heavy rain would pool on the back porch, beneath the gutter that was always clogged, and leak in through the cracked weather stripping of the kitchen door. Whether Josh would think of Izzy even once as he tiptoed past her old room, down the worn carpet of the stairs, over the puddle on the linoleum, and to the stove to make breakfast. Whether he was the sort of husband who'd call Penny down to eat, or whether, on second thought, he'd take a tray up to her—and keep her occupied in bed for as much of the day as she'd let him.

She would think of anything but that.

"How 'bout that rain yesterday?" Sonny called through Izzy's open office door by way of greeting. "I almost built an ark, but then I realized I'd be trapped in an even smaller space with my kids climbing the walls. Then I'd *really* need God on my side to survive the flood!" He laughed at his own joke, and she heard Day join in with one of her signature giggles. They must have walked in together.

"But you only need two of everything for the ark, right?" Day said. "Maybe you could have left one behind!" They laughed again.

Izzy adjusted her face to hide her distaste. As the producer of the station's morning radio show, she was always in the office a solid hour before the rest of the crew. Usually she relished the quiet prep time, even if she did have to wake at 4 A.M. to get it. But today being Monday, she'd found her in-box buried in an avalanche of email—mostly wire service alerts about yet another shooting on a college campus, this one at Saturday night's football game between division rivals in Indiana. She and her neighbors had been chatting under the stars on Clara's new stone patio blissfully unaware of the tragedy befalling dozens of perfect strangers just across the state line. Worse, she'd spent yesterday moping around like the personification of a first-world-problems hashtag, as if her own tragedy even counted as one.

That her job was to sift through all that misery in search of *less real* news that might be *more suitable* for group discussion led by chipper pop radio DJs had filled her cup of self-loathing to overflowing. And now here was the on-air talent, complaining about the rain.

"Good thing today's a Sonny Day!" she called out, forcing cheer into her voice. She gathered her laptop, notes, and printouts of today's agenda and motioned for them to follow her to the conference room for their briefing. She hoped she'd found enough clickbait to fill time—another boy band star posting ill-advised selfies, a survey about what men *really* think of their wives' bodies postbaby, a reason working out less might actually be good for you.

"Oh *boo*!" Day replied. Sonny Keller's name really was Sonny. And Amy Day's surname really was Day. Coming up with their on-air monikers had been too easy—though tolerating them in the flesh was another matter. The listeners seemed to find Sonny and Day to be great company, but Izzy felt their particular brand of energy was a bit much. The fact that this made her perhaps not the best fit for this job was one she chose to ignore. *Freshly Squeezed* had been Dayton's top morning show for five years running. It was an easy twenty-minute commute from Yellow Springs—better than the drive from Springfield had been—paid well, and looked great on her résumé. Not that she had any immediate plans to use her résumé for anything, but you never knew.

Sonny plopped heavily into a swivel chair and rubbed his hands together. "Tell me we've got something juicy for Second Date Update."

Izzy settled at the table and glanced at the clock: 5:45. In fifteen minutes, she'd join the pair in the studio and feed them buzz from their social media accounts throughout the show, but she never spoke on air. Josh used to call her "The Wizard of Iz," the woman behind the curtain—back when they'd been best friends who could tease each other about anything. And talk to each other about everything. Except the one thing she should have said but never did. And then, like a girl in a predictable rom-com, she'd missed her chance. In the movies, the guy always realized, just in time, what had been right in front of him all along: the perfect match of his gal pal, who looked beautiful with her hair down and her glasses off. In the movies, he did not actually go through with marrying her little sister. And if he *did*, what would happen next? How would the film end? It would have helped Izzy to have some model for how to shut off her feelings, though she was desperately trying. If Sonny and Day only knew about the silent drama playing out before them, they'd have a field day. She suspected they found her quite dull.

"We've got something juicy, all right, but we can't air it."

"Oh?"

"Our very first preemptive email requesting that *just in case* a certain woman were to write in about . . . what were his words?" Izzy riffled through her printouts. "Ah, yes. If she were to write in about *what might have been misconstrued as a date,* he does not want a call."

"Yikes. She's that bad?"

"No, he's that married. With four kids."

"That *is* good. Damn. They're beating us to the punch now? Just when I thought this segment was getting *easier* now that it's so popular."

When they'd first launched Second Date Update, "adapted" (an industry term for thievery) from similar segments popular on other networks, the DJs had fallen all over themselves telling the people they called on-air that they didn't mean to put them on the spot. It was just that so-and-so wanted to know why they hadn't returned their texts or calls after their first date had seemingly gone so well. A reasonable enough request, can't we agree? But they'd found that those on the receiving end were often more than willing to talk— because no matter what had gone wrong, the idea that someone found them appealing enough to publicly humiliate themselves over was evidently flattering in some backward way.

Izzy felt differently, but she supposed her lack of any first dates whatsoever disqualified her from having an opinion.

"What poor sap *do* we have on the hook?" Day asked.

"Today you will be making polite inquiries on behalf of a young man who managed to sound sweetly yet awkwardly perplexed in his impassioned email about a magical night at Applebee's, in which he emphasized that he had 'dressed appropriately—really nice.'" She slid a printout of the email across the table.

"I already think he sounds great!" Day chirped. "If this doesn't work out, maybe he can call *me!*"

Izzy rolled her eyes. The calls essentially boiled down to three types: people who really had no way of knowing what had gone wrong (the girl whose ex-boyfriend had warned off her date while she was in the restroom, for instance), people who were genuinely clueless about their own flaws (mostly egotistical gym rats), and people who were about to get a raw deal for no fair reason.

As it fell to her to select their lucky honorees from the submissions that streamed in daily, Izzy would have shown a little bias toward that last camp if she could have. But it was hard to know what you were getting up front.

The first thing she noticed wasn't so much Paul—an uncommon presence on the street these days—but the tension radiating from him as he stood, hands on hips, at the end of Kristin's driveway, a look of confusion plain on his face. She knew Kristin and Paul's divorce wasn't finalized yet—Kristin had mentioned it Saturday night, with a matter-of-factness Izzy admired—but still, it was early afternoon on a weekday. Kristin would be at work, the twins at school. Paul had moved out at the start of the summer, just before Izzy moved in. She thought of the house as exclusively Kristin's, though she recognized him from his stops to pick up and drop off the kids.

She swung the car into her driveway and glanced over her shoulder. He was heading her way, white dress shirt unbuttoned at the collar, hands in his pockets, head down. He must be on a late lunch break. Maybe he needed something from the house, but he was going to be out of luck. Izzy didn't know Kristin nearly well enough to have a key, even for neighborly purposes.

"Hi there," he called out as she swung open the door. "Sorry to bother you . . ." He jogged the rest of the long diagonal across the street and stopped in front of her with an apologetic smile. "Sorry, we haven't officially met—not sure if you remember me. I'm Paul, Kristin's husband?"

He wasn't easily forgotten. An ob-gyn, he looked every bit the doctor even without the lab coat. It was something about the way he carried himself—with the authority of someone who exuded intelligence but the ease of someone with a practiced bedside manner. And he was good-looking—a polished, wealthy sort of handsome. No way would she have chosen him for her gynecologist, let alone as an obstetrician. It would be unnerving having someone so *datable* poking around down there, not to mention shepherding you through the dignity-destroying process of childbirth.

"Izzy." She stuck out a hand, feeling suddenly self-conscious of her jeans and *v*-neck T, as if she hadn't come from a *real* job like his. He enveloped it in a firm, warm shake.

"You haven't by chance seen Kristin today, have you?"

She shook her head. "Not since Saturday night."

He snapped to attention. "You saw her Saturday?"

"At Clara's. She and Benny got a new fire pit, and we had sort of a girls' night, helping them christen it."

"Were the kids there too?"

"No, it was after their bedtime."

He frowned disapprovingly, even though Clara's house shared a side yard with his own, and suddenly Izzy felt defensive on Kristin's behalf. "Your old baby monitor reached," she said. "They did a test run during the day to be sure."

"Did you happen to notice if she was around yesterday?"

"It was pouring. I never even got out of my pajamas."

"Right. Well, if you see her, could you please have her call me? Immediately?"

She nodded. "Everything okay?"

"I don't know. I got a call at the office. Kristin didn't show up for work, and the twins were no-shows at school. She wasn't answering her phone, so I drove over here. And . . . well, they're gone."

"Not home, you mean."

"No. Gone." He ran a hand over his hair. "Kristin had the locks changed, but when no one answered, I was worried—I broke in through a back window. It looks like they've taken off. There are suitcases missing. Stuffed animals. Clothes. Even her mother's china out of the dining room cabinet. And the minivan isn't here."

She frowned. "That's strange. She didn't mention going anywhere. In fact, she was talking about helping to organize some end-of-summer party Abby and Aaron had today."

"That's why the school was so concerned. And there are half-done crafts for that spread all over the kitchen table. Like she just walked out midway through, planning to come back and finish."

Izzy wrinkled her forehead. This didn't seem right at all. "Is her phone going straight to voice mail? I assume you've left messages?"

He removed his hand from his pocket, and in it was a cell phone she recognized instantly. The pink case was customized with a photo of the twins as onesie-clad newborns, curled into one another as if they hadn't yet left the womb.

"Also left on the kitchen table," he said.

A cold chill ran through Izzy.

He turned to gaze at his old house for a minute, then back toward her, looking both paler and more solemn than he had a moment ago. "I guess I'm going to have to call the police."

3

It is not without sadness that I tenure my resignation. The staff here truly has been like a family to me from the start—~~like all families, we've been through good times and bad, and I'll never forget~~—but now that I have my own family to raise, my priorities have to change. ~~I would love to make myself available for freelance work—maybe once the baby is more settled into a routine?~~ I hope you understand.

—Draft of Clara Tiffin's resignation letter, a later version of which was submitted exactly two weeks before the designated end of her maternity leave

Hallie was perched on a counter stool at the peninsula of Clara's kitchen, eating an after-school snack of graham crackers and peanut butter and watching Clara assemble lasagna in a large glass pan. It was not a pretty lasagna, which irked Clara, though she knew Benny wouldn't notice, let alone care. She just couldn't understand why the ricotta, beef, and sauce mixtures had yet again intermingled in clumps rather than thin, smooth layers. She was relieved every time it was the noodles' turn. They produced a clean slate upon which to start again.

"Mama says you used to be an editor," Hallie said, her mouth full.

"That's right." Clara was surprised Natalie had remembered that. She always seemed distracted—though understandably so, with Hallie's dad deployed overseas. Despite its proximity to Wright-Patterson Air Force Base, Yellow Springs wasn't exactly a hotbed of military families—"too many hippies, too many anarchy A's," Natalie joked to her once—but Natalie, who'd gotten married out of high school after getting pregnant with Hallie, had come here to enroll at Antioch College part-time. Clara had been happy to help out by agreeing to get her precocious twelve-year-old off the bus on the days when Natalie had a late class.

Of course, that had been before she'd realized just how *persistent* Hallie's otherwise adorable precociousness could be. But still, she was happy to help.

Mostly.

"Was that before you were a mommy?"

Clara nodded. The girl said it so matter-of-factly, as if it were common knowledge that Clara had been biologically meant to have two distinctive life phases all along: caterpillar, butterfly. It wasn't a bad metaphor if you reversed the order—the shedding of wings and the storing of calories coming in the latter phase. Had it really been just over four years ago she'd found out she was pregnant with Thomas? Looking back, it wasn't the nine-to-five editorial role that felt like another lifetime to her now. It was the fact that she'd showered, dressed, made up her face, and flat-ironed her hair every morning to go do it.

Still, she loved it here in this cozy cocoon, with their snuggly sweet preschooler and chubby-legged baby and same old Benny, who claimed he was *glad* she hadn't touched a blow dryer in a year. She doubted that was actually true, but he really was so convincing when he said it that maybe, it occurred to her now, she should try harder to find out. On the off chance that he *did* prefer it this way, the implications would be revolutionary for women everywhere.

"Perfect!" Hallie chirped.

Clara turned to grab the mozzarella from the fridge, stepping over Maddie, who had emptied the contents of the Tupperware cupboard onto the floor. "Why is it perfect?" she asked, frowning at the mess around her feet. Every lid would need to be washed.

"Because I want to start a newspaper. Like, a *real* neighborhood gazette. And I need someone who can help," she said smartly. "A professional!"

"Oh, kiddo, I wasn't that kind of editor." Clara nodded to the bookshelves bridging the open space between the kitchen and the family room, where Thomas was zoned out on the couch watching PBS Kids. She'd helped Benny knock down the wall that once stood there and could still feel the satisfaction of it giving way, one primitive sledgehammer whack at a time. "See those art books, near the bottom there? The tall ones? I used to work with artists to create those."

Hallie's long, poker-straight blond hair whipped around and back again. "Well," she said thoughtfully, "that doesn't matter. You know about writing. And grammar. And facts!" She splayed her hands dramatically on the counter. "This is about the facts."

"Really." Clara eyed her. "Is there something going on around here I should know about?"

"Probably."

She laughed, then checked to make sure Hallie didn't think she was laughing *at* her. But as usual the girl didn't seem bothered. She'd been the first neighbor Clara and Benny met when they were unloading their moving van last summer. She'd rolled up on her bike and said, "Can I talk to you?" Most people who selected that particular opening had an aim in mind for the conversation, but it turned out that Hallie just really wanted to talk. Responses from the listening party were largely optional.

"I'd have to do interviews to find out, to get to the bottom of things. If you worked with the artists, you've probably done interviews, right?"

"Well, some, but—"

"Great! I even have a name for it: *The Color-Blind Gazette.*"

Clara stared at her blankly.

"Get it? Because the Yellow Springs aren't yellow. They're, like, rust. Orange, maybe, but definitely not yellow. Whoever named this town must have been color-blind."

Having been a little disappointed the first time she'd seen the springs, Clara couldn't argue with that.

"I'm sure your mom could help about as well as I could," she told Hallie. "She's at a writing class now, in fact."

"She said no. She has too many papers of her own to do." Hallie wiped the crumbs from her last graham cracker onto her napkin and jumped to her feet. "Please? I only need, like, a little bit of help— on the days I come here anyway. I just don't want it to be obvious a kid made it."

As she emptied the bag of cheese over the top of the lasagna, Clara tried to picture the sort of adult who might publish something called *The Color-Blind Gazette* but came up empty.

"*Please?*"

Hallie offered her broad, gap-toothed smile, and Clara wavered. These days with Hallie were meant to be the ones she would welcome Benny home from the office with a clean house and an atmosphere of calm control. Not that she had achieved that yet, exactly, but Hallie was capable enough of entertaining the kids, at least, that Clara could avoid that horrible what-on-earth-have-you-been-doing-all-day? feeling that came over her sometimes when he walked through the door, looking handsome and accomplished in his shirt and tie, to find her outnumbered and undone. She still hadn't quite worked out how 1950s housewives had done it, but she suspected it involved far more ignoring of the children and far less guilt in doing so.

Then again, she did miss using her brain for something that didn't involve calculating how many ounces of milk Maddie had had, or whether three-day-old mac 'n' cheese was okay to eat.

"Tell you what," she told Hallie as she popped the dish into the oven. "You write the first batch of articles, or come up with some ideas for them, and I'll take a look."

"*Boo!*"

Hallie jumped, and out from behind her popped a triumphant Thomas, a blanket draped over his head, laughing like crazy. "Woooo!" he yelled, in his best impression of a cartoon ghost. "Wooo!"

Not missing a beat, Hallie took off running, grabbing a throw from the couch and ducking underneath. "The ghost of Hallie thanks you, Miss Clara!" she called, and Maddie got unsteadily to her feet and toddled after them to see what the fuss was about.

"It's Ghosts versus Maddie!" Thomas called, circling his sister with exaggerated steps.

Clara shook her head. She was going to have to pay more attention to what was on these shows he was watching. It wouldn't be Halloween for, what? Six weeks? Seven? Then again . . .

She hadn't quit her job so she could spend all day making lopsided lasagna.

Spotting a basket of laundry she'd meant to fold days ago, she grabbed a pair of Benny's baggy flannel pajama pants, draped them over her head, grasped the cuffs in her hands, and started waving her arms in slow motion. "How about Ghosts versus Pants?" she asked, and Thomas let out a squeal. She chased him around the couch as Hallie threw her blanketed arms around Maddie and yelled, "I'll save you!"

Thomas's stocking feet slid onto the foyer tile, with Clara on his tail. She was laughing so hard she probably wouldn't have heard the knock at the front door if she hadn't been running past it. She flung it open and realized too late that she still had the pants on her head.

A uniformed policeman raised an amused eyebrow even as her heart slowed at the sight of him. She tossed her head back, and the pants fell to the floor.

"Clara Tiffin?"

She smoothed her hair with a hand. "Yes?"

"I'm Detective Bryant, with the—"

Thomas slid violently into her legs and clutched her around the knees. "Wow! A real police officer!" He peered out the door past him. "Where's your woo-woo?"

The officer glanced down at him, then back at Clara. "My woo-woo?"

But he wasn't just an officer. He'd said *detective*.

She flushed. "He means your car. The siren."

"Oh! Well, little sergeant, it's parked down the street. Maybe you can look at it later if I can just have a few minutes with your mom?"

Clara's mouth went dry. "Is everything okay?"

"Yes, I just wanted to ask you a few questions regarding—"

"Thomas!" Hallie thumped down the hallway behind her, holding Maddie, and Clara fought the urge to reach out and take the baby. Sometimes Hallie seemed to forget she was a real live thirteen-month-old and not a doll. "Oh." She stopped short when she saw the officer.

Clara turned, careful to keep her face calm. "Hallie, could you please play quietly with the kids in the living room? Maybe show them some books or puzzles? I need to have a quick grown-up talk."

Hallie nodded, her eyes wide. Clara gave Thomas a pat on the shoulder, and he followed Hallie reluctantly down the hallway.

"Full house," Detective Bryant said.

"The oldest is my neighbor's daughter. But yes. Quite full."

"Which neighbor is that?"

"Natalie King, directly behind me."

He nodded. "I'm here to ask about Kristin Kirkland. Next door. I understand she was here Saturday night?"

"Yes, I hosted a—" Clara stopped short. "Is everything okay?" she asked again.

"Just a few moments of your time?" He gestured toward the formal dining room to their right.

"Of course." Clara led him to the table, took a seat, and watched uneasily as he settled himself across from her and flipped open his notepad. He looked to be about her age, which made her feel a certain skepticism for no fair reason. Clara still expected authority figures to be significantly older than her, a fact she felt as strongly in her midthirties as she had in her teens and twenties. One of these days she'd get used to the idea of growing up.

"Have you seen or spoken to Kristin since she left here Saturday?" He looked up expectantly. His face was boy-next-door friendly, without a hint that he might be practiced at the art of intimidation, and his build was somehow both soft and sturdy, like an ex-athlete who didn't work out much anymore. She wondered how long he'd been doing this job.

She shook her head.

"I understand your son goes to the same school as her twins. You didn't see her or the kids on your way to drop him off this morning?"

"Thomas does preschool part-time, only Tuesdays and Thursdays."

He made a note.

"But I know she was taking the afternoon off work to volunteer at the pre-K Farewell to Summer party." He looked unconvinced somehow, so she continued. "They're big on having it near the *actual* calendar end of the season, not around Labor Day like everyone else."

"I understand she was supposed to."

"Supposed to?"

"We're trying to account for her whereabouts, Mrs. Tiffin. She didn't show at work today, and Abby and Aaron never arrived at school."

She sat up straighter. "She's *missing*? The twins are missing?"

"They look to have packed some things. Her minivan is gone. She didn't mention plans to go anywhere?"

"I can't imagine where she'd go."

"Think back to Saturday. See or hear anything unusual after she left that night?"

"Not at all." Clara didn't mention that she'd been so tipsy from the wine that she'd slept like the dead.

"And what time did she leave?"

"Everyone left around the same time—midnight, maybe?"

"Looks like your backyard might have some of a side view into hers. Did you happen to notice if any lights were on in her house yesterday? Or last night?"

Clara replayed the day in her mind. It had been so miserable outside but so cozy inside. Benny was always *doing* something—weed-whacking, stacking wood, running to the hardware store. Not that she didn't appreciate all he did, but she had come to love the rare days when he was forced to be lazy. She'd made banana pancakes, Benny had done a pan of his famous scrambled eggs with cheese, and they'd had such a feast it made everyone sleepy again. The kids dozed on the couch with Benny through most of the Bengals game while Clara baked zucchini bread with the extra squash Randi and Rhoda had given her from their garden. She didn't remember so much as glancing out the window into the driving rain.

"I have no idea. I'm sorry."

"How close are you to Kristin? Are you good friends?"

"We're getting to be. I just moved in last summer, and we're both busy with our kids. But they love to play together, which has been nice."

He made another note. "Does she ordinarily call or text you on weekends?"

"Sometimes."

"She talk much about her divorce?"

"A little."

"Did she talk about it Saturday night?"

Clara played it over in her mind—the laughter in the firelight, the way the conversation had turned personal as the wine flowed. Too personal, probably. There were some things she'd take back herself if she could. A tirade about her flat chest, for instance. "A little."

"What did she say?"

Clara tried to remember. "Just that it didn't seem to be affecting the kids much, which was a good thing. She said Paul was always getting called into work even when he was around. He's an OB, so anytime someone goes into labor or is worried about some symptom or dials the physician on call . . ." Her voice trailed off. Of course he would already know all this.

"How would you describe her mood Saturday?"

"Her mood? Good. Happy. It was nice to be doing something social without the kids, even if it was only out back. We'd never done that before with the whole group—my husband recently finished laying the patio, and it's sort of in the middle. It turned out everyone's baby monitors reached."

"And who was 'everyone,' exactly?"

"Natalie—behind me, whose daughter is here now. Izzy—Isabel, who lives across the street. And Randi and Rhoda—" She pointed a diagonal through the backyard. "Around the curve."

"They the ones with those rusty sculptures out front? The solar panels, the chicken coop, and all that?" Clara thought of telling him her husband called their home an "art bunker," but thought better of it.

"Yes. They own that boutique in town—Moondance?"

"Oh, sure, my sister loves that place. Didn't they just have a baby?"

"Yes, a couple months ago. Like I said, we all needed a girls' night." She tried to laugh, but it sounded forced.

"So it was just you five?"

She counted silently. "Six, with Kristin."

"Did she seem nervous about anything?"

"Not that I could tell."

"Is she a nervous person in general?"

Clara laughed. "She is cool as a cucumber. She puts me to shame."

"What do you mean?"

She tried to think of a way to quantify her friend. "Well, she'd never answer the door with pants on her head."

"And how well do you know Paul?"

"Hardly at all." He'd never been the type to be out in the yard, throwing balls with the kids. Usually, when she did see him, he was on the riding lawn mower, something he still came by to do in the separation. He always raised his hand in a silent wave, but that was it.

"He friendly with your husband?"

She shook her head. When she'd started getting to know Kristin, she'd tried to nudge Benny to reach out to Paul, but he'd called him "more of an indoor guy" and left it at that. She'd been worried Paul would think them unfriendly, but then he had moved out and she'd figured, *No harm, no foul.*

"I have to ask: Ever notice any signs of domestic abuse next door?"

Clara cringed. "No," she said truthfully. "Never."

"Between the two spouses *or* between them and the kids? It doesn't have to be physical. Any shouting? Threats? A general sense that something's not right?"

She shook her head again, trying to ignore the dizzy feeling sweeping through it.

"Thanks. Well, if you think of anything else significant, here's my card. Call anytime." He slid it across the table. "We can't tell you not to talk to the press, but we'd prefer you didn't. You'll be seeing this on the news. We're issuing an AMBER Alert for the minivan—"

"An AMBER Alert?" Clara felt a jolt of fear. "Is she being charged with *kidnapping*?"

He frowned. "Not exactly. Since Mr. Kirkland never adopted the children, it's probably something more along the lines of 'interfering with custody.' At this point our concern is just to locate them, make sure everyone is okay."

Clara squinted at him. "I'm sorry—what do you mean, he hasn't *adopted* them?"

Detective Bryant seemed to be reassessing her. "I guess I shouldn't have said that. You're friends—I assumed you knew the children aren't biologically his?"

If not his, then . . . "She was married before?"

"She was widowed."

"My God." Her mind raced. It made a little more sense, Clara supposed, how Kristin had seemed a bit blasé about how the kids were taking the divorce. But how—

"An accident. One of those freak things." He was watching her closely, and suddenly she felt defensive.

"That's horrible. Awful." She shook her head. "She probably just didn't want to discuss that, to bring it up in front of the kids."

"Right," he said evenly.

She was still trying to piece it all together. "I thought there was some kind of waiting period, for considering someone missing? I mean, couldn't this all be some misunderstanding?"

"Let's hope so. But there's no waiting when kids are involved. We're treating this as critical, and we have to assume they're in danger until we know for certain that they're not."

"In danger with Kristin?" Clara shook her head. "That's ridiculous. Never."

"We don't know that they're with Kristin." He leveled his gaze at her. "We don't know where any of them are. You hear from her at all, you call my number on that card, okay?"

Clara nodded, and watched him go.

4

Maybe you've had this experience: waiting for someone who's late coming home. Really late. You call and call their phone, and there's no answer. Your mind starts to conjure stories of disaster. A patch of black ice. A jackknifed semitruck. A drunk driver. You look out the window every five minutes. You tell yourself you're being silly. You recheck your phone to make sure you haven't missed a call. You turn on the porch light as it grows dark, praying you won't see a police cruiser pull up to deliver bad news. You stare at the TV, not seeing. You pour a glass of water, realizing your mouth has gone dry.

There's a simple explanation. They come home and tell you so. A dead cell phone battery. A traffic jam. Briefly, you wonder what caused it—maybe another person was in the accident that moments ago seemed such a certain possibility. But it doesn't matter anymore, not really. It wasn't *your* person. Your worry dissolves. It's easily forgotten. By morning, you're bickering again.

I used to be that way. A real basket case. Drove my husband crazy when he'd walk through the door and I'd rush at him, all, "Where have you been and why didn't you call and don't you know how worried I was?" Then one day, I finally pulled myself together. I was too tired for neurotic, needless worry. I didn't wait up.

And he never came home.

5

I hear you're the other one with a mountain bike chained outside. Want to hit the trails Saturday? Buddy system = good. Josh, Room 304

—*Note scribbled on the dry-erase board of*
Izzy's dorm room door, freshman college year,
second week

Izzy could not possibly return her sister's calls right now. She was far too busy incessantly peeking through the blinds, looking for any sign of change over at Paul and Kristin's. The gleaming white Victorian stood defiant in the moonlight, every window lit as if to signal, in a luxury version of the old Motel 6 commercials: *Please come home.* The police had left awhile ago, and Paul had not emerged, but she knew he was in there, waiting. Hoping.

What hell must he be going through?

She'd fill Penny in later, and of course her sister would understand why she hadn't called her back at a time like this. Never mind that Izzy didn't actually know Kristin well enough to be truly fraught over her vanishing act, that she thought of herself as more of a curious spectator, even in the surreal moments of the detective's interview earlier. And no matter that Penny had left messages on both her cell and landline, as well as a text and even an email: *Call me? Miss you. Would love to come see the place again, now that you're settled.* It wasn't the words that stung—it was the sight of Penny's new name in her in-box. The surname was all wrong.

One of these days, she'd get used to it. But the trouble with *truly* moving past things was that certain resentments had a stubborn way of sticking around. For instance, she couldn't help being mildly irritated that Penny had suddenly decided to miss her now, when Izzy had been lying low ever since the wedding back in June. Of course, the impulsive purchase of her house and move to Yellow Springs offered convenient excuses for all involved. Izzy knew she had to do a better job of pretending. Penny and Josh certainly were. But she may have put too much stock in assuming it would be easier to pretend from a distance.

In all those months of furtive wedding preparation, led by her mother as if she'd discovered her missed calling in life as an event coordinator, Izzy told herself that if she could just get through her maid of honor duties—the sickeningly sweet cake tastings, and the who-cares hubbub over the centerpieces, and the uncomfortable dress fittings, and the too-old-for-this bachelorette night—that once the big day had come and gone, things would be better. That would be that, till death do them part, and something in Izzy's brain would send her a signal of closure, of it being time to find a way to move on.

Instead, it got worse. The whole week following the ceremony, she dragged herself miserably through her workaday routine nauseated by the thought of Penny and Josh lying on a Bahamian beach, toasting their good fortune in finding each other. She'd reasoned that she just needed a vacation herself, but she had neither the gumption nor the funds to go it alone, and all her other friends seemed too attached to get away.

Then there was the whole business of her parents downsizing to a condo, turning Izzy's childhood home over to Penny and Josh for a steal—a token price, really, which irked Izzy, as no one had asked her if she, their older child, might also be interested (she wasn't, but still, must *everything* be determined by a race to the altar?)—and her mother filling the void the wedding planning had left in her days by dropping hints about grandbabies.

That much, at least, was futile. Neither Penny nor Josh had ever wanted kids—it was the only thing about Josh that *did* make him more perfect for Penny than for Izzy, really. Sometimes, Izzy would be watching Thomas and Maddie playing outside with Abby and Aaron and catch herself caught up in a certain wistfulness. "You're out of order," she'd chastise her biological clock, chagrined that it was evidently real. "You need to pair up before you can procreate."

She didn't know when Penny planned to break it to their mother that she was in for a disappointment, but she hoped it was soon, before she started preemptively knitting booties. In the meantime, Izzy was starting to find her parents as insufferable as she found Penny and Josh. She wrestled with instant regret every time she dodged one of their check-in calls or cut a conversation short, but she needed a little more time to regroup.

In her restlessness now, she turned on the TV and landed on a prime-time special spotlighting victims of Saturday's shooting and the killer's troubled past. She forced herself not to look away from the blood-spattered band members, the sobbing cheerleaders, the shaking spectators. These were people who couldn't have done anything to prevent their misfortune, aside from arbitrarily choosing to be somewhere else that night. These were people who were allowed to be sad.

Not her.

The most twisted thing about the comparison was that it could be a comfort. *See, what you're dealing with is nothing. Witness real tragedy and be properly ashamed.*

You didn't even have to look far to find it. Now it was right across the street.

She poked a finger between slats in the blinds and peered out again at the dark form of Paul's car, silent in Kristin's driveway. She'd been waiting for other cars to join his there—family, friends, colleagues. It puzzled her that there were none. Nothing about this made sense. She desperately wished she had a clearer memory of Kristin's role in the conversation around the fire Saturday night. She didn't know that anything important had been said, but she didn't know that it *hadn't* been, either.

A flash of movement caught her attention, and here came Clara, hugging an oversized hooded sweatshirt to her body, down the wide front porch steps of her old farmhouse, past the massive oak tree shading her front yard, its solitary swing moving gently in the breeze, and—with a furtive look over her shoulder at Kristin's—across the street toward Izzy's.

She'd only started getting to know the other neighbors, but she had really come to like Clara, who was often outside with her kids when Izzy got home from her bizarrely early workdays. They'd taken to chatting in those hours when it seemed as if they had the neighborhood to themselves. Unlike her friends back in Springfield, Clara didn't ask what had possessed Izzy to buy a house by herself, or make her feel like a special case. And unlike other moms Izzy knew, Clara didn't reassure her not to worry, that one day she'd find a man or have kids of her own. Nor did she apologize for her own happiness, falling all over herself to tell Izzy how annoying husbands and children can be.

When Izzy mentioned that her banana bread always stuck to the bottom of the pan, Clara didn't remark woefully that she remembered the days *she* had time to bake things from scratch, before kids. Instead, she lent her these amazing nonstick loaf pans that make everything turn out perfectly. When Izzy told her about her "new," last-to-the-party infatuation with Cary Grant, Clara didn't comment that it must be nice to have time to sit around and watch old movies. Instead, she disappeared into her house and came out with a special edition DVD of *The Talk of the Town*, which became Izzy's favorite. When Izzy admitted one night that she was feeling lonely, Clara didn't suggest that she set up an online dating profile. Instead, she asked Benny to handle the kids' bedtime and came over with a pint of Ben & Jerry's and a bottle of vodka. Clara was one of those rare people who didn't make Izzy feel like she was in the wrong place in her life.

Even though she probably was.

Izzy rose to meet her friend at the door, slipping her feet into the hand-knit alpaca moccasins she'd bought last week at Randi and Rhoda's boutique. She'd only been trying to be nice—the price tag seemed a bit steep for slippers—but they were wonderfully soft and warm, a surprisingly worthwhile splurge, and it was nice to have some small luxury to revel in.

She whisked open the door just as Clara had raised her hand to knock, and Izzy laughed at the startled look on her face. "Sorry! I'm a bit of a nosy neighbor tonight," Izzy said, glancing again at Kristin's. "Come in and save me from my stalkerish tendencies."

"Not a chance. I'm here to join you. I can't see anything from my own living room. Guess you didn't get my texts?"

Izzy felt her face color at the memory of how she'd silenced her sister's ringtone and shoved the phone deep into her purse, out of sight. The problem with dodging someone was that sometimes you ended up dodging everyone. "I must not have heard it," she said quickly. "I'm glad you're here, though. I've been dying to know what you make of this Kristin thing."

Clara caught sight of the TV as she shut the door behind her. "Oh, no. You can't watch this stuff. It's what these shooters want. Attention."

"I know you're right," Izzy said. "But, in my defense, this channel has the earliest local news, at ten. And it's suddenly gotten *really* local."

Clara crossed to the remote lying on the coffee table and pressed it with a purposeful index finger, muting the television. "'They will always be / more beautiful / than you / the people you are killing,'" she recited.

Izzy stared at her, momentarily stunned by both her conviction and her words.

"Alice Walker," Clara said. "She *blogs* poetry now. In a world where political tweets have taken over the Internet, there's still hope."

They both laughed. As a stay-at-home mom, sometimes Clara struck her as . . . well, *underutilized* was the word that came to mind, though Izzy knew that was ridiculous. What more important job was there than raising children? Especially children who would grow up with a mother who could quote Alice Walker? Moms didn't get much respect when they dedicated themselves full-time to doing it well, but if anything went wrong—even twenty-five, fifty years later—they were always the first ones blamed. Sometimes by the kids themselves.

"I'm clearly reading the wrong blogs," Izzy said. "Glass of wine?"

"Randi, Rhoda, and Natalie are all right behind me. We're ambushing you. Better make it a bottle."

On cue, the doorbell chimed, and Izzy chided her heart for lifting at the sound. Their neighbor and her children were unaccounted for. This was serious stuff, not a social occasion.

But it was so nice not to be alone.

Izzy swung open the door and Rhoda stepped in, looking, as she always did, like a walking advertisement for her boutique—earthily beautiful with her hair twisted back in elaborate braids and her shoulders wrapped in a willowy pashmina. Behind her, Randi appeared cloaked in a long patchwork pullover, a finger pressed to her lips as the opposite arm flexed around the handle of an infant car seat with baby Adele asleep inside.

"She dozed off on the way home—we don't usually close up shop so late," she said apologetically. "Police kind of threw us off schedule . . ."

"Do you want to put her upstairs? Or down here in a quiet corner?"

"Maybe just in the upstairs hallway, so I can hear if she cries?"

"No problem." Izzy was about to reach for the handle, but Randi breezed past her and up the stairs, as if they were old friends and this wasn't her first time setting foot inside.

"Is Natalie going to be able to leave Hallie?" Rhoda asked.

Clara nodded. "Her text said she'd be over once Hallie is asleep. I know Natalie's cautious about parenting on her own, but twelve is that borderline age of *almost* being allowed to stay home alone anyway—"

"And then she can *babysit*," Rhoda said. "It's going to be glorious." Her smile didn't reach her eyes the way it usually did, though, and Clara reached out to touch her arm softly.

"I take it you—"

A soft knock on the door cut her off, and Izzy moved to answer it as Randi padded down the stairs behind her. Natalie looked the way she always did: tired but tough, even as she smiled a greeting. "I can't stay long," she announced loudly. "I have a test tomorrow. I'm telling all of you this so you do not under any circumstances let me stay past my bedtime."

"Noted," Izzy said, standing aside to let her through. "I was just going to open some wine but I also have tea, coffee, decaf . . ."

"It's a math test, not a blood test," Natalie said, grinning. "One glass won't hurt."

The women burst out laughing. Izzy started toward the kitchen and motioned for them to follow.

"Okay." Clara leaned her elbows on the island as Izzy busied herself retrieving glasses and a corkscrew. "Does anyone have the slightest idea what has gone on here? Did anyone see this coming?"

They all exchanged glances, shaking their heads.

"This whole thing is surreal," Izzy said, clunking the glasses down on the counter and going to work on the cork. "I keep waiting for some update that she's been located, that there's a simple explanation."

"The idea that we seem to have been the last people to see her is making me feel guilty," Randi said. "Like we should know something. Or, you know, *was it something we said?*"

"Did anything strike you guys as off?" Clara asked. "I keep racking my brain." She accepted the glass Izzy offered her and stared intently into the wine.

"We remember the whole night exactly the same," Rhoda said, smiling affectionately at her wife. "Except for the foggy parts— which we *fail to remember* exactly the same."

"Seriously," Natalie said. "Who put alcohol in the wine?"

"I'm glad I'm not the only one," Izzy said, handing over the last of the glasses. "It was kind of embarrassing talking to the detective."

"I know you're still getting to know us, but you might have gathered we don't get out much," Rhoda told Izzy as the group returned to the living room. "I swear we're not usually such lushes."

"At least you have the kid excuse," Izzy said, taking a breath to steel herself as she claimed her spot on the couch. Clara sank down next to her, and Natalie perched on the opposite end. Now seemed as good a time as any to clear the air. "Me, I apparently just wait for opportunities to spill my innermost secrets to my new neighbors." She still cringed to think of it. *Hi, what's your name again? Have I mentioned I'm in love with my brother-in-law?*

"No one thought anything of it," Clara said, smiling sympathetically. "We're Team Izzy."

"If anyone should be embarrassed, it's me," Randi said. She slid onto the oversized armchair next to her wife. "I am *way* more of a lightweight than I realized. I've been trying to behave, nursing a newborn, and I guess—"

"No one is judging you either, Ran," Rhoda said. "You were fun! You were neighborly! You even offered to lend Izzy our *tools.*"

Randi burrowed into her pullover as the women burst into laughter around her, and Izzy felt some of the tension in her shoulders subside. It *had* been one of the evening's more memorable moments, when Izzy had worried aloud about being in over her head with the maintenance on her house and Randi had crowed, "Don't worry, you have lesbian neighbors! We have all the tools a single woman could ever need! And I do mean *all* the tools!"

"Oh, God, I was *really* far gone," Randi groaned, her tone turning serious again. "I mean, I slept straight through until morning. Adele must have cried. She must have gotten hungry. She's not even three months old! And I didn't even hear."

"As I think I've mentioned once or twice or a *thousand* times, I didn't hear her either," Rhoda said. "Maybe she *didn't* cry."

"But it's not up to you to hear her cry! You're not the one who's moonlighting as a cow!"

It was clear this discussion had been ongoing between the two since Sunday morning. Clara cleared her throat. "You know, when I was pregnant with Thomas, Benny and I had this take-charge older nurse as our childbirth class instructor. There was an entire session devoted to the never-shake-a-baby lecture, and I remember her talking about how if a baby won't stop crying and you feel like you might lose your cool, you should just put the baby in the crib and go take a shower. 'A baby never died from crying,' she said." She bent to pick up a pacifier that had fallen to the carpet and handed it back to Randi with a grin. "Yours does indeed seem to have survived."

"Thanks," Randi said softly, tucking Adele's Binky into her pocket. "That's the first thing that's made me feel better."

"Oh, sure. *She* says it and you feel better!" Rhoda rolled her eyes.

"Well," Clara said, "if it makes anyone *else* feel any better, I don't think I was that far gone Saturday. And I don't remember anything significant. Just normal stuff. Kristin being Kristin."

"She didn't seem too broken up about the divorce," Izzy said. "Maybe it was somehow easier to take off rather than deal with the bullshit?"

"Uprooting the kids seems kind of drastic, though," Rhoda said, biting her lip.

"Not to sound gossipy," Clara said, "but did the detective tell you they aren't Paul's?"

"They're not? Whose are they?"

"He said she was married before. Her first husband *died*."

The women stared at her in horror. "Gosh," Randi said. "When the twins were babies?"

"I guess they had to have been . . . Aaron and Abby are four, and she and Paul have lived here a couple of years at least." She shook her head. "I felt ridiculous. I'd been going on about how Kristin and I were getting to be good friends, and then obviously had no clue about, like, this major thing. So who knows what else we didn't know." She stuck a finger into the blinds and closed one eye. "Seen anything over there?"

"Not a thing," Izzy said. "I was imagining Kristin's minivan pulling in. And then her flipping out that Paul is in her house when he doesn't even have a key anymore."

The blinds clattered closed. "He doesn't have a key? How do you know that?"

"He flagged me down, coming home from work—before he'd called the cops. Told me he had to break a window to check on them. Said she changed the locks." Izzy knew the words sounded bad even as she was saying them. They always investigated the husband, even when the husband was . . . well, Paul. "I'm surprised he didn't knock on your door too."

Clara thought for a moment. "I was probably at the grocery store," she said. "One of the few luxuries of my lifestyle is that I get to avoid that madhouse on weekends."

Izzy pictured Paul going door to door, getting no answer, his panic mounting with each passing moment. That look on his face as he stood in her driveway, as if she, a total stranger to him, might be able to explain everything . . . "I felt awful for him," she blurted out.

"But why would she have changed the locks?" Clara shifted on the cushion. "Like he's going to, what, start taking the furniture while she's at work?"

Natalie shrugged. "Maybe her lawyer advised her to. Maybe she changed them for an unrelated reason and just hadn't given him a key yet. Who knows."

"Tons of explanations," Clara agreed quickly. "I'm just thinking out loud. It's better when no one can hear me think." She was twisting the end of her ponytail around her fingertips so ferociously that Izzy half expected the whole clump to detach itself from her head in surrender.

"Do you know if they have family in the area?" Izzy asked. "I can't believe no one else has pulled up over there."

The other women stared at one another blankly, and an uneasy silence filled the room. "How is it possible that I'm such a shoddy friend to have never asked that?" Clara mumbled.

Izzy was about to answer when she caught the station logo flashing on the TV screen. "Oh! It's on!" She dove for the remote and turned on the volume.

"New developments tonight in the missing persons case of a local woman and her two children," the anchor said, on cue. "Authorities are broadening their search and issuing the AMBER Alert across additional states, after the estranged husband of Kristin Kirkland has alleged that certain funds are unaccounted for, and she may be traveling with a large sum of cash."

The women exchanged looks again. *Large? How large?*

"Given that it's uncertain exactly when Kirkland and her children went missing in the thirty-six-hour window between Saturday night and this morning, that raises additional questions about how far they may have gotten and how fast. So far, searches for the vehicle in Ohio, Kentucky, and Indiana have come up empty. Let's have another look at the make and model of the minivan . . ."

A photo from a car lot flashed on the screen with the license plate number in bold print beneath it. Then the picture changed to one of Kristin and the kids, taken at a Fourth of July picnic just a couple months ago from the looks of the flags and banners in the background. She had one arm around each twin and was smiling serenely into the camera, as if everything she could ever need was right there in her arms.

"Kirkland is the mother of four-year-old twins from a previous marriage: Aaron and Abigail. Their biological father is deceased. Authorities are calling this a critical missing persons case, assembling a team of detectives and working around the clock, so we expect to know more by our morning report."

"Um," Izzy said, as she clicked off the TV. "How much do gynecologists make, exactly? Do you think she cleaned him out?"

"Her college administrator's salary can't be much," Rhoda said. "They had to have been mostly living off Paul's. How much could possibly be left?"

"What if someone *else* took the money, and took Kristin and the kids too?" Randi asked, tears blinking into her eyes. "What if we've been sitting here joking around when they're in real trouble? It hadn't occurred to me they could *really* be anything other than fine."

"Let's not get carried away," Rhoda said. "I mean, I've never heard of someone staging a crime scene by packing up the china."

"Right," Natalie said. "As a military wife, I've seen some pretty cold divorces. Custody battles can get *nasty* when one parent's home address is at the mercy of their next deployment. Women who seem sweet as pie will do crazy things to cut those ties. And I wouldn't call Kristin sweet as pie. There was always something *too* perfect about her, wasn't there?"

A silence descended. Clara turned and lifted the slats again, and she and Izzy peered out, shoulder to shoulder, like children. No. *Like sisters.* She and Penny used to do the same thing, looking for the curious but regular sight of Mrs. Timmons coming down the sidewalk with her Siamese cat on a rhinestone-studded leash, back when all Izzy coveted of her sister's was her rainbow-colored headband.

"It might be turning out I didn't know Kristin as well as I thought," Clara said finally, turning back to the group. "And I never claimed to know Paul at all. But whatever's going on here, I'm willing to bet she didn't do anything he didn't deserve."

"Team Kristin?" Izzy asked.

"Win, lose, or draw."

6

People who tell you, "Don't sweat the small stuff," mean well, but I've noticed that the more you sweat, the healthier you get!

—Flyers for Clara's mother's aerobics classes, circa 1985

Clara loved Yellow Springs. They'd come here from Cincinnati last year, from a cookie-cutter town house complex she'd never quite felt at home in, and she still reveled in the newness of it. Or, rather, the lack thereof. She loved that the houses here were as eclectic as the people who lived in them, that century-old farmhouses like hers were adjacent to towering beauties like Kristin's, midcentury additions like Izzy and Natalie's, and earthy bungalows like Randi and Rhoda's. She loved that the backyards didn't meet neatly, that even though hers wasn't fenced, she wasn't peering out her kitchen windows into someone else's. She loved the outbuildings—the old art studio that Benny used for his tools and odd projects, the chicken coop behind Randi and Rhoda's that yielded so many eggs Clara would sometimes find a basketful on her back porch, and Kristin's honeysuckle-rimmed detached garage that afforded both of their properties privacy but not total seclusion.

She loved that she could walk Thomas to school and cross paths with other families on the way. She loved that the roads to town weren't gridded out but curved generously, and that what was around each curve might surprise you—even if you'd walked the route the day before. She loved that she could stroll by Benny's accounting firm on the way to the market or the library and surprise him with one of his favorite lattes or join him for lunch. She loved that she could window-shop while Maddie napped in her stroller. She loved the weekend visitors who you could tell wished they lived there, and the college students with their big ideas and sometimes ridiculous clothes, and the mystery surrounding the exact address of their most famous resident, Dave Chappelle, who had traded in an entertainment deal worth millions for *this* and who occasionally could be spotted at Dino's Cappuccinos.

And she'd always loved, as she suspected Dave did, that it was an unlikely place for a media circus.

But it was there in the morning, cluttering the sidewalk to the edge of her lawn. From her vantage point at the window, Clara watched the reporters huddled around their vans drinking four-dollar coffees brought from Dayton as they gave instructions to their cameramen, checked their equipment, and readied themselves for the early broadcasts.

She crawled back into bed. Benny turned to face her and reached over Maddie's sleeping form to lace his fingers in hers. For once, last night Clara had welcomed Maddie's cries in the darkness, had jumped at the chance to snuggle her back to sleep. She'd been awake anyway.

"I guess this means Kristin isn't back," he said softly. "Do you want me to stay home?"

Clara shook her head. "What good would that do? Save your vacation days for something happy."

He frowned. "I don't like this. You know they're going to be knocking on the door as soon as they see a light on."

"No comment." Clara smiled weakly. "Did that sound stern enough? I've been practicing in my head."

His expression didn't change. "It's not that I don't have faith that

Kristin and the twins are fine. I do. It's just that the questions people are asking . . . I'm worried they're going to dredge up bad memories for you."

She didn't blame him for bringing it up—he'd worked so hard to help her move past all that—but she had somehow hoped he wouldn't. "I can handle it," she told him, her eyes begging him to leave well enough alone. But what if that sounded like an admission that there was something to handle? "I mean, they won't," she rushed to add, her voice firmer. "But if they do, I can handle it."

He brushed away a strand of hair that had fallen across her face. "But Thomas. How are you even going to get him to school without him wondering what the hell is going on?"

"We can sneak out the back, through Natalie's yard. Thomas will think it's an adventure." She only hoped the chaos outside wouldn't be mirrored at the preschool.

"He's going to catch wind of it, you know. Even if he doesn't, he'll still be asking after Aaron and Abby."

"We'll tell him they've gone on a trip." Clara squeezed his fingers. They had a pact never to lie to the kids. Benny had caught his own parents in a lie at a young age, and it *still* bothered him. "Best as anyone can tell, that's true."

It occurred to her now that Benny had never made her promise to tell *him* only the truth. She supposed that part went without saying. He was right: It *was* sad that lying to kids was up for debate. Funny how it was their innocence that so often could complicate the truth.

And their questions. Thomas was doing a fine job of picking that up from Hallie, so Clara had a feeling she was in for it.

Benny pulled her to him and kissed her gently on the lips. "Divorce is an ugly thing," he murmured. "Let's never get one."

Oh, Benny. Somehow she could still be taken aback by his sweetness, even though he'd been exactly this way ever since she'd met him. If she was going to keep her vow of honesty, she'd never be able to tell the kids when they headed off to college that nothing good ever came of a frat party. Clara had been leaning against the wall of a crowded fraternity kitchen, killing time in line for keg beer she didn't really want while the friend who'd dragged her there ignored her (quite predictably, it turned out), when she'd heard a chorus of enthusiastic greetings from the brothers—"Benny boy! Hey, Benny's here!"—and turned expecting to see a jazz musician or an old-timey baseball player. And there he was. Benny Tiffin. Dimpled, blue eyed, and soon to be hers.

"Done."

"Done!" The clarity of the tiny voice startled them both, and they looked down at the pillow between them to find Maddie's blue eyes open wide, her jack-o'-lantern grin glistening with drool. All three burst out laughing.

"She's so good at talking, she wakes up doing it now!" Benny beamed. Maddie wasn't *really* talking much on her own yet, but she was on the brink of a successful career as a mimic.

As Clara carried the baby down the hall to the changing table, she heard the shower come on full blast. She closed her eyes and breathed in the normalcy of the morning here inside, trying to pretend that nothing outside was different. Sometimes when it was just the four of them, warm and safe, she'd get this overwhelming urge to lock the doors and keep them here, where everyone was accounted for and together. She knew this time with the kids was limited, that one day not many years from now they'd spend more of their hours away from her than with her, and think of her less and less when they were apart. She wasn't about to let their earliest childhood get away from her unappreciated. Every time Thomas ran to her, arms outstretched, yelling "Mommy!" at the end of his preschool day, something in her heart would click back into place, and she'd realize for the millionth time, with an awe that never quite dimmed, the fierce depth of her love and the maternal fear that came imprinted, like it or not, on the other side of her most precious coins.

Downstairs, she occupied Maddie with some dry cereal in her high chair, turned the wall-mounted TV in the family room to the local news—traffic and weather, over and over, until the top of the hour—and set to work on a ham-and-cheese omelet big enough to share, trying to ignore the anxiety building in the pit of her stomach as the morning anchors droned on.

Benny's footsteps thudded down the stairs, and as he leaned over her shoulder to inspect the contents of the pan, the masculine smell of his aftershave and the dampness of his hair cooling her cheek momentarily eased the lump in her throat.

"There's something very twenty-first-century America about waiting for the local news to give you updates on your neighbor, isn't there?" she asked, forcing a lightness into her voice as he plunked the baby monitor they still used for Thomas onto the counter.

"And to think we thought we left all the excitement behind in Cincinnati." It was the second time *back in Cincinnati* had come up that morning, and it was two times too many.

Benny popped slices of bread into the toaster, humming "My Country 'Tis of Thee," and did a cereal juggling act for Maddie, catching her airborne O's in his mouth as she giggled.

"Your phone rang upstairs," he said, clearing his throat. "It was an unfamiliar number, so I answered—on the off chance that it was Kristin."

Clara whipped around, spatula in hand, only to catch Benny's shoulder, leaving a smear of melted cheddar on his dress shirt. "Shit! Sorry."

"Usually I wait until my first clients come in to start being cheesy." She rolled her eyes, though she suspected Benny knew his lame jokes had brought her back from the brink of fury or exhaustion or tears or loneliness more times than she could count. He crossed to the sink to wet a dish towel and started dabbing at the mess.

"So who called?"

"The police." He seemed to be trying very hard to keep his voice casual, even as her heart kicked into high alert. "Someone on behalf of Detective Bryant. He wants you to stop by the station later this morning. I guess they have some follow-up questions."

She flicked off the burner and busied herself dividing the omelet into two larger pieces and two smaller ones as the blood pounded in her ears. At one point during her career-driven days, she'd considered going to the doctor for what she thought were anxiety attacks. They'd subsided, though, and she'd never known if they were truly beyond what most people experienced as ordinary trepidation. The once familiar sensation rising within her felt foreign now, and she concentrated on breathing normally.

"I'm sure it's nothing to worry about," Benny said, in a tone that *almost* succeeded in being convincing.

She was about to answer when Benny jumped for the remote on the counter. "Go time," he said, gesturing toward the TV. He turned up the volume as Clara set their plates on the counter and slid unsteadily onto a stool.

WOMAN AND CHILDREN STILL MISSING FROM YELLOW SPRINGS flashed on the screen in block letters as the anchors recapped the details, again sharing the family photo and description of the van. "Our own Stacy Sanders is live outside the house where Kristin and her children live. Stacy, what can you tell us?"

The screen changed, and there was Stacy, standing in the driveway next door.

"Well, Margot, it's been a long night for Dr. Paul Kirkland, Kristin's estranged husband and the man who's been helping to raise her boys. He came out earlier and asked if he could speak on camera, address his wife directly. As you can imagine, this is a very emotional time for him, so he asked not to do it live. It took several takes to get through it, but we do want to roll that tape now."

The screen cut to a shot of Stacy standing in front of the Kirklands' porch stairs in the dimmer light of the earlier morning, accompanied by a stoic Paul. He was disheveled in a wrinkled white dress shirt and pleated slacks—Clara guessed them to be his work clothes from the day before. She supposed he didn't have clothes at the house anymore, and it occurred to her that maybe she should have sent Benny over to see if he needed anything. His hair was messed on one side, as if he'd fallen asleep on the couch, though the circles under his eyes didn't indicate much rest. His hands were buried in his pockets, and he shifted from one foot to the other, his typical air of confidence replaced by clear discomfort in front of the camera.

"Dr. Kirkland, how are you holding up?" Stacy asked with practiced concern.

He cleared his throat. "All night, I kept hoping they'd come home." His voice broke, but he forced himself to continue. "You're all here, reporting, and the police are out trying to find them, and I was just sitting in there—" He coughed. "I guess I thought I should come out and say something. You know, in case she's listening."

"I understand your divorce was to be finalized soon?"

He nodded. "I thought it would have been by now. It takes longer than you think." He lifted his eyes to look directly into the lens, and just like that he appeared himself again—the handsome man with the smooth bedside manner who was not unfamiliar with the task of delivering difficult news. "You say things you don't mean. You have to divvy up things you don't want to share. It takes a toll." The camera zoomed in, cutting Stacy out of the frame. "Kristin, if you're watching, I want you to know that whatever this is about, it's fixable. If this has to do with the money, you can keep it, obviously. It's yours. I wasn't really going to make a play for half. All the money I've contributed to raising the twins these past years—it was the best money I ever spent. I don't regret a cent." He looked woefully at the reporter, as if it were worth breaking the spell to explain himself. "Like I said, you say things you don't mean."

She nodded, and he turned his attention back to the camera, eyes wide. "The police say I could petition the courts to make this a more serious charge, but I don't *want* to file more paperwork in the courts. I don't want the courts in our lives at all. Just come home, and I'll make all this go away. I'll give you whatever you want. That's what I set out to do, back from the very beginning . . . Remember the beginning?" He swallowed hard, his Adam's apple bobbing in his throat.

"I know you don't love me anymore, it's over, and I accept that. But the idea of not knowing where Abby and Aaron are, not being able to give them a hug, or even just take them to their soccer game on Saturday—" His eyes filled with tears. "Please come home," he finished.

"I hope she hears you loud and clear, Doctor," Stacy said, turning back to the camera as he jogged up the porch stairs. Flashbulbs lit up the dim morning.

"Doctor, what can you tell us about the money that's allegedly missing?"

"Doctor, why didn't you adopt the kids when you married their mom?"

"Doctor, where do you think she went? Any theories?"

The barrage of questions from the other reporters on the lawn chased Paul up the stairs and into the house, the door shutting quietly behind him, and then the screen flashed back to the live shot of Stacy, standing in the brighter sun of an incongruously beautiful day.

"Police are working this case around the clock, and we've learned that the money Kristin is believed to be traveling with is a *million-dollar* life insurance payout she received when her first husband was killed, along with his parents and sister, in a tragic boating accident at Buck Creek State Park. Having worked in the insurance industry, her first husband left his wife and children well provided for. We don't know how much of that money might have been spent over the last few years, of course, but we do know it's been cashed out little by little over the past twelve months, which could indicate that she was planning this for some time. Unless, of course, the money was used for something else and she's not traveling with it at all. More questions than answers today, Margot."

Benny flipped off the TV, and they began to eat in silence. "I've never cared for the guy," he said, "but I feel for him. He looks awful."

Clara didn't answer. She didn't buy that Paul's speech had been sincere, but if pressed, she couldn't have said exactly why not.

"Wow," Benny said. She looked up from her plate to find him staring at her.

"What?"

"The look on your face right now is something else." She swallowed the bite she'd been chewing a bit too thoroughly and reached for her coffee, averting her eyes. "Penny for your thoughts?"

She took a long sip of the lukewarm drink and met his gaze. "It's not that I don't feel for him, but . . . don't you think the doctor might be a bit of a *spin* doctor too? I mean, I don't think he's *ever* been to one of their soccer games."

"So he was using that as an example. I bet he *does* wish he could go this Saturday."

"I don't like that he's making her sound greedy. The obvious implication is that money is her motive. End of story."

He raised an eyebrow. "Look. I know Kristin is your friend, but if I've learned anything from my years in accounting, it's that you can solve a *lot* of so-called mysteries by *following the money.* Even when good people are involved. It's predictable, and sometimes it's a little depressing, but that doesn't make it less true."

She pushed her stool back from the counter and turned away to rinse her plate at the sink. There was no real reason to be irked at Benny, and yet she couldn't help but think that his buying Paul's story meant that Paul was somehow *winning*. "Don't you think that's a little too easy an explanation in this case?" she asked, her voice tight.

"Maybe." He slid his own plate, unrinsed, into the open dishwasher and gave her a peck on the cheek. "But sometimes the most obvious explanation is the right one. Even if you don't want to hear it."

She waited until he turned away before pulling the crusty plate back out. As a general rule, she tried to reserve nagging for things she couldn't just as easily do herself.

7

The missing, the hidden, the murdered, and the otherwise lost never get to tell their sides of the story. It's the last and sometimes cruelest injustice. Because often the people left behind to shape the narrative have an agenda that doesn't necessarily revolve around the truth.

It's not always out of malice. There's self-preservation to consider. One's image, state of mind, well-being. The human desire to attempt to make sense of a world with no real order to it, to demand to know why when there is no reason—or at least no good one.

The explanations given, the conclusions drawn, might be willfully dishonest, they may be obliviously ignorant, or they could be part of the truth—but rarely are they the whole story. Still, by default, those versions are the only ones that will ever be told.

Consider, for instance, the suicide note. You might think that's an exception, a victim who does get to have the last word. Yet rarely does it satisfy those left behind. They read between the lines and still they ask: But why? They arrive at their own conclusions. As well they should. Who's to say if that note is true? It may have been what they thought you wanted to hear. It may have been what they wanted you to believe. It may have been an act of kindness, one easier than the truth.

What if the rest of us had the luxury of foreseeing our premature exit, one way or the other? Would we entrust our own truths to some-

one else after all? Would we make sure that someone we've left behind could speak for us? Or would we merely curse the fact that no one would ever know?

Because some of us were silenced long before we disappeared from view.

8

Family law focuses primarily on protecting marriage and traditional families. Stepfamilies, it seems, are considered more problematic and often underrepresented.

—"Knowing and Understanding Stepparents' Rights," DadsDivorce.com

Clara pushed the stroller to a stop against the brick wall and knocked lightly on the locked glass door of the boutique. Rhoda glanced up from the counter, where she was filling the register drawer, and Clara raised her hand in a silent wave. She caught sight of Randi, sprawled in a hemp hammock for sale in the corner with Adele propped up on her lap, and her friend turned the baby and pumped her tiny fists in the air in a greeting.

She was reminding herself not to call the baby *Radele,* as Benny always jokingly did at home, trilling his *r*'s whenever he caught sight of them across the yards or down the sidewalk—"Rrrandi! Rrrhoda! Rrradele!"—when Rhoda swung the door open, ringing the whimsical chimes that hung in the doorway. "I was just going to text you," Rhoda said cheerfully, gesturing for her to come in. "Now there won't be a written trail of what a gossip I am!"

Clara lifted Maddie from the stroller and slipped inside, taking care not to disturb the CLOSED sign as Rhoda shut and locked the door behind her. She paused for a moment, as she always did upon entering the aptly named Moondance boutique, to breathe in the feeling of being surrounded by beautiful and somewhat frivolous things.

Clara had once had style. Something close to a signature one, actually. A frugal but patient shopper, she'd delighted in her finds as if they were endangered species she'd tracked through miles of wild terrain: the cashmere cowl-neck with a near custom-fit drape, the vintage dress so well preserved it could pass for a reissue, the distressed gray riding boots that hugged her skinny calves just so. Now she looked down at her khakis and plain navy T with a kind of shock and wondered where it had gone.

To the grab-and-go purgatory where you shopped with kids in tow, that's where.

"I take it you saw?" Clara asked.

"Struck us as quite the performance," Rhoda said.

"But to be fair, we've never really been fans of Dr. Paul," Randi added. She swung her legs over the side of the hammock and carefully laid the baby in the soft center of an oversized throw pillow on the floor. "What did you make of it?" she asked Clara.

"Same." She got to her knees on the floor and settled Maddie next to Adele, marveling at how her daughter, still a baby herself, dwarfed the nearly three-month-old. She couldn't resist running a finger across the tips of Adele's tiny toes.

"Well, I think we're in the minority," Rhoda said. "We ran into Natalie on the way in, and she seemed to think it proved her point from last night. Stay for coffee?" She squeezed Clara's shoulder and disappeared into the back room without waiting for an answer.

Randi took a basket of small felt toys from the shelf behind her and set them in front of a delighted Maddie, who immediately dumped them onto the floor and started lifting them by their price tags, one by one. Clara bicycled Adele's pudgy little legs and was rewarded with a gummy smile.

"I suppose it doesn't really matter why she's gone," Randi said sadly. "Only that she is."

Clara shook her head. "About that," she said. "The police called and asked me to come in. I guess they have more questions."

Everyone had more questions. Clara hadn't known what to expect when dropping Thomas off at school, but what she'd found was sort of a reverent hush—nervous nods and meaningful silences conveying the uncertainty that would seem too real if given voice to. The concern was thicker there, where the twins' cubbies sat with empty coat hooks and crinkly piles of artwork waiting to be taken home. Clara gathered from the teachers' whispers that the detectives had been there and were still making their rounds talking to the enrolled families.

"Really? Have you remembered anything new since last night?"

"I don't think so."

Rhoda reappeared with a tray of cream, agave nectar, and three steaming mugs, and Clara accepted one gratefully. It was one of those sturdy kiln-fired creations that always beckoned her at art shows, until she saw the price tags. "But that's why I'm here," she admitted. "I know you have work to do, but is there any chance I could leave Maddie with you, just for a half hour or so, while I stop by the station? I'm not sure who else to ask . . ."

"Of course," Rhoda said, sinking cross-legged to the floor next to Clara. "In spite of the circumstances, I have to say it's nice seeing you so many days in a row. All day Sunday we were saying we should all get together more often, make it a regular thing, get to know Kristin and Izzy more."

Clara nodded, watching the cream swirl into her coffee. She liked this cozy corner of the store, with piles of artfully arranged pillows on display and quilts strung up on the wall. Soft sunlight streamed through the side windows, creating what felt like a little pocket of warmth and light, though the storefront was still in deep shadow, as was the alcove of more unwieldy sale items in the back.

"Say," Randi said, "would you like to come to our meditation group tonight, at the Intuitive Healing Studio? We got an email from our instructor this morning that we'll be focusing this session on sending safe energy and strength to Kristin and the twins. She said we should bring anyone who might want to join and they could sit in for free."

The idea did sound sort of interesting, though not normally her scene. "You know, I think the kids could use some normalcy tonight—both parents home—but I *love* that you'll all be doing that. Maybe Izzy would like to go?" She had no idea if that was true, but Izzy seemed to be longing for something she hadn't yet found here. Even if it was just friendship.

"Good thought," Rhoda said. "We'll invite her."

"Will anyone be sending energy to Paul too?" Clara couldn't help asking.

"Conspicuously not mentioned in the email."

"Benny felt the same as Natalie, about Paul on TV. He buys his story . . . reluctantly."

Rhoda pulled a face. "I could never put my finger on why I didn't like the guy. I don't know that I've spoken with him since . . . maybe last Christmas? He came in to get gifts for Kristin and the twins. I think things were already on the rocks by then, though."

They were staring intently at Clara, as if she'd been cast in some reality TV show. "It's weird looking back, isn't it?" she said. "But the more I think about it, I guess I'm starting to feel like some things make more sense now."

"I feel kind of mean talking about this," Randi said. "I mean, being a parent has *nothing* to do with biology." She looked meaningfully at her wife, and Rhoda nodded. Clara wondered how they'd decided which one of them would give birth to their daughter. It couldn't have been easy. "But I know what you mean. I always thought he was kind of an absentee dad."

Clara nodded. "It never seemed to bother Kristin, though—even before the divorce. She told me that sometimes he seemed *jealous* of the time she spent with the twins instead of with him. I guess I've heard of other men feeling that way, but Benny is just so not like that."

Rhoda cleared her throat. "Don't take this the wrong way, Clara, but I'm not sure you're the best judge of what is and is not normal man behavior. When it comes to husbands, you hit the jackpot—and I say that as a devoted lesbian with no bisexual leanings."

"Still," Randi said. "Maybe he should have spent more time with Aaron and Abby. And maybe he wanted more one-on-one time with Kristin. That doesn't mean he doesn't care. He's the only father they've ever known. He has a right to know where they are."

"Of course he does," Clara said quickly. She plucked a felt bluebird from Maddie's fist just as she was about to use it as a teething ring. Maddie let out a wail, and Rhoda handed her a little purple butterfly that she chomped down on gleefully and without hesitation. "It's okay," Rhoda told Clara, smiling. "It'll dry."

Clara resisted the urge to snatch it back. Her concern hadn't been as much that the toy was for sale as that it had been handled by who knew how many shoppers' dirty fingers and was now being licked by her toddler. But her leeriness of germs did not play well in Yellow Springs, where the other moms on the playground were unbothered by their children gumming the ladder to the sliding board and would give her dirty looks for wielding hand sanitizer.

Rhoda sighed. "It's just that Kristin never struck me as overly concerned with money, even though she had enough. And we business owners know the spending habits in this town."

Clara thought again of what Benny had said, about following the money. "What were Paul's?" she asked.

"His spending habits? Aside from those gifts?" Rhoda furrowed her brow. "Huh. I guess he didn't really have any. He must have left all that to Kristin."

"The place he's been living ever since he moved out is kind of a dump," Randi said, sitting up straighter. "When the landlord mentioned he'd moved in, I was surprised. I guess I just figured he'd been in a hurry to find something and would move again later."

Clara had never thought to ask where he'd gone. She'd only known it wasn't far. "Unless he thought it was temporary for other reasons," she said.

"You mean like he thought there was a chance of them getting back together? Or hoped there was?" Rhoda stared into her coffee.

"Okay, now I feel like kind of a bitch. Maybe I shouldn't have discounted what he said on TV after all."

"I never got the impression reconciliation was an option for Kristin," Clara said carefully.

"Well," Randi said, "if Dr. Paul couldn't take the hint before, I'm pretty sure he's gotten the idea *now*."

The room Clara was led to looked more like it belonged in a real estate office than a police station. Cushioned chairs, potted plants, even framed line drawings of local landmarks—the old gristmill, the new brewery. Leave it to Yellow Springs to dispense with the cold, surgical feel of the interrogation rooms from televised crime dramas and—Clara happened to know from unfortunate experience—from the precincts in Cincinnati.

Still, that didn't stop it from bringing back memories. Clara pushed them aside to focus on Detective Bryant. He was shaking her hand, thanking her for coming, introducing his partner, Detective Marks, an austere-looking middle-aged woman dressed in slacks and a button-down, her hair back in a tight knot. She brought to mind a school principal Clara had had, one who was always reminding the students of the spelling of her title by assuring them she was their pal. They'd quickly learned that she wasn't, though, as she doled out detention generously and at random, like candy at a parade. Not even the good kids were safe.

"Detective Marks and I are part of a task force working various aspects of the case," he was explaining now. "So I can assure you this situation with your neighbor is a priority."

Clara wasn't sure how to respond. *Thanks?* She nodded.

"I know you were caught off guard yesterday, as everyone was. We've been interviewing friends and family, coworkers, teachers— covering the bases, of course. But we wanted to circle back and see if anything else has come to mind, now that you've had some time to process this."

She bit her lip. "I've been replaying Saturday night over and over. But everything just seemed so normal."

"Your other neighbors don't seem to recall Saturday night very well," he said. "Sounds like you ladies know how to have a good time!" He laughed good-naturedly. "So if you could tell us more about it, that might be a help."

She cleared her throat, hoping she didn't appear as nervous as she felt.

"You mentioned she talked a bit about her divorce, that it wasn't really affecting the kids. What about *her*? Did she say anything about how *she* felt about things?"

Clara thought for a moment. "Just kind of dismissive stuff," she said. "I don't think she really wanted to talk about it, but someone asked."

"What kind of dismissive stuff?"

She shifted in her seat. Being here felt like betraying a confidence. "She said she wasn't cut out to be a doctor's wife. She mentioned the rough hours, like I told you before." Clara tried to picture Kristin in the firelight, wineglass in hand, tangle of dark curls billowing around her head. And suddenly, she *could* see her saying something else. "She said he would sink into horrible moods when something went wrong with a patient."

"And that was often?"

" 'More often than you might think,' she said. I think those were her exact words."

"Okay. Good. Anything else?"

What had happened next was something Clara had been replaying in her mind since yesterday. "At least two good things came from the marriage," Clara had reassured Kristin, alluding to the twins, expecting her to agree. But Kristin hadn't given her so much as a nod. She'd merely stared off into space, allowing an awkward silence to wrap around the fire circle. Clara had suddenly, inexplicably felt so foolish that her face had flushed.

Now, of course, she understood why. The twins hadn't come from the marriage. That would have been as good a time as any for Kristin to tell her. But she hadn't.

Clara shook her head.

"Mrs. Tiffin—"

"Clara."

"Clara. As far as we can tell, you knew Kristin just about as well as anybody did."

If that was a fact, Clara couldn't help thinking it a bit sad. Much as she loved Kristin and their young friendship, she could list a whole host of people who surely knew her own self better than the woman she'd lived next door to for just over a year. There were her college roommates, still tightly bonded though they'd scattered like seeds after graduation, and old coworkers back in Cincinnati, who kept a standing lunch date every other month at a midpoint restaurant, and the wives of Benny's old friends . . .

Although she had to admit, she'd seen less and less of all of them since she'd had kids and followed Benny here, an hour away from their old home base. Maybe the same had been happening to Kristin, for longer.

The detective continued. "I've interviewed a whole group of women who had regular playdates with Kristin and her children, and no one can tell me much about her. It's almost odd."

Feeling a surge of loyalty toward her friend, Clara leveled her gaze at him. "Have you ever *been* on a playdate with kids that age?" she asked.

"No kids."

"Well, take it from me, you can't get a word in edgewise."

He raised an eyebrow. "Then why have playdates at all?"

She had wondered the same thing many times, usually when bundling up kids cranky from an afternoon of overstimulation, her own stomach growling because she'd barely managed a bite of the potluck lunch. "I guess to make ourselves feel like we're socializing with adults, even though really we're just wrangling even more kids than we started with?"

He glanced sidelong at Detective Marks, who hid a smile and shrugged. Clara recognized the look of a fellow mother and relaxed a little. Funny how that was all it took to relate to another person, once you'd had children. A biological similarity. It was ridiculous, if you thought about it, but that didn't make it less true.

"Great," he said dryly. "Okay. Try to think about the words you did get in. She ever talk about the rest of her family?"

Clara had given it some thought after Izzy asked about it last night. "Saturday she did say something about not being on the greatest terms with her sister. I remember because it was the first I'd heard that she had a sister."

"What did she say exactly?"

"Izzy was talking about an issue she was having with her own sister. And Kristin said"—she could still hear it—"*My sister is shit.*'"

He looked at her expectantly. "That's it?"

She shrugged. "That's it. I think someone changed the subject."

He changed tack. "Your kids went with Kristin's to the Circle of Learning preschool. Was Kristin well liked among the moms?"

The twins were so recognizable that everyone in the school seemed to know Kristin. Never once had Clara seen her just rush in and out to drop off or pick up Abby and Aaron. She was always cooing at a baby in the lobby, or talking up a pregnant teacher, or stopping by the director's office to offer help with whatever new activity they were planning. She wasn't one of those moms who seemed skittish about coming too close to anyone else's kid, as if at any moment someone was going to jump out and accuse her of overstepping. She regularly had a crowd of four-and five-year-olds lined up behind her own kids for high fives out the door.

"Very."

"Do you ever read the school's collaborative parent blog?"

"Occasionally."

"She made some guest posts there, and I have to say, some of those comments threads devolved into flame wars over seemingly trivial things. On one, she was getting attacked just for admitting to serving her kids chicken nuggets."

She shook her head. "That has nothing to do with Kristin. Every parenting blog is like that."

Again he looked at Detective Marks, and again she shrugged with a small smile. "What happened to 'it takes a village'?" he muttered.

"The village has gotten pretty judgmental," Clara said. Detective Marks laughed out loud.

He sighed. "What about her dad? Any feelings about not know-ing him, or maybe wanting to find him?"

Clara shook her head slowly, taking it in. If Kristin had grown up without a father, then being faced with raising her own children without theirs must have felt like the worst of ways for a life to come full circle.

"She ever talk about her mom being in an Alzheimer's facility?"

She cringed. Detective Bryant was right. None of them had known Kristin. It had nagged at the back of her mind since his visit yesterday, and it was filling her with all-out shame now. How could these questions be about her most outwardly together friend, who took everything in stride and transformed it into something they could laugh about? She shook her head.

"Did it ever strike you as strange that she never mentioned her parents?"

It was Clara's turn to shrug. "Not really."

"Any reason why not?"

"Well, my mother is a water aerobics instructor in Florida who only occasionally remembers she has grandchildren and calls to check in. So I don't mention *her* much either."

He put his pen down on the table and sat back in his chair.

"I'm sorry," she said, meaning it. Somehow this conversation had taken a cheeky turn. Staying home all day with kids made her oc-casionally impatient with adults, but she knew now wasn't the time for that. "I know I'm not being very helpful."

"You were a little." He gave her a brief smile.

Clara hesitated. "I have to ask," she said. "Do you have any rea-son to think she *isn't* okay? Gone of her own volition?"

"We're exploring every option."

She couldn't resist pressing. "Izzy said Paul told her he broke a window to get in. Do you have any way of knowing that he didn't break it earlier? Like, whenever she went missing?"

His face revealed nothing. "Not really. It's under an overhang, so the rain wouldn't have come in on Sunday. I take it you saw Dr. Kirkland on camera this morning?"

"I did."

"And what did you think of it?"

She hesitated. "I guess something about it didn't sit well with me."

"That's obvious from your demeanor."

Clara sat up straighter.

"We understand you have prior experience as a witness to a domestic violence incident."

Clara was surprised, though she supposed she shouldn't have been. It was probably routine for them to check records, and her subpoena would be on file. "Years ago."

"Would you say that might be coloring your perceptions of things here?"

She looked pointedly at Detective Bryant, and then Detective Marks, whose role in this partnership remained unclear. She'd neither spoken nor taken notes. "No. But I'd say it might be coloring *your* perceptions of my demeanor."

The detectives exchanged a glance.

"Why do you care what I think?" Clara asked, genuinely curious. "What does it matter?"

Detective Bryant sighed. "We don't, necessarily. It's just that you were right next door. And you were among the last people to see her."

"Can I ask you an honest question? Have *you* ever been the last person to see someone? Someone who never came back?"

He hesitated, then shook his head.

"Well, I'm glad for you. Because as I guess you know, I have, and it's not something I'd wish on my worst enemy. I'm certainly not gunning for that to be the case here."

She glanced at the clock, hoping Maddie wasn't wearing out her welcome with Randi and Rhoda. "I guess what I don't get is this picture that's being painted—about the money. If Kristin was sitting on a million dollars, and then had the good fortune to marry a doctor, why would she take a job at Antioch? It's not like admin is the kind of rewarding career you can't pass up."

No one offered a rhetorical answer, so she continued. "Seems to me she wanted to contribute financially and *not* rely on Paul. So to see a mom work hard to try to do it all—especially now that I know what she's been through, being *widowed,* for crying out loud—and now it's being suggested that she left just to deny Paul what he thought was his due? While he's up there alluding to all the money he's spent raising her kids? I don't necessarily blame Paul for grasping at straws, but it doesn't ring true to me."

Clara took a deep breath, realizing she'd been ranting. It was all a roundabout way of getting to say what she was really thinking, "And that leaves the question: If that's not why she left, then why?"

"We do appreciate your help, Mrs. Tiffin. And we encourage you to continue to let us know if you think of anything else that could be relevant. But understand, we can't discuss the details of the investigation with you. It's ongoing."

"One last question." It was the first from Detective Marks, but something in her tone made Clara think it would not be the last after all. "When you were all sitting around the fire, did Kristin happen to throw anything in? A scrap of paper, even?"

Clara frowned. "Not that I saw, no."

"You wouldn't mind if we swung by later to take a look around the patio? We don't need to further infringe on your day. You won't even know we're there."

Another wave of the anxiety she'd felt earlier this morning swept over her. Just how much scrutiny was she under? "Of course not." Detective Marks granted her a smile, but it did nothing to set her at ease. She took a deep breath. "I'd feel a *lot* better if I could leave here with you assuring me that you have confidence that nothing dangerous is going on. Kristin and Abby and Aaron might be gone for the time being, but Paul Kirkland is right next door, and my concern about that doesn't have anything to do with what else I may or may not have witnessed years ago. Any mother would feel the same. Any *friend or neighbor* would feel the same."

"We always look at the husband—or ex-husband—regardless," Detective Bryant said. "But we can't get in there with a forensics team unless he lets us at this point."

"He isn't letting you?"

"Something we said rubbed him the wrong way."

She'd been feeling increasingly unsettled. But now, for the first time, she allowed herself to consider the real possibility, however small, that she should be afraid for Kristin.

"Can you at least tell me if I should be worried?"

"I can," he said. "You should not. That's our job."

9

In 1825, Yellow Springs was inhabited by a co-operative community called the Owenites, and in 1862, the town welcomed a group of free slaves led by the Reverend Moncure Daniel Conway. Yellow Springs became a place for new beginnings and rejuvenation, aided by the healing waters of the springs themselves, as health spas and resorts cropped up in the village.

—Yellow Springs Historical Walking Tour

No-brainer idea for tomorrow's discussion segment," Sonny was saying. "*Share your nastiest divorce stories.* Should make for some great calls, lots of Facebook shares . . ." He'd crashed Izzy's post-show planning period, taking a seat in her office without asking and then loudly calling Day in to join them, and Izzy was trying to swallow her irritation.

"Seems a bit tasteless, don't you think?" she asked, cutting him off.

"Not at all," Day piped up. "It's a natural tie-in to the buzz out of Yellow Springs."

Izzy had chosen not to share that the *buzz out of Yellow Springs* was happening on her street. And this was exactly why.

"What's so bad about asking people to share their experiences of marriage ending in disaster? Everybody knows of one." Sonny laced his fingers behind his head, a sure sign that he was not about to let this go until she gave in, and the back of Izzy's neck began to tense, vertebra by vertebra. She didn't want to be stuck here any later than necessary. She'd hit the motherlode yesterday on clearance at Greenleaf Gardens, where someone who seemed to know what he was talking about had advised her on fall plantings, and she planned to spend the afternoon converting her neglected little fenced backyard of weeds into the sanctuary she'd been dreaming of. The forecast called for flash storms, but she was undeterred. An impulse to sink her fingers into the soil, to plant something that could take root, had seized her with surprising ferocity. She wanted to hang on to this urge, to show herself and everyone else that she could do this—make a life on her own. Maybe later she'd throw her hat into the air like Mary Tyler Moore, for posterity.

Sonny snickered, oblivious. "I mean, I'm as happily betrothed as they come, but I've got a whopper about a friend whose crazy, *and I do mean cuckoo crazy,* wife actually—"

"That's not the point," Izzy said. "The point is that someone should be able to have a personal tragedy without us polling the audience about it."

"Oh, please," Day said. "CNN can't even host a presidential debate without consulting we the people of Facebook. Why should local headlines be any different?"

Izzy was feeling disproportionately testy, she knew. She blamed the tension that had settled over her neighborhood—there was no escaping it. Another day had passed with no developments in the search for Kristin, and no further sign of Paul, who seemed to have gone into hiding since his plea on camera yesterday. With nothing new to report, the network vans had been gone by the time she headed in this morning, and it was an odd relief, though it hadn't stopped the anchors from devoting their early broadcasts to speculating live from their studios.

Speculation irked Izzy. How much nicer the world could be if people who didn't know what they were talking about would keep their mouths shut.

"While we're at it, why don't we recast Second Date Update as a breakup update?" she said. "We'll give people a chance to call bullshit on the reasons they were given for the split. Now, there's a shitstorm people would tune in for, am I right or am I right?"

Sonny cocked his head to the side. "I know you're joking, but actually—"

Izzy let out a grunt of frustration so loud he jumped. "No 'but actually'! Have we really sunk that low?"

Her cell phone buzzed, and she seized it from her desktop, grateful for the distraction. Penny's picture toasted her from the screen, holding up a martini on a long-ago girls' night, and she stifled a groan. Still, if she was going to acquiesce to a conversation she didn't want to have, all the better if it got her out of another one.

"Sorry, I have to take this." She didn't give them a chance to protest, simply put the phone to her ear. "Hello?"

"Izzy! *Finally.*"

She mouthed "tomorrow" at Sonny and Day, and they got to their feet, exchanging a glance that was the optic equivalent of a shrug. Each gave her a silent wave as she pushed the door shut behind them.

"Sorry. I've been meaning to call—"

"Gosh, I hope so. I'm starting to feel like a stalker!"

"I really—"

"And nobody wants to see a pregnant stalker!" Penny laughed loudly. "That's just weird!"

Izzy held perfectly still. Maybe she'd misunderstood. "What?"

"That's why I've been ringing you off the hook! Geez, I was starting to worry you were going to find out from someone else! I've been trying to keep the cat in the bag, but Mom and Dad know now, so not only is it out, but it's running around terrorizing the neighborhood."

Izzy felt faintly aware that she was supposed to summon something—words, a laugh, an exclamation of happiness—but the bottom was falling out of her heart. She allowed the silence to go on a beat too long, and knew she had to speak. She moved her lips, but nothing came out.

"Wow," she said finally. "Gosh, Pen. I didn't think . . . I mean, you used to say you didn't even want kids."

"Oh. I *know*." Penny laughed as if this were the greatest lark of her life.

"Seriously, though. You used to say it a *lot*. Like *every time* you saw a kid."

"I know! But that was before, obviously. I mean, I never could picture it, myself as a mom, but then I found Josh, and I realized I just *could*, you know?"

"And Josh, he's excited? Because he also—"

"Okay, so the full story." Penny's voice was so breezy she might have been explaining why she'd decided to give country music a try after years of singular punk rock devotion. "We met this older couple on our honeymoon. Those all-inclusive places, you end up seeing the same people all week at meals and stuff, and . . . anyway, they were great. Pushing sixty, but they were there to *party*. They figured out we could order top-shelf margaritas even though they weren't on the bar menu, and man, could they dance. People don't dance like that anymore! It's like in those old movies you love."

So Penny had managed to meet a modern-day Cary Grant on her honeymoon. She really did have all the luck.

"Anyway. One night we started teasing them that our goal is to be them when we grow up. And they started telling us more about themselves, how they've just become grandparents . . . and when we said we didn't plan to have kids, they were *crestfallen*. Like, it was almost weird. But then Sheri—that was the woman's name—she said it seems like the people who would be the most amazing parents are the people who decide not to have kids. And how sad that is, what a waste."

Stay out of it, Sheri, Izzy thought. *Go dance with Cary.*

"We both woke up the next day still thinking about it, and we decided they were right. I mean, we have *so* much to offer. We'd be fun parents, right?"

"Fun," Izzy repeated, numb.

"I guess it was meant to be. We pulled the goalie last month and scored on our first try!"

"Wow." This was where Izzy was meant to switch over to something genuine. She'd asked her questions. She'd gotten the answers. On to the happy part.

And yet.

This was why Penny had been trying to reach her. Izzy realized too late that while she'd been smugly dodging her sister's calls, a part of her had been feeling relieved that Penny had finally noticed her absence. She hadn't, though. This was the sisterly equivalent of those obligatory calls she'd gotten for years after college, from friend after friend whom she hadn't heard from in months phoning under the guise of catching up only to announce her engagement. Izzy had minded those calls more than she should have. "What do you want them to do, *not* tell you?" Josh had asked one day.

Of course she hadn't wanted that. She just wanted to be the one with the happy reason for making the call.

"Well! Congratulations. Yeah, that was . . . it was fast, for sure. Good job."

"Good job—ha! That's what I told Josh! Listen, Mom and Dad are beside themselves. I know it's overkill, but they're hosting a thing at their condo's clubhouse next Tuesday. Nothing official, no gifts. Just cocktails—mocktails for me, of course—hot hors d'oeuvres, desserts—they're inviting the whole extended family, and friends. Say you'll be there?"

Izzy stalled. "Tuesday, you said?"

"Yeah, I know it's a weird day. The clubhouse was booked weekends. They just didn't want to wait to get everyone together, I think. Seems like they're sort of empty nesting all over again now that they're alone in their condo, with all new neighbors, and you've left town, and . . . well, dad had this health scare."

"Health scare?"

"They didn't want to worry you. Thought you were already under enough stress, with the house and the move. You're lucky you didn't know. Josh said I was impossible to live with that whole week we were waiting for the test results! He was so sweet, though, taking care of me as if *I* were the one being tested and—" She cut herself off abruptly. "Anyway, don't worry. It was a false alarm. He's fine. But I think it made them a little trigger-happy with their party hats."

Izzy wondered how she'd come to this point where she felt so utterly outside of her own family. Surely they hadn't pushed her out. At least not intentionally. Maybe an accidental nudge. And then . . . well, then she'd left of her own volition. That much she had to take responsibility for. Once her parents became grandparents, she'd be even more . . . extraneous? Forgotten?

No. She'd be an aunt.

"Of course I'll be there," she said weakly.

Penny let out a squeal. "Great! And seriously, we really want to get out there and see what the house looks like now that you've got it all set up. Not that it wasn't cute to begin with, but you know what I mean."

"Sure."

"I have an ultrasound Saturday, and then Josh's parents are having us over, but—"

"We'll pick a day soon."

"Right. See you Tuesday, okay? So glad I finally got hold of you! It was like it wasn't going to feel real until you knew. And now it does!"

Izzy knew how she felt.

Please, tell me that didn't just happen, she thought, staring at the silent phone in her hand. *Please, God, I can't—*

There was a rap on the door, and Sonny burst through. "Good! You're off!" he said, diving for the tiny television on her desk and switching on the local twelve o'clock news. "This proves my point."

Izzy wiped away the tears that had escaped his notice as the anchor's voice filled the room. "Much has been made about this *million dollars* of life insurance money that's unaccounted for, so I'm here with Todd Davis, a wealth manager with Bank of Ohio. I know this situation has raised a lot of questions among our viewers. Mr. Davis, thanks for agreeing to answer a few."

"My pleasure."

Izzy might have screamed at Sonny to get out of her office, but it was easier to just sit there, numb to his rudeness, numb to Penny's excitement, numb to the newscast.

"Let's cut to the chase," the anchor continued. "Dr. Kirkland claims his wife vanished with the life insurance payout from her first husband, in part because she was worried she'd lose half of it in the divorce. Is it really possible the courts would have awarded Dr. Kirkland a share?"

"It's not likely. To some extent it would depend on whether she'd commingled the assets—put the money into joint accounts. In that case it obviously becomes hard to determine what portion of that money has and hasn't already been spent by the parties with access to those accounts, even if she were to then withdraw the same amount later."

Sonny caught sight of Day walking past and gestured wildly. "Day! This is what you were saying!" She stopped in the doorway.

"I see. But it's been reported that we're talking about a separate account that she allegedly was setting aside for the children."

The wealth manager frowned. "I saw that, though I'm not clear on where these details are coming from—"

"So what Dr. Kirkland is stating as his wife's motive for taking the money and disappearing is simply not plausible. Because those funds would not have been split in the divorce settlement."

"I wouldn't call it *implausible*."

"Can you explain?"

"I have clients all the time who make odd decisions about their money simply because they don't understand the law." He leaned back in his chair, clearly enjoying the fact that someone was interested in the topic for a change. "It's like those people who lived through the Depression and now store cash under their mattresses because somehow they feel that's safer than a bank. Obviously, in today's world with more fiscal safeguards in place, the bigger danger to your savings is that your house could catch fire, or you could be robbed, or you could pass away unexpectedly without having told your family where to find it. But that doesn't mean those people don't have, in their minds, a valid motive for stashing their money that way."

"So in this case . . ." Izzy couldn't help thinking the reporter seemed a little slow on the uptake.

"If he threatened her that he was going to make a play for the funds in court—regardless of whether that play would have been successful—she might have been scared enough to take the money and run."

"Because it does seem unfair that your second husband would be able to take the life insurance money your first husband left you."

"It does, and that's why the law is the way it is. But . . ."

"Yes?"

"If that second husband raised the first husband's kids largely with his own money, while all that life insurance money that was intended for them sat untouched in a bank, he might argue that he was entitled to something of a refund." He chuckled as if this were the most fun he'd had in months.

"The plot thickens. Mr. Davis, thanks so much for your time."

"If any of your viewers have concerns with their own finances they'd like addressed—"

Sonny switched it off triumphantly. "So, obviously we're going with the divorce stories segment," he said. "Money, custody, cheating—it'll be great."

He smiled easily at Izzy. "I know what you're thinking, I could produce this show myself." She narrowed her eyes. "Don't worry, we'll let you stay. I'm no good at paperwork."

The wind whipped Izzy's hair as she ran to her car and slammed the door shut against the chaos outside. Summer and autumn seemed to be colliding in the sky, as if it couldn't make up its mind between the two. The humidity was tangible, the heat a twenty-degree leap from this morning, but the wind carried oddly icier blasts that warned of bone-chilling days ahead.

Izzy started the engine, and instantly the front and back wind-shields fogged, a smattering of supersized raindrops dotting them as if on cue. She looked in the direction of home, where the sky was brighter in the distance. She had to get out ahead of the storm. She did not want her coworkers to see her marooned in the parking lot, sobbing pathetically over what was ostensibly her baby sister's happy news. Which she was about to be. Any second now.

Her phone buzzed into the car's Bluetooth system, and Izzy glanced down at the display. Her mother. She couldn't talk to her, not like this.

She flipped the vents on full blast, and the bottom few inches of fog faded. Good enough. Blinking back tears, she whipped backward out of the parking space and heard a sickening crunch.

In the rearview mirror the culprit loomed—a light pole with a large concrete base. The very one, in fact, that she looked at almost every morning thinking, *One of these days I'm going to end up hitting that.* Swiping angrily at her eyes with the backs of her hands, she looked around and didn't see anyone. What were the odds that no one inside had witnessed her gaffe through a window? The thought of it pressed on top of the humiliation she was already feeling, and without even getting out to look at her car—she was confident the light pole was fine—she hit the gas.

Penny and Josh were married. Married. It wasn't as if throwing a baby into the mix was what made him officially and forever off-limits.

So why did she feel as if the sky were caving in on her all over again?

"Auntie Izzy!" Her mother's ecstatic voice mail message was auto-playing through the car stereo now. "I'm so excited Penny finally got through to you with the news! I just called to gush. You're going to be such a great aunt. Not like those *other* aunts." The notes of her laugh were a giddy song, and real tears were trailing down Izzy's cheeks now, fast and hot. This was not how this was supposed to be. She should be just as happy as her mother was. She *deserved* to share in this happiness. Josh had ruined *everything*. "Don't tell your father's sisters I said that," her mother was whispering now. "Call only if you want. Can't wait to see you soon!"

The rain teased her throughout the drive, as if someone were aiming a garden hose over her car in brief intervals, but the downpour never came. By the time she pulled onto her block, her hands still shaking, a patch of bright blue showed itself in the blustery clouds, and she knew with certainty that it was mocking her. Had she actually thought she was doing better, here on her own? She'd only been fooling herself.

The garage was still filled with the largest boxes from the move, the ones she wasn't sure if she should throw away—the too-expensive-to-toss-too-colossal-to-keep wardrobe carriers with the hanger bars, the packaging from binge-ordered décor she still wasn't sure she liked. She hadn't missed the garage until this exact moment, when parking in the driveway meant bearing her scars for the neighborhood to see. She briefly considered backing in, but given the day's track record, that didn't seem wise. *Maybe it's not that bad,* she told herself as she pulled the car up close to the house, cut the engine, and walked around to survey the back bumper.

But it wasn't just the bumper. The left taillight was smashed, surely inoperable, and ugly dents and scratches smeared the side rear panel. The metal of the trunk looked like someone had taken a baseball bat to it. No, something harder and bigger than that.

Like a lamppost.

"Damn it!" she yelled, kicking the tire. With her next kick came a fresh flood of tears, floating her fists into motion as well, and soon she was full-out whaling on the car, pummeling the trunk with the whole of her arms and the tire with the toes of her boots, letting out primal grunts of fury.

Behind her, someone's throat cleared loudly, and she stopped without turning around, heaving to catch her breath.

"You look like I feel," said the voice behind her. And she recognized it as Paul's. "On behalf of me, thank you for doing that. It was quite satisfying to watch."

She barked out an ugly laugh. She couldn't bear to turn.

"Permission to approach the vehicle?" She heard his steps

draw near, and a large hand appeared beside her and slid itself over the top of the trunk. "This one I could hammer out from the inside," he said. "It'll have crinkly spots, like used wrapping paper, but we can get the shape back." He bent toward the taillight. "This one is just a trip to the hardware store. And the side panel . . ." He moved to examine the streaks. "Not an easy fix outside of a body shop, but you could make it less noticeable with touch-up paint."

"Thanks," Izzy said. "Maybe I'll—" She could think of no one she knew who was capable at this sort of thing. "Ask my dad," she finished lamely, knowing he'd never touched a bottle of touch-up paint in his life. Though infinitely interested in getting his hands dirty in the natural world, he cared little for the man-made.

"I could help," Paul said. "You may have noticed I'm not doing much else. For some reason I feel like I can't leave the house, yet every hour that goes by it seems less likely that I'm going to be throwing a welcome home party."

Discomfort washed over Izzy. "I can't ask that of you," she said. She still hadn't looked at him. She knew she must appear wild, her eyes puffy, her hair blown into a tangle, her hands and forearms red and throbbing from their assault on the metal.

"You didn't," he said. "In fact, *I'm* asking it of *you*. I need something to do with myself. I'm going crazy. And this is leaving the house without leaving it. I can see it from here."

Why was he being so nice? Fresh tears filled Izzy's eyes. She shook her head again.

"Please," he said. "Just let me do something nice for someone today. You can stay inside if you want to. I just . . . I need this."

She knew she should be ashamed. If anyone here should be doing something for someone, it should be the other way around. She should fix him a meal. She should offer to help in some way— in *any* way. Where the hell was Team Paul?

But she could conjure no genuine feelings. The stormy skies she'd dodged earlier were still raging in her brain.

Reluctantly, she turned to face him. "Maybe just the taillight, so I don't get pulled over?"

He nodded, touched her arm so briefly she thought she might have imagined it, and was gone as quickly and silently as he came.

She didn't know anything, not really, about being married, or raising kids, or splitting up. But regret . . . regret, she knew. And his voice had been thick with it.

10

Did you make a new friend today?" At the start of each new school
year, my mother would ask that question when I stepped off the bus
every day until she was satisfied that I'd reached out to the whole class.
I never quite understood why I needed to designate myself as the social
chair or the goodwill ambassador of the elementary school. I had plenty
of friends and wasn't pining for more. But still, I complied . . . until I
uncovered a hypocritical streak beneath her line of questioning. Because
apparently her definition of a new "friend" had limitations.

"I swear to God," I overheard her telling someone on the phone one
day, "you should see these ragamuffins she drags home. They're like stray
cats. I'm afraid that if I feed them a snack they might never go away."
Our neighborhood at that point was what some might politely call transitional. Only it was transitioning in the wrong direction. By the time
I hit junior high, we were out of there.

Evidently, though, I took my knack for finding choice companions
with me.

I'm not blaming my mom. I know I have no one to blame but myself. But I do wish she'd prepared me a bit better for the importance of
judging character up front. Because if there's one thing I've learned,
it's this: She needn't have worried so much about the strays. Sometimes
the meanest, most feral cats of all are the ones with a pedigree.

11

There seems to be some confusion about our no-tattling rule. Let us be clear: We appreciate that certain things warrant being brought to the caregivers' attention, for safety reasons. Children at this age, however, have difficulty distinguishing where that line is. Thus, let's focus their energies on a more easily learned line— where the offending party recognizes the need to do the right thing. We stand by our policy: The ONLY tattling we will tolerate is from those who have the good judgment to tattle on themselves. Those who do will not be disciplined, but praised.

—Letter from the Circle of Learning director,
Pam, sent home to all parents

Mommy, you count to ten and I'll go hide behind the curtains in the dining room. Ready, go!"

Clara stifled a laugh. "Thomas, hide-and-seek only works if you don't tell me where you're going to hide. I'll count and you pick a new place, okay?"

"But the curtains are a great hiding place!"

"But you just told me you're going to be there. I already know."

"Okay. Close your eyes—no peeking! I will go hide now—and *do not look behind the curtains.*" Thomas pointed an ultraserious finger at her, then backed toward the hallway.

Clara shrugged and covered her eyes with her hands. "One," she began. "Two . . . Three . . ." She hoped she wasn't being loud enough to wake Maddie. Thomas was usually tired out on the afternoons when he'd spent the morning at preschool, but today he'd only stared at her wide-eyed after lunch and story time came and went. "Do you want to skip your nap just this once and play a game?" she'd ventured. He'd be cranky by dinnertime. But she didn't want to be alone with her thoughts anyway. She'd seen patrol cars come and go from Paul's house again yesterday afternoon, and the uncertainty about what was happening or *not* happening was driving her mad.

Plus, she knew it was selfish, but it wasn't just that she was worried about Kristin. It was that she was starting to miss her.

"Ready or not, here I come!" she called.

Maniacal giggling came from the dining room.

Clara hadn't needed Detective Bryant's reminder of what she'd witnessed years ago to be mindfully grateful for what she had. Even at her most exhausted, she relished the off-key notes of Benny singing in the shower, the Muppet-like form of Thomas's bed head, the new fascination Maddie had with sticking out her tongue and going cross-eyed trying to see it.

The charming inability of her preschooler to grasp the parameters of hide-and-seek.

Loudly humming the *Pink Panther* theme song, she made her way into the kitchen. She opened a silverware drawer and loudly rustled the forks. "Thomas, are you in here?"

"No!" came a loud whisper. "*Mommy.* I'm behind the *curtains.* In the *dining room.*"

So much for putting on a show. Clara rushed around the farmhouse table and threw the curtains back dramatically. An exposed

Thomas dissolved into giggles. "You thought I was in the kitchen! I fooled you! I fooled you!"

"You did," Clara said, bending to fold him into a hug. "You, my clever boy, are today's hide-and-seek champion."

"It's okay, Mommy," he said, patting her primly on top of the head. "You'll win next time."

"Another day," she told him solemnly. "It's time to get Hallie off the bus!" Clara slid the baby monitor into her pocket and Thomas slipped his hand into hers as they headed out and down the front porch stairs.

"Can Abby and Aaron still come to my birthday party?" he asked.

Clara hesitated. They'd simply told Thomas that Kristin and the twins were on a trip and they didn't know for how long. His birthday was still months off, but she'd observed that parties were the weapons of choice in the precarious social structure of pre-schoolers. If someone wouldn't share the fire engine, it wasn't the "You're not my friend anymore" pout she used to see from Thomas months ago. Now it was "You're not invited to my birthday party!"

"I hope so, sweetie." He'd attended the twins' party back in May, at Young's dairy farm, where a whole gaggle of kids—Kristin invited half the school—had climbed giant tractor tires and fed goats and rode the little cow train. Paul had accused Kristin of purposely picking a Saturday he had to work, which of course she had. "What does he care?" she'd muttered to Clara. "This party exceeds his kid tolerance by the small factor of a couple *dozen* kids."

Kristin was radiant that afternoon, her loose curls shining in the sunlight beneath a cowboy hat that matched the little woven ones she'd bought as favors for all the kids. Paul was sleeping in the guest room by then, making arrangements to move out, and that day, she looked more than just happy. She looked free.

Thomas broke his grip on Clara's hand and ran for his tree swing as she headed down the walk. A white van was backing out of Paul's driveway, and she stopped cold as she caught sight of the name on the side: WALT'S WINDOWS. The doctor stood with his back to her, holding a yellow paper she took to be his invoice, and she reflexively stepped back under the cover of the old oak, where Thomas was situating himself between the ropes. "Mommy, can you give me a push?"

She moved to comply, and her eyes flicked toward the corner, where Hallie's school bus was set to appear any minute. A dark sedan was crawling around the bend. She gave Thomas a firm starter shove and stepped aside—he'd protest if she gave him more than one. As the van pulled away, the sedan swung swiftly into Paul's driveway, and through the open window she caught sight of a frowning Detective Bryant.

"You replaced the broken window, Dr. Kirkland?" he called out, putting the car into reverse. "Wish you'd checked with us first." The car backed onto the street, then crawled forward along the curb, headed back the way it came.

Paul's voice was smooth, calm. "I didn't realize it warranted checking, Detective. Certainly if you'd instructed me to leave it, I'd have complied." Clara sucked in a slow breath, feeling the blood drain from her face.

Detective Bryant barked a laugh. "I apologize for getting sloppy with my instructions. I assure you, it won't happen again." Without waiting for a response, he accelerated too fast toward the corner, where the van had just disappeared, and whipped past the stop sign without pausing, close on its heels.

An angry horn sounded in the distance, and Paul turned on his heels without a glance in Clara's direction. She heard his front door slam just as the school bus came into view.

Clara shivered in the warm air. *What had she just seen? An innocent misstep? An overreaction? A cover-up?*

Beside her, Thomas was pumping his little legs hard now, swinging higher and higher, and he let out a whoop as the bus groaned to a noisy stop at the curb and the doors snapped open.

"Hey, Chief!" Hallie shouted, bounding across the lawn. "The first edition of *The Color-Blind Gazette* is underway!"

Clara looked once more toward Paul's house, which remained

still. So much had happened this week that she'd completely forgotten Hallie's idea for the paper. But this was the last thing she wanted to think about right now.

"I've decided Monday's the big day," Hallie announced. "Sunday's already covered. But the start of the week, that's when people will be most receptacle."

"Receptive," Clara said automatically.

"See? This is why I need an editorial adviser!"

Thomas dragged his feet in the dirt to slow the swing. "Is it snack time?"

Clara led the kids inside and let Thomas plant himself in front of a cartoon as she doled out tubes of frozen strawberry yogurt. It was nothing. It was probably nothing. Detective Bryant was just trying to keep Paul on his toes, and to dot his *i*'s and cross his *t*'s. That didn't mean he really suspected that the window was evidence of something. Only that he was good at his job.

Or *not* so good at it. She thought of his own parting words: *Getting sloppy . . . won't happen again.* He'd only been chiding Paul—right?

Hallie hopped onto a counter stool. "I've got real front-page breaking news. Like, when people used to yell, 'Extra, extra, read all about it'? They might start doing that again."

Clara swallowed a smile and let herself relax a little. She had to admit, the kid had enthusiasm on her side. Maybe Hallie would be a welcome distraction after all. "What's the scoop?"

"The *real inside story* behind the police investigation next door!" Hallie squealed.

Clara froze. "Hallie," she said carefully, "breaking news is something that hasn't been reported yet. You should probably—"

"But this *hasn't* been reported yet!" She flipped her notebook open on the counter between them. In it was a not-bad pencil sketch of a windowpane with flowers on the sill. Fragments of notes were scribbled in the margins, underlined and circled with question marks that looked like little curly *q*'s. "Internet search?" "Harassment?" "Not a suspect?"

So much for a welcome distraction.

"What is this?" Clara asked uneasily.

"I was kind of hanging out in Kristin and Paul's yard yesterday, when the police came back, and—"

"Wait a sec. You were 'kind of hanging out' in their yard?"

"Well, yeah. I was on a stakeout."

"Hallie, reporters don't go on stakeouts. That's cops."

"Whatever. I was just kind of lying low, but then the *police* showed up. And the *window* was open. And I got the whole thing on my phone!"

"You *what*?"

Hallie pulled a turquoise smartphone out of her denim jacket pocket and started swiping at the screen. "I found this amazing voice recorder app. You wouldn't believe how well it picks stuff up."

Before Clara could say another word, Hallie tapped the screen, and Detective Bryant's distant but clear voice filled the room. "We did try those leads—nothing has panned out yet. But we have just a few more questions, if you don't mind?"

"Of course," Paul's voice said. "Anything to help."

Her mind racing, Clara motioned for Hallie to turn it off. She complied, grinning.

"Hallie, this is illegal. Recording police conversations without anyone's knowledge—"

"But I was in a public place!"

"Wrong. You were on private property."

Hallie stuck out her lip in a pout not unlike Maddie's. "I could've been at the edge of your yard, and I would have heard it anyway! No one needs to know where I was."

Clara shook her head. "No, I'm going to stop you right there. This is wrong. This isn't how it's done. Whatever is on that recording, you absolutely cannot use. For anything."

"I think you might change your mind if you knew what was on it." Hallie's voice was a singsong, a taunt. Clara tried to let her brain catch up to her escalating heart rate. Of course she wouldn't feel differently once she'd heard the recording, but she did *desperately* want to know what it said. Especially after what she'd just witnessed outside. First the questions about the fire pit, and now the window . . . What did the police think they were on to?

There was no telling what Hallie had heard or how she had taken it. If it was serious, and from the look on Hallie's face she certainly seemed to think so, then the girl might need an adult to explain, to sort it out. Clara knew it was irresponsible to do anything other than delete the file, but wasn't it equally irresponsible not to find out exactly what Hallie had heard, so she could help prevent her from jumping to wrong conclusions, or blowing things out of proportion?

Clara knew too well that witnessing something meant you felt involved, whether you were supposed to have seen it or not.

She knew she was rationalizing, but when Hallie tapped the screen again, she didn't stop her.

There was a minute of small talk between Detectives Bryant and Marks and Paul, who offered coffee and invited them to sit. The screeching of chairs on the kitchen floor, the clearing of throats.

"So, Doctor—"

"Like I said, please just call me Paul."

"Paul, we appreciate you letting us take your wife's phone and the laptop. We were hoping to find some sign of where she'd gone—a route she'd looked up, maybe, or a flight she'd priced, or a hotel, a car rental—"

"And did you?"

"Nothing like that. But we did find a solid two hours of frenzied Internet searching from the very early hours of Sunday morning."

"What was she searching for?"

Papers rustled as Detective Bryant began to read. "'Domestic violence support.' 'Domestic violence assistance.' 'Domestic violence shelter, Dayton.' 'Domestic violence safe housing, Dayton.' 'Ending an abusive relationship.' 'Escaping an abuser.'"

Clara's hand flew to her mouth before she could stop herself.

"I know, right?" Hallie said quietly, filling the stunned silence that had evidently fallen over Paul's kitchen at that moment as well. "I had to look it up, but it means—"

Clara raised a finger, and Hallie fell silent.

It was Detective Marks's voice that chimed in next. "Do you have any idea why she might have been searching for those kinds of resources, Doctor . . . Paul?"

"I really don't. It must have been . . . well, this was after she got home from the girls' night at our neighbor's?"

"Correct. Not long after."

"One of them must be in trouble. She must've been trying to see how she could help."

"That's *one* explanation," Detective Marks said.

"You're not suggesting I ever laid a finger on her? That's ridiculous."

"We're not suggesting it, no," Detective Bryant said quickly. "Would you say she knows these neighbor women very well? They're close friends?"

"She's closest to Clara Tiffin, next door." Clara stiffened. "They're pretty good friends, I guess—I don't know if I'd say *close*. The rest, I don't think she knows them all that well."

"So it would be very caring of her to stay up until three A.M. frantically searching the Internet out of concern for one of them."

"Maybe she was looking on behalf of someone else she knows. Someone at work, or the school . . . Maybe she couldn't sleep. Maybe she got the idea to write a novel about a domestic violence survivor. How should I know? We've been separated for months."

"Does your wife aspire to write fiction?"

"You tell me. You seem to know more about her than I do."

"Well, her computer history is wiped mostly clean, which seems a bit odd." Detective Bryant coughed. "Antioch was nice enough to let us have access to her work machine, and interestingly, it looks like most of her personal activity was done there. Personal emails, online shopping, the occasional guest blog post for the school . . . Can you think of a reason for that?"

"She was bored at work?"

"That's *one* explanation," Detective Marks repeated.

"Back when you were living here, did you do a lot of checking up on your wife's Internet usage? Look at the history, see where she'd been, anything like that?"

"I might have happened to see it sometimes, but I wouldn't say I checked up on her."

"Well, even now that you're separated, you do text her an *awful* lot. Texts that some might classify as checking up on someone."

"Checking *in*, maybe. We're still married. We have kids together."

"An outsider might observe that you text her much more than she texts you."

"I . . . my work schedule is irregular, and when I'm at the hospital, I usually can't talk. It cuts down on phone tag if I take the lead on communications."

"The sheer volume of texts, some people might find it overwhelming. Oppressive, even."

Paul said nothing.

"Do you still love your wife?"

His sigh was audible. "Our marriage is over."

"That's not an answer."

"If you want to know the truth," he said, his voice turning cold, "I'm not sure I ever really did. I felt sorry for her. She'd been widowed young, and there she was, saddled with *twin* babies, totally overwhelmed, and . . . I guess I thought I could ride in on my horse and help the damsel in distress. Sweep her off her feet. Be *that* guy."

"Do you think your wife thought of herself as *saddled* with the twins?" Detective Marks cut in. Clara couldn't help but admire the way she was interjecting doubts with casual precision. Suddenly, her relative silence during Clara's own interview didn't seem like a bad thing.

"My word, not hers."

"So *you* felt saddled by them."

Frustration was almost audible in the beat that followed. "It was the wrong word, okay? My point is, I think I got caught up in playing Prince Charming. But it wasn't a fairy tale. It was a mistake. I was sort of taken in by her, I guess."

"And when you realized it was a mistake, that's when you decided to separate?" Detective Bryant again.

"You know how relationships are. They don't just end one day. Things kind of accumulate."

"Did it make you angry, the realization that she had 'taken you in'?"

"Angry? At myself, maybe. Not at her—not then, anyway. Do *you* think it was fair, her keeping all that money in separate savings, untouched—for the kids, she said—while I spent all mine sustaining our lifestyle—the mortgage, the memberships, those astronomical day care bills? If that was your wife, you wouldn't feel a little taken advantage of?"

"Well, if we're being *fair*, Kristin did work too, though her salary was smaller than yours," Detective Marks said.

Yes, Clara had definitely misjudged her.

"We've already gone over this." Detective Bryant's voice had taken on an air of calm and patience, as if he hoped it might permeate the room. "We have your statement on the life insurance as a possible motive, and we're looking into it."

Paul coughed. "Am I a suspect or something? Do you have reason to think something *happened* to Kristin and the kids?"

"No reason. Of course, we also have no forensics—"

"I told you, I just don't feel right about letting you tear the place apart. I think of it as her house now."

"Even though your name is the only one on the mortgage? Even though you've basically moved back in?"

"I'm just waiting for them to come back! Where else would I wait? I don't know what to *do* with myself!" There was a loud noise, the sound of maybe his hands slapping down onto the wooden kitchen table, and Clara and Hallie both jumped.

"Understandable." Detective Bryant's voice was calmer than ever. "And *we* are just trying to make some sense of this Internet search. Also understandable, I'm sure you'd agree, given the fact that it's the last thing she did before she disappeared."

"I'm a *doctor*," Paul said, incredulous. "I took an oath to *do no harm*. That's all you need to know about me. Are we finished?"

Hallie swiped the screen on her phone, and the recording stopped.

Clara stared at Hallie in stunned silence. Her mind was reeling. She shook her head vehemently, as if to physically jolt herself out of it. She'd think about what she'd just heard later. Right now she had to deal with what was in front of her. Hallie was looking at her expectantly, beaming as if her Pulitzer was surely coming any day.

Clara looked levelly into the girl's eyes. "Hallie," she said sternly, "this is *not* how reporters operate. Sneaking around on private property? Eavesdropping on police? Recording their neighbors without their knowledge?"

Hallie's face fell. She crossed her arms defiantly across her chest. "Could have fooled me," she said. "We learned about Watergate in school."

Clara was caught off balance for a moment, trying to remember exactly which grade Hallie was in. Watergate? Seriously? Clearly the lesson hadn't quite come across, at any rate.

"You have to listen to what I'm saying. Not only is this kind of snooping around illegal, it's *dangerous*." She flashed on an image of an unhinged Paul discovering Hallie outside his window—not while the police were there, but on a dark night, alone. Clara shuddered. "You can't print anything you overheard in your paper, Hallie. And you can't go sneaking over there anymore. Promise me."

"But it shows that she had a reason to leave! It's important evidence! Everyone thinks Kristin was heartless or something. The kids at school are calling her 'stone-cold,' and 'gold digger'! This shows another side to the story."

Clara cringed. *Kristin, stone-cold?* Paul had done that. Paul had made people think that. What else had Paul done? Still, she had to be careful not to show even the slightest sign of agreement that the girl had a point. Hallie was far too easily encouraged. Clara had to focus on conveying that this must not go beyond this kitchen.

"All it shows is that Kristin Googled those things before she left," she said calmly, stealing a glance at Thomas. He was zoned into the television—something Benny often poked fun at by pretending to tap-dance around him, to no reaction whatsoever—and for once, she was grateful. "Like Paul said, she could have Googled them to help a friend. She could be off with that friend right now, helping her. It doesn't prove anything about Kristin, or about Paul."

Hallie's face bore such disappointment and disbelief that Clara wanted to take it all back, to give her a hug, to tell her she understood the urge to plaster this over the front page but they couldn't, because that wasn't the way the world worked, and they had to let things take their course and hope the police would sort it out.

And to tell her what a bunch of bullshit that all was.

"Have you played this for your mom?" she asked.

"No . . ."

"Well, I'm going to get Maddie up from her nap, and as soon as your mom comes home from class, we're all going to walk over there and have a talk." Clara felt a twinge of guilt at her relief that she wouldn't have to keep what she'd just heard *entirely* to herself. Natalie had seemed so unconvinced that there was more to Kristin's story. What would she make of it now?

Hallie stuck out her lip. "She's always telling me I ask too many questions. This time all I did was listen, and apparently that's wrong too. How am I supposed to get *answers* about anything?"

"Sometimes we're not meant to have the answers, Hal. Sometimes the answers aren't any of our business." Clara knew it was the responsible, adult thing to say, but the words pained her.

"If you're not going to let me report on the only real news going on around here, Chief, this paper is going to be L-A-M-E lame."

"Well, maybe now isn't such a good time to be starting a paper after all."

Hallie hung her head. The toe of her shoe thumped the cabinet in a sullen rhythm.

"Listen. If you have your heart set on doing this, why not make your paper different from all the others? Why not report on *good* news?"

Hallie seemed to be concentrating hard on her kicking, her hair falling around her face, but Clara could tell she was listening. "I mean, that's what *I* always think is missing from the other news."

She forced hopefulness into her voice. "I page through all those stories about one bad thing after another and think, *Where's the kind
of stuff that would make me smile?* That could be your role, Hallie.
You could deliver news that gives people hope."

A tiny, sputtering wail came through the baby monitor, then
escalated quickly. "Zero to sixty in a second," Benny would tell
people in restaurants. "We got the model with upgraded horsepower."
They always smiled, no matter how loud or disruptive Maddie was
being. Benny was masterful at defusing tension. She wished for him
now.

"Think about it, okay?" she told Hallie. "I'll be right back."

Up in Maddie's room, she glanced out the window and could
see a light on in Hallie's kitchen. Good. Natalie must have gotten
home from class early. They'd go now.

Hallie sulked as the four of them trekked through the backyards
painfully slowly, so that Maddie could keep up, holding hands while
Thomas sang out, "Five little monkeys, swinging from the tree, teasing Mr. Alligator, can't catch meee . . ." Thomas, a grudging Hallie,
and even little ear-to-ear-grinning Maddie all broke their link to
put their hands together and do the motion of the alligator swimming through the water toward its carefree prey. The song was
all the rage at preschool, but Clara found it disturbing. Whatever
happened to the monkeys jumping on the bed? Was the danger of
bumping one's head not enough of a deterrent?

They made their way across the patio and around Benny's workshop, where the Tiffins' backyard ended and the flat expanse of
Natalie and Hallie's grass began.

The kids clapped their hands in unison and sang, "And it snapped
that monkey right out of that tree!"

The back door in front of them squeaked open, and the figure
that filled the doorway was decidedly not Natalie. Its broad shoulders filled the expanse of the doorway; its gray T-shirt had U.S. AIR
FORCE across the front in faded letters. Hallie yelped and took off
running. "Daddy! Daddy! Daddy!" Natalie's husband ran down the
stairs to the grass and gathered his daughter in his arms. "Daddy,
what are you *doing* here?"

He pulled back to look at her, then hugged her to him again. Clara's eyes filled. It was the best kind of holiday commercial come to life in the middle of September, and she pulled her children to her self-consciously, feeling as if they were intruding on a private moment.

Yet here she was, geared up for an uncomfortable yet necessary parent-to-parent conversation about what Hallie had been up to.

Hallie's dad caught her eye. "Hi," he said, smiling and standing, lifting Hallie so easily she might have been half her size.

"You must be Jim."

"You must be Clara. Don't think we met on my last leave, but I'm happy to have the chance to thank you for helping out with our girl here." He beamed at Hallie.

"She's a great kid." She waited for Hallie to look over at her— maybe she'd bring up the newspaper on her own—but she kept her head buried in his shoulder. "And it's great that you're home. Does Natalie know you're here?"

"I thought Hallie and I'd surprise her coming out of class. You up for that, Hallie-bear?"

Hallie nodded, then brightened as if remembering the most wonderful thing. "Daddy, you said when you came home we could—"

"Go to Lakeside Lodge? I've booked us for a long weekend!"

Hallie squealed. Clara tried not to outwardly blanch. Lakeside Lodge was a resort with a huge indoor water park and conference center—along with, of course, the expansive lake—east of Cincinnati. The worst night of her life had occurred there. Otherwise, it was a wonderful place.

Jim nodded at Clara. "Do you usually get her off the bus on Mondays? I'm taking them for a four-day weekend, so she won't be back to her routine until Tuesday."

Hallie pouted. "Only four days, Daddy? And then do you have to *leave* again?"

"Four days more than I thought we'd have, sweets. And I'm going to spend every second of them with you."

Clara paused. If they weren't even going to be in town, she supposed she didn't need to have the conversation about Hallie's adventures in reporting just now. It seemed insensitive to bring it up to Jim under the circumstances, and knowing that nothing more could come of it while they were away. Best to let them have their family weekend and fill Natalie in right afterward.

"Hallie, ask your mom to call me when you all get back, okay?" Hallie wouldn't look at her, and Clara swallowed the uneasy feeling nagging at the corners of her brain. "Have a fabulous time," she told Jim.

He ruffled Hallie's fine hair. "I've got everything I need for that right here."

As Clara led her own little ones back home, she heard the slamming of a door from Kristin's backyard. Apparently Paul wasn't the most receptive audience for someone else's happy reunion.

12

Regrets only.

—The only comprehensible line, to Izzy, of
Penny and Josh's wedding invitation, buried
under the request to RSVP

Early Sunday morning, frustrated with her inability to sleep in, Izzy slowly opened the door to the spare bedroom where, with no prospects for overnight guests now or in the foreseeable future, she'd stashed everything she either hadn't yet gotten around to unpacking or couldn't bring herself to unload—literally or figuratively—into the untinged space of her new home.

"Be aware of the relics of your reality," the meditation teacher had intoned as Izzy sat riveted by the sheer intensity of Randi and Rhoda's group at the Intuitive Healing Studio. She wasn't sure what she'd expected—soft mats, dark rooms—but the place emanated a glow of warmth and light. Seated cross-legged in rows covering the full expanse of the hardwood floor—with so many of Kristin's co-workers from Antioch in attendance, along with parents and teachers from the Circle of Learning, they'd had to give up on forming a circle—Izzy had obediently followed along the warm-up exercises that the instructor explained would guide them in finding "the most centered spiritual space" from which to send positive vibrations to Kristin and the twins. "I am of my surroundings," they'd all repeated in unison, earnest and transfixed, while Izzy tried not to feel skeptical about how any of this admittedly buoyant energy would ever reach, let alone help, her missing neighbors. She wanted it to work. She wanted to believe.

She wanted to belong.

"Remember," the teacher had concluded the session, glancing around the overcrowded room and resting her eyes, at last, on Izzy, "your vibe attracts your tribe."

Well, here were the relics of her reality. The sliding doors to the closet were open, and even in the dim light she cringed at the sight of the lone bridesmaid's dress hanging inside. Admittedly it was a little Miss Havisham of her to leave it alone in here, but she couldn't bear the thought of it mocking her from her own closet. The gown was quite beautiful as far as wear-them-only-once bridesmaid dresses went and would be a welcome donation at Goodwill, but Izzy couldn't escape the nagging worry that one day Penny would ask her to dig it out and get her feelings hurt if Izzy didn't have it anymore.

She supposed she should be heartened that she was still worried about hurting her sister's feelings. If by Tuesday evening she could manage to conjure an emotion other than despair over her pregnancy, she'd be on her way back to being a decent human being.

Stepping through the maze of unpacked cardboard in her stocking feet, she gently lifted the lone decorative box from the closet's top shelf. She sank to her knees on the worn carpet and pushed the pale blue lid aside. A snapshot of her and Josh dressed as Bonnie and Clyde at a Halloween party stared up at her, Josh's arm slung confidently around her shoulder in a way that had once seemed natural. For a moment she sat quietly, breathing in the remnants of their friendship—the heart-tugging array of ticket stubs and photographs and gallery pins and festival programs and trail maps and guidebooks and the leather-bound travel journal they'd shared for a while. She didn't need to riffle through the box, to touch them or to see them. But she liked to be in their presence, to remind herself that these memories were real, that she hadn't imagined them after all.

Izzy had booked a neuroscientist last Valentine's Day to talk on *Freshly Squeezed* about what happens to your brain chemistry when you're in love—or trying to come out of it. "What a bad deal," the expert had joked, explaining that the regions of the brain most active after a rejection or a breakup are areas associated with love, craving, focus, and deep attachment. "All you want is to forget about this human being and go on with your life—but no, you just love them harder."

Great, Izzy had thought. *Even science is against me.*

If she flipped through the journal, inevitably she'd land on the page where Josh had sketched the Yellow Springs themselves, before she'd ever had an inkling of making her home close by. Even then her mind had wrapped itself around the quick moves of his fingers holding the thick pencil, his other hand cradling the open journal as if it were a fragile thing, the way he'd occasionally stop and lunge for her share of their trail mix. "Not on your life!" she'd shrieked, ravished. As usual, they'd made their plans at the last minute, and she hadn't prepared enough for the journey. Not the right snacks for this length of time, not the right shoes for this much hiking, not the right words for what she wanted to say.

Don't do this to yourself, a familiar voice inside her warned.

Oh, but she had. Done it to herself. From the start. She'd failed to recognize that all of life was like those warnings about being good citizens of this world where extraordinary tragedy could be averted by ordinary people: *If you see something, say something.* And she *had* seen—not at first, but eventually—the evidence no one else seemed to. The image of what was meant to be. It had taken years to come into focus, but when it had, how obvious: It was right there all along. Yet she'd been too cowardly to open up to Josh; neither had she said a word to Penny in the early days when real damage had not yet been done. Things had escalated quickly.

"Explosive," Penny had called her early days with Josh. And everyone knew you couldn't undo a bomb once it went off.

Izzy had kept her feelings to herself then, so she had no choice but to deal with them alone now. She wasn't crass enough to hurt her family with the truth, or naïve enough to think it would do

anything other than make matters worse, or crazy enough to believe that if she missed Josh hard enough, she could make him miss
her too. She knew that her *vibe* was off, that the meditation teacher
hadn't landed on her by accident. But she didn't know how to stop.

She snapped the lid back on the box. She would not waste her
Sunday morning this way, would not squander these rare hours
where there *was* a moment of Zen to be found. At least for a short
time her feet would be rooted to the ground, and hope would be in
the air, and she would not be trapped by her secret sadness. She'd
feel like herself again.

She could come back to this later.

The sun was starting its rise into the sky as Izzy pulled out of the
driveway and caught sight of Paul, bending to pick up a bundled
Sunday paper from the end of his driveway. He raised a hand
in silent greeting, and she rolled down the passenger window
and slowed to a stop.

"Nice to see someone still get an actual newspaper these days,"
she called.

She caught sight of the headline through the thin plastic cover—
"Still Missing: Day 7"—and instantly regretted her words.

"You've got to hand it to them," he said dryly. "They keep putting it out, even when there's nothing new to report."

All weekend she'd had a nagging feeling that she just wanted to
know for sure that Kristin was okay. Which was ridiculous. Of
course Kristin was okay. She'd taken her mother's china from the
dining room. She'd cleaned out her bank account. It was Paul who
was not okay.

"Well, I'm glad I ran into you, because I think you forgot to bill
me for the auto repair services." She offered a half smile. True to
his word, he'd fixed her taillight and left her in peace.

"I didn't forget."

"How did I know you were going to say that?"

"Lucky guess." He looked like a man who had absolutely no idea
what to do with himself. Izzy, for once, *did* know what to do with

herself—and she preferred to do it alone. But the look on his face was so familiar that she knew if she pulled away from this curb right now, she'd leave feeling even worse than she already did.

Paul seemed to have no one, yet for some reason, here she was. Just as when she'd been whaling against her broken car in her driveway, he'd magically appeared. And for that, she owed him a favor. Even if it was one she didn't particularly want to give.

"If you won't let me pay you, how about a trade?"

"For?"

She gestured to the passenger seat next to her. "A change of scenery."

As the words hung between them, she halfway hoped he would say no.

He hesitated, but only for a second. "Why not."

So it would be, then. She looked him over. His jeans and fleece would do, but definitely not the Dockers. "Got any not-so-nice shoes to change into? Old sneakers? Hiking boots?"

He shook his head. "In my apartment. By where you turn toward John Bryan State Park? I've been meaning to go get another load of stuff. I keep hoping I won't need it, but . . ." He coughed into his hand, avoiding her eyes. "It's been a week."

"I'll take you. John Bryan is where we're going. Hop in."

She waited while he locked up, and they sat in precarious silence on the short drive through town until Paul directed her to a non-descript two-story brick building dotted with tiny balconies, identical save for their dingy assortment of plastic furniture. She looked over at him, certain she'd turned in to the wrong place—this seemed so far beneath his pay grade. But he was unbuckling his seat belt, reaching for the handle, unfolding his long legs onto the pavement.

He disappeared inside for a few minutes and emerged wearing a pair of tennis shoes that looked way too new for a hike—practically unworn—and hoisting a bulging duffel bag over his shoulder.

She popped the trunk. He made his way around, and a more conspicuous silence filled the car as she waited for him to buckle back in. He cleared his throat. "I know it's weird, me taking stuff back to the house, staying there still," he told her. "I'm not even working right now. My patients deserve better than substandard care, and anyone can see my mind is elsewhere. I just can't bring myself to—"

"You don't have to explain." She risked a glance in his direction. He was staring at her. "It actually seems weirder to me that you'd stay *here*."

"Yeah?" He barked out a laugh. "I deliver at the hospital in Xenia—the logical thing to do is find a nicer place there. But even though it's only fifteen, twenty minutes away, it seemed too far from the kids . . ." His voice trailed off, and she was seized by a sinking feeling that bringing him along had been a mistake—for both of them.

But no. He needed this more than she did, even if he didn't know it. It would be good for her, too, to think about someone other than herself, to get out of her own head.

She just wasn't sure she wanted to be in his.

Izzy waved at the ranger on the way in and steered the car into the small lot by the campsite supply store. "There's another trail-head that can get us where we're going—via the old stagecoach trail—but I like starting over here instead."

"What's the difference?"

"That one is wide and flat to start, more of a walk than a hike. This entrance through the campground is more like a deer trail." She could tell from the look on his face that he'd have preferred the former, but she pretended she didn't notice. She *liked* the ritual of embarking with blind trust in the barely visible path, the satisfaction of pushing to the point where you could see out ahead of you.

They shut their doors as quietly as they could in the crisp morning. Dome tents of all colors and sizes dotted the drive-in campsites. Some sites were still quiet with sleep, while others had fires going, where campers huddled sipping instant coffee. Izzy inhaled the scent of woodsmoke and felt her blood pressure lower—but only for the fleeting minute it took to remember that the last time she'd sat around a fire had been with Kristin. As she led the way to the hidden trailhead, she hoped Paul wouldn't be reminded of it too.

The last thing she wanted was to spend the morning fielding more questions she didn't have answers to.

Izzy plunged into the woods, eager to leave as much as she could behind, but Paul was stepping over branches and through weeds as if one of them might jump up and bite him. She slowed her pace so he could keep up.

"We're just going to make our way down this hill to the creek, and then the path is more defined."

He nodded, uneasy, and she pressed on with him trailing behind her, hoping he wasn't hating this, hating her, wishing he hadn't come. She just had to lead him to the right spot in time. None of this awkwardness would be worth it unless they made it.

The narrow dirt trail declined steeply, cutting and winding this way, then the other, and she ignored his grunts from behind her until at last the path opened up to the rocks alongside the creek.

Here in the ravine, the otherwise subtle shortening of the daylight hours had had an amplified effect on the slow trek toward autumn. While their neighborhood was still a lush green—it had been a wet summer, with none of the lawn burnouts that Ohio Augusts sometimes bring—these trees were dotted in low-hanging patches of gold, orange, and red. Clusters of soggy brown foliage meandered along the water's surface. A light breeze rustled through the forest, and loose leaves floated down around them like snowflakes.

"Pretty," he said, visibly relaxing.

She smiled. "Just wait."

A short distance upstream, they came to the first footbridge. From here, the trail climbed to a safe height above the riverbank and then wound its way along the bottom of the towering limestone ridge. There wasn't as much undergrowth encroaching, and they had room to walk side by side. When Paul didn't drop back on the other side of the bridge, she didn't step ahead, either.

And now that their paces were matched, now that it was almost odd *not* to make conversation, Izzy's curiosity—percolating like a slow-brewing distraction for the past week—came to a pressure point. If he was here, that might mean he wanted to talk. But even if he didn't, would he blame her for asking? She kept her voice low. "I don't want to intrude, but do you have any family to come be with you? While all this is going on?"

He sighed. "My parents are in Connecticut. They've met Kristin and the kids only twice—once right after we got married, since we didn't really have a ceremony, and once at a funeral. It's not that they're not concerned, but . . ." She stole a look over at him but couldn't read his expression. He seemed to be struggling to keep it neutral. "I guess it's not that personal to them," he finished.

"Not personal? You're their son."

"Well, my dad is—" He stopped himself. "You know, I don't really talk about my childhood. It wasn't happy, but it pales in comparison to the stuff I see in my line of work. I could tell you plenty of stories that no one should ever have to hear, much less live through."

Izzy thought of the hopeless feeling that sometimes overwhelmed her at the news desk, and of how much worse it could be for someone like Paul, who was no stranger to life-or-death scenarios. She pictured him alone in a modest doctor's office, head in his hands from feeling his patients' pain too keenly, and a sense of solidarity filled her.

"I think what you're going through now might qualify," she said gently, and he was quiet for a moment.

"My dad is . . . not a good guy," he said finally. "And my mom goes along with whatever he says." The statement ended flatly, as if he was debating leaving it at that. "When I was in med school at Ohio State, we'd have these weekly calls, Sunday nights, with both of them on the line—ostensibly to save the minutes on the phone bill. *Everything* is money with them. Every call, my mom would hardly say a word while my dad gave me the third degree about my professors and if I was getting my money's worth and whether I was being distracted by any actual fun. But she'd always call back later, practically whispering so he couldn't hear, to ask if I needed any money. That was always the only question. Like if I didn't need money, there was nothing else to know. As if I would have taken her money anyway."

"Maybe they can't afford the airfare, then. Maybe they're embarrassed by it."

But Izzy wasn't really thinking of his parents. She was thinking of the money Paul had allegedly threatened to fight Kristin for. Maybe with a childhood like that, he couldn't help himself.

"They should be," he said, his tone blunt. "My dad has horrible gambling debts. He fell into it when I was little, and for a while it didn't seem bad. We'd go on long weekends to Atlantic City, stay for free in a suite since he was such a *loyal* customer. My mom would play on the beach with me while he sat at the tables. But soon after, we'd be dodging debt collectors. Changing houses, changing schools. It pinged back and forth for years, between the high life and the low life, and then it kind of just stayed low."

He stumbled over a tree root, and Izzy automatically shot out an arm to steady him. He held it for an instant before letting go. "I don't want you to think I've written them off or anything. I love my parents. I paid their way here after the wedding. We would have visited them for holidays, but Kristin wanted the kids to have their own traditions in our house, which I understood. I always offered to fly them down for Christmas or Thanksgiving, but they always declined. I do think you're right that they were embarrassed. And I'd buy them tickets in a second if I thought they'd be a comfort to me now. But I don't. They never showed an interest in my wife or the kids while they were here, and they didn't seem to much care when I told them we were getting divorced."

They made their way in silence under a rocky overhang.

"I get the feeling my dad thinks I should have kept a better handle on my wife, and if I don't know where she is now, that's my problem."

Izzy didn't know what to say. "Your kids are adorable, and so sweet," she ventured. "I've always thought boy-girl twins are something special. How rare it is to have someone who is so much the same as you, but also so different, I mean."

"Thanks, but they're not my—"

"Yes they are," she cut him off. Her voice sounded pointed,

harsher than she'd intended. "Yes they are," she repeated more softly. They walked in silence for another moment.

"Thank you for that," he said, and when she looked over, his eyes were wet.

"They'll be back," she said. "Or the police will find them and bring them back. Don't lose hope."

"I think I lost that even before this happened," he said,

And then, it began.

She looked over at Paul as the soft voices of the choir registered and the first notes cascaded down around them, as if the beams of sunlight streaming hazily through the trees had themselves burst into waves of sound. His eyes met hers first in confusion, and then in recognition. Somewhere, on the ridge high above the ravine, was a church. He stopped short and looked up through the treetops in wonder, just as she had during that first hike of accidental perfect timing.

Paul blinked at her. "Is that—?"

She nodded. "Every Sunday morning," she said softly. "Like clockwork."

It wasn't a hymn she recognized, nor could she understand the words through the echo—and that made it all the more beautiful, almost ethereal, as if the voice of the universe itself was conveying a nonspecific yet unmistakable message of peace.

She closed her eyes in gratitude for the return of this moment, the sublime convergence of the natural world and the spiritual realm and the tug of her heart. Stumbling upon it that first time had been like a miracle, the pure unexpectedness of it. She'd been trudging along that midsummer morning, regretting everything about the hike—the humidity that made her clothes stick to her even here in the shaded ravine, the loneliness of hiking solo not by choice but by default, the knowledge that her living room was still filled with unpacked boxes and yet here she was, seeking some sort of reprieve from the choices she'd made instead of dealing, instead of follow-ing through. And then the harmonies had begun, stopping her short. When the first song had ended, she could have sworn she was a *part* of the forest, both of them perfectly still, holding their breaths, afraid the magic would disappear with so much as a rustling of the breeze. And then a new hymn had started, like a promise: When you think the spell has been broken, when you think you might have imagined it, don't give up. If you wait, there can be more.

"Will we still hear it if we walk on?"

"For at least half an hour."

His eyes glistened. "It *sounds* like hope," he said. And it did. And it was.

"Sometimes it's the only way I know to find it."

He didn't ask why she was looking, and for that she was grateful.

13

A safety plan is a personalized, practical plan
that includes ways to remain safe while in a
relationship, planning to leave, or after you
leave . . . Although some of the things that you
outline in your safety plan may seem obvious,
it's important to remember that in moments of
crisis your brain doesn't function the same way
as when you are calm.

—*National Domestic Violence Hotline*
Path to Safety

Clara pulled open the dishwasher and sighed—because a clean,
wet mess was still a mess. The top rack was a cascade of flimsy plastic medicine dispensers: squat children's dosing cups, tall pour
tubes, and infant syringes in an assortment of measurement scales,
none of which ever seemed to have the right push piece. Both kids
had ear infections. In both ears.

She'd never fully appreciated, before becoming a parent herself,
how even a fairly straightforward childhood illness could shut down
a household, taking adults and kids alike out of commission for days
in a blur. The understanding had come the first time Thomas was

ever truly, miserably, exhaustingly sick, with the wave of trepidation that hit her in realizing that she was wholly responsible for the well-being of this little person who could not yet communicate his needs beyond a pitiful cry. In the days when parenting was a hypothetical, she'd put too much stock in the power of pediatricians. Sure, they could set your mind at ease for a few moments—if you were lucky. But then they passed the buck right back. *Call if he seems worse. Look for the subtle signs of dehydration, of oxygen deprivation, of something more serious. Call me if . . .* Yet who was to say you would recognize that *if* when it came? Those were the watchful days—and, more often, the nights—that laid bare the best and worst parts of this rewarding and terrifying new career.

She thought of Kristin being left on her own with not one but two babies and wondered how she'd ever managed, especially with her own grief. If the sadness didn't drive you to the brink, the sheer exhaustion would push you over.

There was no telling what—or whom—you might say yes to, just to avoid dealing alone.

She unloaded the damp mess of medicine dispensers into the dish drainer and set about trying to match sippy cups with their lids. Much as Clara never would have wished this nasty run of illness on her children—or herself, for that matter—she had to admit it may have been a blessing in disguise. Thursday night's wake-up cries, Friday's trip to the pediatrician, and the subsequent sleepless weekend had kept her busy enough that she'd barely had time to obsess over the implications of Kristin's computer search history, or Paul's accusations and denials, or Detective Bryant's sneer as he'd chased after the repair van, or Hallie's audacious reporting. At least, she hadn't had time to *concentrate* on obsessing. Whereas the revelations on Hallie's recording might have otherwise rendered her glued to her laptop stalking Paul's sparsely updated Facebook page, or to her windowsill checking up on his whereabouts, now she could only play it over in her mind, again and again, while she rocked her crying children, coaxed down chalky antibiotics, and waited nervously for Natalie to return.

Benny had been so calm—so careful—when she'd relayed the whole recorded ordeal as best she could from memory. *I'm sure there's an explanation; Paul might seem clueless, but he also seems harmless;* and the kicker, *we can't let on about anything that we have no business knowing anyway.* Beneath his measured façade, she could see his concern—not for Kristin, but for her.

"Maybe Kristin did what she had to do," he'd finally conceded last night, when she'd risked bringing it up for the umpteenth time. She knew she was pressing him, but she couldn't help it: In some backward way, it was nice to be able to talk to Benny about what she'd learned, even if he was reluctant to talk back. Otherwise, she'd have burst by now. "Maybe we should hope she *isn't* found," he'd said, and she'd clung to the reassurance like a stubborn child.

Yes, thank goodness for Benny, as usual. He'd been her partner in slime fighting all weekend, running to the Amish store for homemade chicken soup and coming home with silly toys from the dollar aisle—flimsy airplanes to be assembled, coloring books to be filled, playdough to be molded. She'd taken over solo on Monday with the still-cranky version of her kids, and the long hours of double sick duty had taken it out of her. Here was Tuesday, though, and the morning had gone better. The antibiotics at last kicking in, Maddie and Thomas both went down for their naps willingly—a small miracle in itself—and now she had serious cleaning to do if she didn't want to be the next one sick. Not that there was any *real* chance of escaping that, but she had to go through the motions, for her own sanity.

And also, for the health of anyone who might happen by. Hallie and her parents had gotten back sometime yesterday—Clara spotted their lights on last night—but Natalie had never called. Clara could guess Hallie would claim she'd forgotten Clara's instructions to ask her to, but then again, it had also been Jim's last night home, and Clara couldn't bring herself to intrude on their good-bye. Now, though, Hallie was back at school, and Jim was back at the base, and Natalie was fair game. She usually worked a shift at the Sunrise Café on Tuesday mornings, then studied in the afternoon.

Clara wasn't exactly looking forward to their conversation—she still hadn't grown comfortable discussing her own children's bad behavior, let alone someone else's—but she knew they needed to talk. And she *was* glad for the excuse to talk with just one more person about the extent of the drama next door, to find out what she made of it all. She'd sent Natalie a couple of vague texts earlier, with no response. If she didn't hear back by the time Maddie and Thomas were up, she was heading over. She'd already waited too long.

She gathered all the hand towels and set the washing machine to hot. She sanitized the doorknobs, the light switches, the remote controls. She ran out to her car and gathered the detritus from the backseat—the follow-up appointment reminders from the doctor and the dropped Cheerios and the wrinkled books and clunky computerized toys she'd dragged along in a failed attempt to distract them from the pain between their ears.

And then she went to the mailbox.

As soon as she saw it, she knew. The gravity of her mistake hit her with full force as she took in the large letters across the top of a crudely stapled pair of trifolded papers: *The Color-Blind Gazette*. But it couldn't be. How could Hallie have *possibly* found the time? Where could she have even done this, without her parents seeing? At the Lakeside Lodge? Or *did* her parents know? If that was the case, at least Clara would be off the hook for not having warned them when she'd had the chance . . .

Though it seemed unlikely.

She unfolded the pages, hands shaking, and alarming phrases wasted no time leaping off the page at her.

A middle-of-the-night search frenzy relating to domestic violence resources . . .

What some might call a lame excuse for not allowing police to search the house more thoroughly . . .

The presumed innocent man seemed uneasy, asked if he was a suspect . . .

The article ended, Clara had to admit, somewhat smartly, considering that its author was a twelve-year-old.

At a time when so much has been made of the missing life insurance money, one must ask: Was more than one kind of life insurance at play?

She turned the page. The next sheet contained a simple calendar of events, a call for submissions or story ideas to be sent to colorblindgazette@gmail.com, and, in the top left corner, a masthead.

Editor and Lead Staff Writer: Hallie King.
Editorial Adviser: Clara Tiffin.

No. Hallie wouldn't have. She couldn't have—

But she had.

Once, when Clara was a child, her mother had yelled at her so terribly that she'd run straight to the trash can and thrown up, right in the middle of the kitchen. It had silenced and shocked her mother, as they both knew Clara hadn't done anything all that wrong—at any rate, surely nothing to warrant screaming or vomiting. What had it been? A missed chore? A missed bus? A missed grade? All Clara could remember was that her mother had apologized, a rare occurrence, and taken her for ice cream, a rarer one.

She was transported back to that kitchen now, filled with that sense of being in terrible trouble that was not completely unwarranted but was far worse than what was due. She wondered if she might deposit her lunch right here on the curb. She wondered if she might pass out. Her vision was tunneling, ever so slightly. She turned toward Paul's driveway and saw his car parked there. A cold foreboding shivered through her.

She was going to have so very much explaining to do. She didn't have the energy for this. She didn't have the time for this. She had a house full of sick children. She hadn't slept in days. All she wanted was to be left alone.

Clara quickly folded the paper and stuffed it into the stack of bills and catalogs she was holding, as if doing so might hide it from the whole neighborhood. She surveyed the street, not bothering to pretend she wasn't. She didn't see anyone. Maybe they hadn't gotten their copies yet? Maybe she could still retrieve them all?

She envisioned herself running along the curb, opening each mailbox, reaching in, swiping the flyer, and running on to the next one. She then imagined Paul pulling up next to her while she had a fistful of *Gazettes*—how she would fumble trying to explain she was not involved in a situation that was the very definition of being caught red-handed. What would he possibly say to her after this? He was her next-door neighbor, for pity's sake!

And not just any confused, grieving neighbor. One who police had reason to suspect might have a violent streak.

It seemed too risky to gather them all up and be seen.

It seemed too risky not to.

She fled up the walk and back inside. She needed a second to think. The door closed too loudly behind her, and Maddie let out a wail from upstairs. Great. So much for her little reconnaissance mission. Unless the stroller could serve as a cover . . . Maybe it could! She'd be just another mom, out for a walk in the fresh air, conveniently stopping at every mailbox to . . . well, to teach her children about the mailman. Or something. She'd come up with a story on the spot, if she needed to. At least the stroller had a pouch where she could stash the vile things.

Maddie's fever had finally broken—her outfit was soaked with sweat. Clara's mind raced as she wrestled the wriggly little arms and legs into a fresh one-piece outfit that snapped up the front, humming "Twinkle, Twinkle" in an effort to keep them both calm. How many houses might Hallie have delivered these to? Surely not the whole of Yellow Springs. Was Clara lucky enough that it might have been just this block? But when had she even done it? The afternoon school bus hadn't come yet. It had to have been this morning, before school. Unless maybe Natalie had kept her home again today? Maybe to compensate for her dad's departure?

There was no telling how much damage had been done, or how much Clara could still undo, but she had to try. And she couldn't leave Thomas here alone, sound asleep though he seemed. Maddie in her arms, she burst into his room. "Naptime's over, buddy," she told him, tickling his tummy. He moaned, and she glanced at the robot clock on his wall. He'd been down only an hour. Hardly long enough, given how sick he'd been. This was not all-star parenting. But neither was having your name plastered on something that could rile up the entire neighborhood and . . . what, get her sued for slander or libel? She tried to remember the difference between the two. It hardly mattered. Could it put her family in danger?

She coaxed Thomas out of bed with the promise of a popsicle if he'd just put on his shoes and come along for a ride in the stroller. With each valuable moment that ticked by as she attempted to wrangle her sluggish children, her fury with Hallie was building. Blind fury—pure, hot, and indiscriminating. What could the girl possibly have been thinking?

Thomas finally fastened the last Velcro strip of his shoes, and she scooped him up, though he was getting too heavy to carry this way, and clumped down the stairs as quickly as she could with a child under each arm. She set Maddie up with a bottle, Thomas with a popsicle, and debated whether the kids should have light coats. The temperature was hovering under seventy, chillier in the breeze, and they'd been sick . . .

Forget it. There was no time. She flew to the front closet, set the children on the bottom step of the staircase behind her, clumsily yanked the double stroller out, and with a flick of her wrist shoved the front door open with her shoulder—only to come face-to-face with Detective Bryant.

"Going somewhere?" he asked, unsmiling. He held up a copy of *The Color-Blind Gazette,* and Clara stopped where she stood.

"I did *not* editorially advise that," she blurted out. "In fact, I told Hallie that she should not, could not print it."

"How did she *get it*?"

Clara looked past him, in the direction of Paul's house. Through the sprawling branches of the trees, she could tell his car was still in the driveway, but there was no sign of anyone.

"Please." She hated that her voice was such a desperate plea. "I can explain, but I was about to go try to—" How to phrase this in a way that didn't sound unlawful? "Gather them up."

"We have someone on that. Let's talk inside, shall we?"

She wheeled the massive stroller backward, and the detective filled the doorway. He caught sight of the children sitting on the step and eyed them uneasily. She half expected Thomas to jump up and ask about the woowoo again, but he was curled into a sleepy ball, his head resting on the step above him, staring forlornly at them.

"They've been sick," Clara told him. "I can't unload them on anyone right now."

"Why don't you give me the short version."

So she told him, right there in the entryway, while Maddie sucked her bottle and Thomas licked his popsicle and she tried to behave as if a talk with a detective was nothing to be alarmed about in the middle of an ordinary day in her ordinary life. She told him about Hallie having the idea for the paper before she'd even known Kristin was missing, and how she'd forgotten about it until the girl showed up with "breaking news." About how she'd stressed to her the importance of going no farther with what she'd heard. About how she'd had every intention of telling the girl's parents, until she'd walked into the Folgers commercial reunion and felt heartless bringing it up just then. About how they were going out of town, and she'd made the judgment call that filling them in could wait until today. Which was obviously, in hindsight, not the right call.

When she was finished, Detective Bryant sighed heavily.

"Look. I'm a cop, but I'm a human being too. I can understand how what you went through in Cincinnati might have made you hypervigilant—"

"I am *not* a vigilante."

He stared at her.

"I'm not. Detective, this is my neighborhood! I can't believe she put my name on this. Given what I was thrust into the middle of against my will once before, I don't want *anything* other than to mind my own business in this case. Or any case. Believe me."

He looked at her for a long moment, then sighed again. "And at no point did it occur to you to let *us* know about this little development?"

"Report a twelve-year-old to the police for eavesdropping?"

She could tell he was debating saying more but decided to let it go. "Any clue whether Hallie's mother has seen this yet?"

"Natalie was going to be my next stop."

"Well. We better get to it."

Clara maneuvered the stroller up Natalie's lone front step and stood awkwardly to the side while Detective Bryant knocked. In unspoken agreement, they'd taken the long way around the block so as not to walk past Paul's house. Clara wondered exactly how Paul himself factored in to the detective's containment plan. She was still clinging to some small hope that he might never learn of the paper, however unlikely.

It took a moment for Natalie to come to the door, and when she finally opened it, Clara's heart sank. Her eyes were puffy from crying. She wore a huge sweatshirt that had to belong to her husband, and half her hair had come loose from its ponytail. She looked from Clara to the detective and back again.

"Oh, God," she said. "What? Have you found Kristin?"

Clara shook her head, and Detective Bryant cleared his throat and held up the flyer. "Have you seen this?" he asked simply.

Natalie shook her head. "I haven't gotten the mail. I'm having kind of a hard day. This isn't the best time—"

"Clara told me about your husband coming home and leaving again. I'm sorry to barge in at a time like this. But it's important."

Natalie hesitated, then stepped aside and held the door open wide. Clara lifted Maddie and took Thomas by the hand, and followed Detective Bryant into the living room. She'd been inside Natalie's house only once before, and she took in its coziness and the obvious signs of sadness—the rumpled blanket on the L-shaped sectional, the family photo album open on the coffee table, the ball of soggy tissues.

"You'd think I'd be used to it by now," Natalie said quietly, coming up behind her. "But nothing can ever soften the fact that you might not see someone you love again." She clapped her hands together decisively. "How about a cartoon?" she asked the kids, her voice bright.

Clara had always admired those moms who could slip into take-charge mode at a moment's notice. In a flurry, Natalie had a pile of picture books on the floor in front of Maddie, Nickelodeon on the TV for Thomas, and the table in the adjoining dining room set with three mugs of steaming coffee, one of which Detective Bryant gladly accepted. Clara kept her eyes on her children, feeling chagrined that on neither of the detective's visits had she offered him a thing. She'd merely blinked at him like a deer on a nighttime highway and complied with his requests. Clearly she'd overestimated her ability to keep it together in times of stress and confusion.

Then again, she hadn't anticipated quite so many such times. At least, not like this.

"Now, what's this about?" Natalie asked, taking a seat across from them.

The detective slid the paper toward her, and Clara watched her flinch at the initial sight of Hallie's name, and the widening of her eyes as she read.

"Oh, my God, I have no idea how she gets these things into her head," Natalie said, groaning. "How many people got this little gazette, exactly?"

"We're not sure yet. A lot."

She covered her face with her hands. "I'm horrified. You have to understand, she has a vivid imagination. I didn't even realize she'd been so affected by what's been happening, by the news of Kristin and the twins gone. I've had other things on my mind . . ." Her voice trailed off, and she dropped her hands to the table. "Surely we can just explain to everyone that this is a fabrication, the product of a child's imagination?"

"I'm afraid it's not that simple," Detective Bryant said. "For one thing, it's true."

"What? What do you *mean,* it's true? How would she possibly know?"

Clara shifted uncomfortably in her seat, and Natalie's eyes locked on hers as if only just registering her presence. "I'm sorry," she said, turning back to Detective Bryant. "Why is Clara here?"

"Turn the page," he said simply. Clara blanched. So he was going to leave the explaining to her. Fair enough.

Natalie took in the masthead. "I don't understand," she said, her eyes not leaving the paper.

Clara did her best to explain, from the beginning.

When she was finished, Natalie's eyes blazed. "I don't give a damn if it seemed like 'a bad time' to tell us on Thursday," she snapped. "It didn't occur to you that it might actually have been a good time? For once, I had my husband here to help me parent the kid! And now I have to deal with this myself. *Again*." She burst into tears.

"I'm so sorry," Clara said, her own voice breaking, her own tears welling. "You have to believe me that I didn't—"

The slamming of the front door jolted them all. Hallie stopped short as she took in the kids in the living room, the adults seated at the table, and her mother furiously wiping at her wet cheeks with her sleeve. The girl's mouth opened, but nothing came out.

"Don't pretend like you don't know what this is about," Natalie said sternly, her composure returning. "Why don't you join us and fill us in, like the reporter you are."

Slowly, Hallie crossed the room and slid into a chair, dropping her backpack with a thud. "I thought you'd be proud of me," she muttered.

"When did you even *write this*? When did you print it?"

"The kids club at the lodge had a computer room. One of the girls working in there helped me. She seemed to think it was pretty cool."

Clara and Detective Bryant exchanged a glance. So someone outside the neighborhood had seen it too. Exactly how "cool" had she found it?

"Do you remember her name?" he asked casually.

"Stephanie. I remember perfectly because I used to want my name to be Stephanie when I grew up, but then Mom told me I would always be stuck with Hallie." The girl glared at her mom, who glared back.

"Hallie," Clara said firmly, trying to steer her back. "I thought I made it clear that making that recording was wrong. Not to mention sharing it with the neighborhood!"

She expected the girl to concede that she'd disobeyed, but to her surprise, Hallie stood her ground. "Yeah, but you also said that maybe my project could be to print only good news. You said that's what this world needs more of. I thought about it, and you were right. And this *is* good news!" Clara stared at her, stunned, and Hallie turned to her mother. "People have Kristin all wrong, thinking she was greedy. This could help clear her name."

Clara shook her head. "You and I both know that isn't what I meant. And you *promised* me you wouldn't print this!"

"I never promised. You told me to promise but I never actually said anything after that."

Natalie wheeled on Clara. "I still can't believe you knew my daughter was over there creeping around that man's house, playing Nancy Drew or Girl Friday or whatever the hell, and you didn't tell me. You didn't want to ruin Jim's surprise on Thursday? Fine. We got home last night! You should have been banging on my door!"

"The kids have been horribly sick . . ." She sounded so pathetic, even to herself, that she couldn't even bother to finish the thought. "I'm sorry," she said again, stealing another look at Hallie, half expecting her to pipe up and apologize, at the very least for having printed her name. But she remained silent.

"We're going to do as much damage control as we can on our end," Detective Bryant said finally. "But you're both going to have a fair amount to do too. Just assume that everyone has seen it. We're gathering up as many of these as we can, but it's out there. We got the initial call alerting us to the matter from the professors down the street."

"Which one?" Clara asked. There were at least three houses she could think of.

"All of them," he said.

14

If you really want me to, I can tell you about the first time I realized he was capable of killing me. The story itself is unremarkable. Not much more than a run-of-the-mill argument, really.

The look in his eyes, however, was something else.

I was already in it, deep—he'd made quick work of that—so all I could do was rationalize. Just because he was capable of it didn't mean he would do it. The circumstances that could drive him that far seemed unlikely. And now that I was learning what they were—the precise buttons to in no event push—surely I could minimize the risk. I could handle this. I could handle him. If anyone could do it, it was me. In fact, I still believe that's why he chose me. All the more satisfying to triumph over a worthy opponent.

The day I knew that he wasn't just capable of killing me, but was very likely going to? That all the wrong buttons were stuck in the On position? That nothing could stand in his way?

That's the better story.

But you won't hear it from me. I've broken enough promises to myself to last a lifetime, and breathing a word of that horrible night would be breaking one more.

The details aren't important anyway. The point is, there's a line. Sometimes you can make it out, sometimes not. I guess in that respect you might consider me one of the lucky ones.

15

People are drawn to Yellow Springs for its au-
thenticity . . .
In Yellow Springs, good vibes bubble up.

> *—Flyer Izzy pocketed on her first visit to the*
> *YS real estate office, on a whim while waiting*
> *for Penny to finish browsing boutiques for*
> *bridesmaid gifts*

The doorbell was ringing.

Not just ringing. Insisting that she answer.

Izzy was cocooned in bed, the blinds drawn against the midday
sun, still wearing only the tank top and underwear she'd slept in.
Cary Grant was on the TV screen, sexy in black and white. Her
popcorn, soda, and half-eaten bag of chocolate chips were in reach
on her bedside table. She'd taken more NyQuil, just for the fog of
it. She didn't want to move, had no reason to.

It rang again. Whoever it was was not about to give up. Grudgingly, she surveyed the floor for the yoga pants she'd discarded there
last night.

She was supposed to be at work. It was Tuesday, after all. But
when her alarm had pulled her crudely from sleep too early that

morning, she'd been stunned to discover tears flooding her cheeks in the darkness. It had taken a moment to orient herself. She'd been dreaming that she was standing silently next to Josh high on a balcony, waves crashing onto the beach below them in the moonlight, watching the stars fall one by one from the sky into the sea.

The world, ending. *Her* world, ending. That was the stuff her dreams were made of.

For a few minutes, she'd lain sniffling into her pillow, suffocating in self-pity and trying to convince herself that her subconscious mind had developed a severely exaggerated penchant for melodrama. When that didn't work, when she was unable to shake the dream, to quell the panic rising that her life really might be at the point of her own personal apocalypse, she'd decided that for once she couldn't face it—not today of all days: the day of the damn pregnancy party. *Pregnancy party.* Since when was that even a thing? Why did Penny seem to get her own custom-made neighboring universe in which to live? She had reached for her phone, groggily called in sick to work, found a bottle of nighttime cold medicine in the bathroom cabinet, drank a double dose, and went back to sleep.

When she came to—an hour ago? two?—the sun was high in the sky, and her shame rose with it. Her excuse for skipping work had become a self-fulfilling prophecy, as excuses were wont to do—the illness of self-loathing was worse than any virus. Her head dizzy from the medicine, her stomach roiling from the emptiness, she texted Penny that she was ill and so sorry she couldn't make the celebration tonight. Then she slunk down to the kitchen for something to right her blood sugar. She tried to make toast, but a fuse blew, and she left the bread there, defeated. Something needed to be rewired in this house. Something needed to be rewired in her life. She was ill equipped to fix any of it, in over her head. Never had it been so clear that running away had only made things worse. Funny how it had taken a dream, of all things, to finally do her in. Her eyes fell on Clara's *Talk of the Town* DVD on the counter, and thus with her arms full of unhealthy choices she hauled herself upstairs to crawl back under the covers. Where she belonged.

The uselessness, though, even now, was an unfamiliar skin; just a half day in it left her squirming, restless. How hard could fuses and circuits and whatever the hell was haywire in her kitchen really be? What would she ever gain by being this easily discouraged—especially if the house really was the metaphor for her life that it suddenly seemed to be? A tentative how-to search on her tablet led to another. Maybe *this* was the way to decipher home ownership woes—with junk food and old movies and a string of hours she had already committed to wasting. She wasn't about to jump up and attempt a fix just now, but thinking on it—well, that was becoming her specialty.

But then came this ringing, followed now by impatient knocking. It wouldn't let up. Her pants were nowhere. Fine, then. She pulled the blanket off her bed, gathered it around her, and padded down to the front door.

She had it halfway open before she realized her mistake.

She hadn't seen Josh since the day the whole family helped her move in, and seeing him now, alone on her doorstep, brought back the sense of a bad omen that she'd awoken with. The force of it hit her again, how the stars had *fallen out of the sky.* And what had the dream version of Izzy done? What had her mind's conjured version of Josh managed? They'd both just watched their world come crashing down. Even in her wildest dreams, she couldn't turn to him and make him really see her.

She squinted and blinked at him. The sunlight was unconscionably bright.

He took a step back. "Oh," he said, holding his palms out. *Don't shoot.* "Sorry. I had this crazy idea you weren't really sick." She followed his eyes to her hand, clasped around not just the blanket but also, to her surprise, a wad of soggy tissues. Oh, God, what must she look like? As her eyes adjusted to the light, she registered the wild mess of hair in her peripheral vision.

"Sorry to disappoint," she said. "Better keep your distance."

Josh must have come already dressed for tonight's festivities. She recognized his light zip-necked sweater from the rehearsal dinner. His hair was artfully misarranged, his khakis ironed, his shoes shiny. Obediently, he took a step back. But he kept his eyes on hers, his head cocked to the side, as if debating whether to speak.

She'd been down with the worst flu of her life when Josh and Penny had gotten together. They'd both been concerned, taken turns checking in at her apartment when she grew too feverish and lethargic to even answer her phone. She still didn't know exactly how it had started. Only that when she came out of her fever-dream state, forty-eight hours later, something had already shifted between them.

Between all of them.

She wondered if he was remembering the same thing.

"Penny was upset, when she got your message." he said. "I figured the least I could do was—"

Izzy raised an eyebrow, and his voice trailed off. She wasn't sure what was worse—that he had suspected she was feigning sickness, or that she looked so awful that he believed her to be ill after all. But given that the unflattering truth was saving her from the horrific lie . . .

"Iz," he said finally, "am I imagining it? That you've been avoiding us?"

She looked down at her feet.

"Maybe I'm imagining the Penny part," he said. "I know you've been tied up with the move. But I'm not imagining the *me* part. I miss you."

Helpless tears welled in her eyes, and she coughed into her tissue-filled fist, trying to hide them.

"I wish I'd known this would be . . . I mean, I suppose I can understand, things getting weird between us. I guess I don't know many people who hang out with their siblings' significant others. Maybe it's not . . . I don't know, is *appropriate* the word?"

She swallowed hard and reluctantly lifted her chin to even her gaze with his. "Some people might say that's the word," she said quietly.

"But I thought we were different. We were friends *first*. Not just friends. We were . . . us."

The words were the ones she'd wanted to hear, but the tone was off, a sidestep to the left of the center she'd had in mind. It was a variation of the conversation she had both most longed for and most dreaded, with every pathetic ounce of her being, since the moment he'd started up with Penny. But everything about it was wrong. She didn't just look awful, she didn't just *feel* awful, she was in shambles—unable to look him in the eye without a deep and self-conscious shame clouding her vision, triggering her fight-or-flight response until it was all she could do not to slam the door and run back upstairs.

And Penny was pregnant.

She couldn't think of a single thing that seemed safe to say in response.

"I didn't think I'd be losing you as a friend," he said. His voice was a soft apology, barely more than a whisper, and in it she could hear a familiar note—in the same key of the hurt she'd been feeling these long months without him. "I thought I'd be gaining you as a sister."

He was almost begging, but he forced a laugh, an invitation to join in or maybe to correct him, an unvoiced *Can you believe how foolish I was?* or maybe a *Can you tell me I wasn't?* and she thought she detected a whiff of bitterness beneath its olive branch exterior. Maybe, though, it was just sadness. She kicked at the doorstep, where the crushed pieces of her heart had been spread to be trampled anew. "I honestly thought it would be *better,*" he said, shaking his head sadly. "You were already my sister. But now you really are—and now you're really not. I can't say I understand why it has to be this way. Does it, Iz? Can we fix it?"

She licked her cracked lips.

She had no choice but to speak. "I . . ."

Josh looked at her, expectant. Waiting.

"I didn't get a chance to congratulate you," she choked out. "On the baby."

It was not the right thing for *her* to say in this situation, but it was *a* right thing for *a person* to say, at some point, and so it came to her, stupidly and all bent, in a moment when every other possible response seemed unequivocally *wrong.* Her voice didn't sound congratulatory—more like one of those robotic assistants that come programmed into cell phones. He looked at her with disbelief. *That's how you're going to play this? As if I didn't say anything at all?*

She looked back at him helplessly. And she could see the Josh she loved shutting down, replacing himself before her eyes with a polite stranger who'd married her sister. Which was exactly what she'd treated him as. How else would she have him act?

"Thanks," he said finally.

"I really am sorry I'm sick. I hate to miss the party."

The polite stranger nodded and took another step back. "Best not to force it. The doctor did warn us that Penny's immune system would be compromised right now."

Compromised. Their continued friendship was not necessarily *inappropriate,* but it was definitely compromised. That was the word he'd been looking for. No point in saying so now.

As he turned to leave, she caught a glimpse of his mouth—and it gave him away, called her back. Because it didn't belong to the stranger. It belonged to Josh. And it was twitching the way it always did when his mind was busy working over a problem. She had a flash of him studying on the floor of her dorm room, his baseball cap turned backward. Driving in bumper-to-bumper rush hour, late for a sold-out concert they'd paid too much for. Sitting in the hospital waiting room the night his grandmother had a stroke. Watching those stars fall in her dream.

"Come back," she said, her voice tortured. Breaking.

He turned, slowly.

She faltered.

"You and Penny should come back. Once I'm well. We can go to the glen—" She caught herself. They both knew Penny didn't really hike. "We can . . . get drinks at the tavern. Before it gets too cold to sit outside."

"Penny can't drink anymore, but—"

Izzy closed her eyes. How much more ridiculous could she get? "We can go to brunch!" She sounded like her mother, who had a habit of clasping her hands together joyfully and blurting out things no one wanted to do. *Wouldn't it be lovely to drop in on Mrs. Sims?*

*Her son doesn't visit much, you know. And she's got that gorgeous par-
lor that never gets used!*

"Yeah." He looked around, and she cringed as she saw his eyes
fall on her car parked in her driveway. Her taillight was gleaming
new, but the area around it looked to have been in a fight with a
tiger. "Yikes. Were you in an accident? Everything okay?"

The longer he stayed, the worse this was going to get.

"It was just some dumb thing." He was staring at her. "Just a
flesh wound," she managed, one of their favorite movie quotes, and
he rewarded her with a small smile.

"If you say so. Almost forgot." He held out a bundle he must
have grabbed from her mailbox—junk envelopes, catalogs, some
sort of rudimentary-looking newspaper she hadn't subscribed to but
would probably get billed for. It was defeating, how things you
didn't want to deal with could show up at your doorstep anyway.

She didn't linger to watch him leave. She closed the door and
retreated to the kitchen, the bundle of mail still warm from his
hands. She hugged it to her ferociously as she gave in to the fresh
tears that had been threatening. Then, with a flick of her arm, she
dropped it in the recycling bin as if it were on fire.

16

Most courts use the "best interests of the child" test to determine whether to award a stepparent requested visitation. Courts review whether continuing the child's relationship with a step-parent enhances the child's life and improves his or her welfare. If the answer is "yes," visitation is awarded.

—Passage highlighted by Paul Kirkland in a "Rights of Stepparents in Custody and Visitation" brochure, with a question mark doodled in the margin

I can't believe you're making me do this," Clara whispered. Benny kept on as if he hadn't heard her. He dashed through the darkness, closing the gap between their yard and Paul and Kristin's with a few long strides, and ducked behind the Kirklands' detached garage, motioning impatiently for her to follow. She stole a glance through the narrow gap between the trees and out toward the street, where reporters, copies of *The Color-Blind Gazette* in hand, were too slowly packing up their vans in the wake of a stern admonishment from Detective Marks. "There is *literally nothing to see here*," Clara had heard her booming. "You can do your reporting without further distressing these families." Beyond them, Izzy's house was dark save for a single upstairs window, and Clara couldn't help wondering if Izzy was hiding up there—possibly even from her. She had no idea what any of her neighbors were going to think of this, what they were going to think of *her,* though she'd received confused, alarmed, "What the hell?" texts from Randi and Rhoda and promised to fill them in later. First, she had to deal with Paul.

"Come *on*!" Benny hissed. She was trying his patience. She'd called him at work and given him the short version of her afternoon with Hallie, Natalie, and Detective Bryant, but that hadn't padded his shock at arriving home to the chaos assembled outside. The reporters had yelled questions at him as he slunk up the walk in a posture that broke Clara's heart with its un-Benny-ness. All she could do was watch helplessly through the window. "Mr. Tiffin, were the Kirklands clients of your accounting firm?" "Mr. Tiffin, what do you make of your wife's involvement with the case?" "Is it true that your wife was with Kristin Kirkland the night before she disappeared?" "If she wanted to be a whistle-blower, why this neighborhood newspaper? Why not do an interview with us?" "What else does she know?"

Clara took a deep breath, patted her jeans pockets to be sure the baby monitors were snug, and leaped ungracefully across the grass, knocking into her husband behind the garage wall and breaking her fall with a fistful of his shirt. "Too bad the cameras didn't get a shot of that," he muttered. "It would lay to rest the questions of your stealth." She punched his arm. Benny would do this, forcing jokes to pretend he wasn't upset when he really was—and usually, his going through the motions would stick. He *wouldn't* be upset anymore. She wasn't sure about this time, though. He hadn't said he held her responsible for getting them pulled into this, but he hadn't said he didn't, either.

A distinctly autumnal chill had descended at sunset, and Clara's shiver of anticipation doubled in intensity. The last of the summer's locusts chorused as she and Benny peeked around the corner toward the sliding glass doors to Paul's kitchen. The new back window gleamed, its pane standing apart from the weathered tone of the others, and the effect was one of someone trying too hard to blend in, failing to recognize that nothing about perfection was normal.

He was seated with his back to them at the table, alone, a low-ball glass in front of him filled with ice and a brownish liquid. Bourbon, maybe. Clara didn't want to be here. She knew it had to be done—Benny was right about that. But still . . .

She didn't want to be here.

"I don't feel right about sneaking up on him this way," she said, stalling.

"It's not like we can knock on the front door."

"But maybe over the phone . . ."

He gently pressed her forward, out of the shadows into the expanse of grass illuminated by the lights of the house. She untucked her hair from behind her ear and let it fall over her face, a futile attempt to hide behind it somehow, and headed toward the low back porch with Benny half a step behind her. The wooden stairs creaked, and Paul turned and caught sight of them before they could knock. Quickly, he stood. He was wearing a T-shirt and pajama pants and had swapped his contacts for glasses. Though he wasn't exactly disheveled, it was so foreign to see him dressed down that she felt a bit taken aback, as if they'd come upon him in an intimate moment.

Which, of course, they had. Sometimes solitude was the most intimate thing of all.

His face registered nothing—not surprise, not displeasure, not dread—as he crossed to the door and slid it open. He and Clara stared wordlessly at each other.

"Hey, man," Benny began. "We can't tell you how awful we feel about this. We wanted to clear the air—" Paul stepped aside and gestured toward the kitchen table. Benny filed in obediently, and Clara followed.

"Join me for a drink? Scotch? Beer?"

"No thanks," Benny said. "Long day at the office tomorrow."

"Clara? Come on, it's bad form to let a neighbor drink alone." She understood that this was a test of some sort. She also understood what he might have added but didn't: *Don't tell me you have somewhere to be tomorrow. You're right over there. All day. Right next to me.*

"A beer would be great," she managed, and as Paul made for the fridge, Benny shot her a look. She flipped her palms open in a way that she hoped conveyed, in the subtle language developed over years of marriage, that she had no fucking clue what he expected her to do.

"What the hell," Benny called after him. "Make it two."

Paul opened the bottles and handed one to each of them. "I have cookies, casseroles, you name it," he said, tilting his head toward a cluster of Tupperware on the counter. "Any takers?" They shook their heads, and he slid back into his seat. "I went back to work yesterday and today. Only half days, but better than just sitting here. The nurses don't know what to do but overfeed me. Then again, depending on what they make of that little gazette, this may be the last of the meals on wheels." His voice was casual but pointed.

Clara wondered if he was turning a blind eye or if he, too, had read the comments threads on the early articles about Hallie's project.

"Shudder. Glad he's not my doctor."

"Ugh. He happens to be mine, but not as of tomorrow."

"This speculation is unfair to Dr. Kirkland. His wife cleans him out, and you're all pointing fingers at *him*? He delivered all three of my children and is the kindest, most caring medical professional I've ever known. I'd recommend him to anyone."

"I had a complication with this pregnancy and would have lost my mind with worry if not for the outstanding care of Dr. Kirkland. Appalling that our police would waste taxpayer money with this kind of witch hunt."

She didn't know whether to feel grateful that the damage done might be minimal, or horrified that arguable warning signs were so easily dismissed.

Clara averted her eyes and sipped her drink. The cool, familiar foam on her dry tongue emboldened her. "I want you to know I had nothing to do with that article," she said. "I was just as surprised as you were to find it in my mailbox." That sounded wrong. Like she was comparing her reaction to his. "I mean, maybe not *as* surprised—certainly not as horrified, I'm sure, though I *was*—really horrified. What I mean is—"

"Bryant told me," he cut in. His dropping of the detective's title seemed to convey a certain disdain. "Tough break for both of us, I guess." He was looking straight at her now, and she looked away, taking in the once-homey kitchen where she'd had many a cup of coffee with Kristin while the kids made a mess of playdough on the floor, or kicked balls across the yard, or zoomed cars around the living room. The house felt different now. Unsettled. Off balance. Abandoned, even with Paul in it.

Benny spun his beer bottle slowly on the tabletop. "I know we don't know each other all that well, but we feel for you. The idea that anything we might have been associated with could add to your stress at a time like this—" Benny shook his head. Clara wished he would stop saying *we*. She wasn't sure she deserved his support just now. Then again, without it she wasn't sure she'd have the stomach to deliver these necessary assurances on her own. "It's the last thing we'd want," Benny continued. "We didn't have any role in what happened here, but still, we're deeply sorry."

Paul was still eying Clara. "The girl played you a recording of that conversation? Between me and Bryant and Detective What's-Her-Face?"

Surely Detective Bryant had already told Paul the whole story? If she said no, would he lie about what had been said, say Hallie had distorted things? What she'd printed in the paper had been out of line, and it had painted him in a suspicious light, but it had been accurate. Behind Paul the too-clean window reflected back to Clara the memory of Detective Bryant chasing after the repair van, trailing behind him the dismal feeling that any potential evidence inside was already tainted. *Inadmissible*—a technical term for *useless*.

Clara nodded.

"You were with Kristin that night." Upon closer examination,

Paul's eyes looked a bit glassy, and Clara wondered how many drinks he'd had and how much they might have lowered his inhibitions. "Do you have any idea what reason she might've had for Googling those things?"

Clara looked to Benny, feeling like a child who hopes her mother might answer a stranger's question, but he remained frozen squarely at the midpoint of stoic and neighborly.

"I haven't the faintest idea," she said, turning her head to meet Paul dead on.

"There wasn't anything anyone said, or—?"

She cocked her head and pursed her lips, and Benny kicked her under the table. *Careful.*

It was an odd place to be, caught between feeling angry enough to call him out and afraid enough to keep quiet. She knew she was lucky to have come to this place as an outsider—she could simply walk to the door and turn the knob. Anytime she wanted. Any minute now. Too many women couldn't, and she wasn't about to gamble on whether Kristin had been one of them. Her eyes bore into Paul's, and he shrugged, letting the question drop.

"Well, I don't know what was up with her search terms either, but I can tell you, they're barking up the wrong tree. She's out there with my kids—*my kids*—and every minute they spend looking at me is a minute they're *not* spending looking for them." He took an angry swig of his liquor and grimaced in the way of someone who didn't typically forgo the mixers.

"I'm sure they're doing all they can," Benny said.

He scowled. "Every day they have a new theory. The latest nonsense is that I was trying to make her quit her job. As if that would even be in my interest now that we're getting a divorce." She wondered if Benny noticed, as she did, that Paul qualified the theory as ridiculous *because* their marriage was over. Was she just oversensitive to that sort of thing? "It's clear they're grasping at straws. I'm *this close* to hiring my own guy."

Clara's mouth went dry again. "A private investigator?"

"I know what you're thinking. She wasn't going to be my wife anymore anyway. I never adopted the twins. If I don't care about the money, why not let them go?"

"Oh, I wasn't—"

"I'm getting all this bullshit about stepparents not having custodial rights. 'Visitation' is all they call it. I need to make a case about my 'standing' with them. My standing! They're children! I'm not some fly-by-night fill-in father. I'm their *dad*. And the fact that I never filed the paperwork to make that official . . ." His voice drifted off as his eyes fell on the corkboard tacked to the kitchen wall, and Clara followed his gaze to the display of the paperwork that came with four-year-olds dabbling in the business of becoming full-fledged kids. Lunch menus. Soccer schedules. A flyer about picture day. Tough though it was to look at, she couldn't help but think what a handy collage it made—something to point at and say, *I want that back.*

There would be no reason for anyone to infer that what you were really after was the board itself, the thing those messy bits were attached to.

"I thought I had time. I never imagined Kristin and I would . . . come apart."

He looked so sad right then, it almost escaped Clara's attention that his fists were clenched on the table, as if barely containing themselves.

Benny cleared his throat. "I can't tell you how many people come into my firm, distraught—about money, of course, which is ostensibly why they see an accountant, but that's just on the surface. What they're really distraught about is a divorce or a death or an investment gone bad or a mistake or an oversight. Every one of them thinks they've missed their chance to set things right. And you'd be surprised how often it turns out they haven't missed their chance at all. Sometimes it just feels that way."

Her husband looked so sincere that Clara wondered what she'd ever done to deserve such a good man. And then immediately wondered why anyone deserved less of one.

"I'm sure it felt like an eternity to you, but it didn't take the reporters long to back away last time," Benny continued. "They will again. Just give the police time to do their jobs."

Paul took a deep breath and let it out slowly. "It's an odd thing, searching for someone who doesn't want to be found," he said. "Even if you have good reason."

Because that someone has a better reason? Clara knew she had to muster some sort of outward sympathy. But now that she was here, she found herself thinking not so much of Paul's reaction but of what hers should have been earlier today. She wished she'd pressed Detective Bryant harder. She'd been so caught up in defending herself that she hadn't asked the questions that had been noodling at her since Hallie first played the recording. Namely, *how much suspicion was Paul under, exactly?*

Clara knew that in volatile situations, the worst imaginable outcome *was* a possibility. She'd seen it once before. And one time had been too many.

"I don't suppose you'd like to look around?" Paul asked abruptly. He was talking to her.

Reflexively, Clara looked around the kitchen. It appeared the same as ever, save for a cardboard box on the floor filled with construction paper cutouts of fall leaves intermingled with brightly colored flowers.

"The crafts for the party," Paul said, following her eyes. "There's a big Farewell to Summer banner in there, too, if the school could still use it. You're welcome to take it."

"I think they're on to pumpkins and scarecrows now," she said, then wished she hadn't. It made it seem as if a whole season had passed since Kristin and the kids vanished.

He nodded. "But maybe you could look around the rest of the house, see if you notice anything out of the ordinary, or . . . I don't know, some clue as to where they might have gone. The police did a cursory search, but they don't know Kristin from anyone. You stopped over often enough. Who knows, you might spot something I missed."

Was he challenging her? It was true that she'd stopped over often enough, but if he wanted a second set of eyes, why not ask before now? Clara's instincts told her this was some sort of game. But which one? An innocent round of *I Have Nothing to Hide* or an arrogant one of *Catch Me if You Can*?

"I'm not sure I—"

"If it would make you feel better, I'm sure Clara would be happy to," Benny cut in, and she blinked at him, surprised. Was he overcompensating for the newspaper incident, or, contrary to his insistence that they shouldn't get involved, was he just as curious as she to see if there *was* anything to be found?

Clara got unsteadily to her feet. Paul looked up at her and nodded. "I've done my share of obsessing over every room," he said. "If you don't mind, I'll hang here with Benny."

Another potential motive for this setup occurred to her then: Was Paul trying to get Benny alone, with her out of earshot? To check up on her, to plant an idea there, to try to manipulate him in some way? Clara hesitated.

"You know where the twins' room is, right? I remember Thomas playing up there." She nodded. Preschoolers were huge on showing each other their bedrooms. They had so little territory they could call their own.

He looked at her expectantly.

"Right, then," she said, backing her way into the dining room. The chandelier above the gleaming mahogany table was already lit, just like the rest of the house. Clara wasn't sure if Paul was sending a message to himself, to Kristin and the kids, or to the rest of the neighborhood, but every night it was the same: Every light in the house on, until . . . Clara didn't know how late. After the late news broadcasts, for sure. From a more distant vantage point, she would have found it heartbreaking.

Dust rimmed the circular impressions Kristin's mother's dishes had left in the mirrored hutch of the china cabinet. It made sense that Kristin would take family heirlooms, especially since the detectives had mentioned her mother's declined mental state and poor health. The question was, would Paul think to remove those items if he were staging his wife's disappearance? Clara doubted it. Benny always seemed surprised by how much she cared about such things, as if it were the first time she was reminding him to be careful with the cookie jar because it had been her grandmother's, and that no, they could *not* throw away the ratty crocheted dolls her aunt had made for her as a child.

She made her way upstairs. The first door was to the master bedroom. She hesitantly poked her head inside. The bedside lamps were on, the bed was made, and the room had the inhuman presentation of a hotel suite ready for check-in; there was none of the clutter of the room she shared with Benny—not a single open drawer, or an item of clothing on the floor, or a mound of pocket change or jewelry on the dresser. She stepped in, tentatively, one foot in front of the other, and realized she was holding her breath. It was eerily quiet up here, and she strained for the low rumble of the men's voices from the kitchen, perhaps a burst of laugher. But there was nothing, and the hair stood up on the back of her neck, as if Paul might come up behind her any minute and . . . and what? Catch her doing something he'd asked her to do?

On the upholstered chaise sprawled under the window was an open duffel bag with a mess of undershirts inside, and button-downs and slacks were spread on the chair's back. So Paul was still living here like a guest; he hadn't unloaded his things into the drawers again. She walked to the open closet and pulled the string of the overhead light. She'd never been in here before, but the number of empty hangers indicated that Kristin had taken quite a few things. She scanned the shoes and didn't see Kristin's trainers, or her black flats, or those knee-high leather boots she'd been coveting herself.

The adjoining bathroom was much the same: almost clinically clean. She pulled open a drawer and found a basket of makeup. Old stuff, probably, though it was hard to say. A couple of eye shadows and blushes were scattered among enough bottles of concealer and foundation to fill a drugstore aisle, in a range of shades. Kristin didn't exactly embrace the natural look, but she never looked heavily made up, either—though maybe she was just more skilled in the art of application than Clara was. Clara touched her fingertip to one of the bottles. It looked almost full. Why so many? To match summer tanned skin tones and winter ones? Or did she use them somewhere other than her face—to hide bruises or scars? Clara rolled the drawer shut and pulled open the mirrored medicine cabinet. Just an ordinary assortment of over-the-counter stuff, no prescriptions. Nothing Kristin couldn't buy wherever she was going.

This is silly, she told herself, snapping off the lights behind her, though they'd been on when she arrived. She made her way to the doorway of the twins' room and stopped to take it in. Though the house had four bedrooms, they'd insisted they *wanted* to share, something Kristin had told her with pure maternal pride that her kids were smart enough to know from the start: *We have each other. Let's stick together.*

Things weren't quite so neat here, books off the shelves, bunk beds unmade, which, as Clara stood in the stillness, was even more eerie—as if the kids might come running in at any minute to pick up where they left off. She pictured Thomas's room without Thomas in it, Maddie's nursery with no Maddie, and shuddered. She didn't want to do this. How much time needed to pass to satisfy Paul that she'd been thorough?

Aaron was attached to a stuffed elephant he called Fante, and she crossed to the top bunk and lifted the covers, checked under the pillow, patted down the length of the mattress. No Fante, which was a good sign. She ducked to the bottom bunk and discovered with relief the same void there. The favorites had gone with their owners. She turned to the bookcases, where the less loved plush animals lined the top shelf, some looking perpetually eager and others downright forlorn. Even stuffed animals could be divided into realists and hopeless optimists.

She had to fight a motherly instinct to gather the books from the carpet and stack them back on the shelves. Paul might not want that. But then, she saw it, tossed carelessly among the discards on the floor: The lone, tattered cover of the *I Can Do It!* board book, its binding and the rest of its pages long gone, the cartoonish fox smiling up at her beneath the title.

A flood of memories: Abby pulling the cover from the pocket of her coat, from the seat of her jeans, from the side of her cargo pants, from her soccer practice bag, from the little purses she liked to carry, and rubbing it like a lucky charm. Abby yelling, "I can beat you—I have *I Can Do It!* power!" as the kids were lining up to race down the sidewalk. Abby answering sweetly, "Don't worry, *I Can Do It!* is coming with me," when Clara asked if she was nervous about the first day of pre-K. And Kristin bemoaning how many well-meaning teachers had come upon the cover, fallen from Abby's pocket or backpack, and thrown it away.

"Imagine them mistaking this for trash," she'd told Clara drolly, standing in the parking lot of the school. "If I wipe this thing down with Clorox one more time, the picture's going to come clean off." She'd gone on to outline the great lengths she'd gone to in hopes of locating a replacement. This version was out of print; it had since been re-illustrated; the originals for sale online were as much as $50 each. "I can't bring myself to pay that for a book I'm going to rip the cover off of!" she'd said, trying to force a laugh even as she looked about to cry. This wasn't just any item Abby clung to: It was her very sense of self-confidence. Clara had felt for her. Neither of her kids had a strong attachment to a toy yet, and she'd been thankful, then, that their toys were basically losable, breakable, tearable, disposable. She knew it wouldn't always be that way, that like everything about childhood, these days of easy-come-easy-go were limited.

And yet here was *I Can Do It!* alone on the bedroom floor.

There was no rationalizing with the tsunami of worry drowning out her thoughts. Kristin might have left in a rush. She might have left in a state of fear or panic or emotion. And parents were bound to forget things. Lord knows Clara did. She'd suffered through trips to the pediatrician with no diaper bag, trips to the grocery with no wallet, trips to the playground with no shoes on Maddie's stroller-bound feet—and those were just the outings that didn't require real packing.

Kristin, though, was the superwoman version of every other mom. She did not falter, not when it came to the important stuff. The idea that she would take her daughter to go and start a new life without her *I Can Do It!* seemed beyond unlikely. Clara lifted it reverently, in both hands, and swallowed the bile rising in her throat.

Down in the kitchen, she found the men watching the Reds game on the wall-mounted TV. They remained at the table, sipping their drinks and contentedly ignoring each other. Neither of them even noticed her, until she cleared her throat.

"Anything?" Paul asked.

Benny stared up at her, his face filled with questions he would not ask until they were safely home. She licked her lips and held out the book cover toward Paul.

"Just this." She tried to hold her voice steady.

He took it from her hands, turned it over, and made a small noise, a grunt, really. "Looks like trash to me," he said, looking up at her. "Did I miss something?"

Clara wasn't surprised. *Only everything,* she thought.

17

No one ever likes to admit that they're desperate. It feels too much like calling yourself pathetic. That's not really a fair comparison, though. The word pathetic has only one real meaning—a sad one. But there are lots of types of desperation.

Test me sometime. I can list them all.

18

If you felt overwhelmed when you learned that you were carrying multiples, rest assured you are not alone. Your partner can be an invaluable sounding board at this time, as he likely shares much of the complicated mixture of emotions you may be feeling. Opening up to him will strengthen your bond emotionally as well as better prepare you for what lies ahead.

—"Twins, Triplets & Beyond" brochure from
Dr. Kirkland's waiting room

Detective Bryant had warned her against going, Benny had encouraged her to reconsider, and Thomas had trusted her, in the way that young children implicitly trust their mothers, to do what was best—but nothing had prepared Clara for the onslaught that awaited her at preschool Thursday morning. Though the public police statement had retracted Clara's involvement in *The Color-Blind Gazette* and beseeched everyone to "respectfully disregard this child's project and leave the families in peace," it had done little to satisfy the news teams. They may have grudgingly complied with Detective Marks's request that they not camp out at the curb, but two days later their vans were still circling Clara's block. Her door-bell rang every few hours like clockwork; she had to leave the land-line off the hook.

If they only knew, she thought. The memory of the *I Can Do It!* cover tormented her. She wanted—desperately—to tell the police what she'd found, but what good would it do? It was, at face value, an item that had simply not been packed. An oversight. And not, even if it was in itself suspicious, one that was likely to lead to some other clue. They could easily postulate that Kristin had just forgot-ten it, and they could easily be right. What's more, if they *did* con-front Paul with questions about the cover, then what? *Then* he knew that his neighbor—the very one who had just been associ-ated with a gazette smearing his name all over the neighborhood—was actively reporting unfounded suspicions about him to the police.

When she'd come home that night, she'd shut the back door behind Benny in the darkness of their kitchen, leaned against it, and cried. Benny had held her while she talked herself, on the brink of hysteria, through all these scenarios and more. *You have to calm down,* he'd said. *It's been a long day,* he'd said. *In the morning, this won't seem so dire.* Seeing how weary he was, how unconvinced, she'd agreed to his gentle but firm affirmation that nothing good could come of saying anything—to anyone.

And he was right. She knew he was right. Yet she'd spent every hour since then convincing herself all over again. It wasn't just the media she was dodging. She didn't trust herself to hold back around Randi, Rhoda, Izzy, even Natalie. So she hunkered down at home to wait it all out—the news vans, the questions, the anxiety, the speculation, the answers.

This morning the family had finally enjoyed a quiet breakfast. At last, the guilt and the tension had eased its grip, and she'd left the house feeling cautiously optimistic that the worst was behind them.

She'd had the good sense, at least, to forgo the walk and drive Thomas to preschool today. She was idling outside the Circle of Learning, waiting with a scowl for an impossibly huge black Chevy

Tahoe to back into a prime parking spot marked FUEL-EFFICIENT VEHICLES ONLY, when a rap came on the passenger-side window. She pushed the button to lower the glass, and Miss Sally, one of the classroom aides, poked her head through.

"Clara," she said. "My God. You'd better park around back." Miss Sally was a retired elementary school teacher who'd once told Clara she couldn't imagine *not* spending her days surrounded by children at least part-time, and Clara had instantly taken to the woman, finding her a nice respite from the revolving door of younger aides from Antioch.

"I don't think—"

Miss Sally cut her off with a firm headshake. "There are a few faculty spots back there, past the Dumpsters. AD Evelyn is on vacation—you can park in hers." AD Evelyn had the initials of her assistant director title firmly implanted in front of her name to distinguish her from Baby Room Evelyn and Kindergarten Evelyn. None of the Evelyns were among the most well liked at the school, and Kristin had once muttered to her, upon seeing them all walking in together one morning, "You know how they say bad luck comes in threes?" Clara had gotten a case of the giggles and had to pretend she'd forgotten something in her car to collect herself.

"Is that really necessary?"

"The only thing more gossipy than a small town is a small-town school," Miss Sally said. Clara should have known last week's respectful hesitation to gossip couldn't last. "The back door will be locked, but I'll let you in." You could always tell the best teachers by their ability to render even a capable adult obedient and eager to please. The Tahoe finally out of her path, Clara steered around the side of the building, even though the precaution felt like overkill. She couldn't imagine another parent actually approaching her about *The Color-Blind Gazette* fiasco. For Clara and Thomas, the school was a voluntary, leisurely foray into early education, but for many others it was a full-time day care, and morning drop-offs, though streamlined into the simple steps of hugs, promises of what fun the day would hold, and affectionate but firm good-byes, were privately a complicated emotional time for all involved. If you bought into the Circle school's New Age insistence that everyone had a detectable aura, from a lone parent on any given day one might glean hues of guilt, relief, love, worry, exasperation, pride, and conflicting urges to flee and to stay.

For this reason Clara did not find the school a particularly social place, nor did she attempt to make it so. Only at playdates, outings, and birthday parties did you maybe get a chance to connect with another parent. Here, it was the kids who were focused, the parents whose attention wandered in countless directions. Was it any wonder Kristin had been the only one she'd talked to much?

"Mommy?" Thomas, who thrived on routine on school days especially, was watching her suspiciously as she swung the car into the spot with ASST DIRECTOR painted on the asphalt.

"This is an adventure," she told him quickly. "Today we get to use a special entrance as a special treat."

"What's an entrance?"

"It's how you get into a place."

"We get into *this* place through the front."

"A place can have more than one entrance."

"I saw Kai go in the front with his mommy. I want to say hi to Kai."

"We'll see Kai inside, sweets." She snapped off the car and reached back to unhook his car seat harness. "You can sit at the steering wheel while I get Maddie out, okay?"

"Yeah!" It was ridiculous how much of successful parenting was about knowing how to head off an argument before it started. Distraction was almost always the key.

Come to think of it, it worked pretty well for adults too. Usually.

By the time they were all out of the car, Sally was waving them through a utilitarian steel door in the brick wall. Inside, they found themselves in the back hallway connecting the pre-K and preschool rooms.

"Neat *entrance!*" Thomas yelled, trying out the word loud enough to turn a few heads.

"Clara?" Kai's mother—Clara floundered to conjure her name—

was beelining toward her, grabbing at the sleeve of Clara's coat as if they were in the habit of speaking intimately rather than merely waving in passing. Maddie clung to Clara's other shoulder, startled, and Clara felt a foolish rush of pride that her daughter's instincts were good. "How is everything? Are you okay? Any news on Kristin?"

She shook her head no. "I mean, yes, I'm okay. No, no news."

"Is it true you supported that article because you suspected domestic violence all along?"

Clara stepped back, shaking her sleeve free of the woman's hand more roughly than she'd intended.

"Where did you hear that?"

"Just a theory among some of the moms. We know you knew her best, and being right next door—"

"I didn't *support* the article," she said sharply. "The police released a statement saying my implied involvement was a misunderstanding."

"Come on. We weren't born yesterday, as my mother used to say."

Clara harbored a dislike for people who preceded or followed statements with "as my mother used to say." Their mothers, she was quite sure, had been insufferable.

"Do you honestly think I'd help a *child* break the *law* by recording and sharing private police conversations?" Clara bristled. "I told her not to, in fact."

"So you did know about it beforehand, though!"

Thomas and Kai were playing a game of peekaboo that was escalating in volume around them, each one giggling from behind a flap of his own mother's coat, and as Thomas pulled her off balance, Clara fixed her eyes longingly on the safe portal of his classroom.

"Sorry to interrupt," Miss Sally cut in, "but I was filling Clara in on our new Good Choices program. Perhaps she can catch up with you another time?" Without waiting for a response, she pulled Clara toward the portal, leaving Kai's mother slack-jawed beneath the BIRDS OF A FEATHER banner stretched across the hallway. Clara had only a moment to fantasize about it coming loose and ensnaring the nosy woman before realizing she was no more sheltered inside the classroom. The three other mothers in the midst of drop-off were staring intently; the lead teacher, Miss Lizzie, was crossing to greet her.

"None of them can decide if you and that Hallie child are heroes or troublemakers," she said, so only Clara could hear. While she'd learned early on to leave the other parents to their own devices, Clara never hesitated to socialize with the faculty. She wanted to know whom her son was spending his day with and for them to feel comfortable speaking with her in turn. Still, the relationship could be delicate, as you wanted to believe you knew your own child best but also had to acknowledge that teachers knew more about children in general.

"That's—"

"I err on the side of hero myself. But I worry for you. Have you talked to Paul? Since the paper, I mean?" Clara was almost intimidated by the exuberance Miss Lizzie brought to every interaction, whether they were discussing the weather, the lunch menu, or an "incident report," as the worst missives home were so diplomatically called ("Thomas was kicking a ball when he fell and scraped his knee; we washed the scrape, gave him TLC, and he returned to normal activity." "Thomas was bitten by a friend who did not want to share; the friend understands that he made a bad choice and apologized." "Thomas drew what he referred to as 'a poop machine' at the art station. We explained that while we value creativity, certain subjects are not appropriate, and worked together to turn it into a Tootsie Roll machine—see attached."). Large gold hoops hung courageously from the teacher's ears; Clara had given up anything that dangled after seeing a friend's infant gleefully rip a teardrop stud straight through her mother's lobe.

"I did talk with Paul briefly, just to apologize," she said, then rushed to clarify. "For the misunderstanding." Miss Sally gave her a reassuring touch on her shoulder before fading into the hallway, her charge turned over to another responsible party. Clara fought an irrational urge to call her new ally back.

"Is he angry with you?"

"He *says* not."

Miss Lizzie looked at her meaningfully. "He's never been a big fan of the school, that much is no secret." Clara wanted to ask what she meant, but the other moms were inching closer, straining to hear.

"Did you tell the detectives that?" she asked, in spite of herself.

"Oh, yes. We've all spoken with them."

"Good." Clara nervously eyed the encroaching mothers, and Miss Lizzie finally seemed to notice.

"You'll recall we have an open door policy," the teacher said smoothly, "to allow parents to sit in whenever they'd like?" Clara nodded. "Why don't you take advantage today?" She lowered her voice. "Until traffic clears."

Clara wavered. She'd been planning to drag Maddie along to the store first thing—now that the kids had their appetites back, her poorly stocked fridge wasn't going to cut it. And Thomas was prone to dissolving into good-bye tears whenever she stayed longer than normal. But anything was better than running a gauntlet back to her car.

"Maddie won't be a problem?" She shifted her daughter's weight to the other arm. Maddie was getting a bit big to hold comfortably for this long, not to mention that she was at this moment rhythmically yanking on two enthusiastic fistfuls of Clara's hair. Miss Lizzie gently touched Maddie's arms, and the baby stopped pulling, as if transfixed by her touch.

"Not today she won't," Miss Lizzie said, and Maddie burst into a jack-o'-lantern smile.

Clara shook her head. So Miss Lizzie was some kind of baby whisperer, in addition to wrangling dozens of preschoolers in a way that put their parents' inability to corral just *one* to shame. Maybe Clara would pick up a few pointers while she stuck around. She knelt to Thomas's level, and Maddie wriggled out of her arms and headed for a pile of oversized foam blocks.

"How about Mommy stays for circle time this morning?"

He threw his arms around her neck. "I will love you forever,

Mommy," he murmured in her ear, surprising her. She pulled back to look at him, expecting him to say something silly, but his eyes were gravely searching hers for a reply, and she found herself fighting tears. That was the thing about kids. Even when they didn't really know what they were saying—Thomas had no concept of yesterday or next week, much less forever—they could melt you with it.

"Oh, sweetie. I will love you forever ever after." She hugged him tight again, and then the moment was over, and he was bouncing in a circle yelling, "Can my mommy read the story? Can my mommy read the story? She reads the BEST stories! She does VOICES!"

And that is how Clara came to be midway through *Desert Rose and the Contrary Coyote*—throwing herself into a thick Texan accent and quite enjoying Rose's exclamations of "Hold your horses!"—when Miss Lizzie's intercom buzzed and a moment later the teacher was whispering to Clara that her presence was requested in the director's office. Miss Lizzie smiled apologetically as she gently palmed the book and took over reading, and she even managed to pacify Thomas when he started to protest, though Clara could see the bravery in his bottom lip as he tried his hardest not to cry.

"Be right back," she mouthed to him, holding up a finger as she swallowed her annoyance that this surely could have waited until Desert Rose got her fences mended. Just to show that her own priorities were straight, she took Maddie by the hand and let her mosey her way through the empty hallways to the lobby, where the director's office was behind a glass wall.

Pam, a sterner variety of earth mother who did not like to be addressed with a "Miss" in front of her name the way the teachers did, stood when she caught sight of Clara and gestured to her visitors' chairs, getting right to the point before Clara had even taken her seat. "You know how much we care about all our enrolled families here at Circle of Learning. It's so nice to see that Thomas seems unaffected by all the distractions in his own circle right now." She was wrapped in gauzy layers of scarves that gave her a sheen by comparison.

Clara thought back to Thomas's tight arms around her neck, his out-of-the-blue proclamation. She knew he didn't really grasp what was going on, but she wasn't entirely sure he was unaffected, either. Still, she didn't like the way Pam said the word *distractions,* as if Clara herself had been throwing rowdy dance parties at bedtime or starting food fights with his snacks. "It *is* a little surreal having so much going on next door." Clara said the last two words emphatically, hoping to punctuate the fact that the distractions were not in his "circle" exactly, but on the outer rim. "We're just trying to stick to as much normalcy as possible."

Pam frowned. "That's what I wanted to talk to you about. Normalcy is important for *all* children in our circle. But there's no normalcy here with Thomas on-site. I've had moms holding up traffic in the parking lot, ringing my direct line off the hook . . ."

"Surely not off the hook. We've been here less than an hour."

"That's exactly my point. Five minutes is all it took. I simply can't have these distractions."

"Pam, the distractions you're referring to are related to another family enrolled here. Not ours. We just happen to be their neighbors. Certainly you can't hold us—"

"You didn't have any problems associating yourself with them *on paper.*"

"I certainly did have a problem with that. And I didn't *associate myself* with it. Someone else associated me. A twelve-year-old, I might add. Surely you of all people know that children have minds of their own."

"Be that as it may, we require a calm and holistic environment for our learning approach to be put into practice." Clara bit down on her tongue. The center had password-protected webcams where parents could watch the classrooms during the day, and she'd seen how very far from calm and holistic many days could be.

"You're not asking me to remove Thomas from the school? He loves it here."

"Certainly not. Merely to temporarily step away. Until the distractions subside."

Clara bristled. "This is a small town. Moms are going to be gossiping in your parking lot about these distractions you're referring to whether we're here or not!"

"Still, in focusing on what we *can* control, we feel an arm's length approach is a healthy approach."

Clara sat up straighter. Pam was *serious*. "There's no such thing as an arm's length approach when two of your own students are missing, your staff members and parents have been interviewed by police—"

"That was last week. Do you or do you not have media parked outside your home as we speak?"

"I do not." They were merely driving past it on a loop.

"Well, that makes one of us." Pam crossed to her window and opened the blinds. At the street entrance, next to the CIRCLE OF LEARNING sign, a reporter was standing, microphone in hand, in front of a camera, talking and gesturing at the building behind her.

"This is a first," Pam said. "We can't have them following you here. As soon as everyone has room to self-center, Thomas is welcome back."

Clara stared out the window. Aside from the news team, the parking lot was half empty now, quiet. The trees around its rim were warm bursts of color in the breeze, taunting her that the season was in full swing and the end-of-summer party that never happened was soon to be a distant memory—and Kristin along with it.

"They were bound to show up sooner or later," she said weakly. "They're reaching, running out of things to say." She turned back to Pam, who merely shook her head. "Come on, Pam. They're out by the street, not storming the lobby."

Pam didn't acknowledge that she'd spoken. "We'll be organizing a penny wars fund-raiser in the twins' names to benefit the Greater Dayton United Way," she said instead. "I'll be sure to send you the information in case you'd like to collect donations from your neighborhood."

The annoyance Clara had been fighting all morning surged into the unfairness of the past couple weeks and overtook her. "A freaking Tahoe was double-parked in your fuel-efficient spots today, and *I'm* the disruption tipping the perfect balance here?"

"Watch your language, please."

She couldn't help it—she rolled her eyes. If *freaking* was not a *holistic* enough variation of what she'd really meant to say, then one did not exist. "It's a *V-8*," she said, in protest.

"Might I suggest you take some time to rejuvenate your own soul as well? To lose a friend is to suffer quite a loss. It's a sisterhood not always acknowledged by the masses, but a very real one nonetheless."

Clara would have been more receptive to the sentiment had the sisterhood not just put her family outside its circle.

19

Iz: Please let me in? Sorry about your sweater but it REALLY wasn't my fault. I'll let you use ANY of my stuff you want. Even my new Janet Jackson CD. Though if Mom hears how dirty it is she will TOTALLY take it away from us both, so you'll have to use headphones. Please?

—Note slid under Izzy's slammed-and-locked
door by Penny, age eleven

This was what Izzy had had in mind when she'd chosen Yellow Springs. And to think that if she hadn't found Rhoda's mail mixed up with her own, hadn't dropped it by before resigning herself to another Friday pajama night, she would have missed her ticket. The invitation came spontaneously but not halfheartedly, and Izzy, in the habit of saying no to so much, had allowed herself to be talked into a yes.

Which is how she found herself, not two hours later, here at Forest Meadow—to Izzy's delight the *actual* capital-letter name of the place, which was indeed a meadow at the forest's edge—for a Harvest Moon Celebration hosted by the Guardians of the Glen. Though Rhoda had explained the Guardians were simply a group of volunteers who maintained the trails in the nature preserve, Izzy was still picturing fairies or sprites, and really she wasn't all that far off, though here they were in human form.

The moon lingered beneath the tree line, but in the glow of the massive bonfire, the party was in perpetual freeform motion. Those who'd brought guitars or bongos had assembled themselves in a semicircle of camp chairs and started to riff in an almost primal rhythm, while a cluster of women on the other side of the fire had begun to dance, their long skirts flowing. A row of people seated cross-legged and barefoot in the grass had formed a chain to give one another shoulder rubs, pausing only to pass a bota bag down the line. There were coolers of strawberry wine, and mead, and cans of craft beer, and the air smelled of clove cigarettes and pipe smoke, with occasional whiffs of something less legal floating in from the dark periphery.

Izzy hung back, huddled in her fleece on one of the thick quilts Randi and Rhoda had spread at the edge of the firelight, taking in the scene as her neighbors walked Adele from one cluster to another, showing her off from the flowered sling wrapped around Randi in elaborate layers. Izzy admired the way they'd simply melded the baby into their lifestyle, rather than recentering their world around hers, and though a part of her wondered how long it could last, tonight in the near utopia of the circle, almost anything seemed possible.

"Whew!" Rhoda flopped onto the blanket next to her. "What do you think? Do you love it?"

"*Love*," Izzy assured her.

Randi glided up with a precarious hold on three paper cups of golden liquid and handed one to each of them before settling herself gingerly onto the ground. She nodded down at Adele, who was sleeping now, and tipped her cup, gesturing for them to do the same. Izzy took a small sip. By the second helping, the honey wine would seem sickeningly sweet, but for now, it was just the thing.

"I'm so glad you came," Randi said, smiling around Rhoda at her. "I've been wanting to run into you for days. That segment you've had going, on divorce stories? *Hilarious*."

"And sobering," Rhoda added. "Almost made me wish we didn't have the right to marry. Well done!" Sonny's idea had been so popular they'd end up stringing the discussion through the rest of the week, leaving Izzy feeling like an imposter in her own life, a producer of things she hadn't quite produced. Truthfully, it was the last thing she wanted to discuss out here in the open, under the constellations, in the midst of all that was good and true in the world.

"Thanks," she said reluctantly. "I was a little worried it might be in bad taste."

"Everything's in bad taste," Randi said, shrugging. "The *world* is in bad taste."

"Not this," Izzy said, gesturing around them. "I think you all have the right idea."

She could feel Rhoda's eyes on her.

"You really *don't* like your job, do you? I mean, you told us, that night at Clara's, but I thought it was more about the Second Date stuff bugging you when you're trying to get over the thing with your sister."

Izzy shrugged. They were *fans* of her radio show. How could she suggest that they shouldn't be? They were her neighbors. And she hoped they'd become real friends.

"It's not the job. It's me. The fluffiness of it weighs on me."

Rhoda laughed. "Okay, by definition, that's the opposite of what *fluff* is supposed to do."

"I know . . . But I'll be looking for *nonnews* to cover, and fall down this rabbit hole of awful headlines, and then it's like, *How can you all joke at a time like this?* Which of course makes no sense, because it's always 'a time like this.' " She made air quotes with her fingers, then felt ridiculous, like a politician at a Grateful Dead concert. She rushed ahead. "Also, I didn't want Paul to think we were making light of his . . ." What to call it? "Situation," she said finally.

Randi nodded thoughtfully. "I get that. I mean, we're conscientious. We spent I won't tell you how much to make our house as sustainable as we could without going off the grid. We raise chickens. We compost. We march in Take Back the Night rallies. We're citizens of the world, damn it!" She raised a fist, then dropped it.

"But the world will drag you down if you let it. Sometimes you have to be happy in the little bubble you create for yourself. And thus we can celebrate the full moon equinox by night and still love superficial morning radio by day."

"Loud and proud," Rhoda said, laughing. Izzy had to admit it made her feel better—if a bit silly—though she noticed neither of them had chosen to comment on Paul.

"Well, thanks for keeping me in a job," she said. "Actually, I'd like to return the favor. Do you have any more of those knitted moccasins you sold me? The *ah-mazing* ones?"

Randi smiled. "Just got more in."

"I was thinking of getting my sister some."

"Birthday coming up?" Rhoda asked.

"No, she's . . . she's pregnant." It was the first time Izzy had said the words aloud. They made her slightly dizzy. "I thought I'd get her a gift. Pregnant women get achy feet, right?" She looked to Randi, who had given birth only months before, but Randi was just staring at her.

"Pregnant? With the guy who—"

Izzy held up a hand. "I *really* shouldn't have told any of you that. I'm well aware that he's off-limits. I hope you don't think I'd ever—"

"Of course not," Randi said firmly, saving her from herself.

"Poor Iz," Rhoda said. "We also got some horribly *itchy* moccasins in. I was going to send them back, but maybe you'd like to gift her those instead?"

Izzy laughed. "That'd be more tempting if I weren't buying this as a peace offering."

"Uh-oh. What happened?"

"Just . . ." Blood flooded her cheeks. "My parents hosted a congratulatory thing for her and Josh the other day, and I couldn't make it because I was sick, and—"

"You were sick?" Rhoda raised an eyebrow.

"Well, I *felt* sick . . ."

"Oh, honey."

"I know. I'm a terrible human being. I need to unterrible

myself." She took a big swig of the wine, and winced. Apparently even honey could burn going down if you weren't careful.

Randi perked up. "Our friend Infinity is offering this new thing at the Humanist Center where she resets your karma."

Izzy blinked at her. "Isn't that kind of cheating?"

"That's what I said!" Rhoda looked smugly at her wife.

Randi scowled back. "It's fine if Izzy doesn't want to do it, but I still don't see the harm in performing the ritual for Kristin," she said defiantly. "Especially now that—"

"Even if you could alter someone else's karma, can you do it when she isn't physically there?" Izzy cut in. She hadn't meant to interrupt, but the idea was so utterly bizarre, and the implications . . .

"She's saying *all* the things I said!" Rhoda smiled at Randi, who offered an exaggerated pout and patted Izzy's knee. "Back to resetting *your* karma, I see nothing wrong with old-fashioned bribery. Those new slippers came in gorgeous colors."

"It's a start. I was also thinking of hosting a brunch—for my whole family. Maybe try to sort of start over. Do you think that would be horribly awkward?"

Randi shook her head. "Better on your own turf, in your own space."

Izzy nodded. She had the idea to do it in the garden, where she'd feel more grounded, less claustrophobic. She was also eager to show off her handiwork. In full-on nesting mode, she'd finally gotten her plants arranged—some perennials in the ground, and varietals in pots that could be moved inside for the winter. This weekend, she planned to clean up the gravel pathways, set up the patio. And she'd need to fix the broken gate in the privacy fence. Not only could animals get in and undo her work, but its banging in the wind was driving her crazy. "Do you happen to know where I can get a new latch for my gate?"

Rhoda nodded. "Come by tomorrow, and we'll assist you with *all* your unterrible-ing needs."

"You carry hardware?" Izzy grinned. "I mean, I remember Randi saying you had a lot of *tools*, but I didn't realize . . ."

Rhoda burst out laughing, and Randi threw her empty cup at her.

"Is anyone allowed to live anything down in this town?" Randi said, her face twisted into a pretend scowl. "Anyway, too bad we don't carry eligible bachelors too. See anyone you like, Izzy? We could introduce you . . ."

"Randi," Rhoda chastised. "She doesn't want to be set up. Come on."

"Who said anything about setting her up? *Introducing.* Being *open to possibility.*"

Izzy found herself scanning the crowd. Why not? But the gathering was largely women, and most of the men seemed tied to someone.

"Maybe on the ukuleles?" Randi murmured. Izzy took in the two long-haired musicians, who weren't bad-looking aside from the fact that they clearly hadn't showered in days.

"Hmm," she said. "Much as I love this field, maybe someone who isn't *quite* so at home in it."

Rhoda cackled. What Izzy needed was more of a cross between those guys and . . . well, someone like Paul. Handsome, troubled, buttoned-up Paul. She was surprised to find herself thinking of him, but decided it wasn't an entirely bad thing.

Because for once her first thought hadn't been: *More like Josh.*

"Randi!" A couple of women Izzy recognized from the meditation class were huddled around some kind of ceramic pot, gesturing wildly.

"Oh! They're going to let me try this nursing tea. Be right back."

Izzy and Rhoda watched her go. The music was getting louder now, and the row of shoulder rubbers had started harmonizing hums in the absence of lyrics.

"You know," Rhoda said, "I dated one of Randi's close friends before the two of us got together."

"You did?"

"This may shock you, but lesbians do not flock to Ohio small towns in innumerable droves. Another of my exes married one of my cousins. A *male* cousin."

Izzy's eyes widened.

"My point is, when it comes to having feelings for someone who's off-limits, it's not so uncommon in my circle. I've seen some delicate situations that could have been handled better, and some handled better than you would've thought possible. But the important thing is, I've seen them handled." She smiled at Izzy. "This thing with your sister—you'll figure it out."

"Thanks," she said, touched.

A woman with a familiar dark cloud of curls ran past them, and they both whipped their heads around reflexively, craning for a better look. She was not Kristin. Not even close, really, aside from the hair. Izzy's eyes met Rhoda's ruefully.

"I thought she would've turned up by now," Rhoda said, shaking her head.

"Yeah. Me too." Izzy didn't admit she had stopped following the coverage of the disappearance after the first week. It made her feel oddly disloyal to Paul to be gawking like some rubbernecker on the highway, and saddened to see the beautiful twins' childhood reduced to a headline. When there was something to tell, she'd hear about it soon enough.

"Speaking of which . . ." Rhoda nudged her shoulder, and Izzy turned to see a uniformed police officer headed down the path toward the clearing. Detective Bryant. *Shit. Were alcoholic beverages allowed out here?* She could still feel the sting of the embarrassment at having had to admit to him that she'd drunk her memory clean on Kristin's last night. She upended her wine in the grass, crushing the conspicuous cup in her hand, while Rhoda hissed, "For goodness' sake, be cool!" and offered him a friendly wave.

The detective's face broke into a boyish grin as he approached. "I'm not here to ruin anyone's fun," he told Izzy, and she flushed with the childish sensation of being caught.

"Of course not," she said, laughing nervously, trying not to grimace as the remnants of the sticky wine oozed between her fingers and dripped onto the blanket.

"We try to let Yellow Springs be Yellow Springs." She craned her neck up at him, nodding, wondering if she should stand. He gestured at the bonfire. "All our 'official' festivals get overrun by out-of-towners, but this is one of the few gems we've managed to keep secret for the locals. Glad to see you found your way here."

Izzy flushed with pleasure at the thought of a *real* local—could you get more "local" than a small-town cop?—considering her one of them. Even if she did still feel like an outsider most of the time.

"Here to join us?" Rhoda said brightly, though it was obvious from his attire that he wasn't.

He shook his head, his eyes still on Izzy's. "Just a cursory check-in." She smiled uneasily, wondering if he was checking in on how the festival was coming, or on what Kristin's neighbors were up to.

"I've been wanting to thank whichever of your colleagues posted those signs about cracking down on shoplifting," Rhoda bubbled on. "They seem to be helping." She was indeed the queen of *being cool, for goodness' sake.*

"I'll pass it on." He frowned. "If only the signs *I* created would have the same effect." Izzy had seen them all over town, with that now familiar photo of Kristin and the twins at that summer picnic, bright eyed and innocent: *Missing. If seen, please call . . .* A few people nodded the detective's way as he casually but methodically scanned the crowd, raising their hands in greeting, but most of them ignored his presence entirely. "Clara Tiffin here tonight?" he asked.

"She decided to stay home." It was news to Izzy that Clara had thought of coming at all—but why was he asking about her? She looked from the detective to Rhoda and back again, trying to discern if she was missing something.

He nodded. "Well." He tipped his hat in a gesture that fell somewhere between nervous habit and old-fashioned farewell. "Now I can say I came, I saw, I checked. Have fun tonight. Don't make me look bad to the boss."

His eyes met Izzy's again. "Notwithstanding a refill of whatever was in that cup," he said, giving her a wink, and she looked away quickly, her cheeks burning in the darkness.

"Poor Clara," Rhoda said softly, downing the rest of her drink as they watched him go.

Izzy realized with a start how long it had been since she'd checked in with her neighbor. God, she'd been so self-absorbed. Clara must be feeling bereft with no signs of Kristin—and Thomas without his playmates too.

But still. Why not *poor Paul*?

She was about to ask Rhoda what she meant when the crowd let out a collective whoop, and they looked up, startled. The moon had appeared in full above the canopy of branches. Randi came spinning toward them, pulling them to their feet. All around, people were laughing and embracing as if something wonderful had occurred—which, Izzy supposed, it had.

The dancers began to widen their circle around the fire, and she closed her eyes and joined in, letting go of her questions, her worries, her doubts. She'd almost forgotten how good it felt to simply allow herself to be pulled along.

20

If you want to know why I'm resigning, ask my
husband. Maybe he can explain it to us both.

—*One of several unfinished and unsent letters,
dated over a two-year period, from Kristin
Kirkland to her supervisor, found in the trash
folder of her office computer*

Had the woman arrived even a day earlier, Clara never would have
answered the door. She had to admit Pam hadn't been quite as off
base as she'd thought; the attention was relentless. At the grocery
store, she'd been accosted in the dairy aisle by a fellow shopper who
seemed out for Paul's blood, and then lectured by her cashier, who
was quick to *tsk* "the parents who are supposed to be responsible
for that Hallie girl." At the library, she'd grown sure she wasn't
imagining the curious stares, and especially not the accusatory ones.
At Benny's office, his appointment calendar filled with "free initial
consultations" that turned out to have little to do with accounting.
Some people were just being nosy; others wanted the Tiffins' take
on how concerned they should be about Kristin; and a shameless
few were stringers from Dayton media.

The weight on Benny bothered her most. Clara knew it was her fault just as sure as she knew that no amount of perfectly layered lasagna could make it up to her husband. By last night, she'd given up and canceled on Randi and Rhoda for the Harvest Moon Celebration, much as she'd have welcomed the friendlier company. She'd filled them in as briefly as possible on what had really happened with the *Gazette,* and the subsequent visit with Paul—leaving out the bit about the book cover—and was relieved when their response was only sympathy, not judgment. Maybe if she stayed out of sight for a while, the rest of Yellow Springs would put her out of mind.

When morning came and Benny left to put in some Saturday hours to catch up on the real work he'd been kept from, she answered the knock at the door without thinking, a reflex, and froze when she saw a stranger standing there, holding *The Color-Blind Gazette.*

"Please," Clara pleaded. "Leave us alone." She had the door halfway shut when the woman put out a hand to stop it.

"I'm Kristin's sister," the woman said simply. "Rebecca."

Clara hesitated. What tactics might the media try to get her to talk? But then she caught sight of the two children at the end of the porch, kneeling to examine Thomas's dump truck with a reverence common to young boys coming upon construction equipment.

"Sorry," the woman said. "My husband is away for the weekend, and I work during the week, and . . . well, I had to bring them." Clara looked her over. Rebecca's shoulder-length hair was lighter than Kristin's, but it had a familiar unruly curl, and she held her petite stature in the same delicate way Kristin did. She was dressed simply but stylishly in a fitted corduroy blazer with a gauzy infinity scarf looped around her neck.

"I probably shouldn't have come," Rebecca continued nervously, and Clara realized she was meant to have responded by now. "My husband didn't think I should—'If she didn't want you in her life before, she doesn't want you there now,' he said. But . . ." She held up the paper. "Please, I've driven an hour, through construction. Can we talk?"

Clara looked over at the boys again. Thomas would be glad to see them, having lost his playmates in phases these past weeks. The twins gone. The preschool on hiatus. He hadn't even had his usual entertainment in Hallie. Natalie had gotten permission to bring her daughter along to her afternoon classes until this thing with the paper blew over, so Hallie was taking the school bus directly to Antioch now. Clara had received a terse voice mail to that effect, and she had no idea whether they'd eventually revert to their old routine. Even through the recording, it was clear Natalie's anger toward Clara, whether misplaced or not, hadn't faded.

Rebecca's boys were standing and staring at her now, and she smiled. "If you like trucks, you're in luck," she told them. "Would you like to see what else my son, Thomas, has inside?" They ran to duck under their mother's arms and nodded up at Clara, wide-eyed. Rebecca placed a gentle hand on the head of the taller boy. "This is Shawn," she said. "He's seven. And Jeff. He's six."

"Nice to meet you, Shawn who's seven and Jeff who's six," Clara said, opening the door wide for them to file inside. She led them to the family room, where Thomas and Maddie were constructing a tower of oversize Legos. It was only a matter of time before Maddie would knock it down and Thomas would burst into tears, but still, she loved these rare moments when they focused on something together, and hated that she was about to break the spell.

The boys instantly teamed up on plans for a Lego fort while Maddie gummed a block, warily eyeing their guests. "Love that name, Maddie," Rebecca said. "Short for Madison?"

"Madeline."

"Even prettier."

Clara nodded toward the counter stools dividing the room from the kitchen. "Tea? Coffee?"

"Coffee would be great."

"I don't mean for this to hurt your feelings," Clara said, moving to reheat the pot from earlier that morning, "but I had no idea Kristin had a sister, until that last night I saw her."

"Oh? And what did she say then?"

Clara turned her back and stood on tiptoe to retrieve her best mugs, glad Rebecca couldn't see her face. *She said you were 'shit,' actually. Mind telling me why? Seems she could have used a sister around.* "Just that she had one," she said, careful to keep her voice even.

Clara plunked cream and sugar onto the counter as she stole a glance at the kids. Seeing those little heads of curly hair bent so intently over the blocks next to her own blondies tugged at her heart. From this angle Thomas and Maddie might have been playing with Abby and Aaron.

When Rebecca finally spoke, her voice was hesitant, shaky. "When Kristin was widowed, I felt so awful for her. Too awful. I was almost afraid of her grief, like it might be contagious." She peered at Clara through eyes thick with years-old guilt. "I always had this irrational fear of something like that happening—that one day someone I loved would just never come home. As a teenager, I'd be babysitting Kristin—well, not really babysitting, but you know, I'm two years older, I was responsible—and thinking, *What if Mom is in some horrible car wreck on the way home?* Or, *What if she gets mugged in an alley like Batman's mom?*" She laughed stiffly. "I even remember this one time, when my husband and I hadn't been dating all that long, that he ran out for condoms. It was a short drive to the gas station, but he was gone for what seemed like forever. And as the minutes ticked by I was thinking, *The cops are going to show up to inform his next of kin and find this girl who barely knows him naked in his bed!*"

She dropped her head into her hands. "That was wildly inappropriate. I have no idea why I'm off on this tangent. I'm sorry. I'm nervous for some reason."

Clara smiled and set a cup of coffee in front of her. "What took so long?"

"What?"

"To get the condoms."

"Oh!" Rebecca laughed again. "The gas station was out. I'd have come back empty-handed, but he wanted the goods bad enough to go to the drugstore."

"Ah, youth," Clara said, still smiling.

Rebecca frowned. "But then it happened for real. To Kristin. Ted went out on the lake with his parents, and he never came home.

She said the worst of it was that she *wasn't* up waiting for him. She usually did, but that night she fell asleep on the couch. The police knocked and woke her up, hours beyond the time she should have missed him."

Clara cradled the ceramic warmth of her coffee, imagining a day Benny failed to walk through the door, home safe. She couldn't fathom how Kristin had been able to bear it.

"I think she had some survivor's guilt too," she continued. "She would've gone along that day, but she wasn't feeling well. It wasn't long before she found out that the reason she'd felt sick, and the reason she'd been unable to stay awake that evening, was that she was pregnant with the twins. Ted never even knew he was going to be a dad."

A wave of sadness washed over Clara. The twins hadn't been babies when their dad died—they'd been *babies in progress*. The time line made more sense now. So, too, did the fact that Kristin had never mentioned Ted.

"I don't know if that makes it better or worse," Clara said, shaking her head.

"Neither. It's the same amount of awful either way." Rebecca sighed. "I tried to stay close to her those months. She didn't live far from me in Dayton. I had a baby and a toddler of my own—they were all-consuming—but I really did think I was trying. I did a rotten job, though. I think about how I should have handled things differently after she met Paul, but really I had already failed her by then. Those months were when she needed me most, and I just . . . I was there, but I wasn't there enough. Mom was already in the Alzheimer's facility, hardly knew us, and I was struggling with that, and I—" Her voice broke. "I didn't want to see my own perfect little family damaged the way Kristin's had been. I was worried about them being affected if I spent too much time with her, or had her around too much in the state she was in, but I should have been far more worried about *her*. I was horrendously selfish."

"I'm sure that's not true," Clara said, though she knew what Rebecca meant about how people seemed to think grief might be catching. It had proved true enough back in Cincinnati, after the incident that, while a far less intimate loss, had devastated Clara in other ways. "How *did* she meet Paul?" she asked. Rebecca had seemed to be almost shrinking into herself, but she sat up straighter then and tossed her hair back.

"He was her OB," Rebecca said.

Dots connected in Clara's mind. How had she not drawn the lines sooner?

"I think he felt sorry for her at first—took her under his wing, gave her his cell number to call any time, that sort of thing. She'd been so overwhelmed to discover that she was pregnant, and *then* that it was twins. I tried to tell her what a gift it was, to have these pieces of Ted now that he was gone, but it never outweighed her sense of overwhelm. Not that I blame her." She looked over at her boys, then back at Clara, and lowered her voice, though the children didn't seem to be listening. "It was 'Dr. Kirkland says this' and 'Dr. Kirkland says that.' No one but him seemed to be able to make her feel better about anything. She developed a sort of unhealthy attachment. *I* thought it was unhealthy, anyway. She thought it was romantic."

"Isn't that in violation of some kind of patient-doctor code or something?"

"Or something. He transferred her to another doctor before the birth. They were an item by then. He was promising that her twins would have a father, saying the things she wanted to hear."

Clara hesitated. "Didn't that seem a little fast?"

"It seemed a lot fast. I told her as much, but it was not a popular opinion. She used all the typical lines—*you can't control when love strikes, he was there when she needed him, how could she turn away this second chance at happiness,* you name it." Rebecca shook her head. "She'd been close to Ted's family. They were high school sweethearts, had been together forever, and I think things would've been different if his parents or sister had been around to help her. But they were all gone, all on the boat that day. And Kristin— she'd *always* had Ted. It made sense that she was more afraid of being alone than she was of getting involved too soon. I'd like to think I wouldn't have made the same mistake, but in her shoes, who knows?"

Clara nodded. She knew better than to judge.

"They got married quietly, soon after the twins were born."

"What was he like with the twins back then?"

Rebecca frowned. "I remember thinking that for an OB, he didn't seem all that enamored. But then I thought, *Well, it's not like he's a pediatrician—he's caring for the mothers.* And that's about how it was at home too. I wasn't surprised to learn he never adopted the children, because he seemed to think of them as hers. He was helpful enough, but even when everyone else in the room was focused on the kids, he only had eyes for Kristin. And I don't necessarily mean that in a sweet way. I saw less and less of her, which of course is understandable when someone has newborn twins. Only—" She stopped.

"Only what?"

She shrugged. "My husband thought I was being paranoid. But I had a feeling there was more to it. She stopped going to see Mom, and she'd always been better about that than I was. I mean, our mom raised us all by herself. We never knew our dad. When my kids were babies and my own visits started to taper off, Kristin was the one lecturing *me*: 'After everything Mom sacrificed for us, you can sacrifice an hour and go see her.' I would've thought she'd be taking the babies to see their grandmother every week, even once they moved to Yellow Springs—the twins were a year old then. It wasn't *that* far. But nothing."

She sipped her coffee in silence and seemed to be steeling herself against whatever she was about to say next. "One day she showed up at my house unannounced, maybe a year after she'd moved—and I was kind of annoyed, honestly; it was one of those days I had so much to do I didn't know where to start—and she alluded to feeling trapped in the marriage. I look back now and realize how much courage it must have taken for her to try to open up, after I'd basically criticized her for getting remarried too soon."

"Did she *say* she felt trapped?"

"Not exactly. But she said she might have made a mistake. And she *looked* trapped. Her eyes—" She shuddered.

"So what happened?"

"I basically said, 'I told you so.' Not very sisterly of me. By then I was resenting all the extra time I was putting in at the nursing home. There was a barrage of calls at all hours of the night: Mom was being disruptive, refusing medication . . . Alzheimer's doesn't just affect your memory, you know; it's your whole personality. Awful disease. They always said there was no answer when they called Kristin, and she always had some excuse when I'd ask her about it—as if she were the only one with kids. She'd say it was a longer drive for her, and I'd point out that she'd *chosen* to move away, and she'd say that Paul didn't have the same opportunity to fill a real need in Dayton, and off we'd go on this circular argument. Once she actually said, 'It's not like she knows who I am, Rebecca. It's not like she even knows if I'm there or not!'"

Rebecca bore the weariness of someone who had lost her sister long before her sister had disappeared.

"I should have put all that aside that day. She was reaching out, and I shut it down," she said, tears welling in her eyes. "Like it was more important to be *right*. I never imagined that would be the last time I'd see her, but it was. Complete silent treatment. They call it 'ghosting' someone now, to go cold like that. Can you believe there's a term for it? It shouldn't exist at all!" Clara handed her a napkin, and Rebecca dabbed at her eyes. It came away black with mascara.

"A couple years go by, and next thing I know, the Yellow Springs police are at my door. And the local media is having some field day about her dodging a divorce settlement, uprooting her kids. And none of it sounds like Kristin. Then I heard about this." She tapped her finger on *The Color-Blind Gazette* she'd laid on the counter. "This is the first thing I've read that makes any sense, and that terrifies me. I've been *pleading* with the police to look more closely at Paul, and I can't tell whether they think I'm a quack, or what. They keep coming back at me with questions that have nothing to do with him. *Did she ever discuss having tried to find our real father?* No, but I sure wish she had. *Did I know anything about her visiting our mother, unannounced, the day before she disappeared?* No, but I sure wish I did. I feel like a dolt."

Clara wasn't sure she agreed that the questions had *nothing* to do with Paul, nor did she like this fleeting glimpse into the investigation's direction—or lack thereof. "I just wanted to talk to someone who really knows my sister," Rebecca continued. "I just wanted to talk to someone who would make me feel like I'm not crazy."

"You're not crazy," Clara said. Her coffee had gone lukewarm, though she hadn't really wanted it anyway. "But there's not much else I can tell you. Kristin and I were friends—we talked a lot, our kids played, we swapped books and recipes—but in hindsight, I'm not sure I really knew her." Clara had had plenty of time to reconsider the terms of their friendship. "She was like a master of friendliness through nondisclosure—always asking about *your* holiday plans, or what *you* thought about the new school policy, or how *you* were feeling after that flu took out the whole block. She was funny, she was warm, she was great to be around, she was a devoted mom, and ninety-five percent of the conversations we ever had were completely superficial. She was just so good at it that they didn't feel that way."

"What about the divorce?"

"It seemed to roll off her back. Although that part . . . I'm not sure that part was an act."

"She was happy to be escaping."

"I never thought of it as 'escaping' until—" Clara caught herself. "Until recently. But yes, I suppose so."

"It's classic behavior, in a violent or controlling relationship, to isolate someone from her friends and family."

"I know." Clara did know. But *had* Paul isolated Kristin from Rebecca, or had a wedge simply come between them in those difficult years? Either seemed possible.

"He couldn't isolate her from you—you were right next door. Maybe that's why they seem to think you knew her best. But now I'm here, and you tell me you didn't know her at all." Rebecca looked as if she might cry again. Clara wished she could comfort her. But she also couldn't help but feel that Rebecca should have had this out with Kristin long ago. And that now, yes, maybe it was too late. She wondered uneasily how Kristin would feel about the women sitting here having this conversation.

"I want to help you make peace with this," Clara said carefully. "But I'm not sure I can."

"I took the paper down to Xenia, to the hospital," she blurted out. Clara froze. "One of the nurses took pity on me, agreed to talk on her lunch break."

"And?"

"She didn't know anything about Kristin, never met her. But she said Paul is a favorite among the patients. Women get distraught if he isn't on call when they go into labor."

Clara frowned. It figured.

"She said something about his relationships with them struck her as oddly narcissistic, though. Almost as if he gets off on bringing babies into the world, acting out some kind of God complex. She said he was noticeably colder when their husbands were around."

"Did she tell the police so?"

She shook her head. "She emphasized that hers was a minority opinion. And she values her job too much. But *I* told them what she told me, though I'm not sure that means anything."

"Have you tried to talk to *him*?"

She shook her head. "I came to try to see Kristin last year. Paul turned me away. I asked him to promise to at least tell her I'd been there, and he only laughed. I have zero reason to think he'd be forthcoming with me now. And frankly I don't *want* to see him."

Clara hesitated, an idea suddenly occurring to her. Maybe some good could come of this visit after all.

"Don't ask me why—I don't actually *know* why—but Paul invited me to look around, to see if anything was amiss."

"And?"

"There was this book. The cover of an old one, actually. *I Can Do It!* With a red fox on it?" Rebecca looked at her blankly. "It was something Abby used to take with her everywhere. It seemed odd that it had been left behind."

"Have you told anyone?"

"You have to understand that I have children of my own and I live right next to that man," Clara said, forcing conviction into her voice. *I'm trying to pass the baton here,* she wanted to scream. Kristin was Rebecca's responsibility by *blood.* Surely blood trumped proximity.

"But it might help Kristin if—"

"*Mom!* She's trying to knock down the *walls!*" Maddie let out a cry and came running, her little bare feet pounding the tile. Clara bent to scoop her up and hugged her daughter to her, shooting a warning look toward Thomas before turning back to Rebecca.

"If you can find a way to tell them without involving me, please do. That's why I'm telling you." She smoothed Maddie's hair. "I'm just as concerned as you are. But I don't know if anything we do or don't do can actually *help* Kristin now."

Rebecca stared at her, looking despondent. "Please don't say, 'We just have to hope she helped herself.'"

"Okay." It was exactly what she'd been about to say.

Maddie placed her tiny hands on Clara's cheeks and pulled her face up close. "Poop," she said, blue eyed and earnest.

Rebecca laughed dryly. "My thoughts exactly."

21

If I told you I felt trapped, you'd probably doubt me. Trapped by your own decisions, maybe, *you might tell me.* Take steps to change things. Ask for help if you need it. Speak up. Be a grown-up. *"Use your God-given brain" was always a favorite admonition of my mother's.*

I'm not self-possessed enough to say you'd be wrong. I can take constructive criticism. I get a lot of it from myself, in fact.

There are all kinds of traps, for all sorts of purposes. Animals, people, even whole societies walk right in. In our defense, by the very nature of most traps you can't tell you're in one until it's too late. So you really shouldn't point fingers from the outside the way you do. It could be you, you know. And sometimes there really is no way out. At least, not by breaking through its ironclad engineering.

You have to outsmart the thing.

Most people who try, fail. At worst, they pay the consequences. At best, they're simply out of options.

Either way, they're out of luck.

22

The unseasonably warm late September sun on Izzy's bare arms was a parting gift. Any day now, rains would blow in, a cold front would decide not to lift, and thus would arrive the chilly gray slog leading up to winter. She could never understand why so many Ohioans declared fall to be their favorite season. Fall weather itself was like a rare delicacy—it did live up to the hype when it came, but often it wasn't on the menu. The past few years it had seemed as if Mother Earth decided not to bother with autumn at all, simply flicking a switch from summer to winter. Izzy didn't blame her, mistreated as she was. When no one appreciated the careful preparation you'd put into a feast, eventually you were going to give up and order takeout. The leaves would change and drift to the ground, of course—a lone inevitability no matter the temperature—but nothing else need move so lazily from one phase of the calendar into the next. Izzy usually felt unsettled by these transitional weeks, in which she'd rediscover the futility of trying to plan for a hike or a camping trip, but this year the unpredictability of the shift fit her mood.

She tried to focus on the warmth of the sun rather than the hard-to-place nerves churning in her stomach as she headed up Paul's walk. It was probably just that she'd never really liked asking for help—from anyone. But it *might* have been that she felt skittish about asking for help from Paul in particular. So far they'd run into each other only incidentally; she had yet to seek him out. She needed help, though, in a physical way she couldn't Google her way out of. She'd come from Moondance earlier, so knew Randi and Rhoda weren't home, and she'd seen Benny pull up in his work clothes awhile ago—not like him on a Saturday—and hated to interrupt his abbreviated family time. So here she was. She took a breath and knocked.

"Izzy." Paul smiled and swung the door open wider. He looked dressed for the office too—button-down, pleated pants.

"Sorry," she said automatically. "Are you on your way to work? I was just hoping for a second set of hands, but I can—"

"I'm home early. Had some cancellations." A frown flickered across his lips, then disappeared. "My hands are available. What do you need?"

She laughed self-consciously. "I'm afraid you're going to make fun of me. The latch on my gate is broken, and I've bought this ridiculously girlie replacement. Rhoda warned me it was hard to install, but I was blinded by its cuteness."

In retrospect, Izzy should have known the boutique didn't carry *ordinary* hardware. Like something out of *The Secret Garden,* the oversized gate lock was itself shaped like a tiny arched door and came complete with large weathered brass keys, the kind with loops at the end so you might string them on a rope or hang them on a nail. Whimsical but functional, it looked meant for someone who lived alone and liked it that way. Which was precisely why she'd chosen it.

"Happens to the best of us." The corners of his mouth twitched in amusement. She briefly wondered if he looked *too* put together for someone whose wife and children were unaccounted for, then dismissed it. It had been nearly two weeks now, and nothing. What could he do but go through the motions, and hope, and wait?

"It's too heavy for me to hold steady one-handed. I think it's a two-person job."

"Then I'm your number two. Do you need a drill? Tools?"

His attention was so *focused* on her. For no reason at all, Izzy blushed. "I think I just need brute strength."

"Hmm. Would a doctor's precision do?"

"Even better."

"Just let me change—be over in five?"

Slow down, she scolded her heart rate as she headed home. It was pulsing the way it had when she was a teenager on the few occasions she'd gotten up the nerve to talk to a cute boy at his locker. Not that anything but high blood pressure had ever come from those conversations. She ran her fingertips over the pleats in her braid. It didn't *feel* like it looked bad. Looking down at her embroidered purple tank and flowy black gauchos, she gave herself a B. Not bad for working in the yard, and it wasn't as if she could change now anyway—he'd already seen her.

But wait. What was she *thinking*? If his current breed of crisis didn't render someone emotionally unavailable, she didn't know what would. Plus . . . She'd be crazy not to be wary of Paul. For Kristin to have run off that way—who knew what that might say about him? It wasn't fair to *assume,* but you couldn't deny the red flag.

It was just nice to know that someone, *anyone* other than Josh, could still give her butterflies—even meaningless ones. The very thought of it was like finding out a fun old toy wasn't broken after all, only out of batteries.

She was stirring a preemptive pitcher of neighborly thank-you lemonade in the kitchen when a knock came at the front door. "Come on in!" she called, bending to retrieve an ice tray from the freezer. "I'm making some—" She stopped short. The figure in the doorway was not Paul. "Oh! Hallie, you startled me."

The girl took a step back. "You said to come in . . ."

"That I did." Izzy was good with her friends' very many very small kids, but she hadn't spent much time with this older species and was never sure how to speak to them. "What can I do for you?" She emptied the ice into the pitcher and refilled the tray at the sink.

"I'm working on this newspaper project—my second edition. You might have seen the first one?"

Izzy shook her head. "Don't think so." Was that relief on Hallie's face?

"Well . . . The idea is for me to report on good news. And I heard you work for that radio show, where people go on a second date?"

Good news. While Izzy was spending her days getting *paid* to sift through the bad in search of the meaningless, here was someone—a child, no less—pushing for something better, something more.

"Cool," she said, trying to sound like a peer without being too ridiculous about it. "I take it you're as bothered by the endless stream of bad news as I am?"

Hallie looked annoyed. "Of course I'm bothered by it. My dad is in Afghanistan."

Izzy blanched. How had she become so self-absorbed that even a kid could make her feel like a dolt? Unlike her, Hallie didn't need to seek out perspective checks to put her life up against real tragedy—she lived with the knowledge that she was always a breath away from one.

"An-y-way," Hallie said, singing each syllable. "The dating show?"

She nodded, for once glad of the change of subject to her least favorite one. "Second Date Update. But more often, they *don't* go on a second date." She slipped the tray in the freezer. "I agree that we could all use more good news, but I'm not sure you're likely to find it on Second Date Update."

Hallie's face fell, but she recovered quickly. "Well, could I ask you a few questions about it anyway? Our teacher says that often the real story is the one people don't set out to cover."

Izzy stole a glance out the window into the yard. No sign of Paul yet. "I'm working outside; let's talk in the garden for a few. Would you like some lemonade?"

Hallie nodded. Izzy loaded the pitcher and a stack of plastic cups onto a tray and motioned for her to follow, out the back door. The patio table she'd just bought was in pieces on the ground, its six chairs stacked with the tags still on. "Sorry for the mess," she said. "I'm still setting up back here." The tray was just small enough to fit on the little mosaic stand between her chaise lounges, and she set it there and poured Hallie a glass. The girl perched awkwardly on the edge of a lounge and took a pad and pen out of her pocket.

"What's your favorite part of working at Second Date Update?" she asked, chewing the pen's lid earnestly. Izzy grabbed a pair of scissors from her toolbox and started cutting the tags off the chair legs.

"Well, I don't actually work *at* 'Second Date Update,'" she said, stalling. "It's part of a morning show called *Freshly Squeezed*."

"You don't like it, do you?" Hallie asked pointedly, and Izzy laughed.

"You're going to make a great reporter. No, not really. But you probably shouldn't print that. Sometimes part of being a grown-up is doing things you don't want to do."

"And pretending you like it?"

She laughed again. "Yes, sometimes that's the most important part. Although this expression you might have heard: 'Fake it 'til you make it'? Sometimes that kind of works."

To her amusement, Hallie was writing it down. "Um, you probably shouldn't print that either," she said.

"All right!" a voice called over the fence. "I have to say, I'm dying to see what a 'girlie' gate latch looks like." Paul appeared in the open gate, wearing a polo shirt and nice dark jeans, and Izzy raised an eyebrow. Did the man not own a T-shirt or a pair of gym pants? He stopped short when he saw Hallie. "Hi there," he said, his smile frozen in place.

Hallie didn't answer.

"Hallie, you know Paul . . . er, Dr. Kirkland? Abby and Aaron's daddy?" The girl looked at her wide-eyed, seeming to shrink back into her chair. Was she shy? She'd certainly had no problem marching in here, even though Izzy had talked to her only a few times before.

"I can come back later," Hallie blurted out.

Maybe she was one of those children who are bashful among men—which would be natural, with her father away so much. "Let's just pause the questions for a quick sec, okay? He's going to help me with this latch." Paul picked up the package from where she'd left it on the ground and scanned the back.

"You might be better off with *bigger* hands rather than with *extra* hands," he called over. "Go ahead with whatever you two are doing. I'll let you know if I need help."

Izzy smiled her thanks and began unstacking the chairs. "Okay, Hallie, next question," she said, trying to sound more patient than she felt.

"Um . . ." She rustled the paper of her notebook, her eyes darting anxiously to Paul and then back to Izzy. "Maybe you can just tell me about something nice or good on Second Date Update recently?"

Izzy frowned, thinking, then brightened. "Well, there was one call this week that had a *sort* of happy ending . . ."

Hallie lifted her pen.

"The story starts out pretty bad. This couple hits it off on a dating Web site, decides to go out to dinner, has a great time, the check comes, and the guy lays down his credit card and goes to use the restroom. When he gets back, she's gone. Won't answer her phone, and he can't even guess at a reason."

Hallie rolled her eyes. "Was the good news that she didn't take his credit card with her?"

Izzy laughed. So the kid was street savvy too. "Close. It turned out she'd looked at his card and saw his last name—they'd exchanged only first names—and—"

"I know the last name of every single person in my class."

In a universe where dating was a thing among children, they'd probably be better at it than adults were. "That's great," she said weakly. "It would've been especially helpful here, because it turned out they had the same last name.

"They were *related*?"

"Probably not—it was a common name. But the possibility of it creeped her out."

Hallie looked skeptical. "Why didn't she just tell him?"

Izzy averted her eyes. "You'll find there are a *lot* of things in life that could be cleared up with a simple explanation, but never are."

"Why?"

"Let me know if you find *anyone* who can answer that one."

Paul had pulled the gate shut so he was hidden from view, but she noticed that Hallie stiffened at the sound of his muffled chuckle. She felt self-conscious too, knowing he was listening in.

"But you said it was a common name. Maybe they weren't related. Maybe they could have dated."

"She just didn't think they could be sure. And even if they could, she didn't like the idea of getting teased about the name thing through their whole relationship. She figured the best thing would be to find someone else to date."

"Did he change her mind on the air?"

Izzy shook her head.

"But I thought you said this story was *good* news."

"By Second Date Update standards, it was."

"*Why?*"

"Because the reason she didn't want to date him had *nothing* to do with him. He hadn't done anything wrong." Hallie was looking at her blankly. "Imagine bracing yourself to hear someone say, with thousands of strangers listening, what they think is wrong with you, and then hearing instead that you're great, you just happen to have the wrong name. He seemed pretty relieved, just laughed it off."

"He wasn't disappointed because he still liked her?"

"Well, a little."

Hallie looked as if she might launch the notebook across the yard. "So if it's public, being friend-zoned against your will counts as a happy ending?"

Put that way, the call was swiftly downgraded to Izzy's all-time *least* favorite, but she was in too deep now to back out.

"I think the good news angle from my perspective is that it's rewarding to help people clear up such a simple misunderstanding. Much better than serving as a mouthpiece for the more mean-spirited stuff we hear." Izzy forced a smile.

Hallie got to her feet. "Well, thanks anyway."

Izzy felt as if she'd let her down. "If you'd like to come to the station with me sometime, I'm sure the *Freshly Squeezed* DJs would be happy to answer your questions. Sonny and Day are their names, and they're much better at talking about this stuff than I am. I leave for work super early, though. Before the sun comes up."

Hallie brightened, but her face quickly fell. "I'd have to miss school for that, though. It's only weekdays, right?"

"Yes, but—"

"My mom wouldn't go for it."

"Why not?"

Hallie didn't answer. "Thanks again for your help," she said. "I'll let myself out the front."

Izzy watched her go, feeling a pang of guilt that she would have been more likely to call her back, to try again, if Paul hadn't been here. With a mixture of reluctance and relief, she waited until she heard the door shut, then went to see how he was managing.

"What was that about?" he asked lightly.

"Some school project. I don't think I was much help, unfortunately. How's it going?"

He swung open the gate. "Ta-da!" The little door-shaped lock was perfectly in place, the giant key inside. He turned it both ways to demonstrate that it worked.

"That was too easy," she said, grinning sheepishly. "Like asking someone else to open a jar after I've, uh, loosened it myself."

"You *did* drill the holes right," he said. "But this thing is ridiculously heavy to hold in place. It could be like its own fairy-sized gate instead of a lock."

"Exactly!" she said, clapping her hands together happily, and he laughed.

"Well, you're right that it was too easy. I'm here now, so what else you got?" He eyed the table she was about to assemble.

"Oh, you don't have to—"

"I mean it sincerely when I say that I have nothing better to do," he said. "Let's pretend that's not pathetic, okay? Plus, is that lemonade?"

"When life gives you lemons . . ."

Paul wound the cord around her drill and gathered the random tools scattered in the grass, and she unplugged the extension cord and went to retrieve the pieces of packaging, hiding a smile. As much energy as she'd spent telling herself that she was perfectly capable of doing these sorts of projects alone, she had to admit it was nice to have company.

"You know, most people buy outdoor furniture in the spring," he said, crossing to her patio and throwing the tools in the box.

"Ah, but it's on sale in the fall."

"Fair point. But it'll need to be moved inside for winter. Sure you want to assemble it now?"

"You know how it is, when you're trying to get settled, to put your own stamp on a place. Plus, I'm trying to have a thing for my family."

"What kind of thing?"

She was combing her fingers through the grass, on her hands and knees now. "Wasn't there a second key? To this lock?"

"I only saw one."

"I could have sworn there were two."

He crossed the yard and dropped to his knees outside the gate, patting around on the other side of the fence. "It's not as if they're small," he said. "Only in Yellow Springs does a lock sized for fairies come with a key sized for giants."

She laughed. "One of the few benefits of being single is that I get to pick out my own stuff. Don't ruin it for me!"

She poked her head around the corner, and pain clouded her vision in a way that made her realize where the expression *seeing stars* came from. Paul moaned from the force of their head butt, and they lay curled on the grass, like football players downed on a field.

"Oh, God, I'm so sorry," she groaned, hands to her head. "I don't know how goats do it."

"They eat sweaters too," he mumbled. "Dumb animals."

He crawled to where she was still in the fetal position and swiped her hair out of her face. "Let me get a look at that forehead," he said softly. She looked up into his eyes—she'd thought they were hazel, but up close, she could see flecks of deep green. She'd read that it was the rarest eye color, the hardest to find.

"You're handy to have around, aren't you, Doctor?" The thumping pain was subsiding a bit. She tried to smile. He ran a fingertip across the throbbing spot on her forehead, and for a fleeting second she thought he might kiss her. Instead, he touched his own.

"We're going to have matching goose eggs," he said.

"What will the neighbors think?" she joked.

His eyes clouded, and she realized her mistake. She'd broken the spell. One wrong joke, and he was no longer a back-on-the-market man helping a single new neighbor in her garden. He was an estranged husband, a hurting father, a subject of neighborhood speculation, with an empty shell of a house filling the space where his home used to be just across the street.

She supposed she should let the awkward silence descend, send him on his way.

But it felt oddly safe being in the presence of someone who was even more unavailable than she was.

23

For Father's Day, we hope you'll enjoy this questionnaire where the children's responses to oral prompts were recorded verbatim. "1. My daddy is good at: Fixing things (but only our things, because when he lets other people borrow his tools they mess them up)."

—*Laminated list from the Circle of Living, hanging on the door of Benny's workshop (to remind him to stop being such a softie about lending people things)*

The dog seemed to sense he was auditioning for a part he hadn't gotten yet, the way he pranced in circles, barking happily, as Thomas raced him to his tennis ball, launched it across the yard, and gave chase all over again. Clara imagined that she saw a gleam of mischief in the animal's otherwise soulful eyes, as if he knew he was going to win her over, and when he did, he'd have a few surprises under his collar. The mischievous air should have pitted her against him, but somehow it only endeared him to her more as she and Maddie giggled and clapped from their spot sprawled on a picnic blanket in the center of the action. Today was Thursday, marking a week since Thomas had been asked to leave school, and it was a relief to see him smiling as if he had not a care in the world—which, at his age, was exactly as many as he should have.

"Where'd you get him?" a voice called out. Clara turned to see Hallie cutting through the side yard, her backpack slung over her shoulder, and registered the rumbling of the school bus as it pulled away. Without awaiting a response, Hallie tossed her bag into the grass and jogged to join Thomas, matching his squeals of delight at the dog as if all had been forgotten. Clara sneaked a look at Natalie's back porch, expecting her to burst out the door and call her daughter home at any moment. But until that moment came, she wasn't about to send the girl away. Torn though Clara was between a knee-jerk dread and a genuine happiness to see Hallie, it didn't matter which emotion would win out, because being the one to back away was akin to admitting wrongdoing—something she would not do.

"We got him yesterday at the farmers' market," Thomas told her proudly. "Can you believe it? We only went for corn on the cob!"

Hallie raised a disbelieving eyebrow at Clara, but crazy as it sounded, he spoke the truth. She hadn't given serious, immediate thought to adopting so much as a goldfish until they'd come upon the rescue shelter booth. Clara should have turned on her heels when she saw it; the volunteers had a knack for trotting out the cutest contenders, and she and the kids had been instantly, overwhelmingly smitten. The tricolored mutt was shades of blond, medium sized and medium haired except for his head, which was disproportionately large and covered with what amounted to overgrown bangs. She'd had a stuffed animal that looked just like him when she was a kid.

"I don't know . . ." she'd told the adoption liaison, a kind-looking man whose tie-dye shirt and neat cornrows exuded an aura of calm. "Even if he's as good with kids as you say, my daughter is only a year old. This probably isn't the best time to introduce a pet. She might test his limits."

He'd waved a hand in the air. "Try him out for a few days," he'd said. "On loan. He's young, but he isn't a puppy. I wouldn't offer him to you if I thought he was more than your family could handle." And thus Clara had found herself standing in the kitchen that night explaining the "loaner dog" to Benny.

"Does this have something to do with how much easier animals are to rescue than people?" he had asked once the kids were out of earshot. She'd denied it, of course, though that might have had something to do with it. The rest had a lot to do with the fact that Thomas seemed to have found himself a new best friend.

Hallie flopped onto the blanket and smiled up at her almost bashfully, a look she'd never seen from Hallie before. "I have some notes to show you," she said. "For my next edition." She started riffling through her backpack, and Clara stiffened, her eyes again flitting to Natalie's house and back.

"I'm not sure another edition is a good idea, Hal," she said carefully. The first had brought the police storming her living room not two weeks ago—could nothing discourage the girl? Clara wasn't sure if the emotion collecting in her chest was anger, admiration, or a little of both.

"If I don't do another one, it's like admitting I did something wrong," she said, jutting her chin out. "If that's, like, my *only* edition, people are going to think I did the paper just to get that one story out. I think it's actually better if I keep going, don't you?"

It was an uncomfortably sound argument, but even so, another edition was the last thing Clara wanted. No, what she wanted was to be off of her neighbors' minds, and that meant being out of their mailboxes.

"That might be so, but I don't think it's a good idea for me to be involved," she said.

"Last time I didn't run it by you and got us both into trouble. This time I'm trying to stay *out* of trouble. Please."

Clara had to hand it to her: If she was old enough for the debate team, she should definitely join. Hallie placed a notebook in Clara's lap, and Clara sat staring at it, as if an alarm bell might ring if she touched it.

Thomas plopped down next to them, dragging the dog by his collar. "Gentle," Clara told him, noting that the animal did seem remarkably unfazed. She reached out to pet his head, and he licked her hand happily and panted softly.

"Can you do reporting on our new dog, Hallie?" Thomas asked her. "He doesn't have a name."

"That's because he's only visiting," Clara reminded him.

"If you were *going* to keep him," Hallie began, looking slyly at Clara, "what would you call him?"

At that moment, the phone in Clara's pocket chimed several times, and she took it out to see a string of photos from Randi: a colorful braided leash, a hemp chew toy, even a crocheted canine sweater. "Moondance is now offering free delivery to favorite neighbors . . ." the text taunted her, and Clara laughed. If it was obvious to everyone else that the dog wasn't going anywhere, she'd get Benny's official sign-off tonight. She knew if he was truly against it, he'd have already said so.

"How about Aloha?" Clara asked, trying to act as if she'd only just begun giving it any thought. She and Benny had honeymooned in Hawaii, and she loved how three melodic syllables could not only mean *hello, good-bye,* and *love,* but also could conjure a sense of hanging loose, of no worries. She could already see herself calling it out the back door, maybe even getting a little tiki-style sign to hang on the wall over the dog bed.

"I like Pup-Pup," Thomas announced. Apparently she wasn't the only one who'd been thinking ahead.

"Well, that's rather . . . I mean, that could be *any* dog. Shouldn't we choose a name that suits *this* dog?"

He nodded gravely. "Pup-Pup," he repeated.

Clara's mother had admonished her about turning decisions over to the kids, even before Clara had been confronted with the opportunity to do so: "I'll never understand how people let their *children* rule the roost these days." She'd been pregnant with Maddie, Thomas was a baby, and they'd just announced that Benny had accepted the offer to partner at the Yellow Springs firm when her mother had initiated one of their sporadic and generally irritating phone calls. The comment seemed to come out of nowhere, and

Clara had mistaken it for a judgment of her decision to leave her job and stay home after the move.

"Far more women stayed home in your generation," Clara had pointed out.

Her mother scoffed. "I'm not talking about the decision to *care* for the children. Of course you have to *care* for them. I'm talking about letting them call the shots. Melissa's grandchildren were just visiting the complex last week, and I'll tell you . . ."

It should have come as no surprise that it wasn't really about Clara. As a child, she'd spent evenings and weekends being dragged along to the step aerobics classes her mother taught to keep herself occupied around her father's workaholic schedule. While her friends were taking ballet or playing soccer, she'd spent countless hours under protest in the corners of mirrored studios, reading her way through stacks of library books while trying to drown out the re-verberations of eighties pop. *If you're looking for a physical outlet, you are welcome to join the class,* her mother would say when she complained, missing the point entirely. She supposed that was part of what endeared her to Hallie: She recognized in the girl a familiar loneliness, a solidarity shared among only children with varying de-grees of absentee parents.

Clara reached over and rubbed the dog's soft belly. Her mother also never would have allowed any kind of pet, so the question of who would've been granted naming privileges was too far-fetched to contemplate. *Sorry, pal,* she told him telepathically. *No island style for you.*

Hallie shrugged. "I think Pup-Pup is a fine name." She patted Thomas on the shoulder. "If you keep him, I'll take his picture and put it in my paper. He'll be famous."

"Wow!" Thomas said, throwing his arms around the dog's neck. "You have to stay, Pup-Pup. You'll be a star!"

"Staaah!" Maddie yelled. "Wo!" Clara had to laugh. True, kids shouldn't run the show, but there was no denying that the whole show was for them anyway. She'd grown used to going without sleep, trading in her alternative playlists for sing-along songs, and monotonizing her dinner menu. Why should it make her feel like she was letting go of something to hand over naming rights to a dog, of all things?

She turned her attention back to the notebook and reluctantly opened the cover.

At the top of the first page, she saw that Hallie had added a tagline. "*The Color-Blind Gazette*: Where No News Isn't Good News." "Get it?" Hallie asked hopefully.

"I get it," she assured her. "Clever." It was.

The first article, "Moondance Pays It Forward," was about a new display of Damask weavings Randi and Rhoda had for sale, where proceeds would support Syrian refugees. "The first story came to *me*," Hallie said importantly. "Rhoda stopped me on the street and asked if I was going to do another paper, She said they could use a way to get the word out. That's when I knew I was definitely going to do it again." Skimming the article, Clara could tell its reporting had been a good education for Hallie. She'd covered the history of the patterns in Damascus and beyond, and how the fine craftsmanship was a worldwide luxury, often imitated but never duplicated in the detailed beauty achieved by hand.

The second was a little piece on the fall festival at Young's Jersey Dairy and how much money it brought in for the farmers before the slow winter. Hallie had quotes from several workers, and Clara had to admit she was impressed. The third was called "Up to Date with Second Date Update" and talked about how one of Yellow Springs's newest residents was the producer behind the segment, which did occasionally manage to produce a happy ending—though Clara had to hide a knowing smile at how conspicuously sparse the details were.

"I told you there was good news to report around here," Clara said when she'd finished skimming. "Nice job, Hallie. Has your mom seen this?"

"Not yet, but I promised to show her. She isn't too happy about me doing another one, but once I found out she'd enrolled in 'Censorship in Literature,' she had a hard time rebutting my freedom of expression."

Hallie was almost too smart for her own good. All she'd have to do was cry "censorship" anywhere within a generous radius of Antioch's activist-filled campus, and troops would assemble behind her as if she'd gotten hold of the Pied Piper's flute.

"Well, you're doing great. You don't need me after all." It was a relief, really. "And it would be disingenuous to put my name on this. It's wholly your effort."

She jutted out her lip. "You're just saying it's good because you don't want to help me make it better."

"Not true." Clara shook her head. "If you're really fishing for feedback, just one thing—and for this no credit needed." She landed her index finger on the last paragraph of the article about Izzy. "I don't think it's necessary to point out that the show's producer happens to be 'beautiful and single.' I'm sure she'd appreciate the compliment, but aside from that, she might prefer you didn't."

Hallie's chin raised in a defiant posture that was becoming too familiar to Clara. "It's not like it's a secret," she said. "I'm trying to help. Maybe someone will see this and ask her out."

"I'm sure she's doing fine with that on her own, honey."

"No. She's not." Hallie's statement was so firm that for an instant Clara worried someone had mentioned Izzy's problem with her brother-in-law in front of the child.

"What makes you think that?" she asked, hand on her hip.

"Paul." Hallie spit out the word as if it were a mouthful of gristle, and an uneasiness overtook Clara.

"What about Paul?"

"He was there the other day," she said.

"At Izzy's?"

Hallie nodded. "Helping her fix something. I think he likes her."

Clara could not recall ever having seen the two so much as exchange a word. "I'm sure he was just being helpful," she said. "That doesn't mean he likes her."

"I think it does. I could tell. He seemed kind of nervous."

"Was this while you were interviewing Izzy for this article?" Hallie nodded, and Clara narrowed her eyes. "Well, maybe he was nervous about *you*. And your notebook." The girl looked away and shrugged. Clara had been so worried about Kristin, and Rebecca, and herself, that she realized she'd almost forgotten to worry about Hallie. In her mind she'd sort of left that to Natalie, but who knew, really, how Natalie was handling things—or not handling them. "Did you talk to him?" she asked more gently.

Hallie shook her head. "I tried to leave, but I couldn't figure out how to do it politely." Clara lifted an eyebrow. "What?" Hallie said defensively. "I'm precocious, but I'm still polite." Clara stifled a laugh. Clearly she hadn't conjured the word *precocious* on her own. Adults really did need to watch what they said in front of kids. Even if the kid was . . . well, Hallie.

"Grown-up boys and girls are different," Clara said, trying to convince them both. "Just because they're talking or doing something together doesn't mean one likes the other. And Paul is worried about Kristin and the kids right now. I'm sure the last thing on his mind is—" Hallie rolled her eyes so dramatically Clara couldn't even bring herself to finish the statement.

"You're friends with Izzy, right?" Hallie asked, and Clara nodded. Hallie looked into her eyes with such intensity Clara was taken aback. "You need to get her away from him."

Clara's first instinct was to tell her she was being overdramatic, to brush it off, to correct her, but what was the point? Hallie got enough of that from everyone else. Besides, they both knew that if there was any truth to some sort of bond, however casual, budding between Izzy and Paul, Clara would feel the sense of alarm for her friend just as acutely as Hallie did.

Still, if that was Hallie's aim with this story, yet again, she wanted no part of it.

"Hallie, I'm going to be firm with you: Take my name off the paper. And take out that line about Izzy." She had a flash of inspiration to appeal to the girl's journalistic sensibilities. "You don't want to be seen as some gossipy tabloid."

Hallie leaned closer, seemingly ignoring everything she'd just said. "I got the feeling Izzy hadn't seen my paper." That hardly seemed possible. Clara hadn't heard about anything *but* the paper ever since this mess began. "She might not even know—"

"Hallie?" Clara looked up to see Natalie coming toward them and got quickly to her feet.

"Hallie just stopped to see the dog," she called out reflexively.

Pup-Pup was running to greet Natalie, nuzzling her legs and then turning back toward Clara as if to say, *See how neighborly I can be?*

"Well, aren't you cute," Natalie said, bending to scratch his ears. Her demeanor softened, and Clara met the dog's eyes with a conciliatory look of her own. *Yes, we know, you've come along at a good time.*

"I've been wanting to talk to you," Natalie said to Clara, without looking up at her. "Hallie, can you give us a second?"

The girl pouted. "You mean go home? Can't I just play with Thomas and Maddie? And Pup-Pup?" Without waiting for a response, she hurled the tennis ball across the yard and took off after the dog's bushy tail, Thomas yelling, "Wait for me!" and trailing behind.

"Up," Maddie said at Clara's feet, and she lifted her daughter and smoothed her hair.

"I'm sorry," Clara said. "I didn't expect Hallie to—"

Natalie waved her into silence. "Did Hallie tell you *why* she wanted to do this newspaper? The first time, I mean?"

Clara thought back. "Just that they'd been learning about journalism at school. She said it was 'about the facts,' I remember."

Natalie nodded slowly, and when she spoke again, her voice was serious, low. "The facts of war reporting, evidently. I wish her teacher had given me a heads-up, but she didn't know about our . . . situation."

Their situation. *Oh.* Clara's heart sank. "I had no idea—"

Natalie shook her head. "Turns out they talked in class about the role reporters have played in keeping governments honest, keeping soldiers safe, even bringing them home. She seems to have gotten it into her head—" Her eyes filled with tears. "Not that she thinks she's directly doing that, of course. But she really believes that what she's doing is noble."

Clara hesitated, thinking of how one-sided public opinion on

Kristin—and Paul, for that matter—might have been without that ill-advised edition. Not that public opinion as it was had swayed or affirmed anything, necessarily, but still. "Maybe in a way, it is."

"Maybe. Maybe not. Either way, I can't bring myself to discourage her. I tried, and she cried 'censorship.' What's parenthood if not censorship at this age?" She threw up her hands. "Still, even when I know I'm being played, it's the fact that in some backward way she's doing this for her dad that gets me. So maybe if you did help her after all . . ."

Just like that, the door between them was reopened, and an odd combination of heartache and relief flooded Clara. It had been eating at her, this invisible rift with her neighbor. "I'm happy to help if she ever needs me," she assured Natalie. "But for the most part, she seems to be doing fine on her own."

Natalie shot her a look.

"This time, I mean!" Clara handed over the binder with a nervous laugh. "*This* one is good."

Natalie paged through it, and when she looked up, the raw emotion was gone from her eyes, and something unreadable was in its place.

"This one is good," she conceded. "For now. But I still don't want her doing this alone. I tried to offer to help, but she doesn't want me—she wants you. She seems to think it's your name that is lending a legitimacy to this. That without it people will write it off as a kid project."

Clara bit her lip. "Hardly anyone even knows I used to be an editor," she said, but Natalie only shrugged.

Clara sighed. She knew Benny wouldn't feel any better about her name staying on the masthead than she did. But it seemed crass to resort to the old my-husband-wouldn't-like-it excuse to a wife and mother who was holding down the fort on her own.

Besides, maybe Hallie was right that it was better to move forward than back down. She nodded once, crisply, and Natalie seemed to relax a little.

"About Paul," she said. "Did you talk to him? I put a note of apology in his mailbox but couldn't bring myself to face him."

Clara filled her in on the visit she and Benny had paid next door—minus the choice part where he'd invited her to look around—and the gist of the surprise cameo from Kristin's sister, all the while clinging to Maddie, who busied herself playing tug-of-war with Clara's necklace. When she finished, Natalie crossed her arms.

"I'm on my own with Hallie so much, it's important that I feel our neighborhood is safe. I know I pooh-poohed this whole thing at first, but now . . . I don't know. I don't like feeling caught up in a real-life *Dateline* episode."

"I don't like it either." What else was there to say?

Natalie nodded. "I can't apologize," she said, "for reacting the way I did the other day."

"I wouldn't expect you to." *And I can't apologize for not telling you every last detail. It would only make you worry more.*

Clara looked past Natalie at the patio, neglected since that last night with Kristin. Benny had worked so hard getting the bricks laid just right; they'd stood and admired it upon its completion, imagining the nights of camaraderie those chairs around the fire pit would hold. But they'd gotten only one before it took on an air of . . . not foreboding, exactly, but something like it.

Damn you, Paul, she thought. *And what the hell do you want with Izzy, anyway?*

"She liked coming here after school better than trailing me to class," Natalie said, nodding almost sheepishly toward Hallie. Clara flashed back to herself curled in the corners of so many fitness studios.

"She doesn't have to stop unless you want her to."

Natalie nodded again and, their unsteady truce established, called for her daughter, who obediently came running. So Hallie *did* occasionally have a sense of when she was pressing her luck. Natalie raised a hand in a silent wave as they turned toward home. "Keep me posted," Natalie said. "Assuming you continue to lie low so unsuccessfully." She smiled weakly.

Hallie twisted to look over her shoulder at Clara. "If you decide not to keep the dog, maybe you should see if Izzy wants him," she called, her eyes intent.

Just as they both knew she was keeping the dog, they both knew Hallie was using him as a stand-in for what someone should really talk with Izzy about.

"Maybe I will," she answered quietly. But Hallie was far enough away that she wasn't sure the girl could hear.

24

Earth calling Iz...paging Iz...Rumor has it
you've fallen off the face of the planet, but I'm
calling anyway because we miss you at our girls'
nights. Any chance you might orbit back toward
Springfield for the next one? Tell us when you
can make it, and that's when we'll do it!

*—Three-week-old voice mail from a cousin who
was also in Penny's wedding, undeleted but
unreturned*

Friday night, while her *Freshly Squeezed* colleagues attended the
grand opening of a new comedy club in Dayton, and her neighbors filled the crisp windows-open-weather air with the clinks and
clangs of dishes being done and the jangles of laughter being shared
and the bangs and screeches of movies being streamed, strangers
the world over were aching with yearning, and Izzy, frozen in front
of her laptop when she should have been in the kitchen prepping
for tomorrow's brunch, ached and yearned along with them. She
grieved with the family of a kindergartner who'd been caught under
the wheels of his school bus, tears welling in her eyes as she flipped
through the slide show of his five short years. She shook her head

at the growing list of those who'd been claimed by a massive earthquake in Nepal, curling tighter in her chair as she watched footage of childless couples awaiting word on the fate of their unborn babies—the agency housing for their surrogate mothers reduced to rubble in the frame behind them. She prayed, though she was less and less sure if her idea of God matched anyone else's, for hostages in a hotel overtaken by men wearing explosives in the name of a higher power.

Hours under all that heartbreak and strife left her properly put in her place. She had a home with a garden she'd made beautiful, ready to host a feast that, though decadent, was comfortably less than she could afford. She had neighbors who looked out for one another through those open windows of their living rooms and kitchens, even while inside they faced problems of their own. She had a good job with upbeat coworkers who many people less cynical than she would love to spend their mornings with. If she couldn't face Penny, or Josh, or most of all her parents tomorrow with a genuine smile on her face, she would prove only that she was undeserving of their love.

Josh's words from their last encounter had been on repeat in her mind, playing over unbidden at moments she least expected them. She heard him while driving to work with the glow of the dawn on the horizon, pounding her pedals down the bike trail with her breath heavy in her lungs, shampooing her hair in the white noise of her empty house: *I didn't think I'd be losing a friend. I thought I'd be gaining a sister.*

The words were not just a picture of what might have been between them; they were an honest and befuddled encapsulation of what *should* have been. Worse, there was no real explanation for the fact that it had *not* been except for the truth—the one explanation that Izzy could not give and that, in the absence of any other plausible stand-in, Josh could very likely guess. She'd narrowly escaped their encounter with her ability to go on pretending intact. But she was going to have to do a better job, starting now.

Saturday morning she woke early to handle the preparations she should have done the night before. She had the new recipe she'd chosen all but memorized, having spent the week stocking the highest-quality ingredients she could find. While the oven preheated and she busied her hands whisking eggs and dicing vegetables, her mind rehearsed things she might say over the meal. She'd make them laugh, set them at ease. She'd talk about work. Just this week on Second Date Update they'd had a run of callers denied another chance for a host of left-field reasons: the man who'd booed a quarterback he didn't know was his date's favorite; the college student whose date had failed the good taste test by wanting to make out in a cemetery. "Deal breakers" was their shorthand for these calls at the station, as in these cases, it mattered not how hot the chemistry, how fluid the conversation, or how persuasive the disc jockeys. These daters evoked a strict one-strike rule that unnerved Izzy, if she was being honest, at her own prospects.

Maybe dating wasn't such a good topic to bring up at brunch after all.

She could stick to local gossip, she supposed, but felt unsavory doing so. Her mother had called Izzy in a flurry after recognizing her street on the news, but Izzy quickly rebuked her questions, brushing the incident aside as a nasty divorce blown out of proportion. She didn't want her parents to worry, to think anything about her new living situation unstable or unsafe.

She popped the quiche into the oven and raced upstairs to don her sundress, which she layered over leggings and topped with a cardigan. It seemed a very Yellow Springs sort of outfit, one she hoped would exude a bohemian independence, and she pulled her hair back in a loose ponytail that was nothing if not nonchalant. Looking in the mirror, she *almost* convinced herself that she was entirely at home in her new lifestyle. Even as the host, she'd somehow come to feel like the guest among the rest of her family, but she knew the fault was her own. Today would be different.

And why had she been wasting time worrying over the conversation, anyway? The rest of them had far more interesting things to contribute. She'd pepper them with questions; she'd be so engaged in the baby and her parents' new condo and anything else they deemed of import that they wouldn't even notice she hadn't said a thing about her own life. She'd taken note of this technique watching the most popular girl in her high school, back when she'd longed to be one. Ask everyone around you about themselves, and they'll love you for it, no matter that they don't learn a thing about you in return.

Come to think of it, Kristin had reminded her a lot of that girl.

Out in the garden, Izzy put up the umbrella to shade the full morning sun and felt a rush of pleasure as she carried out her new place mats and votives. The five of them would fit comfortably around the circle, and her arrangement of the table came together with a refined, simple beauty that, for once, was just as she'd imagined. She was topping the yogurt parfaits with berries and fresh granola when the doorbell sounded. She glanced at her watch. Her parents were five minutes early, which for them was right on time.

"Oh, Izzy, look at all this! Your house looks just as pretty as you are."

Izzy stood at the open door and looked around the front yard in search of what "all this" might be. "Thanks, Mom, but I haven't changed anything out front since you moved me in."

At least her mother hadn't noticed the banged-up car, which Izzy had taken to backing tight up to the garage. If her mother had caught sight of even one small scrape, she'd have come to the door "all fretted up," as her father liked to say. She was the type who was so good at fussing over things that she almost seemed to enjoy it—and thus didn't bother to adjust her intensity for big problems or minuscule ones, or for those within her control or well outside it.

"Well, it's always been pretty. And so have you. I keep telling people what a waste it is that you're on the radio. You should be on *television*."

"Mom. I'm not even *on* the radio! Just behind the scenes."

"Every time I hear the smart parts, I know it was you." Pride was radiating from her mother, as usual, and Izzy had to laugh. There were exactly zero "smart parts" on *Freshly Squeezed*, which she knew for a fact her mother did not listen to. Much as she loved to boast to her friends about Izzy's role, Izzy knew she found Sonny and Day just as grating as Izzy did. Her mother might dote on her two daughters unconditionally, but outside of her relationship with her children she lacked neither judgment nor good taste.

As her mother patted her arm and stepped through the open door, Izzy turned her attention to her father. While she'd been dodging everyone else's calls, she'd been fighting the urge to dial him directly and demand the details of this so-called health scare. A part of her was waiting to see if they were *really* going to not tell her, while another part insisted that if he was fine, as Penny had assured her, then there was nothing to tell. "I've missed you, Dad." She breathed him in as his hug wrapped her in warmth. He was just as she'd left him in Springfield: solid, quiet, reassuring, and dressed for a hike.

"Come see the garden," Izzy said, leading the way. Her parents shuffled along behind her, and she tried not to think about how old they were getting. They qualified for *senior discounts* now. "Josh and Penny drove separately, then?" She purposely said his name first, as if to prove to herself that she could.

She heard her mother *tsk* behind her. "Oh, they're not coming, dear. Penny has been having some difficulty in the mornings, you know. They send their love."

Izzy had the back door open now and turned to squint at her mother. "Not *coming*?"

From the counter, the perfectly wrapped slippers she'd meant as a peace offering mocked her, and she recognized herself as a hypocrite even as she said the words. Of *course* Penny wasn't coming. And certainly not Josh. Nothing was ever that easy. Why had she deluded herself into believing otherwise?

"She could have given me a heads-up," she said, sounding more curt than she'd intended, trying to maintain her balance. Even as she recognized that she was choking down the bitter taste of her own medicine, it still seemed a valid point. At least Izzy had had the decency to text Penny when she'd bailed out of her get-together rather than sending a message through a third party.

A third party.

Had Josh told Penny he'd come here? She'd assumed not—assumed he wouldn't want to implicate himself in that humiliation any more than her—but if she was wrong and he *had* . . . If he and Penny truly had no secrets between them . . . What might he have said, exactly? Could things be even worse than she'd feared?

"Well, I don't think she was expecting not to feel well, dear. You know how these things can come on with pregnancy." Her mother clasped her hands and looked past her at the spread in the garden. "But this is so lovely! We'll enjoy it enough for everyone, just the three of us."

Izzy swallowed hard against the betrayal. The useless effort of obsessing over how she'd smooth it all over, how she'd act, what she'd *say*, the foolishness of having put so much stock, so much hope of redemption, into a single event that could be blown off as easily as she'd skipped her sister's own celebration last week. She had convinced herself she couldn't face them that day because of a *dream*, of all things. When would she learn to stop giving so much credit to her subconscious?

Her dad wandered over to the table, hands in his pockets. Why had she gone and set all the places in advance? It looked like she'd been expecting a miniature banquet.

"Camilla, you should tell Penelope to call next time. Look at all this trouble she's gone to." The use of Penny's full name was a telltale parental sign of displeasure. Izzy might have enjoyed it if not for the fact that he'd surely feel differently if he knew the whole truth. "I didn't know this was a *fancy* brunch, Iz." He looked down at his outfit apologetically.

Izzy set about gathering up the extra place settings as quickly as she could. "It's not fancy. It was no trouble putting it out, and it's no trouble to put it away." She tried to balance the two spare yogurt parfaits in the crook of her arm while she restacked the plates, but one of them tumbled loose, showering her sleeve with yogurt and the pavers with a crash of broken crystal.

"Oh, what a gooey mess," her mother said. "Let me get it. Just show me to your paper towels and a broom. Do you need help in the kitchen too? This'll take but a second."

Izzy turned her back so they couldn't see the tears welling in her eyes. "I don't need help," she said, as much to herself as to them, but she didn't argue when her mother showed herself to the pantry and headed outside armed with cleanup supplies.

She served up mimosas and coffee, pulling herself together in time to get the quiche out of the oven and set the singers and standards channel to stream through the wireless speakers she'd set outside. By the time they were settled at the table, all her preparation had lent itself seamlessly to this smaller-scale, lower-pressure Plan B. Her parents were happy, anyway, and seemed not to think anything at all about Penny and Josh's absence.

"Their loss!" was her father's only remark, as he went for his second bite of the quiche. "This is delicious, Iz."

"It's no wonder having your own house has turned you into such a cook. Space to come into your own. That's what I tell my old-fashioned friends when they ask about it, anyway."

"It's the ingredients," Izzy said, seizing the opportunity to steer the conversation off unsteady ground. "So much here is locally sourced. You pay for it, but it's worth it."

"Are you listening, Todd?" Her mother glowed with triumph. "That's exactly what I keep telling you about our grocery bills." She turned back to Izzy. "Tell us everything. Are you making friends?"

Izzy nodded. "I really like the neighbor across the street, Clara. And also these women who own a boutique—I bought Penny a gift there, actually, to celebrate her news. You can take it to her."

"Oh, how nice. And what about that woman who's disappeared?" Her face turned serious. "You don't hear much on the news in Springfield anymore."

Izzy tried to maintain a neutral front. "I don't think there's anything new to say. Though I've stopped following it myself. It makes me feel . . . I don't know, nosy or something." She thought of the detective's brief appearance at the bonfire. *Was* he still trailing Kristin? Had he been doing it even then? Were there any new theories? Everyone knew that the more time ticked by, the less likely they were to be found. She'd been trying to demonstrate a certain respect by letting the questions go, by not prying, but now she felt willfully uninvolved, as if her parents might reasonably expect her to know more.

"I could understand that. Especially if you've met her husband. Or ex-husband, was it? Either way."

Or when I had a moment where I thought he might have been about to kiss me.

"Have you?" she asked. Izzy stared at her blankly. "Met her husband, that is."

She nodded. "He moved back into the house when they left."

"Well. That raises the issue of boundaries, doesn't it? I remember when—"

"Camilla." Her father's voice was firm. "She said it made her feel nosy. Which you are now being."

Oh, how Izzy had missed her father. If Izzy had yet to find her kindred spirit in this world, it was partly because no one could measure up to their born-in solidarity. He never dug into her personal life the way her mother did, nor was he purposefully aloof like so many of her friends' dads. Rather, he'd taught her about life simply by showing it to her: striding through the woods, or floating downriver, or even huddled in a tent during a rainstorm. Penny had been a far less willing participant in these little demonstrations, and thus Izzy had doubled her own enthusiasm to compensate, and gladly.

"Now, Iz," her mother was saying, "you've got to visit soon. Remember Samantha Greene from down the road? She bought the old Gingham Café, and it's amazing what she's done with the place. I stopped her just the other day to say . . ."

Izzy reveled in the normalcy of her mother's running commentary. Now that the mimosa had taken the edge off her annoyance, she could appreciate that Penny and Josh had given her a reprieve from the tense morning she'd been anticipating. Though granted, this did nothing to make amends with her sister. Or Josh. A part of her had needed to get their next meeting out of the way, to override the taste left by the last one.

As she relaxed a bit more with every bite, she hardly even minded that her mother was now going on about the baby. Izzy's niece or nephew, who would be half Penny, half Josh—combining in essence some of her *own* DNA with Josh's. Not that she and Penny looked alike, though they did have the same almond shape to their eyes. If the baby had those eyes too, set in a face like Josh's—

No. She couldn't think that far ahead.

She wasn't ready yet.

And then her mother was excusing herself to "powder her nose"— a too-polite expression she habitually used even at home—and her father's eyes were on her, and they were not comfortable or familiar anymore. They were stern.

"Isabel." He leaned forward. "Your mother seems content to fret happily away in her own oblivious world, so I'm going to make this quick."

She pulled her cardigan around her futilely as the cold wave of his words sent goose bumps racing across her skin.

"Whatever it is between you and your sister—and Josh—the triangle of you, or the line of you, or whatever shape it is, it's going to stop."

Her mouth went dry. "I don't know what you mean . . ."

"You might well not. You might not know how to put your finger on what's gone wrong, but it's still up to you to fix it. Because I'll tell you this: Penny can't take responsibility for anything she didn't knowingly do now that it's too late to *undo* it. Can she?"

Izzy sat stricken. To have her father call her out this way on anything was unprecedented. To have him call her out this way on this particular thing was unthinkable. Worse, even, than Josh showing up at her door. She managed what she thought might be a shake of her head.

"She's hurting, and I think Josh is too, though I don't care so much about that. He might have it coming, for all I know. And I don't want to know," he added quickly, his hand in the air, his head shaking vehemently. "But Penny does *not* have it coming. And I'm not going to see her hurt. Not anymore, and especially not now."

A noise came from inside, and they both turned to look at the door, which remained closed. "I love you like none other, Iz. I'm imploring you—out of your mother's earshot—to find a way to fix it. It's the best thing for everyone, most of all you."

Her eyes filled with tears. No one had ever asked how she felt about Penny and Josh getting together, though she, not Penny, had been the one dragging him to family outings for years. She wouldn't have told them if they'd asked, but she'd always been a bit hurt that they hadn't.

Now it seemed that perhaps her father had guessed, at some of it, anyway. And this would be the beginning and the end of the discussion. A swift shutting down of feelings she had no right to give voice to and yet wanted to scream at being denied.

He tapped the top of her hand with a fingertip. "I don't want to see you hurting either. And that's why I know we won't have to speak of this again."

Her mother reappeared, grinning naïvely, just as her father moved to help himself to another croissant from the basket she'd so carefully warmed earlier. She didn't need to touch it to know that it had gone cold.

25

Here's what I know about waiting: It starts as agony, as anxiety. When will the proverbial second shoe drop? It keeps you up nights. But then it gets easier. Because outside of the worry churning in your brain, life is happening. You can't only *wait. So the waiting fades to the back burner, and you can leave it there, moving it to the front occasionally for a stir and then putting it back where you hope it belongs.*

Until one day, when something wakes you up from your perch at the stove, and you realize that the wait won't be much longer. The drop is no longer a distant possibility, it's a likely outcome. And that's when you face the facts you've been avoiding: That even at the lowest setting, the burners are too hot to stay on forever. You'll either slowly scorch, or burst into flames—and either way, it won't be pretty.

That's when you know deep down that you have to run.

26

Your dog seems stressed. Have you gotten insights from an animal communicator?

—*Question called out in the glen from a fellow
hiker, at which Clara, exhausted from the baby
pack on her back and her own many stresses,
laughed too hard before realizing it was
serious*

Clara didn't need to see the other mother's face to feel her fear.
She sprang into action, leaving Maddie half unstrapped from the
stroller—because Maddie, at least, was a mere foot or two off the
ground. This child, not much older, had scrambled out of reach at
the top of the playground's highest ladder before his mother had
registered the danger—the perilous open sides of the small rectan-
gular platform—and was headed in determined caveman steps
toward the alluring sliding board tunnel at the far end.

"Wait for Mommy! Wait for Mommy!" the woman was crying,
lunging to grab one of his limbs, coming up empty, and Clara
watched her body jerk in indecision between running along the
ground beneath the edge and climbing up after him. She herself

had long cursed whatever clueless engineer had designed this breed of playground. The fireman's pole, rope ladder, and stepping pads were great fun for older kids, but the vertical drops surrounding them were a nightmare for any parent trying to keep hold of one of the younger, eager-to-follow set.

"Need a hand?" Clara called, and without waiting for an answer took off running toward the opposite end of the platform, arms outstretched as if she were a seasoned pro at catching free-falling children, something she had no idea if she could actually do.

The boy was mere inches from the edge now, oblivious of the danger. Catching sight of the fireman's pole, he reached out a curious hand, tottering.

My God. She wasn't going to make it in time. He was really going to fall.

Clara lunged. There was a clank, a collision of bone on metal, an underwater popping in her ears, a spear of pain. She stumbled back, her hands flying to her forehead, a moan escaping her clenched jaw.

"Holy hell, are you *okay?*"

Clara blinked in confusion, registering the horizontal monkey bar she hadn't seen, perfect for practicing chin-ups, or hanging upside down from, or head-butting at full speed.

With some effort, she lifted her gaze upward—and into the eyes of Detective Marks, whose arms were now wrapped tightly around the child, safe on the platform. And who looked curiously unsurprised to see that it was Clara who'd just rattled the structure to its core.

"Way to be a hero," the detective said, a smile in her voice. Out of the harsh bun, her hair was wavy and full, and along with her street clothes had transformed her like a chameleon into an ordinary mother. Or an undercover one.

"Next time, he's on his own," Clara groaned, blinking back tears, trying to regain her composure. A brief but intense ringing filled her ears as she pulled her hands away from her forehead, and she willed it to stop. This wasn't the time to *not* be clearheaded.

"Oh, shit." The detective's smile was gone. "I didn't realize you're really hurt." Clara looked down at her fingertips and saw blood. "We should get you looked at. You might have a concussion."

Clara squeezed her eyes shut again—everything seemed so *bright*. She was fine. She didn't have time for this. She had her own kids to look after.

Her own kids. Clara's eyes flew open, and she turned to see Thomas yanking Maddie through her stroller harness in a sort of bear hug as Pup-Pup strained against his leash, which Clara had looped around the handle. The dog was pulling the wheels out from under them as Maddie kicked, half in and half out of her seat.

"Careful!" Clara screeched, stumbling toward them. After a few uncertain steps the pain dulled and she found her land legs again. Thomas looked nonplussed as she untangled Maddie and deposited her on the pavement.

"I was *helping*." Seeing her face, his defiance switched to wide-eyed alarm. "Mommy, you need a Band-Aid."

"I'll get one once we're home," she said as breezily as she could. If she acted as if everything were fine, then everything would be—just as soon as this pounding in her head subsided. "Go ahead, go play!"

She ushered him toward the swings, got hold of the dog's leash, and took Maddie by the hand. Her daughter smiled adoringly up at her as if she was not at all the incompetent mother she felt, and Clara focused on the grounding feeling of the little hand in hers as they made their way back toward the playset.

Detective Marks emerged at the bottom of the corkscrew slide, her son on her lap. "Thank you for trying to help," she said. "I feel like a dolt for that hero comment."

"I feel ridiculous," Clara said. "I'm just glad he didn't fall."

"I don't know why I always think it's going to be this relaxing little outing to stop by the playground when I get off work."

"I don't know why I think *any* outing will be relaxing. Or little," Clara added, then remembered who she was talking to. "Although if anyone needs relief from the craziness of her workday, I'm guessing it's you."

"I'd take a felon over a cranky toddler," the detective said. She had out a pocket pack of tissues, and Clara took one gratefully, holding it to her forehead. Thomas was pumping his legs rhythmically on a creaky swing now, and Clara steeled herself against the grating noise.

Detective Marks had her phone out, typing out a harried text. "It's just a goose egg with some broken skin," she said, "but you should get it looked at, to be safe." The boy slid out of her lap and began digging through the mulch with his fingers.

"That's not necessary," she said automatically. What mom had time to get *looked at* when she was most likely fine? "I know the concussion symptoms—I'll monitor myself."

The detective looked up, considering her. "You *do* seem to have pretty good instincts," she said, sounding suspiciously like a cop again.

Clara peered at her through her daze, wondering whether the words were as deliberate as they seemed. A thousand questions she didn't dare ask spun through her head. It had been over two weeks since *The Color-Blind Gazette* incident, and she'd heard little from the police since, aside from a few "routine" check-in calls from Detective Bryant. She'd felt too sheepish to ask anything in return, and he never volunteered information. Kristin was more than three weeks gone now, and she couldn't help but wonder how hard they were still looking. Or how long they might try. Or whether they had any new clues as to where she might be, or why.

"Anything interesting going on in the neighborhood these days?" the detective asked casually. Her son was seated in the mulch now, coming up with handfuls of wood shards and watching them fall to the ground, and Maddie stood monitoring his behavior with fascination.

Clara thought with longing of the abandoned *I Can Do It!* book cover. But she'd made her decision. Having not mentioned it before, she certainly couldn't bring it up now. She shrugged. "I was trying not to ask you the same thing."

"Why not ask?"

She was surprised by the question. Because she wasn't sure if she was allowed? Because she desperately wanted to but was afraid to know the answers?

"Has the good doctor been around more?" The levity in the detective's voice did not match the question. "Have you noticed him directing any anger toward you, or anyone else?"

Clara shook her head, wincing as a fresh jolt of pain cascaded through her temple.

Detective Marks nodded. "No cause for alarm. But since I bumped into you, I'll *casually* mention that Dr. Kirkland's partners have not reacted kindly to Hallie's little bulletin. They asked him to hang back, let them cover his appointments until it blows over."

Clara's eyes widened. She could guess at his reaction.

"Seems he has a knack for bargaining. They landed on a compromise where his patients can opt for an easy switch if they feel uncomfortable or have reservations. But he's still none too happy."

"*Are* they opting out?"

"Most have not. But his partners came to me because they felt his grudge against those who *have* seemed disproportionate, all things considered. Just be aware, in case that grudge were to extend to you. Can't help but notice he's quick to divert blame."

Bored of the mulch show, Maddie fixed her eyes on Thomas and began yanking Clara toward the swings, while Pup-Pup tried to follow. Clara felt torn between jumping at the excuse to slink away and staying to prod for more. But the detective was on her knees now, bemoaning the condition of her filthy toddler. Game over.

"Thanks for the heads-up," Clara said carefully. "I'm glad I ran into you. Not so much the bar . . ." Detective Marks laughed, and Clara bent and offered a high five to the mulch-covered boy, who instead gleefully handed her a handful.

She'd been peripherally aware of a siren in the distance, but it was growing closer, and to her horror an ambulance appeared, lights flashing. She shot a look at the detective, who held her hands up. "He's a friend. He's just going to look, as a favor to me. If you're okay, he'll go."

The kids whooped in excitement, but all Clara could think about was the way the passing motorists were slowing to gawk at her standing here bleeding with her neighbor's investigator. Whether speculation cast her as victim or suspect, it was looking less like anyone was going to buy her in the role of bystander—the only part she wanted to play.

Clara peered through the curtains of Maddie's room and across the street toward Izzy's dark house. Behind her, her daughter was sleeping heavily, her breaths deep and rhythmic, both tiny fists curled up by her chin in an irresistibly photogenic fashion. On the other side of the hundred-year-old wall, Thomas was sprawled unapologetically on his back, a stuffed jungle animal under each arm, his face slack-jawed and utterly vulnerable. Benny's soft snores came from down the hall, where the sheets were askew and the TV was still tuned to the sports report. Even when so much had gone wrong in Clara's world, the most important things were still right with it.

Her head seemed okay—mostly. She'd been allowed home with strict instructions to be vigilant, one more thing to remain on high alert about. Word had indeed traveled fast—Benny found out about the incident before she could tell him herself. He was too kind, too concerned, to say what she imagined him to be thinking: that every throb of her temple, every brush against her bruise was like a harsh reminder to keep her head out of other people's problems.

Still, she'd do it again. She could still see that boy unsteady on the ledge, still feel her heart-plummeting fear that he was going to fall. She was glad she'd been wrong. If she hadn't, she'd have been too busy reeling from her own blind spot to catch him.

You seem to have pretty good instincts.

So many people went through their lives in a blissful denial that anything truly bad could ever happen to them, or to anyone they knew. Clara wasn't one of those people. And she wasn't jealous of them, either. She felt sorry for them, because she knew how wrong they were.

Clara possessed a vicious animal instinct indeed when it came to protecting her children. So vicious that it coursed almost calmly through her veins even when there was no imminent danger. She had no idea if she felt it more strongly than other mothers, or if it was the same for everyone. The onset of the sensation had been so primal, the unsummoned immediacy of it. She'd been lying in the darkness after one of Thomas's feedings, in those early days when he seemed to eat more than he slept. She was sleepily marveling at how beautiful he was curled beside her bed in his bassinette, his little tufts of hair matted down on the top of his head, his tiny curled fingers peeking out of his swaddle, his angelic pout and rounded cheeks. And the thought had struck her so clearly she might have spoken it aloud: *If anyone ever tries to harm you, I will kill them.* The ferocity of it delighted her.

It was too bad women weren't born with that fire. If biology could program us to guard our offspring, why not also ready us to fearlessly protect ourselves? Where was the sixth sense that would have been so helpful when it came to certain dangers especially— the kind that talked smoothly and smiled handsomely and draped themselves in sexy suede blazers and unassuming button-downs?

Or that coached you through a pregnancy when you were steeped in loss, alone and overwhelmed at facing motherhood times two?

Or helped you with neighborly things when you were in over your head in a new house and a new town, and desperately in love with someone who would never be yours?

It had been so nice, in adjusting to a life of all-day mothering, to strike up a friendship with someone younger and single and bringing news of what Clara sometimes thought of as "the outside world." Izzy had a no-fuss, semiserious way about her that was just on the naïve side of sweet, with an air of inexperience but not without an edge, and Clara liked the edge best.

She'd been trying to push Hallie's insinuations about Izzy and Paul out of her mind, but with Detective Marks's casual warning they had flooded back. It nagged at her now, the idea that maybe she should have said something to Izzy. The idea that maybe she still should.

She padded back to her own room. She felt around in the blue light of the TV for the remote control buried in the comforter before switching it off and climbing in. She had to get to sleep; Benny was to wake her in three hours—a concussion precaution— if Maddie didn't beat him to it. She was settling herself on her pillow when she realized his eyes were open, staring at her through the short span of darkness between them. She smiled sleepily, but his expression was unreadably serious, and she suddenly found herself holding very still.

"I've been thinking," he said.

"Good on you," she murmured, but he didn't crack a smile. She really was incredibly tired. She just wanted him to wrap his arms around her and spoon her to sleep.

He took a breath. "Maybe you should think about going back to work."

She closed her eyes, then opened them.

"I'm concerned all this drama next door is dredging up bad memories. I'm not sure it's good for you right now, being alone here with the kids all day."

"How could you say that?" Conflicted as she sometimes felt, she was surprised at the conviction in her voice. But not at the hurt. "There's nowhere I'd rather be."

"Is that still true, though? Like it or not, this is the state of our neighborhood: investigations, suspicions, for who knows how long. I'm worried you've been obsessing over it—and I'm not saying I blame you. It's upsetting, and it's right here, and so are you. But at the mere sight of the detective today, you concussed yourself. Maybe it wouldn't be a bad idea to keep your brain busy with . . . something else."

She sucked in a breath. "That is *not* how it happened, and you know it."

"On a subconscious level, you don't think it might be?"

Benny didn't sound like himself. He'd awoken possessed by one of *those other husbands,* the ones who said infuriating things and did not know when to stay in their own lane.

"No, I don't. Because one, I didn't even know it was her until *after* I hit my head, and two, *on a subconscious level,* my brain is busy with plenty else. I can't believe you'd have the gall to imply that I don't have enough to do."

She cued up her day in replay. Even before her run-in at the playground, it had been another exercise in not getting through half the things on her list. Maddie's diaper blowout had cut a half hour off their time at the park before they'd even arrived. It had also bumped the towels from the laundry queue, a fact that proved inconvenient during dinner when Thomas upended his milk and she had to soak it up with an old sweatshirt. Never mind that any other person with a bag of frozen peas affixed to her forehead would have been sprawled on the couch to rest.

Benny sighed. "That's not what I said. You're twisting what I said."

"I'm not. First *Pam* yanks Thomas out of preschool, and now *you're* questioning my decision to be a stay-at-home mom, and you think *I'm* the one putting too much stock in 'the drama next door'?" The more she talked, the angrier she got.

"I only want you to be happy," he said more quietly. "I'm just concerned that you've been being pulled in . . . a dark direction. I'm sorry. If you're happy enough, that's good enough for me."

Was she *happy enough*? Was anyone fully happy immersed in cleaning up one mess after another while chasing people who seemed all at once utterly fragile and impossibly stubborn, without a second of head space to hear herself think? Was anyone fully happy going off to even the best of careers every day, when clients could get irrational and bosses could get unreasonable and work could pile higher at the worst possible times?

Happiness, to Clara, was an elusive thing that came in the form of the overall feeling that tucked you in at the end of the day, even when you had a headache. If you were lucky, it was soft and warm, made up of tiny memories of Maddie's first high-speed jog across the living room and Thomas's reliable glee at her same old knock-knock jokes and the scent of freshly cut grass on the breeze.

Benny gave her a peck on the nose and pulled the covers high, turning his back to her with a pleasant enough "Good night."

She hated going to bed mad. One of the more infuriating things about Benny was that he had no problem doing it, and the next day he'd act like everything was fine. Which, to him, it often was.

She could handle herself. Did he not trust that she could? To Clara, trust was so tangled up with love that it made her chest hurt when she thought about it. Maybe she didn't have much sense of herself these days. Her every choice was ruled by the children. But that in itself was one of the few choices she *had* made. What right did Benny have to call it into question?

Even on days when she'd grappled with her stay-at-home role, she hadn't fantasized about going back to work in anything but the most tangential terms: To eat lunch uninterrupted at a desk. To get through a cup of coffee without it growing cold.

If it took Benny questioning her place to make her feel more solid in it, then she wouldn't begrudge the question. She'd be glad of it even as she answered him with an emphatic no.

But she couldn't help but wonder what it meant, really, that he had asked.

27

Campsites designated "walk-in" are reserved on a first-come basis. Stake your claim by displaying your receipt on the numbered site post. Anyone caught tampering with reservation tags will be asked to leave the park. Because seriously, who does that?

—Sign posted at the John Bryan State Park
camp office

A week to the day after Izzy's brunch, Paul rolled tentatively down his driveway, successfully steered onto the street, and sat revving the motorcycle engine at the end of her driveway. He was wearing a bulky black leather jacket, narc-like mirrored sunglasses, jeans, and black boots she'd never seen before—and looking so much like he was playing the role of some parallel universe Paul that she had to laugh.

"Hello, Parallel Universe Paul," she said before she could stop herself.

She let go of the walk-behind aerator she'd been pushing awkwardly through the soil and wiped her sweaty hands on her jeans. She might not have made any progress with Penny, or Josh, or even her parents, but she *had* read up on fall lawn maintenance, and thus here she was. Maintaining.

He laughed. "You could say that. Want to join me on a ride through the other dimension?"

She stepped back to take a better look at the machine rumbling beneath him. It was . . . well, she knew nothing about motorcycles, but this one was quite shiny at the moment. Beads of water trembled in the spots he'd missed wiping dry after its bath.

"Tempting. But this is the first day all week that it hasn't rained, so I feel like I need to take advantage."

He eyed the primitive contraption at her fingertips, its wheel of steel spikes poised to resume its laborious tilling. "I do enjoy a medieval torture device on a crisp fall day. It's a close second to riding through the cool air, the colorful leaves all around you . . ."

"I'll have you know this torture device is going to fortify my lawn before winter."

He looked around. "It's *unfortified*? I didn't realize. Should I dig a moat while you push?"

She raised an eyebrow, trying not to waver. This of all tasks seemed so much like the sort of thing one should enlist either a husband or a lawn service to do that it somehow seemed important—symbolic, even—that she do it on her own. And she'd had a mind to do it now, today—to act on the conviction before it faded.

"I promised my mother I'd never ride on one," she said. It was true—her mother loathed motorcycles—though she'd made the promise only because she'd been quite sure she'd never be tempted.

"Ouch. I should hope not," he said, shrinking back from the aerator, and she laughed. Admittedly, when Randi and Rhoda had agreed to let her borrow the machine—evidence they really did have *all* the tools—she hadn't been expecting something so lethal looking. Or so surprisingly difficult to push.

"I promised Kristin too," he admitted, and he said her name so unflinchingly that Izzy managed not to cringe. "It's one of the old toys I'm not allowed to play with anymore. I was just cleaning out the garage." They both turned to look at his house, for no reason other than the fact that he'd mentioned it. "I don't want to get ahead of myself, but it's been a month. Something about that benchmark makes it seem like they're really gone. And if they are . . . I can't hang on to this house. It's too much."

She wasn't sure if he meant in the physical sense, as in the house was too big, or the emotional sense, as in too many painful memories resided inside, but she suspected both applied. Halloween was approaching, the Little Holiday That Could in that it spanned weeks of festivals and events here in small-town Ohio, and she imagined him busying himself to avoid thinking of a year without his own duo of costumed trick-or-treaters. Avoidance would be a hard trick.

"This might be its last spin," Paul said, turning the grip so the engine revved again. "I should have sold it years ago, and I can't start riding again now that I'm allowed to. It would look too much like I'm having a midlife crisis."

"Are you, though?" He had reason enough.

"Yes, of course. But it would *look* like it."

She laughed. He wasn't as unlike her as she'd once thought, really. If nothing else, they were both misunderstood.

"Sure you don't need a break?" he asked once more. "Or a hand? I don't have to go."

Again Izzy wondered if she should feel more hesitation about Paul. But what she felt was the opposite: the sort of compulsion toward forward motion that could finally pull her out of her funk. If she couldn't do it herself, why *not* let some external force give it a try? And the only force that had been making itself available was again right here before her.

"I'll get my coat," she said.

The ride was exhilarating. It made Izzy feel alive. And not so much because of the wind tangling her hair or the road rumbling beneath them as they headed away from town, following the county highways that curved intermittently through expanses of farmland and patches of forest, but because of all the reasons she *perhaps* shouldn't be doing what she was doing—her arms tightly wrapped around Paul's waist, as he'd instructed—and all the reasons she had every right to do it anyway.

She'd always thought that a bicycle on a beautiful day was pure freedom. If that was true, then a motorcycle was a notch above freedom into the realm of danger. It was rebellion. No wonder every stereotype put a rebel at the handlebars and a gritty girl along for the ride.

Ahead was an overlook, a simple semicircle on the side of the road, and Paul slowed, pulling the motorcycle onto the patch of gravel and cutting the engine. They dismounted in silence, unstrapped their helmets—which Izzy had insisted they wear, in spite of his halfhearted grumbling—and walked companionably to the stone wall. Izzy must have driven past this spot a dozen times going to and from Springfield, but she'd never stopped. The drop was dizzying: Far beneath them, a rocky creek disappeared into a canopy of trees clinging defiantly to their brightest leaves. In the vacuum left by the sudden silencing of the motor, she could hear the calling of a single whippoorwill.

She said the word aloud, almost involuntarily. "Whippoorwill."

Paul cocked his head to listen. "How can you tell?"

"It's saying its own name." The bird paused as if waiting for Paul to catch on, then started up again. She never heard one without thinking of the first time she'd noticed the bird's song. Her father had pointed it out one summer evening as they'd been sitting around the campfire, just the two of them, neither her mother nor Penny having an interest in the overnight, and it had suddenly seemed so clear to her that the bird was relentlessly asserting its place in the forest. *Whip-por-will, whip-por-will, whip-por-will . . .* She liked to think that even if her father hadn't been there at all, she'd have recognized the birdsong for what it was.

If only she had asserted herself so clearly in the landscape of her own life, rather than waiting for it all to fall into place around her, who knew where she might be now.

"So it is," Paul said. The bird was hitting its stride, picking up steam. "And the song *is* long. Like Randy Travis promised."

She smiled. "I had the same thought first time I heard it." She'd felt gratitude toward the whippoorwill that night, her tired feet propped on the fire ring next to her dad's, as she took in the reminder that knowing something existed wasn't the same as experiencing it for yourself. Like reading about love: You couldn't fully understand it, no matter how brilliant the prose, until you had your first taste.

It was the memory of her father's easy company that delivered the sharpest pang now. Her humiliation at the way he'd called her out last weekend still burned; her fear that he thought less of her than he once had was almost more than she could bear.

"What do you think about out there?" Paul asked. "On your hikes, I mean. I don't know how you spend so much time alone. I'm still getting used to it." He coughed, and his cheeks colored. "That sounded insensitive. I didn't mean—"

"It's okay." Izzy wasn't offended. He was right. She did spend a lot of time alone. And then she wandered into the woods in search of more solitude to top it off.

Only now she was pining for those days when companionship—with her father, Josh, Penny—had been more or less a given. How audacious she'd been.

"To tell you the truth, I think a lot about the fact that I think too much."

He burst out laughing, and she grinned sheepishly. Just as well. A normal person would have *meant* it as a joke.

"I wish I could be more like that," he said.

"No, you don't." Her eyes were on the shadows quivering on the patches of water below, but she could feel him watching her and knew she shouldn't have sounded so adamant.

"I do," he said. "To tell *you* the truth, I don't think enough about the fact that I don't think enough." She dared to look at him then. His eyes had turned serious, but a faint smile still played on his lips. He must have run a hand through his sweat-dampened hair to undo the helmet's flattening job; it stuck out in all directions, putting her in mind of a child watching morning cartoons in his pajamas.

"I should try that," she said. Of the two of them, by all rights Paul should have been the one having more trouble leaving his burdens behind. The fact that he was not might have said something about him—but instead she had the feeling it laid bare her own flawed tendencies.

"Want to try it now?"

He moved a lock of her hair away from her face, and she didn't have *time* to think. His kiss was gentle but not tentative. She took a step back, surprised, but his face never left hers, and she let him follow. When was the last time anyone had followed her anywhere? The brush of his hands against her arms made them buzz with near-electric current. It had been so long since anyone at all had touched her this way—or, more to the point, touched her any way at all.

But what were they doing? Where could this possibly go? What would anyone think—Clara or Rhoda or Randi, let alone the rest of the town?

Then again, did it matter? Where had caring so much about what other people thought gotten her, other than alone and unhappy?

With that final thought, she did try it. She let her mind go pleasantly blank and drank from the void.

When the kiss ended, there was no seismic shift beneath their feet.

"Ready to head back?" he asked softly. She nodded, and he smiled, and then it was almost as if it had never happened.

Almost.

Giving herself over to a moment was one thing. Avoiding deep thought in a more real sense would take some doing. And probably a lot of practice. *And maybe,* a nagging part of her brain was already whispering, *rethinking*—though that was contradictory to the point, obviously.

She was still telling herself not to think about what had happened with Paul as he steered them back toward town, racing against the rain as the cloud cover thickened without warning. She was still telling herself not to think about it as they approached the final turn, his house majestic on the corner, and she found herself imagining what might transpire or how she might feel or what Paul would do if Kristin were to materialize just now at the front door, her hands disapprovingly on her hips, her twins at her side. She was still telling herself not to think about it as she caught sight of Clara—sidewalk chalk in her hand, children and that flopsy new dog at her feet, jaw dropped slightly—watching Izzy dismount the bike. And she was beseeching her mind to revert to that moment of blissful blank as she handed Paul his helmet, gave him a shy wave and a smile, her face burning, and lifted the waving arm higher to include Clara, who only stood expressionless until she finally looked away.

28

You sound so innocent, the way you say your
kids weren't "happy" in their rear-facing car seats
anymore, like that's actually justification for
facing them forward a full six months before
the recommended age of two. You're literally
risking their lives just so they can be "happier"?

—*Anonymous comment left on one of Kristin
Kirkland's posts to the school's Circle of
Parents blog, to which Clara anonymously
replied, before Kristin had a chance, "Fuck off"*

Izzy?" Clara's voice was drowned out by the rumble of Paul's motorcycle maneuvering up his driveway. Thank God her head was back to normal now. Only the bruise remained, and at least the bruise didn't mind the racket. Izzy was fumbling with her keys, about to disappear through her front door. Clara called out again, not a question this time. "Izzy!" Her voice sounded disproportionately frantic, and when Izzy turned, her keys clattering to the concrete stoop, she looked taken aback.

"Sorry!" Clara yelled good-naturedly, taking a few steps toward the curb. "Loud!" She gestured toward Paul's house just as the engine went silent, and Izzy nodded.

"I just wondered if you wanted to come for dinner. Benny's going to fire up the grill."

Izzy looked up at the cold front whizzing by overhead, and Clara's eyes followed hers. The thick clouds were moving with such determination they almost looked like time-lapsed freeze-frames of a sky. "Looks like rain," Izzy called.

"Oh, Benny doesn't mind," Clara said easily. "Actually, he has no choice. He does this every fall, buying out Tom's Market when he thinks it's nice enough for one last barbecue. I won't tell you how many 'one last' barbecues we had last year."

"Well," Izzy said, "if there's one season worth being nostalgic for, summer's it."

It seemed to Clara that Izzy was capable of being nostalgic for just about anything, but she wouldn't have said so. "That's why you should come!"

Izzy glanced at Paul's house, then away. Clara was banking on the fact that she didn't have plans tonight, or any way in such close proximity to pretend that she did. Because when she'd caught sight of Izzy a moment before, on the back of Paul's bike, her head turned into the cranny between his shoulder blades, what she'd felt wasn't nagging worry or niggling concern.

It was fear. A jolt of fear that made her fingertips go numb.

And as she'd watched her friend wave halfheartedly, and watched Paul purposefully not look in her own direction, and watched Izzy turn and head up the walk, the frozen grip that held her under its siege had hissed into her ear, *Don't just stand there, do something*.

She might have hurled a warning at the retreating form of Paul's poseur leather jacket. She might have run across the street to seize Izzy by the wrists and ask, "What could you possibly be thinking?" But instead, she had opened her mouth, uncertain of what to say, and out had come a polite dinner invitation.

"Twist my arm," Izzy said with a weak smile. "What time?"

————

Benny caught his wife's elbow gently at the top of the stairs, steering her back into the dark hallway that ran the length of the old farmhouse's second floor. She could hear the kids giggling from Thomas's room, where they were awaiting one of Daddy's famous stories—no book required. It wasn't that Benny made them up; rather, he stole plotlines from movies they were too young to watch and adapted them to suit his audience. Clara always protested that the kids were going to grow up and realize their childhood had been full of spoilers without the alerts—that he'd ruined key scenes from *Rudy, Star Wars,* even *Forrest Gump.* Benny argued that kids would grow up to find out that *all* their youthful fairy tales were not what they'd once seemed.

Fatalism was where they differed.

"I really don't think you should mention it to her," Benny said. Downstairs, Izzy was awaiting Clara's return, a fresh bottle of wine open on the counter, the soft sounds of Southern blues floating up the stairs. Once they'd cleaned up dinner—the rain held out long enough for a spread of veggie kabobs, barbecued chicken, Amish-made sausage, even perfectly charred corn on the cob—Benny volunteered to handle bedtime so Clara and her friend could chat.

"Mention what?" Clara asked, trying to remain stone-faced.

"You know what. It's none of our business."

Clara narrowed her eyes. "It is. It's our business because we live here, and it's our business because I'm her friend."

"Let me rephrase. It's not your responsibility, Clara."

This was not a new argument between them. Because there was a universal question at the root of it: *What responsibility does anyone really have to someone else, aside from family?* It wasn't just that Kristin's disappearance had left everyone who'd known her wondering what, if anything, they should have sensed was going on behind closed doors, or what, if anything, they might have done to prevent her from vanishing. And it wasn't just that her persistent failure to reappear with the twins had thickened and stagnated in the air of their old house, though that was true enough too. This was a question that had taken hold of them years before and never quite let go, because there was no answer they could agree upon.

Benny was the sort of person who could leave an unanswerable question unanswered.

Clara was not.

"If it's not my responsibility," she said coolly, "then whose is it, Ben?"

He frowned. He *hated* to be called Ben. That the short form of Benjamin was too much formality for Benny was one of thousands of things she'd loved about him from the start. She rarely pushed this particular button, and when she did, it wasn't to goad him.

It was a warning.

Benny sighed as a louder peal of giggles erupted from Thomas's open door, and they both instinctively moved to peer through, as such spontaneous laughter was more often these days soon followed by a cry of protest or pain. Clara and Benny watched from the hall as Thomas handed a bright orange stuffed lion to Maddie, who tossed it over his bedrail to the floor with such gusto that both kids burst into laughter. He then patted her sweetly on the head and handed her a blue elephant to launch. Their assembly line had already relocated half the contents of his bed, always a plush jungle, to a pile on the floor.

Benny and Clara exchanged a smile in spite of themselves. In truth, Clara would have preferred to follow Benny back in to cuddle the kids, listen to his stories and sing them song after song until they drifted off. It never ceased to amaze her that even when she'd had Thomas and Maddie to herself for most of the day—or for too much of it, with them driving her to the brink of sanity with their competing demands—it still stung her to miss bedtime, for any reason.

It wasn't that Clara would rather talk to Izzy. It was that she had to.

"I could go down and tell her the kids wanted only you tonight," Benny said softly. "Make your apologies. Tell her you'll see her tomorrow. Buy you time to sleep on it."

She shook her head. "I won't sleep otherwise," she said. "That's the problem."

"You don't even know that anything is going on between her and Paul."

"Exactly," she said. "But I'm going to find out."

She backed quietly away from Thomas's door and headed downstairs before Benny could stop her. She felt his eyes on her back, willing her to turn and give him one last chance at exchanging the kind of meaningful look that might change her mind. And so she didn't look back. She and Benny had done enough test runs on this argument—in more theoretical and less pressing scenarios—to know they could agree to disagree.

Never mind that in the ambient tension that was becoming their new norm, nothing seemed sure anymore. While she wasn't still mad about what he'd suggested the other night, she wasn't *not* mad, either—nor was she completely convinced he'd dropped the matter for good. But she also wasn't about to walk on eggshells around her own husband.

She found Izzy and Pup-Pup standing side by side in the area that joined the kitchen and the family room, staring through the window toward the dark patio, where the circle of chairs remained, untouched, around the fire pit from that early September night. Izzy had been a hit with the kids at dinner, challenging Thomas to a corn on the cob eating contest and clinking her cup to Maddie's sippy with a "cheers!" roughly every thirty seconds, indulging the baby's favorite new mealtime trick. And she'd been an even bigger hit with Pup-Pup afterward, playing an endless game of tug-the-rope while Clara and Benny brushed off her offers to help clean up. Now, in the dim track lighting, she looked relaxed, if a little sad, swaying slowly with the music. Hearing Clara's approach, she turned and smiled, her eyes already turning glassy from the second—or was this her third?—glass of wine. It was impossible not to think of that last night with Kristin, around the fire. Of how at home they'd all seemed in their neighborhood then. Of how it hadn't felt the same since.

Izzy gestured at the fire pit. "I was going to suggest we light one, but it's starting to sprinkle." A beat of silence passed between them, and Izzy gave an almost apologetic smile. "Might be weird, any-way," she said softly.

"It's not as if I'm never going to use the patio again . . ." Clara began. For some reason, the idea of taking their seats around the circle with Kristin gone still made her shiver. "But yeah."

It was silly. Kristin would likely never know, much less care, whether Clara and her other neighbors removed her chair and tight-ened their circle around the fire. It wasn't all that different from the way Izzy punished her stubborn heartbreak by drowning it in morbid headlines, and Clara turned away from those same stories on the principle of not giving the bad guys the satisfaction. She sup-posed the joke was on both of them that none of it mattered. Nei-ther the perpetrators nor the victims knew if you watched their footage all day or feigned ignorance. All they knew was that the headlines were there, and for many of them that was enough.

So when Clara took the obvious segue, she tried to sound non-chalant. "Making friends with Dr. Paul isn't weird, though?"

"Oh, that was Parallel Universe Paul," Izzy said quickly, and she almost succeeded at sounding dismissive. Almost.

Clara wrinkled her forehead. "A universe where Paul and Kris-tin never happened?"

"No. I mean, yes." She laughed uneasily. "I didn't mean any-thing that deep. Just one where he wears leather and drives a motorcycle."

"Would that make him more your type?" Clara moved to pour herself a glass of wine at the island behind them.

"In what way?" Izzy wouldn't look at her.

"Oh, you know," Clara said. "Benny always said he was 'more of an indoor guy.'"

Izzy gave a little laugh. "Truer words," she said. Her eyes met Clara's then. "Still. I thought handsome doctors were supposed to be everyone's type."

"Men with missing wives, though . . ."

Clara couldn't believe she'd said it aloud. She held her breath.

"Ex. Soon to be ex." Izzy's voice had an edge to it, which Clara had expected. What she hadn't anticipated was that the part Izzy took issue with was the word *wife*, not *missing*. She checked herself, deciding to back up.

"You've been spending time with him, though?"

"Here and there. We run into each other." Pup-Pup abruptly turned and left the room, and Clara heard his tags jiggling up the stairs, as if he'd already heard enough. Somehow, in spite of the fact that Clara was the one home all day, he seemed to have designated Benny as the alpha. They'd go for long walks in the dark before bed and Pup-Pup would come home panting with glee.

She took a breath. "I have to say, Iz, I'm not sure it's the best idea."

"It's just neighborly stuff," Izzy said. "I can't see how that would be a bad idea."

"I didn't say *bad*. I said *not the best*." Clara's lips had gone dry, and she licked them nervously. "How much time together are we talking about, just out of curiosity?"

A small smile played on Izzy's lips, then disappeared.

"Not enough to warrant an intervention," Izzy said, trying to laugh it off. "Let's not blow it out of proportion."

"Am I?" Clara bit her lip. "Forget what I think, or what I'm worried about. Think about how it might look. It's not as if no one's paying attention to what Paul's up to these days."

A light in Izzy's eyes was going dim, clouded out in a way that reminded her of a movie line Thomas liked to quote. It had to do with being between sad and mad. *Sad mad.* "You think I don't worry about how I look to other people? The also-ran who left town after her sister got the guy, who resigned herself to spinsterhood with a mortgage. The stick-in-the-mud behind a happy radio show. The loner on an early-bird schedule. I'm *tired* of it. I thought you were different. I thought we were friends."

Clara blinked at her. "We *are* friends," she said firmly. "I've never thought any of those things about you. And if anyone does, screw them."

"Who are they to judge, right?" Izzy said pointedly.

"Iz, you're taking this the wrong way. It's just that . . . for starters, Kristin's sister came to see me. She had some choice commentary on Dr. Paul."

"Of course she did. Her sister was divorcing him."

"But they were estranged. It's not as if Kristin colored her perceptions."

"I'm not one to be throwing stones where sisters are concerned. Or putting too much stock in one's opinion on the other, frankly."

"But Izzy. You saw Hallie's newspaper. I mean, I wasn't at all on board with distributing it, but what she wrote *was* true . . ."

"Hallie, the kid? What newspaper?"

"*The Color-Blind Gazette.*"

Izzy shrugged and shook her head.

How was it possible she'd really never seen it, never even heard about it? Hallie had suspected as much, and Clara had dismissed the idea. She felt almost relieved. All she had to do was explain—

"Wait a second. She did interview me for something . . ."

Clara brightened. "Yes! That's it."

"I thought that was a school project. It was distributed?"

"To put it mildly."

Izzy was frowning now. "But she said it was about *good* news. You're saying there was something in there about Kristin and Paul?"

She took a deep breath. "Good news is her new angle. Let's just say the original got her into some trouble. I can show—"

"Did you invite me over just to warn me off of Paul?" Izzy's voice was sharp.

"Of course not."

Izzy shook her head. "Your life is very full, Clara," she said softly. "You might have noticed that mine is not. I'm not exactly in a position to turn down offers to help me repair something, or to have someone keep me company for an hour or two. In fact, I think it's better I'm not left with my own thoughts more than necessary right now."

"But Benny and I are here. If you ever—"

Izzy put up a hand. "I'm not talking about intruding on other people's lives. I know Benny would be glad to lend a hand, but I also know he has plenty of better things to do. And Paul, you might have noticed, does not."

Clara cleared her throat. "But maybe there's a reason for that . . ."

"Sure there's a reason! His ex ran off with the kids he'd been raising for years. Honestly, if anyone's behavior here should be chastised, maybe it's the rest of the neighborhood, turning their backs on him, pretending he's not still here."

He's not *still here,* Clara thought. He's *back.* "You don't understand," she said instead. This was going all wrong. She'd expected Izzy to brush off her concerns, even to deny having more than passing contact with Paul. But why was she being so defensive? Unless . . .

"Did something happen between you two?" Clara blurted out. Izzy didn't answer, and the fear Clara had been trying to swallow came flooding back.

"Please, Izzy." She stopped short and glanced over her shoulder, toward the foyer, straining to hear any signs of Benny. The house was quiet. "When I pictured this conversation in my head, we were not standing in a dark kitchen. Let's sit down. Really talk."

Izzy looked at her strangely. "Why are you working through conversations with me in your head?"

Clara swiped the wine bottle off the counter with one hand, took her glass in the other, and crossed to the couch, where she deposited them on the end table. She switched on a table lamp, pressed the remote to lower the music volume, and curled at the end of the sectional, hoping Izzy would think it rude not to join her. Izzy's sigh was perceptible as she made her way to the opposite end, but she didn't sit, only stood there awkwardly, letting her question hang between them.

"Something happened," Clara said finally. "To change the way I talk through things with friends."

"How did you used to do it?"

"I didn't, actually."

"But now you do."

She sighed. "Not very well, evidently. But I try. If you think it's none of my business, Benny would agree. He subscribes to the keep-your-eyes-on-your-own-paper theory."

That they had walked away from the same tragedy having opposing reactions was one of the curious things about their marriage. But then again, maybe it was just a curious thing about tragedy. About how *individual* it can be, to everyone it touches.

"And what theory do you subscribe to?"

"More like *better safe than sorry.* Or *ask forgiveness, not permission.*" The caveat, of course, was that it had not escaped her attention that these particular theories could rationalize good deeds and bad indiscriminately.

"Hmm. Sure you don't want to go put the kids down? I'll hang out with Benny."

Clara laughed, grasping at the chance to maintain any trace of levity. "Izzy," she said, her eyes pleading, "I care about you. Just sit down and let me tell you this one story, okay?"

Izzy sighed. "I know she's your friend, but I think I've heard enough about Kristin."

"It's not about Kristin," Clara said, fighting to keep the desperation from her voice. "It's about me."

29

P.S. Has anyone ever told you that you'd make an amazing wife? I'm serious.

—*Last line of an email from Benny thanking Clara for a wonderful third date, in which she'd attempted to cook for him, burnt the pork chops so badly they seared themselves to the pan, and called out for Chinese delivery*

The ring sparkled so brightly on Clara's finger she couldn't stop staring at it. No matter that she was meant to be mingling with her colleagues and their guests rather than admiring her own hand like a mannequin in a Benetton window. Five years after graduation, six years after they'd become inseparable, seven years since she'd first set eyes on him, she was *really, finally, and forevermore* going to be Mrs. Benny Tiffin. Around the three-year mark her friends had started questioning if it would ever happen at all. But Clara had always known that there could be no better match than her and Benny, and that he would propose when they were both good and ready. The fact that he'd chosen to do so right before the holidays meant she had ample opportunities to show off her platinum-set proof.

She stole a glance across the hotel lobby, where her company holiday party was assembling before dinner. Benny was in line at one of the bar carts, talking congenially with her boss and looking eloquent as ever in a three-piece suit purchased for the occasion, his red tie and vest a precise match to her new cocktail dress. While they were by no means a large publisher—a collection of fine art imprints that just happened to call the Midwest home—the execs had gone all out this year, compensating for the previous Christmas's no-budget-is-met-so-no-party-we-get fail by renting out a whole wing of Lakeside Lodge. She'd heard some of her coworkers with kids grumbling about the implication that they were to stay overnight, the complication of finding babysitters this time of year, and on and on. But she was happy to have the chance to drink without worrying about the drive home. She and Benny had even packed swimsuits to make fools of themselves in the indoor water park come morning. Why not? They were giddy in their love, untouchable.

Her boss, Graham, was a nice man—almost too nice for good management, really. You could tell he had a hard time drawing lines where lines were customarily drawn. But then again, he'd started out as an artist, then worked in academia, and *then* taken the job overseeing their high-end coffee table books. That wasn't exactly a trajectory toward toeing the corporate line.

As she watched Graham clap a congratulatory hand on Benny's shoulder, she felt a jolt of pride in them both. Graham's team at the young imprint was composed of fairly green, overeager professionals, and they played right into the "work family" dynamic, both squabbling among themselves and covering for one another like siblings.

Clara was part of the foursome in editorial, along with Matt, the before-his-time hipster with so many computer monitors in his cubicle they called it Mission Control; Steve, the frat boy–turned–pseudoresponsible adult; and Liv, who always seemed unduly nervous about everything but then again probably should have been, given her penchant for both contributing to and distributing office gossip. They had a standing weekly happy hour, their quartet plus whomever else someone might rope in, and were at ease with one another in a way Clara took for granted. She was too young to know to be self-conscious, too naïve to worry the next morning about that comment she maybe shouldn't have made after that third beer she maybe shouldn't have had. She hadn't yet learned that age and experience had a way of making you guarded, even in aspects of life you didn't necessarily need to guard. And that when it came to things truly worthy of such protection, they could make you wide-eyed with insatiable worry.

In that moment, the whole of her thoughts were occupied by her fun work friends and her sparkly diamond ring. Matt and Steve had just reappeared and were scanning the crowd for their dates, and she raised an eyebrow at their telltale glassy eyes betraying their not-entirely-legal smoke break.

"The banquet room's ready for us," a voice from behind her said. She turned and caught the teasing glint in Liv's eye. "And not a moment too soon. If I had to watch you lovingly gaze from Benny to your hand and back again much longer, I'd be sick."

Clara bit her lip. Liv was newly unattached—she'd broken up with her boyfriend over Thanksgiving—and still feeling the sting of having no plus-one. Although she *had* brought a date, Dale, a good-looking gay friend who'd already earned his meal ticket just by drawing looks of envy at Liv from female staffers who didn't know better. Clara herself had mistaken Dale for a boyfriend when they'd first been introduced, at a pool party last summer. He was the kind of guy who was almost everyone's type, with an outgoing personality and a quick athletic build that had him carrying their half of the sand volleyball court to easy victories. She'd thought it was sweet how playful and affectionate he was with Liv, though she came to realize he was like that with most all of his friends.

"Sorry," she said. "You should probably keep your distance. I can't seem to help myself tonight." It was true. She blamed the twinkling lights strung overhead, the garland catching the simulated candlelight from the chandeliers, the drinks flowing on her employer's dime, the piano player in the corner who was doing a damn good job crooning Bing Crosby–esque Christmas classics.

Liv smiled at her, only a hint of wistfulness showing through. "I know that look. This is one of those perfect moments for you, isn't it? When you suddenly look around and just *love* everyone? When you feel that everything seems so wonderful you just want to freeze-frame it in your brain?"

Clara gave her hand a squeeze, then dropped it as Dale approached. She was glad he was here for Liv. Clara had been the designated postbreakup sounding board at work, but Liv's ex-boyfriend had come off as such a creep—always stirring up some sort of on-again-off-again melodrama—that weeks later Clara was having a harder time mustering a sympathetic ear. One of the warmest people she knew—at least, when she wasn't licking her wounds—Liv so clearly deserved better. But she wasn't going to reassure her of that for the one hundredth time tonight. No, tonight belonged to her and Benny. She was going to go ahead and be nauseatingly happy, and anyone who didn't like it could go be nauseated somewhere else.

"It's time for Graham to carve the roast beast!" Matt called out, and the crowd around them laughed.

"Graham the Grinch?" someone called out. "Hardly!"

"He was the big-hearted version by dinner," Graham shot back, and a second ripple of laughter followed him.

Matt and Steve had located their girlfriends and were strolling gallantly toward Liv and Clara, arm in arm, like they belonged in an old-fashioned formal promenade.

"I will allow the giddiness from *you* tonight, but these clowns better tone it down," Liv mumbled, and Clara laughed.

Then Benny was wrapping his arm around her waist, and Dale started doing a Yellow Brick Road dance toward the ballroom that made Liv laugh harder than she had for weeks, and they all filed in to find their place cards at the circular tables. Their company was not particularly large, but when everyone had a guest, the doubled crowd was impressive. Soon the room was loud with clanging silverware, clinking glasses, chatting, and laughter. Salads were ready at each place setting, warm rolls were passed, and entrees under silver domes were gallantly served. The top managers stood and gave year-end toasts during dinner; Graham went last, speaking over the bustle of the waitstaff's valiant efforts to unobtrusively clear the plates, beginning with, "A word from our sponsors . . ." and ending with Clara and Liv teary eyed with gratitude, and Matt and Steve rolling their eyes in a way that only half hid their own emotion.

"Are you guys hiring?" Benny murmured into her ear. "Because I suddenly realize my company has a way bigger stick up its ass."

"We're creatives. It's not our fault the stereotypes about accountants are true."

"And yet you're marrying one."

"I guess there's no accounting for taste." She winked at him. "Get it? Accounting?"

"I wonder if it's too late to get my own room?" Benny mused.

"Where *is* your room?" Liv asked, leaning across the table so only Clara could hear. "And do you have any clear nail polish in it? I've got a run in my nylons, but we're a hike to the end of the wing."

Clara self-consciously crossed her bare ankles beneath her. "Sorry. Can't stand the feel of those things on my legs! And I'm lazy about my nails."

Liv turned to Dale. "I'm just going to slip out now, before the real fun starts." A band had been setting up in front of the small dance floor, and they looked to be about to get started. Liv shot Clara a smile. "For once, I have a date who can dance! Will you guys get me more wine if they come around? And if they're taking dessert orders, my order is YES."

"I can't promise not to eat yours," Dale said, "but I can promise to order it."

"Fair enough."

As she disappeared into the hallway, the singer took the microphone and introduced the band. "We're going to start nice and slow while you all enjoy some coffee and cheesecake," he crooned, "but stick around for the real show." The opening notes of "Hotel California" filled the room.

"Is this a Christmas party, a wedding, or a bar mitzvah?" Dale asked. "I've lost track."

"If the 'real show' is 'Hava Nagila,' we can rule out Christmas," Matt said, and the table erupted.

"If it's 'Twist and Shout,' we'll assemble a bridal party," Clara said with a laugh.

Benny leaned in so only she could hear. "I'd marry you right now," he said, nuzzling her ear. She felt so full, so warm.

"Cheesecake?" A server was hovering above them, trying not to look impatient. Clara waved him away. "If I eat another bite, I'll never get up. But Dale here will have two."

"So will I," Benny said, and Dale let out a whistle of approval.

Clara folded her cloth napkin neatly on the table. "I'm going to hit the ladies' room," she said. "Who wants something from the bar on the way back?" All the hands at the table went up, and she lifted her own in surrender. "Too many! I'll meet you in line."

There was no wait for a stall, and Clara lingered at the sink, perusing the courtesy lotions and sprays and helping herself to a mint. As she meandered back through the lobby, she stopped at a display of a porcelain street scene from *It's a Wonderful Life,* nestled in white mounds of soft cotton meant to look like snow. She bent to peer into the lighted windows of the little Victorian on the end, admiring the detail, right down to the miniature "George Lassos the Moon" art print inside. Maybe she and Benny should come here, party or no party, *every* Christmas. They'd bring their children one day, gather around the communal fireplace to eat sugar cookies, delight in the water park's mash-up of indoor palm trees strung with white lights. She felt like a child herself. What a magical place her boss had chosen. She should find him and tell him so.

But she didn't need to find him. Here he was, rushing into the hall, his eyes wild, as the hotel manager and a pair of uniformed security guards rushed toward him. "A disturbance in your block of rooms," she heard the manager say, his tone low but brusque. "The police have been called."

Clara's feet were moving now, following them, not stopping to think. Benny filled the doorway of the ballroom, a look of confusion on his face, and wordlessly fell into step next to her. The men were almost running. "What's going on?" she heard Matt call behind them. But none of them turned to answer. At the end of the hall, a security guard threw open a stairwell door.

"One flight up," he barked, as his partner rushed past him. "Us first," he called over his shoulder to Graham, before charging up the stairs.

Clara could already hear the screaming. No, *wailing.* She couldn't discern if it was male or female. But she saw soon enough. It was Dale, his hands over his face, just inside the door to the second-floor hallway. He lifted a shaking arm and pointed to the opposite end of the corridor. "It was her *ex-boyfriend*!" he screamed. "He ran that way! Oh, God, why . . ."

The uniformed guards charged off. Clara reached the top step and looked past Dale into the hall. Smears of red on cream flowered wallpaper. A woman standing frozen in the doorway of an open room—somebody's wife, Clara couldn't remember whose. "I'm the one who called," the woman said, her voice far away. "I heard her screaming—I was scared to open the door—but I should have . . . I should have . . ." She looked pale enough to faint.

Midway down the hall, a crumpled form on the floor. One security guard dropped to his knees beside the tangle of arms and legs, and the other kept going, in the direction where Dale had pointed. The manager yelled, "Stay back!" but Graham pushed ahead, and then he was screaming too. The word *no. Please no.* Over and over.

There were so very many smears of red on the walls. Both sides, some of the doors too. Benny put out an arm, pressed Clara behind him, just as her toe kicked something hard.

She sank to the floor, still not understanding, and her fingers closed around something smooth and cold. She knew before looking that it was a bottle of clear nail polish.

30

If you knew today might be the last day of your life, would you be less snippy with the slow bagger at the grocery store, even though you were running late? Would you tell your neighbor you didn't mind the intrusion, rather than showing that you so obviously did? Would you donate money to the person in need who asked for it?

If, in my absence, people reflect upon my day-to-day and remark that I was kind, this is why. A daily visual of sand slipping through an hourglass can do wonders for your social skills. Try it sometime.

It was never that I cared what people thought of me. It was that I'd made such a mess of things, I wanted to try to be good in some small, other way. To give the bagger faith that not every customer was rude. To give the neighbor a feeling of living among goodwill. To extend a courtesy to the person in need—because I knew too well that kindness could be in short supply at home. Besides, as they say, you can't take it with you.

Of course, there was also the need to keep up appearances for my husband's sake. Come to think of it, take the two factors combined, and I bet I look like a saint. Except for everything he's undoubtedly done his best to undo since I've been gone. Painting himself as the victim. Pointing fingers at the money. There was a time it would have made me sick, filled me with a rage that might even rival his own.

But it doesn't matter anymore.

He can't touch me now.

31

A grief counselor will be on hand throughout the week, by appointment, in the human resources suite. It can take time to fully realize the impact such a sudden and shocking event may have on those involved. If you find yourself questioning whether you might benefit from this service, please take advantage of it while it's available.

—Monday morning corporate memo to all employees

Clara had finished talking, and it was clearly Izzy's turn to say something. It was just that she couldn't imagine what the appropriate response to such a story might be. Clara's eyes had a faraway look, and she'd grown pale, as if the story had taken her back to that hallway.

"She was . . . ?"

Clara nodded, and the lump in Izzy's throat bobbed closer to the surface.

"I'm so sorry. Did they catch the guy?"

"He didn't get far. I don't think he had much interest in not being caught." Clara hugged herself and shivered, though the room was almost muggy from the overexcited furnace returning from its summer hiatus. "Dale wouldn't stop beating himself up that he hadn't gone back to the room with her, but it probably saved his life that he didn't. *He* was hiding there, waiting. He had a big knife. He didn't know that she and Dale weren't more than friends. He point-blank told the cops that if he couldn't have her no one could."

"Jesus." Izzy was trying to remember if she'd heard about this on the news. She hadn't always spent so much time swimming in tragic headlines—and domestic violence stories were so sadly common they had a way of running together. "What was his name?"

"I don't like to say his name." Clara's eyes were steely. "It doesn't matter."

Izzy thought back to that first night after Kristin's disappearance, the way Clara had come in and muted the TV coverage of the mass shooter. What was that line of poetry she'd quoted? Something about victims rising above with their beauty. Fraught as that night had been, Izzy had never seen Clara so serious as she was now. Gone was her self-deprecating humor and fully in-the-moment presence. In its place was a jittery hand-wringing Izzy had never seen in her friend before. And most unnerving of all, it was being directed at her.

And Paul.

"It haunted me, for a long time," Clara said quietly. "It wasn't just the *unthinkableness* of it. It was the unfairness, that somehow I ended up with Benny—God, I spent that whole damn night mesmerized by the ring on my finger—while Liv, who was not very unlike me at all, ended up . . . you know. There's *no* reason one of us deserved one fate, and the other . . ."

Izzy tried to imagine what it might be like to try to wipe the picture of a blood-streaked hallway from your mind when the image wasn't one you'd simply seen on the news but one you'd stood in the middle of—and when the blood belonged not to an anonymous victim but to a friend who moments before had been sitting with you at dinner, laughing, smiling, breathing, living. She felt small by comparison, hung up as she'd been on her own brush with unfairness. Just this afternoon, she'd managed to let go. The wind turning her cheeks pink, the warmth of Paul's leather coat soaking into her core. And now . . .

"This is a horrible story," she said cautiously. "But what does it have to do with Paul?"

Clara bent to open the drawer at the base of the end table, removed a stapled stack of paper with *The Color-Blind Gazette* laser-printed across the top, and handed it over without a word. Izzy started to read, feeling her heart tighten. How had she missed this? It had gone out to the whole neighborhood? She lifted her eyes to Clara, who nodded.

Her hair fell over her face as she forced her way from one paragraph to the next and questions flooded her mind—too many to voice.

But while the details of the article were troubling, they also could be circumstantial. One thing was certain: This was *not* "good news," and even as she read, a back corner of her mind worried over her own interview with Hallie, and whether she'd given the girl any reason to try to seek out the "real story" behind her day-to-day—a thought she impatiently shoved aside. This wasn't about her. It was about Kristin.

It was about Paul.

She thought of his mention of canceled appointments, his quickly disguised frown. Was this why? What humiliation for him, to have this out there.

She sneaked another glance at Clara, but her neighbor was no longer watching her read, only staring blankly toward the large back windows. A short distance through the darkness, Paul was probably sprawled on his own couch, alone, his ears burning.

When she reached the end, Izzy took a minute to absorb the sight of Clara's name in the credits and set the paper on the couch next to her.

"Same question," she said, trying to keep her voice flat. "How does what happened to your friend Liv have anything to do with Paul?"

Clara met her eyes with a look that said she'd hoped she wouldn't have to spell it out for her. "Izzy, I've seen how quickly a relationship can turn deadly dangerous. When no one would have suspected." She seemed to be choosing her words carefully, though clearly she'd planned to deliver this speech all along.

Izzy thought back to that hike weeks ago, side by side in the ravine, how mystified Paul had seemed as to why he could have been left, how despondent without any lead on the twins. What he'd said about his childhood—it had seemed to her that all he really wanted was a second chance at a family. And to give someone else a second chance at one too. It hadn't worked out, but plenty of marriages failed. When people got defensive about "blaming the victim," they didn't usually mean the man in the relationship. But that was how Izzy was feeling on his behalf now. It just didn't seem to add up.

"You're not implying that Paul did off with Kristin and the kids?" Izzy forced a laugh. "There'd have been more to this if the police really suspected such a thing."

"I'm implying that we don't know *what* went on, but the worst is always possible. I'm implying that I've missed my chance to recognize the signs of trouble, to intervene and help a friend before, and I'm not about to do it again." Her voice was taking on a decidedly un-Clara pitch, high and tense.

"You told me yourself, that first night after she left, that you never saw any evidence of domestic violence next door. Don't you think we would have seen or heard *something*?"

"I was blindsided by what happened to Liv. In hindsight, I've learned abusers don't always have obvious red flags—bursts of temper, the stuff you see on made-for-TV movies. With Liv's ex the warnings were more subtle. Always checking in with her, keeping tabs, in a way that seemed a bit obsessive to the rest of us but to her seemed sweet. Trying to keep her to himself—talking her into skipping our happy hours to meet him, for instance, instead of him just joining the group. He had an ego, gave off a vibe that she should be more grateful for things he'd done, even though it was just ordinary relationship stuff no one else would expect a medal for."

"But plenty of men who are like that *are* just being sweet, and *do* just have fragile egos."

"They usually mellow out as the relationship gets comfortable, though, right? With Liv, this guy got more intense as time went on." She leaned forward. "I told you Kristin's sister came to see me. She blamed Paul for their estrangement, said he isolated Kristin from her family, manipulated things, made her overly reliant on him from the very start."

The last part seemed to be directed at her, which was ridiculous. A gate latch and a taillight were hardly the equivalent of fatherless twins. "That's her side of the story. Like I said, when it comes to sisters . . ."

Izzy found herself blinking back tears. She was in no position to be judged through her sister's eyes—and Penny would rightly say the same of her. Had their closeness *ever* been what it seemed? Surely if they'd truly been in tune to each other, things would have turned out differently.

"You're right," Clara conceded. "But still, with Paul, there's reasonable doubt. Why did Kristin follow him here, when it meant being farther from her mom, who was terribly sick? She went all in on their life together, so even when it didn't work out, why would she take the kids from him? Why search online for domestic violence help right before she disappeared? You know as well as I did it didn't come up around the fire that night."

Izzy was tired of people trying to figure out why things happened. Why that first date didn't call back for a second date. Why someone would go into a crowded place with a loaded gun to punish the wrong people for things beyond their control. Why certain lives are rocked by crisis while others glide peacefully by. Why anyone should risk falling in love at all. So much, too much, of our lives spent fruitlessly searching for explanations where there are none.

Clara seemed insatiable in her search for answers. Or maybe she was just caught up in it so tightly she couldn't break free. But Izzy was tired.

Maybe it was time to stop harping on the *whys* of the world and instead look for a new *who* or *what*.

"I don't know any such thing," she told Clara, trying not to let irritation show. "Like I told you, I can't remember the whole night. I don't even remember going home."

Clara shook her head at her. "Well, I can assure you no one mentioned the subject."

"You were drunk too. Maybe it was you." Clara stared, the blood draining from her face, and Izzy felt she'd pushed something she shouldn't have, but she was too irritated to back down. She shrugged. "Maybe you mentioned Liv?"

A weighty silence filled the room, and when Clara finally spoke, her voice was soft and cool, but clear. "I do not talk about what happened with Liv. When I do, it's for good reason. In this case, the reason is this: The very *possibility* that something is not right with Paul should be enough to keep you away. The stakes are too high. I'm telling you, from personal experience I wish I didn't have, that the best line of defense against men who are programmed this way is *not to get involved with them from the start*. Once you do, it can be incredibly hard to get away. Maybe impossible. Look at Liv. Look at Kristin."

Izzy considered Clara—who always seemed so thoughtful, so self-possessed, if a bit scattered at times. But she didn't seem that way now.

"Do the police know about this . . . this thing you were involved in?"

Clara sighed. "They do. I'd been interviewed as a witness, subpoenaed to testify, though it never went to court. He ended up pleading to a lesser charge."

"A lesser charge?"

"Eighteen years from now, he *could* get out. Depending on what the parole board decides. These people, they're out in the world, Izzy. They don't always get what they deserve—not even when they get caught."

She could see how Clara would be overcautious. She could.

But she could also see how Clara would be *paranoid*. Fearful of perfectly harmless men. She didn't love the idea of her hurling accusations around. Not here in the quiet of her living room, or on the pages of this newspaper, which Izzy tapped with a brusque finger now.

"Your name is on this."

"I had promised to help Hallie with the paper—in general terms—before I knew what she planned to put in it. When she brought it to me, I told her *not* to publish it."

How had Hallie even known? Izzy shook her head. That seemed beside the point, since this was old news to everyone but her. No *wonder* the girl had frozen up that day in the yard when Paul had appeared. Izzy, as usual, had had no clue.

"I know it doesn't look good that my name is there," Clara said, "but frankly I don't care about that. I care about you. I lost a friend all those years ago, and I lost another when Kristin vanished—for whatever reason. I don't want to risk losing you too."

Maybe Izzy really was the only one with *any* sympathy for Paul. Maybe that was why she always seemed to be the one to cross his path—from that very first day he'd come across the street, worried and confused. Because no one else was interested in being anywhere near it.

"I appreciate the sentiment, but who I choose to spend my time with isn't up for debate, okay? There's another side to this in which Paul could really use a friend right now."

Clara sighed. "I'll say it again—I don't care about him either. I care about you."

"Well, maybe *I* care about him." Izzy didn't know whether it was true on anything but a surface level, but Clara looked as if she'd been slapped. "He's lonely, Clara. He's probably the loneliest person I know. He even has *me* beat."

Clara's eyes filled with such pity and concern that Izzy had to look away. "Loneliness is not a bond upon which to build a relationship," Clara said quietly.

Izzy blinked at her. "Could have fooled me," she said. "Seen a rom-com lately? They make it seem far less pathetic than it is in real life. Where it happens *all* the time. Hop on Match and see for yourself."

"So you're saying there are plenty of lonely people to choose from, then," Clara shot back. "If that's what you want, choose one of them. I'm begging you, Iz. I have a bad feeling. Kristin's sister did too—all along."

Izzy sighed. Earlier today, unexpected and strange though the whole motorcycle ride had been, Izzy had gone inside, shut the door, and *smiled*.

It had felt so good. Just to smile a genuine smile into an empty room. To be a giddy girl home from a date, if only for a moment. She had expected that kissing anyone but Josh would feel like . . . well, like giving up, she supposed. It was ridiculous, really. He'd given her up long ago. But the fact that she *hadn't* felt that defeat but, instead, a spark of energy, had given her a jolt. And a good kind of jolt. Not necessarily one that was specific to Paul—she wasn't sure about that yet—but one that hit her like the beam of a searchlight.

Now, only a few hours later, she was already ruining the small thrill of the afternoon. She was ruining *all* of it. Izzy had heard enough.

"I promise, if *I* get a bad feeling, I'll stay away."

She stood to leave. Clara looked defeated, and in spite of her simmering anger Izzy felt a pang. Clara was only trying to be a friend. "I'll keep all of this in mind," she added weakly. "I'll . . . I'll think about it."

Clara bit her lip and nodded. Silently, she walked Izzy to the door.

Izzy was starting down the front porch steps when she caught Clara's final words in the cold night air.

"Think fast. *Please*."

But by the time Izzy turned around, the only thing there was a closed door.

32

As shoppers but also as humans, we have a tendency to confuse wants with needs. Wonderfully, the new charitable shopping initiative at Moondance boutique combines the two.

—*Intro to "Much-Needed Moondance for Syria," in* The Color-Blind Gazette

Mommy? When can I go back to school?" Clara reached to clear Thomas's empty breakfast plate and he pouted up at her as he had every morning that week. It figured. Most kids wake up asking why they *have* to go to school, but Clara had the one who wanted to go and couldn't.

She'd been playing a long game of phone tag with Pam at the Circle of Learning, and Clara, too, was growing restless. Benny had marched down and unleashed a rare fury in the school office the instant Clara had told him what happened, but it only dug them in deeper with the director, who then emphasized the need for a "cooling period." Still, some three weeks had passed, and the "distractions" had come to a lull—surely enough was enough. Yet Pam persisted in dodging her calls.

"I'm sure it'll be soon, sweetie. I left another message yesterday. I'm just waiting for them to call back."

"What about Abby and Aaron? When will *they* be back to school?"

Clara sighed. Her answer was always the same—that she didn't know and, more gently, wasn't sure they *would* be back to school— yet he kept asking.

Halloween decorations had transformed the neighborhood into a mischievous version of its former self, cottony spider webs stretched across porch railings, billowy ghosts dangling from tree branches, jack-o'-lanterns in bay windows, and it had dawned on Thomas that he'd more than likely have to trick-or-treat without his usual companions this year. He'd been especially pouty ever since, and Clara was determined to have him back at school for the class parade and the "Being healthy is a treat—no trick!" party afterward. Though Clara, too, had lost her Halloween compadre in desperately seeking recipes for said party that did not involve candy or, heaven forbid, food coloring. Last year Kristin had saved them both with an idea for scarecrow veggie skewers. She and Clara had giggled as they assembled the awkward creatures, drinking hot apple cider with spiced rum on a Saturday afternoon right here at this table. It might as well have been a lifetime ago.

Maddie triumphantly hurled a handful of Cheerios from her high chair, and for once it was a welcome distraction. Pup-Pup came running in a skittle of nails across tile, and she couldn't resist a smug smile that for all the new messes the dog had brought into their house, there were also a few she no longer had to clean up.

Frantic squawking cut through the morning air so suddenly that Clara jumped, half expecting to turn and find a gaggle of chickens *inside* the house. But no, they were sounding through the window she'd cracked when the toaster had unleashed a random burst of superheated aggression on Thomas's frozen waffle.

"Oh, shoo! Shoo! Wait, not you! Come back! Oh, hell . . ."

From the adjoining backyard, Randi's exasperation was drowned out by the sound of a crying baby.

Clara raised her eyebrows dramatically at Thomas. "Uh-oh," she said. "Should we go see if Miss Randi needs help?" He nodded obligingly, and she moved to unstrap Maddie from her high chair. A fresh chorus of angry clucks was accompanied by more frantic rustling, and Adele's wails grew even louder.

"Maybe baby Rrradele was trying to eat the eggs, and the mommy chickens got mad," Thomas guessed. Clara would have found this explanation more entertaining had she not been horrified he'd picked up on Benny's behind-closed-doors name for the baby.

"*Ah*-dele," she corrected him, leading him by the hand through the back door as Maddie wrapped her pajama-clad drumstick legs around her other hip. "And I doubt it."

She extended a foot to stop the dog from following them—"Sorry, Pups, not now"—and shivered as she slid the door shut, Pup-Pup's dejected face peering up at her through the glass. The morning was on the cold side of crisp, the smell of burning leaves was in the air, and there was no mistaking that fall was decidedly here, with winter not far behind. She tightened her arms around Maddie, feeling guilty that she hadn't stopped to grab their coats.

"I only have two hands!" Randi was yelling, futilely, into the commotion of clucking and wailing. Clara ushered Thomas along beside her as they rushed toward the coop, which was obstructed by yellowing honeysuckle.

"Randi? One get loose again?"

"Oh, thank Buddha." Her frazzled neighbor's head appeared around the bush. "Kitchen door's open—Adele's in the swing—can you run in? I'm so afraid she'll thrash her way out. I have to get them . . ."

"Of course!" Clara corralled the kids as quickly as she could to the screen door, through which she could see the metronome of the plush baby swing ticking soothingly side to side, while Adele defiantly screamed her head off, her face red, her tiny fists clenched with rage.

Thomas ran ahead in with arms outstretched, fingers wiggling, intent on tickling the baby's bare feet. "I'm not sure she's in the mood for that," Clara called out, depositing Maddie on the tile and setting about unstrapping the flailing ball of flesh. She pulled the baby to her chest and bounced her rhythmically. "There now," she said. Adele sniffled into her collarbone, her runny nose leaving a sticky trail across the front of Clara's thermal, just as Randi rushed in and slid the door shut behind her.

"Oh, your poor shirt. No good deed goes unpunished," Randi groaned.

"Now it matches the other side," Clara said. She'd been joking, but she glanced down for effect and discovered that it was in fact offset by tiny fingerprints of maple syrup. She smiled ruefully at Randi.

"And Rhoda thinks *she's* doing the 'real' work, getting up early to open the store."

"That's just a thing people say so they can play the martyr while saving their sanity. It's a win-win for the working parent."

"Stay for a cup of coffee? It's been one of those weeks. Ooh! And I'm waiting for the second half of one of those Second Date Update segments Izzy does. Right after this set list." Clara turned to hide her frown, ostensibly scanning the room for something to interest the kids so she could stay. She hadn't seen Izzy for over a week now and was worried that she'd offended her with the heart-to-heart gone wrong after their dinner. But more than that, she was worried that what she'd said hadn't swayed her.

Randi reached to turn up the radio that was mounted under a cabinet. One of the more annoying hit songs of late was playing, and Clara was reminded of why she didn't tune in very often. "Thomas!" Randi clapped her hands brightly. "Adele got some new activity centers. She isn't big enough for them yet, but I bet you and Maddie could help us figure out what cool things they can do!" Clara was content to snuggle the baby while Randi ducked into the hallway and reappeared with two of those little plastic tables toddlers can use to pull to standing. Soon she had Thomas and Maddie situated, testing every button, light, and lever, and was filling a steaming mug for Clara. "It's free trade," she said as she handed it over, as if Clara would have refused it otherwise.

The voice of the DJ piped into the kitchen over the closing notes of the song. "Good morning! If you're just tuning in, you're here with Sonny and Day on *Freshly Squeezed,* and we've got Michelle on the line, waiting to find out what's become of Kevin. Michelle, are you ready as you'll ever be?"

There was a nervous giggle of affirmation and then some dialing.

"Fill me in," Clara said, shifting the baby so she could stir a splash of milk into her coffee. "Do we like Michelle? Do we think we're going to like Kevin?"

"I don't really know. The chickens drowned her out. But that's okay—the second half is where you get the real story anyway."

"If you *ever* get the real story."

"Don't be such a skeptic." Some obligatory chitchat with the elusive Kevin was coming from the radio now, but Randi still had her eyes trained on Clara's. "With a guy like Benny, what do you have to be so cynical about?"

Clara shrugged. "You're not my only neighbors, you know."

"Ah. The good doctor. Sometimes I forget he's over there. Selective memory, I guess."

"I wish I had that."

"Well, I figure listening is about supporting Izzy. Did you get Hallie's new edition of *The Color-Blind Gazette* yesterday? With that great profile of her on the second page?"

Clara smiled. "I would have settled for the kid not breaking any more laws, but she did a nice job with this one, didn't she?"

"Between that and the little spotlight on our charity sale, I was quite impressed."

"Wait, wait, *wait!*" Day's voice cut through the kitchen, sounding positively euphoric. "So you actually *lost your cell phone?*"

"I did." Kevin's laugh was pretty good-natured for someone who'd been put on the spot. He sounded young. Randi's face lit up, and she lifted a silencing finger, waiting to hear what he had to say. "My replacement finally came in yesterday. I was able to keep my phone number, obviously, but they couldn't retrieve my contacts. I've been kicking myself all week for not knowing how to reach her otherwise. I guess that's the downside of meeting someone in a bar when you're drunk . . ." He stopped and laughed more nervously, as if it had just occurred to him that his mom might be listening.

"So you never got my texts?" Michelle's voice through the phone line was thick with amazement. She might have just been told that fairies exist.

"I never did. And I never would've blown you off."

Day laughed merrily. "Kevin. This is a landmark case. I mean, this gives hope to jilted women everywhere! Do you realize that is *the* number-one excuse we invent for you guys when you don't call? *Maybe he lost his phone—he wants to call, but he just can't!* Am I right, Michelle? Tell me you haven't thought that about, like, every guy who ever hasn't called you!"

Clara leaned back in her chair, trying to decide whether this guy was telling the truth. Maybe they'd finally just hit on someone who didn't have the guts to tell the whole listening area, "Hey, I really just was trying for a one-night stand and never had any intention of following up." She couldn't help but wonder how this was going over with Izzy. She couldn't picture her *not* rolling her eyes behind the scenes.

At the other end of the phone, Michelle was laughing too now, giddy with the prospect of a second date after all. "*So* right," she said emphatically.

"Thanks for breaking the mold, Kev," Day said.

"Speaking of breaking the mold," Sonny said. "We've never done more than one Second Date Update in a morning, but we have a special case here. A surprise involving one of our own staffers. A silent partner, if you will. Izzy, say hi to our listeners."

Clara and Randi exchanged a look.

There was a bit of scuffling on the air—Clara pictured a microphone perhaps being offered, headphones perhaps being waved away—followed by an awkward silence. "Hi to our listeners," a meek voice said finally. Randi gripped Clara's arm in an excited squeeze.

Sonny laughed easily. "Izzy is one of our producers, and what you don't see—or don't hear, I should say—is that Izzy helps make

Second Date Update possible. She does all the work behind the scenes so we can have all the fun on the air."

"That's right," Day chimed in. "Anyone out there with a happy ending from Second Date Update, you really have Izzy to thank. It starts with her."

"She knows how to pick 'em," Sonny agreed. "Which is why we couldn't resist when we got a private message from someone who's hoping Izzy will pick him—for *herself*."

Clara's eyes widened in alarm. It couldn't be. Surely Paul couldn't be clueless enough to call a radio show over another woman while Kristin was missing.

"I thought Izzy secretly hated this segment?" Randi whispered, as if they might be disturbing the rest of the listeners.

"She does."

"Been holding out on us, Iz?" Day's voice was breezy, though Clara could only imagine how Izzy must be glaring at her right now. "Any dates you'd like to tell us about?"

Izzy cleared her throat. "No," she said, sounding genuinely confused. "No dates, period."

"Well, it wasn't *exactly* a date," a male voice cut in. Clara and Randi cocked their heads, like puppies trying to distinguish their owner's footsteps from the rest. Behind them, an activity table burst into song, and Thomas and Maddie shared a delighted laugh.

"Kind of an unconventional format we're rolling with here," Sonny said, "without Izzy to pull it all together offstage. So forgive us for any bumps. But let's back up and start at the beginning. Paul, welcome! Pretend you're an ordinary caller, and we don't have Izzy on the line yet. Tell us about your date, or . . . what would you call it?"

"I don't know. She called it a parallel universe. I kind of liked that."

The doctor's voice was smooth, well suited for radio, and Clara closed her eyes. Her grasping-at-straws hope that it was anyone other than him faded. When she opened them, Randi was staring dramatically at her. "*That* Paul?" she mouthed, pointing in the direction of his house, and Clara nodded, dropping her forehead into a hand.

"The timing's all wrong, I know that," he continued. "I've been going through a divorce and there are . . . complications. It's taking longer than it should, and I can't say I blame anyone for keeping their distance from that."

"Things with your ex, though, they're done for good?" Day was using her best suspicious voice, though she was clearly oblivious of the gravity of what Paul had left unsaid.

Paul's laugh almost disguised his bitterness. Almost. "No question."

"So if the timing's bad, why pursue Izzy?"

He sighed. "Have you ever met someone who just makes you feel . . . different? Better. She never judged me for . . . you know, the drama. She's kind, and easy to talk to—she really *listens.* She's her own force in the natural world, though I can tell she doesn't think of herself that way. She's like . . . like the call of a whippoorwill high in the trees. Like a river cutting through a ravine. Like a ride on a fast bike, that feeling of freedom."

"Whoa, buddy. No need to lay it on so thick!" Day and Sonny erupted in laughter.

Izzy still hadn't said a word.

"We've had a few moments," Paul said. "A good connection. And then we had one *great* moment. At least, I thought so."

"Ooh, we're getting warmer!" Day said.

"Are we talking about something physical here?" Sonny asked, adopting his best man-to-man tone.

"I don't kiss and tell, so to speak," Paul said. "But I thought there was . . . a spark."

"And then what?" Day again.

"Then nothing. It's been over a week. I've tried going by her house, stuck a note on her door. Left a couple of voice mails. I don't have her cell number, only what's in the phone book. But she hasn't gotten back to me. Then I saw her leaving for work and I thought— you know what, she's off to this Second Date Update thing, what the hell, why not call. This is what you do, right?"

"Izzy!" Sonny laughed. "I have to say, I did *not* know you had it in you to ghost someone. You always seem so . . . I don't know, approachable. Accessible . . ."

"I'm not *ghosting* anyone," she said. Her irritation was unmistakable, but Clara couldn't tell if it was directed at Sonny or at Paul. "I've been busy, is all."

Clara bit her lip. Izzy had promised to think on what she'd said about Paul. And evidently that had been enough to keep her away for at least a week. But now he was putting her on the spot. She wanted to cry.

"He called you a mountain stream, Iz," Day said. "He called you a whippoorwill. Freedom. This guy is like a walking Garth Brooks song."

"Or is it Randy Travis?" Sonny mused. "John Denver?"

"Whatever it is, I think it's sweet," Day said.

"I wasn't trying to turn it into a joke," Paul said, and Sonny's laughter stopped at the edge in his voice. "She's very different from me is what I mean." The edge softened, and Dr. Paul reappeared, polished and smart. "Izzy has a calming effect. I like being near her. And *she* knows what I mean about the whippoorwill."

"Well, I have to say, that speech alone would knock most women I know right off their feet," Day said. "Okay. So what gives, Izzy? You know the drill. Paul is calling because he wants to know why you haven't been responsive."

"Actually," Paul interjected, "I don't so much care why. She doesn't have to say. I just want to change her mind. I just want a chance."

"Well, I—" Izzy gave a nervous laugh. "Paul, I didn't even know you actually wanted to date. Like you said, it's not great timing."

"I just . . . I don't want to put my life on hold anymore. I've already wasted so much time."

"I'm not sure you're thinking it through. I don't think this is the venue to discuss this . . ."

"You caught me. I was trying not to think it through. Like we talked about?"

"We talked about *me* not thinking things through so much. Not you."

"Even better."

Adele had fallen asleep on Clara's chest, and she wrapped her arms tightly around the baby, evading Randi's eyes. Paul had laid his trap with impressive cunning. What choice did Izzy have but to say yes?

"Why don't we just try one real date," Paul said.

"*Freshly Squeezed* picks up the tab," Sonny reminded Izzy. "What do you have to lose?"

"Well . . ." An awkward silence filled the kitchen.

"Did you know about this?" Randi hissed.

"Why not," Izzy said. She sounded . . . well, not *un*happy.

"Smart move," Day crooned. "This one sounds like a keeper, Iz."

Randi switched off the radio and looked wide-eyed at Clara.

"I saw her pull up on the back of his motorcycle last week," Clara said. "That was the first I ever saw them together. Though Hallie had mentioned to me that they seemed to be friends. She was worried."

"Well, yeah." Randi was shaking her head.

Clara shifted the baby's weight. "I tried to talk to her about it, and she was pretty defensive. I ended up feeling awful. But maybe it worked, if he hadn't heard from her . . ."

There was a scuffle over by the play center, where Thomas and Maddie were at the end of their attention spans for peaceful parallel play. They were battling over a plastic phone receiver, and Randi pulled a face at Clara, who sighed and held out the baby, reluctant to trade in the sleeping bundle for the arguing toddler-preschooler combo.

"I don't want to get stuck in mom mode," Randi said softly, setting Adele back into the swing. "And I know Izzy isn't *that* much younger than us. But I like her a lot. It would be helpful to know how worried we should be."

"Two minutes, kids," Clara called. Maddie had come away with the phone and was gumming it greedily. Thomas scowled at her, but she ignored him and turned back to Randi.

"Kristin's sister came to see me," Clara said. "She seemed to think we're right to be worried."

"Oh, God. Why?"

"Nothing definitive. She just . . . had suspicions all along."

Randi shook her head. "You kind of keep getting pulled into this, don't you?" There was sympathy in her voice, and Clara wondered why she hadn't been spending more time here, with women who intuitively understood more of what she'd been feeling. Benny's more distanced approach was practical, she knew, but it had left her sort of . . . well, alone. Ever since he'd brought up the idea of her going back to work, to find something else to focus her energies on, she'd tried not to mention Kristin. The subject of his suggestion hadn't come up again, and she wanted to keep it that way.

"Kristin's been gone five weeks, six?" Randi asked.

"Somewhere in between."

Randi looked out across their backyards, and Clara followed her gaze toward Kristin's pretty white Victorian. A strong wind had kicked up, pulling leaves from the suddenly skeletal tree branches with alarming speed. Clara hoped whoever had lit that fire she'd smelled earlier had extinguished all the sparks.

"It's gone kind of quiet. Do you think they're even still investigating?"

"Excellent question," Clara said. "Maybe we'd better find out."

33

Husband Drowns After Pulling Wife From Rip-
tide | Heroin Epidemic a "Red Level Threat" | Fa-
tal Maternity Ward Fire Raises Safety Questions
| Protests Draw Crowds, but Not Change | No
Sign of "Black Box" in Flight Wreckage | Famed
Couple Announces Split After 20 Years | Failing
Grades for Water Quality Were Not Disclosed |
Consumer Data Hack Has Deeper Implications |
U.S. Gun Violence Year to Date: An Infographic

—A string of email subject lines moved from
Izzy's work email in-box into her trash, unread

The irony was that she'd come to work just hours ago with Paul's face in her mind, a smile on her lips. She'd been planning how she'd make her way over later, maybe with something homemade to share—was dinner too much? Or would dessert be better?

She'd gotten his note, but it had only made her feel awful. Though she'd promised Clara she'd think more carefully about Paul—and had thought of little *but* him in the week since their kiss—it wasn't doubt or caution that kept her away. It was guilt. She couldn't help feeling as if she'd betrayed him by so much as listening to the ugly comparisons Clara had drawn. She needed the cleanse of a little time, like a hot shower or a good night's sleep.

Finally, this morning she'd felt ready. The sting of her own betrayal by proxy had faded enough for the tingle of possibility to take its place.

And then he'd gone and called Second Date Update.

It wasn't the humiliation of being laid out like a buffet to Sonny and Day, though there was that too. Worse was the simple fact that he'd placed the call at all: glaring evidence that he didn't know her in the least. Anyone who did would know there was nothing she'd have hated more.

The clarity cut sharply through the flush of self-consciousness. In all their conversations, he'd asked almost nothing about her life, or where she'd come from, or where she wanted to go. It was evident from his words that he was focused entirely on how she made *him* feel, not on what made *her* tick. And while that was understandable with what he was going through, it was also not likely to change anytime soon, and was not at all what she wanted.

Never mind the painful contrast with Josh, who knew her better than anyone else.

Paul was a smooth talker, she'd grant him that. Maybe's Clara's picture of him as a manipulator had a shade of truth in it after all. Or maybe not. It didn't really matter, now that she was no longer interested.

She just had to figure out how to back out of it.

Izzy baked an entire batch of soft pumpkin cookies, the cakey ones she could never stop eating, then thought better of taking them with her. She didn't know what she'd been thinking—only, she supposed, that when she'd awoken that day she'd had a mind to bring something homemade to Paul.

Back in college, she'd once delivered chocolate chip cookie bars to a boyfriend only to be dumped on the spot. Having planned to cut her loose, he was not about to be deterred by a sweet gesture, nor did he see anything wrong with asking, "Is it okay if I keep the

cookies?" as she'd headed out the door. Stunned, she'd merely nodded and scurried away. Only when her roommates echoed their
collective "*What?*" of disbelief around her dorm room did she have
the presence of mind to be enraged too.

"We could be stress-eating them right now," one of them had
lamented.

"You should have thrown them in his face!" another chastised
her.

No, cookies and breaking things off did not go together.

And how would she look to her new friends now? Randi and
Rhoda had yet to miss a beat when it came to the radio show. She'd
go from being the pitiful neighbor who was stuck on her brother-
in-law to the third wheel in the domestic drama playing on the public stage. Just great. She felt a flash of annoyance at Paul for putting
her in this position, and used it to propel herself across the street
before she lost her nerve.

It was darker and colder than she'd expected as she made her
diagonal to Paul's. Soon they'd change the clocks and be plunged
into blackness by dinnertime—but maybe this year, in her little
nest of a house, she'd find the longer nights more cozy than depressing. She'd been thinking of enrolling in yoga at the studio
where Randi and Rhoda had their meditation class; perhaps its
warm glow would follow her home.

Paul's face lit up to match the garish brightness of his foyer
when he answered her knock, and she swallowed hard. "Are we
doing the date now?" he asked, grinning. He seemed relaxed, in
uncharacteristically worn jeans and a flannel, and she couldn't
help feeling a pang that she'd never seen him look so good. "The
sooner the better."

She steeled herself to stick to the script. "I was just hoping we
could talk for a minute. Can I come in?"

If Paul sensed what was coming, he didn't let on, merely stood
to the side and gestured gallantly for her to enter.

Glancing into the dining room, Izzy stopped short. Large rub-
ber storage bins were stacked on all sides between the table and the
walls. Each was labeled in stereotypically messy doctor's handwrit-

ing: *Aaron clothes. Abby clothes. Kid books. Outdoor toys.* "What's all this?" she asked, unease hovering over her. Who packed up his kids' stuff when they were *missing*? Her eyes flickered up the stairs, where cardboard boxes lined the hallway more haphazardly, with *Kristin* scrawled angrily across the sides in thick black marker.

"Sorry about the mess. Come around, into the kitchen."

The dread that had been accumulating since morning collected in her throat as she followed him to the eat-in area adjoining the family room. Only then did Izzy realize she'd never been this far into the house before. Straight ahead, sliding glass doors were closed against the black nothingness beyond. The kitchen itself was cheery and appeared largely untouched—with the twins' crayon and construction paper creations covering the fridge and a bulletin board. But she caught sight of a stack of empty bins on the other side of the couch, their lids propped against them, waiting to be popped into place as they were filled.

"Doing some housecleaning?" she asked, as he pulled out a chair for her.

"It's what it looks like—packing," he said. "Glass of chardonnay? Or an IPA, maybe?"

"Just water, thanks."

"Cheap date." He took a glass from the dish drainer and filled it at the dispenser in the refrigerator door. "There are a few factors," he began. "One, as much as I hate to move anything from just how they left it, the fact that I'm living in a shrine is wearing on me. It's hard to disturb it, but it's hard *not* to disturb it, you know?" He cracked open the door and took a bottle of beer in his free hand. "Two, I had anticipated a divorce settlement being, you know, *settled* soon."

Izzy nodded as he handed her the water and took a seat across from her. "I'm stuck paying rent on the apartment until the lease runs out, plus carrying the mortgage on this house alone. Presumably either she was going to buy me out of the house, or she and the twins were going to wind up moving too. And delaying the inevitable is expensive. Especially with legal fees, plus the cost of hiring a private investigator."

"You're going to do that?" Izzy sat up straighter. "What do the police think?"

He looked at her strangely. "Who cares what the police think? They haven't found them. They can hardly object that I'm not content to let this just fade into the forgotten files."

"Is that what's happening?"

He shrugged. "I think we've at minimum segued into a 'Sorry, pal, we tried!' phase. No one's exactly been jumping to my defense as stepdad of the year, right? Aside from having better things to do with their time, they probably think I had it coming."

Everything he was saying made sense. So why did Izzy suddenly feel almost panicked, as if he'd trapped her here at the table? Just over a week ago, she'd been kissing him on the overlook. But that slight should-I-be-doing-this? thrill she'd felt then was taking a different form now. She looked out into the night, wondering if any of the neighbors could see in.

No one knew she was here.

"I have better things to do with my time too," he said softly, smiling at her.

"Paul, listen. That phone call, it was—"

"A little over the top, I know. But I couldn't get it out of my head after I came to fix your gate and heard the end of your interview with Hallie. I have to say, that was a pretty pathetic excuse for a happy ending on your show. I had a feeling we could do better." Oh, Paul. He was *proud* of himself. "Good ratings for the show are good for *you,* right?"

She sighed. Maybe his heart had been in the right place, but everything else about it was still all wrong. Even that day in the garden, he'd come in too late to hear her admit she didn't like the job at all. At best, he had habitually horrible timing. With her own history of the same, they were either a perfect match or a laughably bad one.

"I was flattered. I mean, I *am* flattered. But—" She took a deep breath. "I don't think a date is a good idea."

A self-assured disbelief surfaced in his eyes, then was gone. "You said yes just because people were listening?"

"No. I mean, you did kind of put me on the spot—but no." He

held his smile, as if he thought she might be setting him up for some hilarious punch line. "Now that I've had time to think about it, though, without being caught up in what you were saying . . ."

His face clouded over. "Did I give the impression a moment ago that I didn't mean what I said? I meant it all. Those aren't just words to get caught up in. That's how I feel."

"And it's sweet. Really. It's just—"

He gestured emphatically toward the dining room. "Don't say bad timing. You can't accuse me of not moving on. You can see that I'm moving on."

It was so close to what she'd been telling herself about her time with Paul—*Hey, look, I'm moving on!* And so equally insincere.

"It's me," she blurted out. "I'm sort of on the rebound myself. I'm not sure I'm ready."

"I have always believed," Paul said quietly, "that with all that self-analytical stuff, if we don't let it hold us back, it will work itself out." There was still hope in his expression. "I say that as a trained medical professional, you know."

She couldn't bring herself to humor him, but she didn't know what to say. This was turning out to be harder than she'd imagined.

He faltered, looking down at his lap, and when he peered up at her, it was with such intensity that she couldn't look away. "I'm sorry. I've been . . ." He gave a nervous laugh. "Those relentless DJs already called me John Denver, and now I'm going to botch this too."

They *were* relentless—he had that part right. "John Denver was a great lyricist. And you don't have to—"

He put up a hand. "I *want* to say this. This past year has been the worst of my life, and then came rock bottom. It's meant so much to me that you've been there. Everyone else looks the other way when I come by, but not you. That alone makes me feel like I'm still the person I've been all along. That alone makes me believe I'll be able to crawl out of this."

Oh, God. He seemed to have feelings for her—not just the possibility of feelings, but actual emotions. How could she add to his disappointment when he'd already lost so much? She couldn't help the way she felt—or, rather, didn't feel—but had he really done all that much to deserve it? So he'd called the radio station. Plenty of other women would have swooned.

"It's not just about me," she heard herself say.

"Whatever it is, it doesn't matter. Let me be there for you the way you've been there for me."

"It's not like that."

"Then *what* is it like?" He threw his hands up in the air, looking so despondent that she faltered.

"It's . . ." She couldn't do it. And there was something more to this tightening in her gut than run-of-the-mill discomfort. She needed to be out of here, *now*. For good. Her mind presented her with an emergency exit, and without stopping to see where it might lead, she took it. "My dad—he's sick."

He frowned. "Oh, no. Sick how?"

What was she doing? "We're still not sure of the, um, stage, but . . . well, I can tell my mom knows more than she's letting on, and it's not good." Even as the words escaped her, she wanted to take them back, to start over. "They're going to need me. My sister is starting a family, and I'm the one who's available to help. It'll be a lot of back-and-forth to Springfield." She could already see the depth of the hole she was digging, but there was nothing to do but press on. "I need to focus on my family right now. It just doesn't make sense, in my head space or on my schedule, to be starting a relationship."

"I could be a support." He leaned in. "I know I'm not that kind of doctor, but I know more than you might think about—"

She held up a hand. "I don't doubt it," she said, with surprising conviction. "But I like to do things with my whole heart, and my heart's just not in this right now. I'm sorry."

"With your whole heart," he said, his voice low and impassive. He seemed to finally accept this explanation, the hint of anger receding, the will to protest ebbing away.

"I like that, the way you put that," he said finally, smiling a little sadly at her. "I might steal that."

"I hope you don't need it," she said. And it wasn't a lie, exactly.

34

The realization that someone is not just capable of killing you, but very well may, is surreal enough that you can almost talk yourself back into a state of denial. When he breaks in through your kitchen window and you jolt from sleep to find him standing over your bed, eerily holding the stuffed elephant that signifies you're not the first one he came to see, you wake up in more ways than one. You have two choices: You can stay, biding your time, but knowing he'll always be a threat. Or you can go, hoping he doesn't find you but knowing he will try.

It hardly seems fair that he'd go to so much effort to track down someone he seems to hate with an intensity he equates with love. But he is that proud, that determined to have what he considers rightly his.

Or that determined that no one else will have it.

35

Thanks for making time to see me." Clara accepted the steaming paper cup Detective Bryant handed her as he took his seat across the table. She felt ill at ease being back in the station, willingly risking more of the scrutiny that was finally starting to fade, and a bit let down, too, that it was not the more forthcoming Detective Marks who'd taken the appointment. He'd offered to meet her out for coffee, but the idea of being somewhere that Paul or Izzy might see them together the day after the Second Date Update call was a far worse thought. They might think she was intervening, doing something drastic.

She wasn't.

Not really.

She didn't want to *do* anything, she just wanted some answers.

And she had a valid enough cover story, one that happened to be true.

"Your kid's school seriously said he couldn't be there because of the case?"

She nodded. "Too distracting to the learning environment."

He rolled his eyes. "By those standards, no one in an urban school would ever get an education."

"I thought if I could give them a little more information on where things stand, they might relax."

"Well, there's nothing *distracting* about it. I wish there was. A couple of times I thought we were on to something, but no dice."

"So you've stopped looking?"

"Not yet. But unless we turn up something new to go on soon, we'll have to shelve it with the cold papers." He seemed to be measuring his words, waiting for her to protest.

"How much longer?"

"Usually we'll work a missing persons hard for about a month. In this case, with the children involved, I pushed for two. Resources are tight around here. Halloween is a busy time, thanks to the petty idiocy it inspires. My boss met me in the middle at six weeks."

"So not quite a week left, then."

"It's getting pretty chilly."

"That helps to know, thanks. Is it, um, okay to share that?"

"Between you and the ridiculous school director, yes. I wouldn't, you know, start your own newspaper or anything."

Clara flushed, but when he laughed, she granted him a weak smile. "Too soon," she chided him. If they were on good enough terms to get this far, maybe she could nudge him just a bit farther.

"I'm curious: What sort of thing might prompt you to reopen the case, down the line?"

"When a missing persons case goes cold, it isn't like with a homicide," he began.

"Even if you don't know that it *isn't* a homicide?" The words stuck uncomfortably in her throat, and his eyes narrowed. Still, she couldn't regret asking. It was now or never.

"It's a missing persons case until we have reason to think that it isn't," he said, and she wondered if the exhaustion in his voice was thanks to her, or the process, or his job in general. "And when it goes cold, we need a reason to open it back up."

"What kind of reason?"

"A sighting. A credit card purchase. Some sort of traceable activity." Clara nodded. They both knew anything that concrete was unlikely.

"Look," he said, "I know you care about Kristin and the kids. But you might need to accept that you just need to move on from this, questions unanswered. So does the school. The whole town, for that matter."

She nodded, and a beat of silence fell between them. "Just one more thing I've been wondering, since I'm here." He crossed his arms but didn't object. "If something *was* going on with Paul, would there have been a . . . a better way?" she asked. "I mean, if she'd come to you for help, if she'd come to you and said, 'I need to get away from my husband, I need to disappear,' would you have helped her?"

The detective looked genuinely surprised by the question. "Us? Help someone disappear? No. But there are proper measures. We could issue a restraining order—"

She shook her head. "You know as well as I do those things don't stop anyone with a strong enough desire to be *unrestrained*."

"You get cynical working these things, year after year. These women, you feel sorry for them, but . . ."

"But what?" Clara squared her shoulders.

"Most of the time they don't really want help. They call us to intervene in the middle of a fight, but as soon as we try to arrest the scumbag, forget it."

She bristled at the stereotype even as she checked herself that her own experience with the subject was more limited than his. More limited, maybe, but also more personal. "So you might argue that if she did take off for that reason, she did the sensible thing."

He shrugged. "You might. Unless you're me, with the open file stuck on your desk."

"Or Paul."

"Yes, or Paul. He's not likely to give up so easily, though."

So he might go through with the investigator, then. She nodded, trying to keep her expression impassive. "I'm sure he, uh, misses the kids."

He raised his eyebrows. "Like I said, you get cynical working these things." He stood. "You might see me around the neighborhood this week, dotting *i*'s, crossing *t*'s. You've saved me a trip to your front door, so thanks."

Clara's mind was racing as she collected her purse from the floor and got to her own feet. "My neighbor across the street, Isabel. Were you going to check in with her?"

"With everyone I can get to. Why?"

It wasn't as if she could tip him off without involving herself further. The best she could hope for was that Izzy would let slip something that might prompt the detective to warn her away from Paul. "Oh, I think she was just wondering, too, what would happen from here. That's all."

He nodded, holding her gaze. "I just wish someone who knew something that could actually help me was wondering about it too."

She made her way to the door, then turned once more.

"You said you couldn't help someone disappear. But do you think disappearing is *possible*?"

"For someone who has money, resources? Yeah. I can't say I haven't given it thought. I think I could do it. It's definitely possible."

A warm reassurance spread over her. This, then, was what she'd choose to believe. That Kristin and Abby and Aaron were gone of their own volition. Safe. No matter about the broken window Paul had jumped the gun to repair. No matter about the tattered book cover Abby wouldn't have left home without. No matter about the computer search history, or the plea from her sister, or the other odd threads found dangling. No matter about this feeling of unease that had taken up residence the moment they'd left and grown in intensity as small, heart-tugging truths had been revealed.

She had to listen to Benny, to the detective, even to Izzy. There was truth in their admonition to stop projecting her own past on the present. Kristin was not her unsuspecting coworker from the holiday retreat.

In fact, it was obvious that by the time she'd vanished, Kristin had suspected plenty.

Clara had to try to stop worrying that something had gone awry. She had to believe the best, whatever that was. She had to let go.

Leaning against the conference room doorframe, she flashed Detective Bryant a sad, sideways smile. "So *how* would you do it?" she asked.

"Disappear? Start over?" He shook his head. "Why don't you ask any of the thousands of illegal immigrants who do it every year."

With that, he raised his hand in a wave and strode past her, down the corridor that led deeper into the station. The strange smile stayed on Clara's lips as she stepped out onto the sidewalk, the sunlight warming her face. What an unexpected relief, that there was nothing left to ask, and nothing left to answer.

36

Please join us in welcoming Adele to the wide world. Can't you just see it in her eyes—her whole life ahead of her? We can't wait to watch her grow.

—Printed birth announcement from Randi and Rhoda, captioning a stunning baby photo

Izzy caught sight of Randi through the boutique window and slowed her stride, clinging tighter to her slim hope that she and Rhoda had somehow missed hearing her on Second Date Update. Randi was sliding a new cash drawer into the register, likely just starting her late-afternoon shift, and the store appeared empty. Here it was, a chance to face something head on for once, to clear up any misunderstanding or gossip, and before she could stop and think about it she found herself pushing through the door with a sheepish wave.

"Izzy! How've you been?" Randi tossed her long braid over her shoulder. Even as her face lit up in a genuine enough smile, something in her eyes seemed to be weighing her options.

"Well, it hasn't been a boring week," Izzy said cautiously, approaching the counter.

"I guess not," Randi said, her forehead wrinkling. Izzy nodded. So she *had* heard it, then.

"I hope you didn't think that I—"

Randi shook her head. "I didn't think anything about *you*."

The words were a small kindness, and gratitude washed over Izzy. The only person she'd talked to, even a little bit, about anything to do with Paul was Clara, and that conversation had so much to do with Clara and so little to do with Paul that it hardly counted. She felt an urge to explain it all to Randi right here at the register, from the beginning, and realized with a start her own unlikely synergy with Kristin, albeit on a much smaller scale. For both of them, Paul's side of the story was the only one anyone had heard. And far too many people had heard it.

She'd tried too hard not to let that bother her about Paul and Kristin's situation before—a fact she was realizing too late. It *should* have bothered her then. And it bothered her now.

She cleared her throat. "Well, in case you did, it's not happening. No second date. No first date, for that matter."

"Well, good," Randi said. "I mean, it's none of my business, but the whole thing made me a bit nervous." She laughed uneasily. "I guess I shouldn't have said that, I'm sorry. I don't even know why you backed out. It's just that ever since Kristin disappeared, I feel like the whole energy of the neighborhood is off balance."

"It's okay," Izzy said. "I know what you mean. And that's not exactly the reason why. Or at least, it wasn't. But then it kind of became part of the reason. I don't know." She sighed. "I told him later that same night that I'd changed my mind. To tell you the truth, I've been feeling horribly guilty about it. I can't shake it."

"Guilty?" Randi shook her head. "It's not *your* fault he decided to stage the whole thing on the radio. If you ask me, you need to be braced for *some* degree of embarrassment if you're foolish enough or brave enough or *whatever* enough to make that call."

"Oh, I don't feel guilty about him. I feel guilty about me." Izzy leaned on the counter and peered into the pretty basket of impulse buys. The contents rotated, but today it was filled with little felt flower pins. She rubbed the leaf of one between her thumb and forefinger. Its fibers were unexpectedly rough against her skin. "I wasn't entirely honest, with the reasons I gave. I said . . . oh, God, I don't even know why I did it. In the moment it seemed like some kind of external factor would make everything easier for him to take."

"What did you say?"

Izzy tilted the basket to get a better look at the array inside. She could picture her mother pinning one to the lapel of a coat. "I said my dad was sick, that I was going to be focusing on my family, driving back and forth to Springfield to help. It just popped into my head. I wanted to extract myself—*completely*, you know?—and I kind of panicked."

"But your dad, he's—?"

Izzy shook her head. "He had tests run recently, and you know how the subconscious works. It was a false alarm, but now I'm afraid he's going to *get* sick. I'm terrified I've conjured bad juju—putting that out there, just *asking* for the lie to come true." Izzy met Randi's eyes in a reluctant attempt to gauge the scale of her disapproval.

"Oh, Izzy. No one will ever know you said that. Forget it. You did what came to mind in the moment. And if it did the job, got through to him, then that's what matters. Obsessing—that's where the bad juju comes in. And trust me, I know juju. I *sell* juju for a living." She gestured to the wall of charms, stones, and crystals on display behind her, and Izzy was enjoying her first genuine laugh in days when Rhoda burst through the curtain from the back room and looked around expectantly.

"Hey, Izzy. Man, busy day for the neighborhood. Where did he go?"

Izzy and Randi both frowned at her. "Who?" Randi asked.

"Paul. I just went to check something for him, in the winter inventory—"

"Right here." To Izzy's left was the alcove of garden things and other oversized décor, and Paul stepped out from around the partition into her peripheral vision. She froze, not turning to greet him, not moving even to breathe. Randi's eyes bored into hers with all the questions Izzy herself was thinking: *How long had he been standing there, so close? How much had he heard?*

"Sorry that took so long!" Rhoda was using her saleslady voice, reserved for strangers. "But yes, we did have more of those come in this year, so it's no problem to accommodate the late return. Happy to help."

"I appreciate this." Paul held out a woman's scarf and matching hat with the tags still on, and Rhoda took them. "I know she thought they were beautiful," he said, his voice thick with apologetic charm. "I can't imagine why she didn't even take the tags off. She must have just misplaced them."

Izzy stood to the side so Paul could step to the register. "Hi, there, Izzy. I didn't realize that was you."

"Hello." Her cheeks were burning.

"I'm always doing that myself," Rhoda said, "getting all these Christmas gifts I just love and then forgetting about them. I have such a big family, it's always chaos, and I'm sure it was the same with the twins." The four of them collectively cringed at the mention of Abby and Aaron, none of them doing a very good job of hiding it, and Rhoda's fingers moved hastily as she processed the refund.

"Yes, it's quite the project packing it all up for storage now. So thanks again for taking this much off my hands. It's a small dent, but at least it's something." Paul took his receipt and nodded his good-bye at Rhoda. "Take care," he said to Izzy, his face neutral as he pushed through the door in a tingle of wind chimes.

"They weren't her style at all," Rhoda muttered. "I tried to talk him into this gray pattern she would have loved, but he already had his mind set on the display he'd seen from the street, without even taking a closer look."

Izzy let out a loud breath and dropped her head, groaning as Randi reached out a hand almost involuntarily. "I don't think he heard, I think I would have seen . . ." Randi's reassurance was weak, and she didn't even bother to finish the sentence.

Rhoda looked, confused, from one to the other.

"What? What did I miss?"

Izzy was plopping her purse on the kitchen counter when the knock came at the front door. She froze, keys still in her hand, her muscles reflexively tensing. Finally, she'd cleaned the last of the boxes out of the garage so she could pull the car in, and she hadn't seen anyone on the street. Who could it be but Paul? But even if he had overheard what she said to Randi, would he really put them both through the humiliation of having this out again?

If it was him, he'd seen her arrive home. She had no choice but to answer.

Detective Bryant stood on her step, hands in his pockets, brown leather jacket zipped tight against the cold. He cleared his throat and said her name, her full name, as if it were a question. Had *he* heard the Second Date Update too? What if he thought . . . Oh, God, what if he suspected she and Paul had been involved all along, even before Kristin's vanishing act? She managed a blink of a "Hello" even as she looked past him, scanning the street for a vehicle she didn't see.

"I'm around the block," he said, following her eyes. "Going door to door is not one of the more glamorous parts of my job, but I spend more time doing it than I'll ever admit."

She smiled politely. "Has something happened?"

"Just doing due diligence. May I come in for a moment?"

"Of course." Izzy led the way into the kitchen. "Coffee? Tea?"

"A glass of water would be great, if it's no trouble." Izzy wondered if Paul had taken her request the other night the same way the detective's sounded—unobtrusive, as if aware that by the end of this beverage they would still owe each other nothing. The detective hung back in the doorway and took a lengthy drink from the glass she handed him as she settled herself onto a counter stool.

"I don't suppose you have any new thoughts on the Kristin Kirkland case? Anything you've remembered? Or seen or heard since we talked last?"

Did Paul whisking her away on the motorcycle Kristin had forbidden him to ride count? What about him being so ready to date again, and thinking nothing of saying so publicly, when anyone in town listening might recognize him from his voice and first name alone? What about him boxing up his family's belongings? What about the fact that Clara seemed convinced that something wasn't right with him, that he was, at minimum, an unnecessary risk?

It was all just gossip where she didn't have any room to talk, and judgment where she didn't have any right to throw stones. Izzy shook her head.

He nodded, running a hand through his close-cropped hair. Leaning on the doorframe, he looked more casual and less official than when she'd seen him last, out of place at the bonfire, and a bit more fit, as if maybe he'd taken up a new regimen at the gym. "I won't be actively working the Kirkland case beyond this week, unless something else turns up. I'm just going over everything again before I file it."

She shifted in her seat. "Is that frustrating, having to move on from something that's unresolved? Or is it more of a relief, to tackle something new?"

"Even when I'm tired of banging my head against the wall, it still drives me crazy," he said. She knew the feeling.

"Do you get hunches about things?"

The memory of Paul's forced nonchalance when he'd overheard her in the shop crawled up the back of her neck.

"In my experience, the more hunches I get, the better I am at my job. I do wish I got more of them."

All this time she'd been priding herself on being somewhat re- moved from the situation—the only neighbor who *didn't* take sides, didn't speculate, didn't butt in. But maybe she'd been wrong. Maybe what was going on across the street was, just by that very fact, her business.

And maybe there *was* some risk involved with proximity.

Suddenly she desperately needed to know what Detective Bry- ant thought of it all. So she decided to be blunt.

"If I had a friend who was interested in spending some time with Paul Kirkland, do you have a hunch how worried I should be?"

He frowned. "Too much of what I've said about this case has already gone public. I shouldn't speculate more." He looked weary, and she caught herself glancing at his hand—no ring. What must it be like to do a job like his without someone to come home to?

"Of course," she said quickly. "I'm sorry." Her eyes fell on the two tins she'd filled after returning from Paul's the other night and gorging herself on the feast she'd left cooling on the counter. "Do you like pumpkin cookies?" she asked. "I overbaked. You could take them back to the station."

"Oh, I couldn't—"

"Take them as a token of the neighborhood's appreciation."

He rewarded her with a laugh. "I admit, tokens of appreciation are less common than you might think."

She bent and rummaged through the closest cupboard in search of a disposable container with a lid, then crossed to the sink to wash her hands. Her back was to him when he said, "So as I said, I won't be working the case anymore."

She nodded, dried her hands, and began filling the container with cookies.

"That being a nonissue now, I wonder if you might let me take you to dinner."

Izzy looked up and blinked in surprise, taking him in—the cut to his jaw, slightly on the rugged side of the boy next door, and the way he carried himself, as if only *trying* to appear as if he wasn't on alert. In truth she hadn't given him much thought after their initial meeting, aside from panicking and throwing her wine into the grass when he'd approached at the festival. She wasn't sure she'd ever been caught so off guard by such an innocent request, though now she was remembering the way his eyes had lingered on hers in the glow of the bonfire, and his parting wink. Had what she'd taken as his attempts to put her at ease instead been an on-duty version of *flirting*?

"Maybe you don't like formal dates," he said quickly. "I saw the feature about you, in the new edition of that kid's paper? Reading between the lines, I got the feeling maybe you weren't exactly enamored with that part of your job. The radio dating thing."

Hallie had dropped off her two "contributor copies" last week, and Izzy had been relieved at how much tamer it was than the earlier edition Clara had shown her. Still, though her own feature had been wiped mercifully clean of personality, it was nice to know he'd *seen* her in what Hallie had written.

She managed a smile. "You *do* get good hunches," she said.

He lifted a hand as if to say, *There you go.*

But she was already thinking of the bleak headlines in her inbox every morning—the crimes gone wrong, the mistakes turned deadly, the errors in judgment, the evil, the corruption. She knew that the stories were already too personal to her, the way she soaked up the sadness as if it were her own. And she knew that if someone she cared about was involved with so many of them, she'd never be able to stop. She'd carry the weight of it all; she'd worry day and night.

"That's a kind invitation," she stalled, busying herself with the cookies again.

Not a date in years, and now two offers in the same week. One from a potential suspect, and one from the lead investigator. Izzy could picture herself as a caricature, a little angel on one shoulder, a devil on the other, her eyes looking upward for help from above.

Which she was going to need to turn him down.

"What I'm about to say is completely unfair."

He cleared his throat. "Okay."

"But I know myself—at least, certain things about myself—and I'm ashamed to admit that I'd be a horrible match for a police officer. I'm not built from the right stuff."

There was a weighty pause. "In a town like Yellow Springs, the job isn't what you might think . . ."

She shook her head. "It's not just that. It's . . . well, part of it comes from my own job. Some people in the media get desensitized to the news—I'd guess it's similar in your profession. But the reverse seems to be true for me. Let's just say I'd be the opposite of a comfort to you. And I'd drive myself insane."

It felt good to follow through with something that was entirely the truth, for once to feel sure, even if it was with a certain sadness.

He tilted his head, then nodded once. "If that's a line you need to draw, better to know now."

"I'm touched that you considered me," she said, handing over the cookies. What *was* it with her and baking? Now she could use it to summon the end of relationships she hadn't even known were a possibility.

He moved to leave, and she followed, to see him out. "About your friend and Paul Kirkland," he said as they reached the front door. "The friend isn't you, is it?" She could feel color rushing into her cheeks. In front of a detective. Damn it. She couldn't have him think she was passing him over for *Paul.*

"I'm not interested in him," she said quickly. "But it might be the other way around." Come to think of it, her initial relief aside, she really was surprised the detective didn't know about the Second Date Update call. It had been aired with only the thinnest veil of discretion. What else could the authorities, even the most earnest of them, have missed?

He looked at her for a long moment. "In that case," he said, "between us, as friends? Since you asked . . ."

"Friends," she repeated, nodding.

"If I did have a gut feeling, it wouldn't necessarily be that Kristin and the twins are gone because he put them in the ground. But it might be that the reason they're gone has more to do with him being who he is than it has to do with money."

"And who do you think he is?"

"I can only say who I think he's not: The good doctor who means well but is wrapped up in his work, the prince charming who swoops in and saves the day when she's widowed and pregnant. Those descriptions don't add up for me, at least not in such simple terms. I'd be careful."

She knew that in some ways she'd been horribly selfish lately. But in other ways maybe she should have thought of herself a bit more. Or at least in a higher regard.

"I was a terrible witness for you," she blurted out. "I remember so little of that night—only flashes, mostly of things *I* said, not anyone else. I was embarrassed to admit it, when you questioned me . . ."

"I got the gist."

"I hope I didn't let Kristin down. Or you."

He touched her arm. "If you're going to have too much wine, from an officer's standpoint a neighbor's backyard is the perfect place to do it. No rowdiness, no driving. You didn't let anybody down. You didn't do a thing wrong."

"Well. Thanks for trying so hard to find her. And the twins. Nothing is the same without them."

She opened the door, and he started down the walk. She used to watch Abby and Aaron from here, pedaling their bikes as Kristin trailed behind them, and think how cozy it was. How quaint. Now she thought of Paul packing up the remnants of their lives there. Clara revealing her tragic, traumatized side. Hallie launching an underground newspaper. Randi and Rhoda holding court in their shop. The neighborhood really was a different place now. What was it Randi had called the energy? *Off balance.* She supposed scrutiny could do that to a group of people.

"Detective?" He turned, and she saw that he somehow already had a half-eaten cookie in his hand. He shrugged guiltily, and she laughed. "I know it's not likely, but call me if you ever leave the force."

He took a few steps back toward her. "You're right," he said. "It's not likely." He grinned mischievously. "But call me if you ever bake too many of these again. They're delicious."

He was standing close enough now that she caught a whiff of his cologne—something run-of-the-mill, maybe an inexpensive drugstore spray, but still nice. He caught her hand in his, and before she even registered his touch brought it to his lips and gave it a gentle kiss. She couldn't help smiling as she headed back inside.

It was an oddly gallant end to a mess of a day.

37

Items in the Lost and Found will not be held in-definitely. Please take inventory of your child's belongings daily, as well as of your own (coffee carriers, keys . . .). We cannot be held responsi-ble for anything gone missing, or for authenti-cating claims of ownership.

—*Memo to all Circle of Learning parents*

Halloween had never looked so friendly as it did at the Circle of Learning. The lobby was filled with artwork assembled with a level of care that Clara would have been hard-pressed to replicate with her lone one-year-old underfoot, let alone a whole building full of toddlers. Maddie loved nothing more than to rip paper, no matter whom the paper belonged to—and thus Thomas was understand-ably losing his enthusiasm for art while his sister was on the prem-ises. But here, the youngest children had made orange paint handprints that the teachers had cleverly transformed with black marker into five little fingertip pumpkins sitting on a fence. The preschoolers had pressed googly eyes and pipe cleaner hair onto silly monster shapes formed from homemade playdough, which had then been carefully arranged in a miniature pumpkin patch shelved in a Plexiglas display case. Clara smiled at the few that had more eyes than hair. Glittery bats hung from the ceiling, and in the corner a few bales of real hay framed a plywood mural of sunflowers with holes for the children to poke their faces through.

Clara was overcome with affection for the place in spite of herself. As much as she'd joked with Kristin about the over-the-top policies—why not let kids be kids and eat a little Halloween candy?—the truth was, she loved the school. Thomas had been well cared for within these walls, and as a first-time mom whose own mother was several states away, so had she. She wasn't ashamed to admit that she'd turned to the preschool teachers for advice the way other parents consulted pediatricians. *Do you think this is just a heat rash? Is it normal for his letters to be backward sometimes?* And the Circle of Learning's coordinated cuteness eased some of the pressure to achieve a perfect Pinterest parenthood, freeing her to focus on her own kind of less photogenic but never wavering love.

It had been easier to be angry with Pam than to feel hurt or betrayed. But now, she felt none of those things. Only determined.

Miss Sally was standing just inside the office, laughing with the director, when Clara stepped in. She immediately recognized this as one of their "Silly Hat Days"—Pam was in a wizard's cap while Miss Sally wore a crown of flowers, ribbons trailing her shoulders. Thomas loved these days, even though he always wore the same thing—his red plastic fireman's cap, really not very silly at all. At the sight of her, Miss Sally's smile brightened even as Pam's faltered.

"Clara! Oh, Miss Lizzie and the kids have *all* been missing Thomas. How is he? Will he be ready to come back soon?"

Ready to come back? Clara frowned. Had Pam not had the decency to tell the staff she'd *asked* Thomas to leave?

Never mind. It was better, perhaps, if she hadn't. Clara didn't want any lingering tension with anyone. A lack of communication might work in her favor if she played along.

Clara matched the wattage of her smile. "Absolutely. He wouldn't miss next week's Halloween party for the world! And neither would I. The lobby looks amazing."

Sally clapped her hands together in delight. "You know, I think I have a few extra dough monster kits, if you'd like to take a couple home to him and Maddie? You'd just have to watch that she doesn't try to mouth the tiny eyes."

"Really? They'd love that!" She wasn't being polite. They *would* love it.

"I'll run and get them. Have him bring his monster when he comes back, and we'll add it to the display." She disappeared through the doorway in a flourish of rustling ribbons, and only then did Clara take the seat Pam was gesturing toward with barely masked reluctance.

Clara perched on the edge of the chair, not wanting to seem too comfortable. "You probably gathered I'm here to tell you Thomas will be back next week." She held her smile.

Pam cleared her throat, and Clara could tell she was trying to work out how she might holistically tell Clara that the decision was not up to the parent.

Clara lowered her voice. "Not that it should matter, but—off the record—I have it on good authority that the investigation *next door* won't be actively ongoing after this week." She leaned forward, careful to keep any smugness from her voice. "Ergo, we won't be associated, however tangentially, with any more 'distractions.'"

Pam dropped her professional façade and knitted her brow in concerned lines. "But that means they'll stop looking? For Abby and Aaron?" She wrung her hands on the desk in front of her, and Clara sat back in her seat, caught off guard.

"Not necessarily," she said. "Just until something new comes in."

"Is that as unlikely as I think it is?"

Clara shrugged. "The twins' father might be hiring his own investigator." She wasn't sure why she said it. She was trying to distance herself from this, not reestablish herself as the closest contact to the drama.

"Whatever for?" Pam snapped. Her hands clenched into fists, and she looked up toward the ceiling. "Never mind," she mumbled. "I know what for." She shook her head. "Sorry. It just strikes me as . . . insincere."

Clara nodded carefully. "Detective Bryant did say he thinks we all need to accept that things might be left as they are. To move on. Which is what I'm here trying to do. I'm sure you can understand . . ."

But she could tell Pam's mind wasn't on Thomas. She took the wizard hat off her head and sat it on the edge of the desk, sighing heavily as she ran a hand over her hair to smooth it. "Frankly, I was hoping you might turn something else up," she said. "That newspaper was such a gift to Kristin, though no one can say it out loud. I think I even thought that seeing you and Thomas out playing, without his usual playmates, might get to Dr. Kirkland. Convince him to own up to . . . whatever there might be to own up to."

In all the times she and Kristin had chuckled about Pam—from her oxymoronic "rules for fun" to the political correctness of even the most benign holiday parties ("the notion of a leprechaun may be perceived as disrespectful to little people")—and as much as Clara had been missing those chats more than ever, she had never, until now, stopped to consider Kristin through Pam's eyes. The impeccable parent with impeccable children who made everything look easy. The doctor's wife who had it all but made sure to pay it forward. The all-star activities volunteer with a table full of handmade party favors, right until the end.

How many hours must the women have spent together? Clara could picture them standing on chairs, laughing, after the recycled newspaper streamers hung for Recycling Week had come loose and tangled the twins as they walked through the door. And though there were several sets of twin parents at the Circle, Kristin had been the one Pam stopped, en route to the parking lot with Clara, to ask if she might meet with a new mom to offer tips on managing the morning drop-off. (Clara had often thought that if she could not so much as drop her kids at day care without enlisting the aid of a massive double stroller, she'd never have the energy to leave the house.) It was Pam who had, with expert efficiency but also empathy, handed Kristin the whole box of tissues the afternoon Aaron sprained his wrist and Kristin burst into tears at the mere thought of him in such pain. Pam might not have known the real Kristin—or, rather, the *whole* Kristin—any more than anyone else did, but of course she'd cared about her, and especially her kids.

Maybe Clara wasn't the only one with certain blind spots.

Clara blinked at her. "Surely that's not the real reason you asked us to stay home?"

She stared back for a beat too long. "Of course not." Clara wondered if she knew something more than she was letting on, then decided to let it drop. She could hardly fault Pam for having Kristin at the center of her thoughts. Frankly, if she'd known the director had felt this way all along, she might have thought of her as an ally. But that wasn't why she was here. This wasn't about Kristin anymore.

It was about Thomas.

"I want you to know I get your earlier point, about how your job is to have the best interest of *all* the children at heart," Clara said. "And I know you requested a cooling period after Benny reacted badly to your judgment call. I've respected your wishes, but now I need to get back to doing *my* job. Which is to have the best interest of *my* child at heart. He wants to come back. I want him to come back. His dad wants him to come back. Please."

Pam studied her for a moment, then nodded. "I'm sorry if—" She grappled for the right words, then gave up.

A whoosh of ribbons announced Miss Sally's return. "Two kits," she announced triumphantly. Clara stood, and Miss Sally met her eyes as she took them. "Thomas usually went trick-or-treating with the twins, didn't he?"

Clara nodded, glancing at Pam for good measure, lest she rethink what she'd just agreed to. "That's why he's so excited for the Halloween party here, I think," Clara said. "There aren't a lot of other kids on our block."

"I was thinking about that," Miss Sally said. "I know it's a small town and you could head anywhere, but you have an open invitation to start and finish at my house, if you'd like. I'm on the other side of campus and can't pass more than a couple of driveways without running into a Circle of Learning kiddo out playing. He'd have plenty of company, plenty of fun. Maddie too."

"That's really kind," Clara said. "Thanks. I'll run it by Benny."

She tucked the craft kits into her purse and turned to leave.

"About the Halloween party," Pam called out. Clara turned, and the director's all-business smile was back. "There's still time to sign up. Thomas's class is set on snacks, but there are open slots for party favors."

"Oh, sure," Clara said, relieved at escaping another year of veggie scarecrow assembly. This sounded easier: Grab and go. "What's the head count now—eighteen?"

Pam nodded. "Of course, we want to be sensitive about how some families choose not to celebrate Halloween per se. Nothing too blatantly scary—witches, vampires, things that could be associated with death, or the occult."

"Nonscary Halloween. Got it."

"We're also trying to steer away from superheroes and princesses. We don't want to encourage violence, or dated gender roles, poor self-image . . ."

"Of course."

"Wonderful. Oh, and none of those temporary tattoos. Some parents are having an issue with the fact that they can only be properly removed with rubbing alcohol."

Clara hid a smile even as she wondered what was left. If someone had to step up to fill Kristin's shoes, it might as well be her. And if she fudged the rules here and there, or if what she contributed was a little uneven, so be it. At least it would be honest.

She swept the wizard hat off the desk and placed it gallantly on her head. "Challenge accepted."

38

Izzy was cocooned sleeplessly in bed, the house dark around her. But for once she wasn't awake because she was stuck thinking about Josh. And it wasn't the sweet detective who'd taken his place, nor was it Paul, much as the run-in at Moondance had left her cringing and uneasy.

It was Penny.

After Detective Bryant had left, she couldn't stop thinking about one of the last things he'd said: "I can only say who I think he's not. Those descriptions don't add up for me." It put her in mind of what Clara had told her of Kristin's estranged sister, who had felt all along that something wasn't right. And Izzy had pooh-poohed it. Sisters don't always know.

But often, they do.

Her first memory of Penny was of complaining to her mother, "Penny is a pain in the bum." Or maybe her mother just told the story so often that it had become a false memory. As the older sibling by a mere two years, Izzy didn't remember Penny coming home as a newborn, or life before her arrival. She suspected she'd largely ignored the baby, as toddlers tend to do. But that changed when Penny turned mobile and could insert herself into Izzy's space, knocking down her block towers, yanking the headbands out of her hair, trying on her shoes and leaving them strewn around the house. She supposed, from watching Maddie at Clara's, that Penny had been around one, which would have made her three.

The louder moments of her memories were of Penny shadowing her with infuriating innocence, imitating her, sabotaging her, but what she couldn't stop thinking of now were the quieter moments in between. Whenever she'd be put on time-out—even if the time-out was for being unkind to Penny—Penny would creep quietly into the dining room and sit with her, her diaper rustling as she plopped down cross-legged so their knees would just touch. Their mother tried to separate them, to explain that Izzy was being disciplined, but Penny wouldn't budge.

Even as a baby, Penny would stop what she was doing and come pat Izzy's shoulder if Izzy was hurt or sad or angered by the unfairness of a world ruled by grown-ups. Her parents would sometimes do the same, but with them there was exasperation, judgment about whether the tears were proportionate to the situation, an adult perspective that by its very nature was not her own. It was Penny who brought the real comfort, the wordless, unconditional support, the sense of a shared station in the world that no one beyond the two of them, with these specific parents in this specific house in this specific time and circumstance, could ever fully understand.

Sure, they butted heads. Once they got into school, they had phases of closeness punctuated by periods of eye rolling. Such spats might last a day or a year, but they became obsolete when that quiet support was needed. When Izzy was blacklisted by the in-crowd, or landed in the emergency room thanks to those awful roller blades, or left the back door ajar and their cat wandered off and never came home.

By the time Penny joined her at college, they'd hit what Izzy had assumed to be their now permanent phase in which Penny was her best friend by default—even during the years Josh had been her best friend by choice. And then Josh had chosen Penny.

Penny was a pain in the bum.

"Stop moping around like you've lost your best friend," her mother used to say on the girls' off days. But in this case, Izzy had been moping like she'd lost her best friend because she *had*.

Actually, she'd lost two.

And one of them, she had to admit, she wasn't going to get back—ever. Her relationship with Josh could be distant or it could be jovial, but it could never exist outside of Penny. She didn't know what that might eventually look like, but she wasn't going to figure it out if she carried on the way she had been.

Penny was a different story. What they'd had was still retrievable, or at least there was still a *chance* that it was retrievable, and Izzy had to try. Because another of the very few things she knew for sure was that if something were to happen to her tomorrow, if she were to vanish the way Kristin had, she didn't want her sister to be left saying, "Sorry, I don't know what's been going on with her these days." Things *had* been happening with her lately— remotely interesting things, for a change. But here she was living a life where not one person was a close enough confidante to know all the sordid details of her Second Date Update call and the visit later that night and the detective later that week and everything in between.

She'd been so focused on how badly she missed Josh that she hadn't even let herself consider how much she missed Penny.

She'd been wrong that she didn't have any option but to resign herself to the way things were, to get used to this new normal. She could do something to change it. At least, she hoped she could. She had, after all, been the one who'd destroyed it.

She was buzzing, thinking of Penny now, as if the molecules of her resolve were rearranging themselves in a new, more solid order. She didn't know what to do to make things right, but she knew that she wanted to try, and that was something.

No. It was everything.

But it wasn't going to resolve itself overnight. She swung her legs over the side of the bed. She would pad down and make a cup of chamomile tea, and she would mull this over for exactly the amount of time it took to drink it, and then she *would* go to sleep. She had only hours until she had to beat the *Freshly Squeezed* crew to the studio.

That's another thing, she thought as she made her way to the kitchen, not bothering to turn on the lights, not wanting to send any more "awake" signals to her brain than it already had. She ought to get a new job. One with a schedule that allowed her to share her waking off-hours with people other than ob-gyns and stay-at-home moms and police detectives. And one with less conflict and crisis in her in-box. And fewer opportunities for public humiliation, for herself or anyone else on the line. Really, what *had* she been doing with her life?

The moonlight was bright enough that the quartet of rectangles projected onto the floor through the over-sink window illuminated the kitchen. She took a mug from the cupboard, turned on the tap, and peered out into the night. A few lone clouds were passing, white and fast, across the sky, as if lit from within. The silvery garden looked almost magical. She should refill the bird feeder in the morning, though just this week she'd seen great flocks in formation, migrating south. Soon it would be time to haul in the furniture. But that was okay. She was already looking forward to spring.

Turning off the tap, she squinted at the gate, frowning. It was open, just a little. Odd. She always left it locked, rarely entered or left the backyard from the side. She glanced at the wall, where the ornate fairy garden key hung on a hook.

She must have overlooked securing it last time, probably when she'd hauled out the leaves. Or maybe a squirrel had landed just the right way on the interior latch. Either way, it would nag at her now to leave it that way. If the wind kicked up, the gate would bang open like it used to and drive her mad. She was hardly going to get any sleep as it was.

Sighing, she slid the mug into the microwave and set the timed cook to warm the water for her tea. Her garden clogs were by the back door, and she pulled her coat on over her nightshirt. Palming the key, she opened the door and stepped out.

She was halfway down the walk before she saw him, keeping to the shadows by the fence, slinking back from her and yet closer still to the house. A gasp caught in her throat as she stopped midstep, her hand flying to her chest.

There was no mistaking Paul's face in the moonlight—clean shaven and white. He looked as alarmed as she was. Caught. Their eyes met.

Something in her mind took flight, as if watching the scene unfold from above. The moon was a crescent poised above the tree line, a stoic fraction of its former self. What an odd sensation, to be stalling for time when there was none to waste, to be actively deciding whether to scream, to be gauging the threat of an intruder who was known.

"What are you doing here?" Izzy was breathing hard.

He took a step back, startled, as if the fact that she'd spoken had made the encounter real, and something clanked to the stone patio pavers at his feet.

Izzy's eyes followed the noise; the moon found the object for her. It shone. A faint beep from the microwave came from inside the house.

It was an oversized key.

And suddenly, she knew exactly how her gate had come to be open.

39

*W*hen you finally confront the fact that you have no choice but to leave, you will contemplate how best to fit your life into your car. You know that all you really need is your children—they are *your* life, even more so now than ever before. And yet, you want them to have what will make them happy, what will make them whole. It will not be easy on them, you know. How can they understand the reasons when you don't comprehend how you got to this point yourself?

Feeling sentimental, you will take something of your own mother. You haven't thought of her enough these years. Being forced to live in survival mode does that—it consumes you. It makes you a shitty daughter, sister, friend.

You'll need just enough familiarity to help the kids not feel completely displaced: favorite pajamas, blankets, a few toys. And then there's your daughter's I Can Do It! nothing more than a scrap of cardboard, but one she has cherished, one that has made her brave. At times you've wished for such a talisman yourself.

"It's for babies!" She'll lash out, surprising you. Then comes the root of it: "Stephie and Andrea say it's for babies." Her friends at school. She won't even have these friends come tomorrow, won't likely see them ever again, but how can you tell her that?

You'll pack it anyway, in your own bag. She will see it just as you're zipping it closed. She will hurl it in frustration through the open doorway of her room. "I don't want it!" she'll scream. She is four, but she *might as well be fourteen. You have no choice. You have to go. The designated point of no return has arrived.*

By the time you cross state lines, she'll be crying for it again. "We have to go back," she'll sob. "We have to go back for it."

But you'll keep your hands on the wheel of this unfamiliar preowned van you've paid cash for to replace your own—a switch made with surprising ease. Far from any town, the promise of silence comes at a bargain price. Your eyes will not waver from the road ahead. Because you can't go back. And this is what you have sacrificed: a tattered piece of your daughter's childhood for survival. You already know your search for a replacement will be futile, but it doesn't matter. You can't do it over, you can't turn the car around, you can only move on. If you go back, he will kill you.

40

There's no shortage of safety gear on the market, but you'll find that the two things most likely to save your life are free: common sense (or at least the good sense to remain calm and trust your instincts), and the buddy system.

—*Introduction to the final chapter in the*
Outdoor Preparedness guide gifted to Izzy by
her father, flagged by her mother with a sticky
note bearing a single exclamation point

Izzy stared at the metal shape at Paul's feet, identical to the one clenched in her palm, as comprehension wrestled with confusion. So the other one *had* gone missing the afternoon Paul helped her install the lock. She'd convinced herself it had never existed at all.

Or, rather, she'd let *him* convince her.

An icy fear gripped her, but she pushed it aside. She was on her own. She couldn't afford to be afraid.

"Where did you get that?" she snapped.

"I found it—" He was stammering lies before she even had the question out. The truth was obvious: He had pocketed it, back then.

Even then.

But why?

Her mind conjured the beginning of his Second Date Update call—the part that had struck her as odd for exactly one instant before she'd gotten caught up in the rest.

I saw her leaving for work and I thought . . . what the hell, why not call.

She left for work so very early. This time of year, that hour was more night than morning.

"I'm returning it," he said lamely. He stooped to pick up the key, and she pocketed her own, expecting him to hold it out toward her—but he didn't.

She took a small step back toward the kitchen, then another.

If she turned and ran, could she beat him to the door?

But what if this was some kind of misunderstanding? There she'd be, fleeing in panic from a harmless neighbor, exposing herself as silly, helpless, hopeless. He did keep odd hours. He was on call at a hospital, after all. Briefly and ridiculously, she wondered how many people met their demise out of politeness.

"What are you doing here?" she repeated. Her voice shook.

And then, to her horror, he seemed to come to. To assess the situation, to regain control. His whole demeanor of slinking away, of fading in, changed as if he'd flipped a switch, and instead he took a step toward her, then another.

"I was out for a walk," he said, his voice low. "I guess I got to thinking."

She swallowed hard, waiting for him to elaborate. He didn't. "About?"

"This and that. A bit about how you changed your mind after agreeing to our date. A bit about how you lied, about your dad being sick." He advanced another step; she continued her slow retreat. "A bit about how Detective Bryant was kissing your hand out front this afternoon."

So he *had* overheard her in the store. But he had the wrong idea about the detective.

Had he been watching her—again? Or had he just happened to see—again?

And why should any of it matter? What business was it of his?

"That doesn't answer my question," she said as firmly as she could. He took another step toward her, and as she retreated reflexively, her ankle turned on the paver behind her. She wobbled, then caught her balance, and he didn't bother to hide his smirk.

"I don't really know. I just . . . ended up here." He was so clearly in the wrong—nothing about this was right, none of it was okay—and yet he didn't move to apologize, didn't move to leave.

"If you wanted to talk, Paul, you could have rung the doorbell."

He closed the gap between them, and his eyes were dark. "I don't want to talk."

A final step back and she made contact with the cold siding of the house, jagged against her spine through the too-thin barrier of her coat and nightshirt. She glanced to her left. The back door was several strides away. She had not retreated wisely.

"Then what *do* you want?" It was impossible to keep the terror from her voice now. He hesitated, his eyes unchanging, and she could see that he had no plan, and then, just as quickly, that he didn't seem to mind—that acting on passion rather than logic was not a new side to him, but a second skin.

He laughed mirthlessly. "I will never understand women. My mother never recognized that she could have done so much better than my father. Kristin never recognized that she *couldn't* have hoped for better than me. What's the happy medium? Does it exist? Because I thought you were different, but now I see that you're just the same."

Izzy glanced sidelong at the door again. There was no graceful escape from this wall she'd been backed into, but she had to try. "I *am* sorry. But we'll talk about this in the morning, when you aren't so upset. Good night, Paul."

She whipped around and made for the handle as quickly as she could without downright lunging. She supposed a small corner of her mind was still keeping up the appearance of civility. She reached out, visualizing how she would yank it open and then slam the door shut before he could push his way in after her. But she didn't get that far. Hands grabbed her shoulders roughly from behind and slid expertly down her arms until Paul had her at the joints, his fingers closing easily and completely around her thin elbows.

"You *are* sorry?" He yanked her against him, and she cringed at the firmness of his chest against her back. Had he always been so much larger than her, so much stronger? "Why do you all seem to think you can let me in, lead me on, and then be rid of me so easily?"

"Let me go!" she cried. She screamed it out again, and his hand clamped over her mouth from behind as his other arm tightened around her waist. His fingers were firm against her mouth and nostrils. Her chest constricted as she struggled to breathe.

"You can go when I say you can go," he snarled into her ear. "But I have to tell you, I'm tired of being left."

41

People often don't see their new dog's true personality until weeks after adoption. If your dog had a relationship with a previous owner— especially a neglectful one—you may find him to be the product of mixed signals and unrealistic expectations. The best way to build trust is by demonstrating patience.

—"Your Rescue Dog in His New Home" tip sheet, posted on the Tiffins' refrigerator

Clara. You did *what?*"

She shot Benny a look. The kids hadn't been asleep long enough not to be startled by raised voices. She'd waited until they were snug in bed to fill him in, so he could get the full story out of their earshot.

"Benny. This is *good* news. Thomas can go back to school."

"I think we could've found a way to achieve that without another visit to the police station."

She dried the last of the dinner pans and maneuvered it into the overfilled mess of a drawer beneath the oven. "It was no big deal. Detective Bryant said he was making more rounds this week anyway, before shelving the case." She forced the drawer shut with her foot. "He said I was doing him a favor."

"All it takes is one person to see you coming or going from the station, and we'll be getting it from all sides again!" He shook out a new kitchen trash bag with an angry snap and slammed the lid onto the can. "Your priorities are out of whack."

"My only priority was to get my son back at school where he belongs, to get a sense of normalcy back to our lives. What is *out of whack* about that?"

"Do you honestly expect me to believe this didn't have *anything* to do with Paul declaring his affection for Izzy on the radio? You weren't grasping for an excuse to get back in there and guilt the detectives into giving you a status report? What do you take me for?"

She glared at him.

"Tell me you didn't stick around long enough to ask a few extra questions after he told you they were about to stop investigating."

When she didn't answer, he raised his hands to an imaginary audience in the adjoining living room. "That's not fair," she protested. "I was there anyway—anyone would have asked. It doesn't mean that's why I went."

"Clara, Kristin isn't Liv. I don't think it's healthy, the way the two seem to have become entwined for you. This man is not perfect, but he's a doctor, by all accounts a good one. He's been a father to those kids when they might have grown up without one. I can't see what he'd have in common with Liv's psycho ex-boyfriend— and thank God for that. I understand why the whole thing worries you, I do. But you have to stop assuming the worst, just because of what we went through before. I am imploring you to stop bringing this other family's problems into our own."

She opened her mouth, then closed it.

"I understand that this is a sensitive issue for you, which is why I've *tried* not to be so blunt about it. It's sensitive for me too. I was there, remember? But getting pulled into things inadvertently is one thing. Marching down to the police station and playing Nancy Drew is another. Not healthy. Not good for you, not good for me, not good for us."

She stepped back, startled, as tears filled her eyes. "Benny, it had nothing to do with *us*. Don't talk like that."

"You're *making* it about us. Whatever I have to say to get through to you, I'll say!" She saw then—really saw—how serious he was. A wave of sudden sadness stopped her where she stood, and the breath went out of her lungs, leaving her empty.

"Okay," she said desperately. "Okay. I'm sorry, Benny. I'm *sorry*."

"Promise me that will be the last time you ever check in with that detective. For any reason."

"I promise." She meant it. There were no reasons left, anyway. That was it. "I'll stay out of it."

"And stop panicking poor Izzy."

Clara took a deep breath. It was a promise that went against everything she'd come to stand for. It was a promise that could mean endangering her friend.

Then again, Izzy wouldn't want to hear any more from her anyway. Clara had done what she could. And she had risked enough.

"I promise."

"No matter what."

"No matter what."

A hard knock startled them both, and through the darkness on the other side of the sliding glass door she could see Hallie, standing with a coat pulled over flannel pajama pants, her feet clad in rubber-bottomed slippers, a frantic look on her face. She was pointing and mouthing something Clara couldn't understand. Benny rushed to the door and flung it open. "Hallie? What—"

"It's Paul," she blurted out. "He's sneaked across the street to Izzy's, through her fence. I saw him, out my window. Her house is dark, she must be asleep, and . . . I'm scared for her."

Clara froze.

Benny squinted at the girl. "You just happened to be looking out your window?"

"I didn't just happen to be. I've been keeping watch."

"Over Izzy?"

"Over Paul. Or his house, anyway."

"Why?"

"Because *someone* has to!"

Clara felt a fierce urge to hug her—whether to offer comfort or gratitude, she wasn't sure.

Benny sighed. "Hallie, you've promised your mom you'd stay out of this . . ."

"I was out of it. I didn't even leave my bedroom. I just happen to have a good view of his house out my window. And *can we talk about this later,* after someone checks on Izzy?"

She looked pleadingly at Clara.

"Hallie." Clara needed to speak carefully, even as her thoughts raced. "You have to be absolutely sure of what you saw. Maybe Izzy invited him over. Maybe they're trying to be discreet. When grown-ups date . . ."

"They're not dating. Izzy turned him down after the radio show. Randi and Rhoda came over for dinner tonight, and they told my mom everything. They said Dr. Kirkland overheard something he shouldn't have today. They were joking about it, but I could tell it made them nervous."

Clara looked past her, toward Hallie's own dark house, as her growing sense of unease hovered over the unsteady ground of her tentative truce with Natalie. "Then why are you telling us and not your mom?"

"I was afraid she'd go out by herself. She'd be reluctant to call the police, after what happened with me."

Benny was looking helplessly from one to the other. It was so obvious that Hallie was terrified, how could he not do *something*?

Clara's promise from just moments before caught in her throat. The only person who had *not* promised to stay out of it was reaching for the leash hanging by the door and sliding his cell phone into his back pocket.

"I'll take Pup-Pup for a walk," he said.

Clara squeezed his hand tight, then turned back to Hallie.

"Let's call your mom," she said. "I'll make us some hot choco-late."

42

I can't imagine my life without you in it, and I'm so glad I don't have to. What's the next adventure? Make a wish, and we'll make it happen!

—*Josh's inscription in a birthday card to Izzy,*
five long years ago

She'd been so stupid. She'd been so wrong.

If she ever got out of this, she'd do everything differently.

She *had* conjured bad juju with her lie to Paul, but it hadn't landed with her father. It had come straight for her. Straight for the source.

"Scream again, and you'll be sorry," he hissed into her ear, and his palm pulled away from her face. She gasped for air.

What if she hadn't lied? Would this never have happened, or would it have happened that night, in Paul's kitchen, when he wouldn't take no for an answer?

"I know you've been going through a hard time—" she tried.

He cut her off with a bitter laugh. "That's one way to put it."

His arm around her waist squeezed tighter, and she forced herself to stop pushing against it, to lean into him instead. Maybe if he sensed submission, he'd ease up. "I'm sure what's happening now . . . this isn't you. You're under a lot of stress. I understand. Let's just step away."

"Away, away, away." His voice was a cruel singsong. "So eager to get away."

Oh, God. She should have listened to Clara.

She should have listened to a lot of things.

"I never meant to hurt your feelings—"

"I didn't come here for an apology. Do you think I care about apologies?" He spun her around and pressed her roughly against the house, the siding cutting across her back in hard lines. Tears finally found their way into her shocked system, and they spilled out in ugly streams.

"You're scaring me," she whimpered.

He laughed, cold and mocking. Izzy's mind flew through everything he'd ever told her about himself, looking for a way to get through to him, or at least to keep him talking.

"I know it's hard," she sobbed. "Not being able to control things in our lives that we don't like, or people who we wish felt differently. I can relate. I *do* relate."

That neurologist guest on *Freshly Squeezed* had made it all sound so *scientific,* how brain areas for craving and love were activated by rejection. Izzy had thought only of how it applied to her. But what about someone whose brain was wired differently from the start?

"I'd say I'm pretty in control right now."

The moon moved behind a cloud, and his face darkened so that she couldn't quite read his expression, which only made it more ominous. She continued as if he hadn't spoken.

"What I mean is, I can imagine it's extra hard for you, after spending your childhood at the mercy of your dad's gambling . . ."

"Don't pretend you know me."

A dog barked. It sounded close. If it was with its owner, maybe someone could hear. But Paul seemed to sense her intake of air, and before she could belt out another scream he clamped his hand over her mouth again. She struggled against him, squirming, kicking one leg and then the other, trying to make any kind of noise at all.

She'd never felt so powerless.

"No one knows me," he snarled, ensnaring her tighter. Her kicking seemed to have little effect, and she cursed herself for all the times she'd thought of enrolling in a self-defense class but never followed through. He was dragging her now, toward the back door. He was trying to get her inside.

Where no one could hear.

Where no one could see.

She couldn't let him.

Something jabbed into her gut. The key. Her key. In her coat pocket. Was it sharp enough to do any damage?

It was all she had.

She grunted and squirmed as hard as she could, even as she struggled to breathe against his sweaty palm. Her left clog fell away on one thrash, and her toes crunched into something hard with the next. Sharp pain blinded her, but she couldn't let it. She'd hit the doorstep. They were on the threshold.

The knob was old, not an easy one to turn, and the door always stuck in the warped frame. If Paul wouldn't risk uncovering her mouth, he would have to let go of her waist to get it open. He might even have to give it an extra shoulder, or a kick.

He began to wrestle with the handle, his elbow jamming into her ribs, and she twisted, drawing her hand as close to her pocket as she could.

Then the thick arm pulled away from her, and she swung around, not free but loose, as her fingers found the key. She heard the sucking sound of the door reluctantly giving way. He yanked her by the hair, over the step and into the doorway, and she swung blindly with the makeshift weapon, left and then right, frantic not to disappear inside.

She heard him howl.

She was free for an instant.

She lunged forward, back outside, sucking greedy gulps of air.

But he had her again.

His fingers were tightening over hers.

Over the key.

She'd never be able to hold on.

"*What* is going on?"

The voice was calm but deadly serious. Paul's arms released her instantly, and Izzy stumbled, gasping, away from him. The floppy four-legged form of Pup-Pup was heading toward her, dragging a leash. And behind the dog, standing in the open gate, was Benny.

"Nothing is going on." Paul laughed breezily, and Izzy stopped, doubled over to catch her breath, amazed at how smoothly he slid back to center. "Izzy is just playing hard to get. She's quite good at it—I gather she's had a lot of practice."

"I wasn't asking you," Benny said. He didn't crack a smile. "Izzy? My God." Pup-Pup nuzzled at her hand with a whine, and she crouched and put her shaking arms around the dog, breathing in the animal's compassion.

I'm safe, she told herself.

For now.

I think.

"Oh, Iz will tell you we were just playing."

She looked back at Paul, who was peering at her so innocently it seemed he believed his own lie. *Holy hell,* she thought. *This is what he's used to. Being excused. He's so accustomed to getting away with this kind of behavior, it hasn't even occurred to him that I have no reason to cover for him.*

The thought that followed, she realized, should have been the first one to enter her mind the instant she'd seen him lurking in the shadows.

It hasn't even occurred to him that I'm not Kristin.

Still hugging the dog, she watched Paul's brown leather shoes make their way closer, until she could see how finely made they were, how well stitched, how well polished.

"Not another step toward her," Benny warned, and the shoes stopped.

She was only an arm's length away now, and the fear flared anew. *You will not make me feel threatened. You will not make me feel ashamed.*

She found the end of the dog's leash and stood, smiling uneasily at Benny. "He's right," she said. "Just a game." She extended her arm, as if she only meant to hand the dog back, and began to cross to Benny, who was making his way toward her. Only after a couple of awkward steps did she realize how off balance she was, one foot still secure in its clog, the other naked, the pain taking its time receding. She did not avert her eyes. She stared straight into Benny's and saw that he understood. In spite of her uneven gait, she did a good enough job of pretending to play along that Paul didn't reach for her. He let her go.

When she got to Benny's side, she held fast to the leash. "A sick game," she said, her voice strong and clear. "He stole the spare key to my gate—a month ago, when he helped me install the lock. Tonight I got out of bed for some tea. Through the kitchen window I noticed the gate was open, came out here to shut it, and he attacked me."

She stepped behind Benny, putting him between her and Paul. Fresh tears came into her eyes. She was shaking harder now, absorbing the vibrations of what had just happened—of what might have happened—and Benny reached a hand back to steady her.

Paul laughed his easy laugh again. "That's ridiculous. I was out walking, found the key, used it to open the gate just to verify that it was in fact Izzy's, and was going to leave it here on the patio for her. She caught me by surprise and got the wrong idea."

"For the past month, my missing key just happened to be lying on the sidewalk?" Izzy's horror was giving way to anger.

"It was in the grass down by the road. Maybe a squirrel or something made off with it the day we lost it. They like shiny things, don't they?"

Izzy looked pleadingly at Benny. What would she do if he didn't believe her? What would she do if no one believed her?

"Well," Benny said, matching Paul's easy tone, "I was out for a walk too. Not sure if you met our new dog yet, but he *loves* our nightly strolls. He makes such a racket at the sight of the leash that I end up taking him to the porch and tying my shoes out there so he doesn't wake the kids."

Paul nodded amicably. "Let sleeping babes lie. Beautiful dog," he added.

"That's how I saw you head directly from your door to Izzy's back gate. No leisurely walking. No stooping to pick anything up. A man on a mission."

Izzy stared at Benny. For some reason, she wasn't entirely sure he wasn't bluffing, but Paul's smile wavered almost imperceptibly.

"That's why I followed you," Benny said. "I can't say I saw the whole thing, but I saw enough."

"Whatever you think you saw, you're mistaken."

"Oh, I was mistaken all right. Do you know I've actually convinced people to give you the benefit of the doubt? I even doubted my own wife, and for what? Because I pitied you! Because I thought: Well, his *job* is to care for women!" Benny was emitting an anger— no, a disgust—that sent a chill through Izzy. "I feel sorry for any child who came into this world and had to see you first."

An ugly fire flashed in Paul's eyes, and Benny put a protective arm around Izzy's shoulders, sending a wave of gratitude washing over her.

"Let's not blow this out of—"

"Save it for the police. I've already called them."

Paul's hands balled into fists at his sides. "Not very neighborly of you, Ben," he said through clenched teeth. "Don't you think I've been through enough?"

"No," Benny said, sounding almost his jovial self again. "I definitely don't."

"Neither do I," said a voice from the open gate behind them.

Detective Bryant *was* pretty nice to have around, after all.

43

I wasn't going to do anything—she never would have even known I was there if she hadn't come outside.

—Sentence most repeated (five times) throughout the course of Paul Kirkland's statement to the police after his arrest

There was not even the slightest hint of a question anymore: Izzy knew what she had to do. And the sooner the better. Never mind that she'd barely slept last night, the adrenaline unrelenting long after she'd waved Benny away, declining his offer to send Clara over to stay with her, saying she just wanted to be alone when really the thought of it made her queasy. The bandages on her foot had chafed as she'd tossed and turned, though fortunately it was only badly scraped. She had other bruises, welts shaped like fingers, and the process of having her injuries photographed and cataloged by the police—as apologetically invasive as they were heartbreakingly practiced in the matter—had driven home the odd combination of relief and horror that came with knowing she'd gotten off easy. She'd finally fallen asleep not long before dawn and had been awakened by the phone not long after.

But she'd rest more easily than she had in far too long once this was done.

She dug through her closet until she found the oversized canvas tote she was looking for, a freebie from a book fair she'd dragged Josh along to, and steeled herself as she slung it over her shoulder and crossed the hall to the guest room.

The things stored here were *not*, as she'd once lamented, "the relics of her reality." They were relics of . . . something else.

Into the bag went the journal she and Josh had kept. Never once had he asked about it, from the second he'd started seeing Penny. She made quick work of concealing it from view under a stack of her own sketchbooks from their years of wandering the woods together, and on she moved to the box of jumbled ticket stubs and park maps, admission bracelets and snapshots. She filled the bag slowly but with determination, ignoring the pangs of protest from somewhere within as she gathered every memento she'd kept from their years of friendship. For so long, it had felt like her closest one, but she had to accept that, for her part, at least, it hadn't really been friendship at all. It had been unrequited love all along. And she couldn't hold on to what was left of it anymore. Never had it been so obvious how unhealthy it was. She supposed she had Paul to thank for that, in some contorted fashion.

Working her way down the checklist that had formed overnight in her mind, she returned to her room and flung the closet door open wider. She tossed in that T-shirt from the concert they'd driven all the way to Indianapolis for, wired on gas station coffee. The sweater she'd bought with the remote hope that he'd notice how it matched her eyes. Her old worn hiking boots, the tread still muddied from all the trails she'd followed him down. From the jewelry box she retrieved the clover charm he'd chosen for her birthday, her favorite one on her silver Pandora chain. She knew without trying the bracelet back on that her arm would feel lighter without it.

Josh was wrong. He *hadn't* gained her as a sister. He *had* lost her as a friend—or, at least, as a close one. It would never be that way again, between them. But that didn't mean she had to lose Penny too. She never wanted to be like Kristin's sister, stuck wondering how she could have handled things differently once it was too late to make amends. In a once-removed kind of way, she owed it to Kristin to take her own second chance.

She could only hope that Kristin, wherever she was, was doing the same. In the garish light that last night's events had shined on Paul, she didn't know whether to be more afraid for what might have become of Kristin and the twins, or more relieved for what they might have escaped. She'd decided on the optimistic outlook—where *all* of them were concerned.

Penny would forgive her for these months of distance. She was sure of it. Her sister would never know the real reason behind her absence, but she'd know Izzy was back, and that was the part that mattered. They had a lot to look forward to. And Izzy was going to be a damn good aunt, as a matter of fact.

When she could think of nothing else to purge, she took the bag down to the garage and heaved it into the trash bin with a thud. Pickup was first thing tomorrow, leaving little room for a lingering temptation to dig it out, for sensing its presence there like a stowaway on a ship. She topped it off with the garbage from the kitchen and pressed the button to raise the garage door so she could wheel the bin to the curb before she lost her nerve. No matter that it was only midmorning.

As her ears filled with the sound of heavy plastic rolling across pavement, it was no surprise to see Clara's front door open and her friend bound out. Clara jogged across the street but paused at the end of Izzy's driveway, as if it had occurred to her to wait for an invitation. They hadn't spoken since the night Clara tried to warn her off Paul, though Izzy had seen her huddled with Natalie and Hallie on the Tiffins' porch last night, watching Detective Bryant guide the handcuffed doctor roughly into the backseat of his patrol car as Izzy and Benny retreated inside to give their statements to another officer. Izzy had been too shocked to register Clara's presence with anything other than embarrassment—she had every right to be thinking *I told you so.* The lights didn't flash, there wasn't much of a scene, but this wouldn't be the end.

Izzy would never back down from pressing charges—there was too much at stake.

Issuing a restraining order against your neighbor was mathematically challenging, it turned out, where yards as literal rectangles of grass made more sense than as units of measure, and there weren't nearly enough of them in between. Detective Bryant had called first thing and told her that since Paul had already been making moves to put his house on the market, he'd been ordered to relocate back to the dingy apartment. Evidently, they expected him to cooperate fully now that his medical license could be in jeopardy. He'd warned Izzy, though, that the media weren't as likely to keep a safe distance once they got word of his arrest. Any time now.

Oddly, for the first time in a long while, Izzy wasn't worried. Not about Paul or anything else. It was as if the impossible sadness and fear she'd been unable to hide from in the world around her had arrived on her doorstep and she had looked it in the eye and turned it away.

Not here.

Not me.

The fact that help had arrived when she needed it, and had put its faith in her and in the truth, had restored her belief in something. The world was not against her. The right people, evidently, were on her side.

She waved Clara closer. "It's freezing out here," she called. "Come drink something warm and non-nonalcoholic with me."

It took only a glance to know that of course Clara wasn't feeling smug about being right about Paul. She was feeling *sorry*. She hadn't wanted to be right. Izzy never should have bristled the way she had.

She led the way into the garage and held open the door to the kitchen. "Irish coffee?"

Clara shrugged. "Top o' the mornin' to ya."

The brewer's burner light still glowed warm, as if expecting company all along. She moved to get the Baileys from the fridge while Clara settled onto a counter stool.

"Of everything that ever bothered me about Second Date Update," Izzy told her, "I now know firsthand the *worst* thing." In the cupboard by the sink, her hand hovered over a set of stemmed dessert coffee glasses, then chose two larger, cozier hand-fired clay mugs and began to fill them. "Sometimes you can get a read on the callers right away. I've seen it all—and a lot of it, I've seen coming."

She carried the mugs to Clara and handed one over.

"But sometimes," Clara finished for her, "you *can't* tell."

"Not even when you're really trying." She fixed her eyes on Clara, hoping to convey something not unlike an apology. Clara waved it away as if she'd spoken the words aloud, and just like that, the air was cleared.

"Please tell me they aren't going to make you do some kind of follow-up on the air."

"They're not going to make me do some kind of follow-up on the air. Because I'm not going back."

Clara's eyes widened. "You're going to quit?"

"Would you believe Yellow Springs Public Radio called this morning and offered me a job?"

"91.3 WYSO?"

Izzy nodded.

"I love WYSO!"

"They saw Hallie's profile in that gazette thing. I guess their morning producer resigned and they're desperate for a new one who requires minimal training. Didn't even want to interview me. Just asked if I was tired of commuting to Dayton and offered to match my salary."

Clara let out a delighted squeal. "And here I thought we were drinking our sorrows away. We're celebrating!" She clinked her mug to Izzy's, and they both took a sip. "You've got to tell Hallie. She'll be so excited to hear something good came of the paper! Natalie too."

"I take it you're back on good terms?"

"She was at my back door this morning with muffins. I get the sense she views neighbors the way I do—sort of like family. You don't get to pick them, and you're stuck sharing space whether you like it or not, so you might as well try to get along."

Izzy laughed. "So you admit you're only nice to me because I'm across the street! I always suspected."

"Just because you don't pick your neighbors doesn't mean you can't be grateful for the ones you get."

"Randi and Rhoda are like quirky fun cousins, then."

"And you're like the *slightly* younger sister I never had."

"I have one of those," Izzy said. "But I haven't done a very good job as big sis lately."

"Well, that makes two of us."

"You meant well." Izzy turned serious. "Actually, so did I."

Clara took a long sip of her drink. "You know, when I married Benny, everyone was giving us all this unsolicited advice. It's like an invitation to a wedding is an invitation to unload all your baggage in the form of wisdom onto the couple."

Izzy laughed. "I noticed that with Penny and Josh. I kept hoping people would quit telling them what to do right so they might screw it up." She clamped a hand over her mouth. "Oh, God, I can't believe I just admitted to that. I've been awful."

Clara laughed too. "No one involved in a wedding is exempt from engaging in some kind of awful behavior. I think it's a bylaw." Izzy wished she could let herself off the hook so easily. "Anyway, it was annoying. I didn't think we needed any advice. We were perfect together, one of the lucky couples. I would have made you throw up in your mouth a little."

Izzy gave her a look. "You still sort of do sometimes. No offense."

"None taken. But there was one bit—and I don't even know who said it—that stood out as useful and true: On your wedding day, you're choosing to love that person forever, but that's just the beginning. You have to continue to choose them, every day. It's not like your other options are going to go away—it's up to you to *turn* them away. Marriage isn't what it once was to a lot of people. And if you really want it to work, you're not making a one-time vow— you're committing to a lifetime of remarrying that person every day.

That's not the most romantic thing in the world, but it made sense to me then, and it makes even more sense to me now."

Izzy nodded at her blankly.

"If you can choose to love someone every day," Clara said, "maybe you can choose *not* to love them, for as many days as it takes until it sticks."

"Funny you should say that," Izzy said. "I just packed everything I have of Josh into the trash. I'm literally kicking him to the curb— not that he'll ever know."

"Do we have *Paul* to thank for this?"

"I'd prefer to credit his better half."

Clara nodded slowly, staring into her coffee. "What happened last night . . . I suppose it's only a matter of time before the reporters catch wind?"

Izzy nodded. "Detective Bryant said he'd appeal to them to keep my name out of it, but that I should brace for the worst." She raised her cup to Clara. "Liquid courage."

Clara was quiet for a moment. "If it comes, it will blow through." Izzy nodded. She was dragging her feet about calling her family, operating in one-step-at-a-time mode. Her mother would be a basket case. "Hard as it is," Clara went on, "without *any* kind of coverage he'd be just . . . just *out there,* for some other unsuspecting woman."

"That will probably be the case—eventually, anyway—whether I'm a blip on the local news or not. Although Detective Bryant said they might have probable cause to get a warrant to search Kristin's house now. He's going to try for one, though he didn't seem particularly hopeful of finding anything, even if it's granted. So much time has passed, and so much has been packed up."

Clara looked like she was about to press the issue, then checked herself with a nod.

"He knows my favorite place to hike alone," Izzy said quietly. "Guess I can't go anymore."

"I'll go with you," Clara said automatically, and Izzy found herself biting back a grateful smile. She'd been spending too much time dwelling on relationships she didn't have. The ones right in front of her held so much potential when she stopped being so self-conscious and allowed for the fact that her new friends knew her faults and still seemed to like her. For a moment, she and Clara sipped their coffees in companionable silence.

"You know," Clara began, "Detective Bryant, he seemed *really* concerned about you. Sweetly concerned."

Izzy sighed. "He asked me out, actually—before all this."

Clara opened her mouth to speak, but Izzy held up a hand.

"Maybe the timing will be better down the road," Clara rushed to say.

"I know I have a lot to sort out," Izzy said quietly. "But it's not just that."

"He's not your type?"

Izzy hesitated. For months she'd been lamenting that if life were like the movies, Josh never would have gone through with marrying Penny. Likewise, a Hollywood version of Izzy would have jumped at a second chance with Detective Bryant, disregarding her better judgment with a shrug. But really, it was too bad that *the movies* weren't more like *life*.

If they were, maybe people wouldn't spend so much time waiting around hoping for alternate endings, or deleted scenes.

She shook her head. "For once, I just want there to be a story with a happily-ever-after that does *not* involve ending up with a love interest. Do you think that's possible?"

"Absolutely," Clara said without a hint of hesitation.

Izzy decided to believe her.

44

I couldn't be more glad for you—and not just
because your happy ending gives me hope that
I'll find mine too.

—Liv's handwritten note in the engagement
card discovered in Clara's in-box the Monday
after the Christmas party

Ohio's November skies usually struck Clara as unforgiving, but
as she turned her eyes upward on her way to the mailbox, this evening's offering seemed more sympathetic. A full spectrum of blues
blended itself into the darkening gray as if to say, *I'm sorry this is
the best you're going to get until spring, but I'm trying.*

Soon Thanksgiving would come and go, and Christmas would
bring enough cheer to distract from the slog of winter ahead. Then
they'd all resign themselves to it for the dreary months to follow.
She'd adopt a shameless wardrobe of fleece pants and thermal shirts,
and hunker down. It wouldn't be the same without Kristin and her
brood crunching across the snowy yard to share hot chocolate after
school, but maybe there'd be new friends for her and the kids next
door. The pretty Victorian remained the perfect picture of a place
to raise a family.

The FOR SALE sign in its front yard was swinging almost imperceptibly in the breeze as a shiny red car slowed to a stop in front of Izzy's house. Penny's coat fell open as she stepped out of the driver's side, revealing the baby bump that was just starting to show, and waved a silent greeting to Clara. Penny had become a fast regular on the street these past weeks, but for the first time she wasn't arriving alone. The messy-haired, fresh-faced man who offered his hand as she stepped over the curb was smiling at her with such adoration that Clara had to look away at the pang she felt for her friend awaiting their arrival inside. It was *almost* a shame Penny didn't know what Izzy had sacrificed for sisterly love, though clearly it was better this way.

Sometimes keeping something from someone you loved really was the best thing—the bravest thing—uncomfortable though it may be.

At the mailbox, Clara peeked at the only real letter in the thick stack of mail, slid it into her pocket, and gathered up the bills and Black Friday circulars, so many that she hugged them to herself as she went back inside, suddenly feeling abuzz with possibility. Benny was in the kitchen, Thomas hanging on one of his legs—"Daddy, want to see what I can do? Want to see what I can do?"—and Maddie on the other—"Daddy do! Daddy do!"—as he attempted to open the fridge with a look hovering between amusement and annoyance. Clara knew that amusement would win out, but also that not all wives and children were so lucky.

And before she could lose her nerve—the images of Penny and Josh and the FOR SALE sign next door intermingling with the one in front of her—an idea that had existed only in her brain was bubbling over.

"All this stuff with Kristin and her sister, then Izzy and her sister, has me thinking about my own family," she blurted out. Benny looked up at her in surprise. "I know my mom drives me insane, but for my part, I could do better." She expertly relocated Maddie 180 degrees around Benny's leg, opened the door, and handed him the five o'clock Friday beer she knew he was after.

"You're getting good at this June Cleaver thing," he said, taking it gratefully, and she shot him a look. He'd been apologetic in his shock after the incident with Paul and Izzy, and she'd told him the only apology she was after was one for having questioned how she should be spending her days. He'd backpedaled fiercely.

"What does *insane* mean, Mommy? Your mom is Grandma, right? Grandma drives you insane?"

She really had to start watching what she said around Thomas. She hugged him to her, hoping futilely that he might forget the question. "June Cleaver, at your service," she told Benny over his head, rolling her eyes.

"Maybe I was just thinking of cleavers in general," he said wryly.

"Funny. But really. I could get a cheap midweek flight after Thanksgiving, maybe? The kids will have cabin fever before long— Florida sunshine will do them good." Thomas had turned his attention back to his relentless pursuit of interesting Benny in watching the same Hot Wheels trick for the tenth time, and Clara was practically shouting over him to be heard. "Maybe you'd like a few quiet evenings too," she added with a smile.

"If that's what I have to sacrifice for you to reconnect with your mom, so be it."

She helped herself to a beer too, overcome by one of her increasingly frequent urges to wrap herself in the cozy ordinariness of it all: the banter at the end of a long week, the grilled cheese on sourdough she'd throw together with soup, the movie she'd picked up for after the kids were in bed. "I'll be the one sacrificing my sanity after one night with my mother. Prepare to defend your actions when I ask why you ever let me think it was a good idea to go."

He kissed her on the cheek. "Has anyone ever told you you're really good at doing the right thing?"

She shook her head, pretending she wasn't still hoping that someone would.

Christmas lights wound around palm trunks in their best impression of a holiday Corona commercial. Glittery oversized snowflakes hung in windows and storefronts, which puzzled her. Santas and reindeer she'd expected, but why evoke snow? Part of the charm of Christmas this far south was that it didn't have a thing to do with being cold but was festive anyway.

Clara found she liked it here this time of year. The joy had drained out of the holiday when they'd lost Liv, and she'd been trying to redeem it ever since. Having Thomas and Maddie had poured the magic back in, but seeing Christmas come to life so far from home was like an accidental healing salve to a wound she hadn't realized was still open.

But maybe it wasn't accidental. She was here seeking a kind of peace, after all.

"Mom?" Clara stepped into the tiny living room of her parents' condo and found her mother clad in a hot pink jogging suit that made swooshing noises when she moved, demonstrating for Thomas and Maddie how to use her water aerobics equipment.

No wonder Dad spends every waking minute golfing, she thought, then chastised herself for the cruelty. Her parents had spent so much of their marriage apart that it seemed they'd forgotten how to spend time together, even though now they had nothing *but.*

"I know this weight is just foam, but you'd be surprised how much water resistance it gives you in toning your core," her mother was telling Thomas, who nodded solemnly, touching it with his index finger as if it were a curious alien object fallen to earth. Maddie was busy trying to balance what looked like some sort of armband on her head, giggling each time it slid to the ground.

Her mother hadn't exactly figured out how to employ a more grandmotherly version of her uninspired mothering strategies, but the kids didn't seem to mind. Everything about this trip was novel to them—the plane, the rental car, the condo complex arranged as a maze of balconies and shuffleboard courts and, at the center, a pool so heated it was like bathwater. Clara was enjoying the change of scene, too, so much that she almost felt guilty for leaving Benny at home, where winter was blowing in no less bleak than the tension on their street that had not quite subsided. He was hopeful, though, that the extra hours he was squeezing in this week would afford him more family time during the holiday, and for Clara, getting the better end of both deals, that was a pretty good tradeoff.

"Would you mind watching the kids for a bit?" Clara asked "There's something I was hoping to run out and do."

She fixed her face in a look meant to imply that Santa had a mission afoot—as so many looks did this time of year—and fortunately her mother wasn't so far removed from parenting that she missed the reference. Tucking her cropped silver hair behind her ear, for a second she almost looked like an elf.

"Take all the time you want," she said. "If we aren't here when you get back, check the pool."

The drive to the coast was short, and Clara followed the two-lane road along the Gulf through stop-and-go traffic for a few miles farther, until she reached the pier. She pulled the rental car into a spot and put more money in the meter than she'd need, just to be safe. Before her was an array of shops filled with impulse buys and guilty pleasures, and she set about browsing through one boutique, then the next, running her fingertips over racks of first-name key chains and palm tree magnets and sunset postcards. She stopped to examine miniature chests carved from driftwood, beds of perfect tiny shells inside. Colorful kites with long tails, fashioned to look like exotic animals turned airborne. Pretty flower-print sarongs, the kind that always seemed like just the thing until you got them home and realized they never fit *any* occasion in the Midwest.

There was nothing here that the kids would want, not really, and it was all priced too high. Besides, Thomas was going through a nosy stage. Sneaking anything past him into the luggage would be difficult, probably not worth the effort.

But there *was* a gorgeous array of irresistible sun hats. The aisle was empty, the store about to close, its off-season hours limited to daylight, and Clara took her time choosing a black woven one with a wide, curved brim that conveyed more glamour than whimsy. She fitted it onto her head and surveyed herself in the wall-mounted mirror, arranging her newly bobbed hair—the unfamiliar result of having accompanied her mother to her salon yesterday—to curve smoothly around her chin. She slipped on her sunglasses and nodded at her reflection once, in brusque approval, before striding to the register.

"It suits you," the cashier said, smiling, and Clara thanked her, wondering if it was true. She wasn't sure what suited her these days, but she could already see Benny's reaction to the hat, placing it on his own head and posing, making some wisecrack about the Kentucky Derby. Maybe they'd go this year—it was only a few hours' drive away. She hoped to return from this trip with a weight shed, and who knew what surprises the lighter, freer Clara might have in store?

The shop door closed behind her with a familiar wind chime jingle, and she caught herself imagining what sort of boutique Randi and Rhoda might own if Yellow Springs were seaside. She liked to think they'd shun the pressure to trend toward the tacky, instead finding a beachy variation on the homespun offerings they curated so well back home.

The pier beyond the shops stretched over the water in a long, wide T, its odd hybrid structure formed from sections of traditional wooden slats reinforced by concrete slabs. Clara wandered out, her eyes on the spot where the glassy water met the sky. A mass of clouds had gathered, but the ethereal glow around the perimeter signified that somewhere beyond them, the sun was about to set. She made her way to the left tip of the T, wrapped her arms over the railing, and peered down to the water below, looking for signs of life.

"Nice hat."

Clara turned, her poker face fading in spite of herself, a smile already playing on her lips. Kristin was wearing a clean white tennis visor, her dark curly hair gone sleek and auburn blond, her mirrored sunglasses impenetrable from the outside. But there was no disguising her voice, smooth and sardonic as ever, thick with a blend of amusement and emotion.

"One can never be too careful," Clara said, her voice confidentially low. "The good doctor may have hired his own investigator, though I'm not entirely sure if he went through with it. He ended up getting a bit . . . distracted."

Kristin nodded. "Well, we figured as much."

"Where are the twins?"

She pointed, and Clara squinted in disbelief at the pair of kids pushing for turns at the rotating metal binoculars at the far end of the pier. She'd been prepared for Kristin's disguise, had even had fun playing along with one of her own, but seeing two four-year-olds rendered unrecognizable made the reality of their running away snap into focus. Even with their baseball caps, she could tell their hair had been chopped and dyed.

"I gave them a whole pocketful of quarters," Kristin said. "It's not the end of the world if they see you, but it's probably best if they don't. They've finally stopped asking endless questions."

"How are they?" she asked, fighting the urge to run and hug them.

"Really good. It was hard at first. But I think on some level—a very primal level—they know we're better off."

Clara nodded, unable to take her eyes off the twins. They were smiling, laughing. The force of the relief might have knocked her back—all three of them safe, within reach.

"I miss their curls," Kristin said, sighing. "And mine. But keratin is pretty amazing. And they don't even bat an eye at doing it to a kid. Really, other parents ought to be ashamed of themselves."

"But not you," Clara said firmly.

"No. Not me." She shook her head. "I took your advice—I didn't look back. No Internet, no TV. But I have to ask: How did it go over?"

"About like you thought it would. Everyone was mystified—no one saw it coming. No one heard anything or saw you go. And he was angry—about the money, at least."

"He was under suspicion?"

Clara nodded. "But that was as far as it went." It was a small lie of omission, and out of kindness. Clara tried not to think about how many of those she'd been accumulating. There was no point in telling her what she'd missed. Her missing it *was* the point.

"You managed to stay out of it?"

"I did my usual bang-up job." Clara tried to laugh. "Nice touch, by the way, not actually telling me anything. The life insurance money, the kids not being Paul's, how the two of you met, what he was really like, the rift with your family . . ."

Kristin's eyes took on a familiar stance, between defensive and apologetic. "You were genuinely surprised when you needed to be, weren't you?"

Clara nodded. "I wasn't being sarcastic. It *was* a nice touch." They watched together as a pair of pelicans rose from the water's surface in a quick, graceful splash and glided, with a few effortless wing flaps, low and parallel to the shore. A nervous energy crackled in her throat, and she had to work up a bit of courage to speak again. "If you want to know the truth, I was terrified. The broken window, the Internet search, Abby's *I Can Do It!* cover—I didn't know what to think. I was legitimately worried that our plan hadn't gone off."

"I'm sorry. It had to be that way." Kristin hesitated. "The window, he'd broken it two nights before. I was terrified, but in the morning, the kids were barely even fazed. When I realized shattered glass was becoming normal to them . . ." She shook her head.

So that was what had made Kristin finally crack. Friday after work, she'd stopped by to drop off some things Clara was borrowing for the next night's patio party—a platter, an ice bucket—and burst into tears. As Clara had taken in her awful confession, she wasn't sure which of them was more surprised, more horrified.

"The Internet search started as a last-minute freak-out," Kristin admitted. "I think I was trying to convince myself there had to be another way. But all it did was affirm that you were right."

You have to go, Clara had told her. *You have to go now. Tonight, or tomorrow . . .* A divorce sure as hell wasn't enough. Her experience in Liv's sad case had raised questions no one had been able to answer. Namely, what anyone might have done to prevent the whole mess.

"And don't even get me started on the damn book cover."

Clara and Kristin had shared the language of motherhood long enough for her to recognize that there was a story there, one to do with a stubborn child, and just the idea of it calmed her, that the reason it was left behind had been something as ordinary as all that.

The flash of anger that she'd been worried over nothing was easily checked, disregarded. But still . . .

"You could have told me *some* of it—I mean, along the way," she said quietly. "I feel like a horrible friend."

"You would have thought differently of me."

"I wouldn't have."

"You wouldn't have felt sorry for a desperate widow who'd gotten herself into something scarier than loneliness, something emptier than grief? I'd already had enough pity, which was why I allowed myself to be brought to Yellow Springs in the first place. Though I'll grant that I was a little too eager to leave everything behind. By the time I knew deep down it was time to leave again—farther and faster and forever—I was doubly scared to do it."

Clara tried to ignore the bruise of her hurt feelings, dulled but still tender to the touch. She nodded with what she hoped looked like understanding but kept her eyes on the water. It was impossible in this light to guess at how deep it was.

"I *did* tell you the one thing I never told anyone else," Kristin said more softly, her voice breaking.

"You told me the one thing that was important to tell." It was true, and it was all that mattered. Glancing sideways at her friend, she caught her look of concern. "Don't worry," she said. "It worked. You did it. You're officially a cold case, until and unless Paul manages to turn something up."

Kristin nodded. "I don't know if this feeling of looking over my shoulder will ever go away, but that's one less thing to worry about, I guess." She pushed her sunglasses tighter up on her nose and stole a glance back toward the beach, for good measure. "It's been hard, not feeling guilty—even about that last night. I still can't believe we actually went through with drugging everyone. I couldn't stop thinking about Randi and Rhoda, sleeping through the baby crying."

"A baby never died from crying," Clara said almost automatically. "The same could not be said of your situation." They fell into a companionable silence, and somber as it was, Clara couldn't help smiling. She'd been imagining this meeting for months, wondering if it was really going to happen—if she'd ever see Kristin again—and worrying how, if it never came to be, she'd ever deal with the not knowing.

They'd predetermined this last checkpoint standing in Clara's kitchen, just before the bonfire that night, as Kristin nervously watched Clara crush the pain pills and carefully distribute the powder into the wineglasses awaiting their guests.

"I'm not sure—Randi is nursing . . ." Kristin had begun to protest.

"These are left over from my C-section recovery. So I know they're safe for the baby."

"But maybe the wine by itself would be enough?"

Clara had been the firm one. She had seen firsthand what kind of crash could occur at the intersection of so-called love and simmering anger. She wasn't going to see it happen to anyone else. She'd shaken her head fiercely. "This is what we agreed. Randi and Rhoda are up at all hours with Adele, and Izzy's job has made her half nocturnal. We can't risk anyone seeing anything, and you need the biggest possible head start. This is the only way."

Seeing the look on Kristin's face, she'd softened. "Where will you go?" But then she'd recovered herself, shaking her head. "Never mind. It's better that I don't know."

Kristin's eyes had filled with tears. "I'm ready to walk away from Paul. But leaving the rest of my life—and the kids' lives—that's going to be the worst part. Never seeing you or Thomas or Maddie again . . ."

Clara poured a splash of wine into a clean glass. "I know we decided on grape juice for you tonight, but a little this far in advance won't hurt."

Kristin downed it all at once.

"Are you sure you don't want me to just *tell* the police when they come asking, assuming you're long gone by then? Yes, he was violent. Yes, she ran. No, I don't know where." It wasn't an entirely unselfish question.

But that's where Kristin was adamant. "If you do, they'll focus the investigation on me. What kind of wife I've been, what kind of

mother, what right I had to disappear, what I should have done instead." She'd already made this argument, that the uncertainty
about where she'd gone and why would focus the scrutiny on
Paul, where it belonged. "I've covered his tracks—and mine—too
well. I don't want him to get away with a simple he said–she said
dismissal. I want there to be doubts about him, real ones. I want
him to sweat it out. I want him to be branded with a warning."

Clara wouldn't press her again. "It's going to be awful, not knowing for sure that you're okay." Once they'd been released into the
kitchen air, the words seemed incredibly insensitive. "I mean, you
will be. I know you will be. I just won't be able to see it."

"Maybe you can," Kristin had said. "Once everything has died
down. Name a time and place. I'll be there." Clara could tell she
was bluffing. Not that Kristin herself wouldn't want to arrange to
meet, but that she didn't believe Clara would care enough to travel
so far, to risk so much, just to see her again.

How low Paul had managed to knock her sense of self-worth.

"My mother lives in Florida," Clara said. "Not that you'll be
there, as far as I know, but you could treat the kids to a little vacation. Early December would be three months out."

But then Clara had been so nervous she'd ended up drinking
more than she intended that night. It went fuzzy—and nothing
after it was clear, either.

Not until that letter had come in the mail before Thanksgiving,
bearing only two cautious yet hope-filled words: *We're on.* She'd
wanted to cry from relief right there on the curb, but instead she'd
let the tide of emotion sweep her into action. All along, Clara
had dreaded the necessary excuse of visiting her mother, but by the
time she'd found herself breathless in the kitchen, trying to seem
cool as she floated the idea by Benny, she almost meant what she
said, about making amends.

"Your sister misses you," she blurted out now.

"She came to see you?"

She nodded. "I know she regrets pushing you away, judging
you . . ."

Kristin didn't say anything. Finally: "She's used to me being out of the picture. She'll be okay."

"If you can think of a way you'd feel comfortable with me relaying a message . . ."

She shook her head. "I can't risk it. I've come too far. I just wanted to survive, but Clara, it's the most wonderful thing—we're *happy*."

Clara watched as Aaron put his arm sweetly around Abby, both of them perched on tiptoe at the binoculars, to steady her on the circular rail. What a good example he would have been for Thomas. Just last week she'd heard him complaining to Hallie that he still had to "train" Maddie. "We miss you," she said softly. "Me, the kids, everyone."

"Has Benny ever suspected, do you think? That you know more than you let on?"

She shook her head. "Much as I've hated keeping this from him, I never actually lied," she said. "To him, the police, anyone. I was careful with what I said. But he'd be furious with me if he knew. He hates secrets. Also, he thinks I need to learn to mind my own business." She laughed. "Which, in a way, I probably do."

Kristin's fingers circled tightly around her wrist on the railing between them. "I needed help," she said. "And I'm glad I wasn't flawless at making sure no one could tell."

Clara clapped her own hand over her friend's and squeezed.

"Breathe that sea air," Kristin said, her smile broad, her eyes wet. "If it wasn't for you, I don't know if I'd ever have gone through with it. Who knows where I'd be. Or if."

The twins came running, then, a mass of bare arms and legs, and Clara turned away, the wind off the Gulf whipping her hair and chilling the tears that had come into her eyes. She took one step away, then another.

"I'm glad we did this," she said softly, not sure if Kristin could hear.

"Me too," Kristin replied, her voice a hush from behind. "*All* of it."

Clara forced herself forward, toward the opposite corner of

their end of the pier, where she could look back toward the shore, and watch Kristin go.

"Who were you talking to, Mommy?" Abby asked, just as Aaron called out, "Can we get ice cream?"

"Someone I used to know," Kristin said, the false nonchalance in her tone failing to disguise the emotion beneath it. "And yes. Ice cream sounds great."

"When, Mommy?" Abby's sandals made little scuffing sounds as they retreated down the pier, and Clara had to resist the almost panicked urge to turn, to throw her arms around them all, to say what the hell, she'd go grab the kids, and they could all have one last cone together—with sprinkles—just like old times. Their secret.

"Right now, sweetie. There's a parlor over there—see the lit-up sign?"

"No, I mean when did you *know her?*"

Such a long beat passed that Clara thought maybe they'd moved out of earshot.

"In another life," she said finally.

Clara turned her back to the beach in time to see the clouds on the horizon pull apart in the middle, two divided, billowy clumps of atmosphere, alike but not the same, revealing the brilliant pink-orange of the sunset in between. One moved slowly toward the curve of the coast, a dense, hovering mass seeking land, and the other churned and allowed itself to be blown out to sea. Soon, both would all but disappear in the fast falling night, but they'd show themselves again tomorrow, taking form at first light over another place, where with any luck someone might be undistracted enough to stop, turn her eyes upward, and look—really look—and see the beauty that Clara saw now.

There were so many ways to begin again.

Author's Note

While most of the excepts at the start of the chapters are fictional, a few bits draw from real sources.

In depicting Yellow Springs, "Everyone's Favorite Place!" is indeed the tagline of the chamber of commerce, and www.yellow springsohio.org is a wonderful resource for anyone planning a visit. The narration of the walking tour at the start of Chapter 9 was adapted from the tour housed here, and the copy beginning Chapter 15 is not in fact from a real estate brochure but is drawn from the "Explore" page of this helpful website as well.

The National Domestic Violence Hotline Path to Safety does include the quote cited at the start of Chapter 13, and can be found in its entirety at www.thehotline.org/help/path-to-safety. If you or someone you know is in a dangerous, concerning, or uncomfortable situation at home, know that resources like this one save lives. Readily available help ranges from hotlines to escape plans to shelters. Telling someone, even anonymously, is the first important step. You don't have to do this alone.

Regarding interpretations of law concerning stepfamilies, The DadsDivorce.com article "Knowing and Understanding Stepparents' Rights" that opens Chapter 8 is real. And the highlighted passage from Dr. Kirkland's "Rights of Stepparents in Custody in Visitation" brochure, cited in Chapter 16, is taken from an

Attorneys.com article of the same name. Both resources proved valuable in my research.

The Alice Walker poem from which Clara quotes is titled "They Will Always Be More Beautiful" and is available in its haunting entirety at AliceWalkersGarden.com.

There are at least two radio stations in the Cincinnati/Dayton area that have featured "Second Date Update" segments, and many more nationwide. For the record, my local radio hosts have a knack for handling these calls with respect and good humor, and I wouldn't want anyone to mistake Izzy's distaste for her colleagues as my own. *Freshly Squeezed* and its hosts are purely imagined. The show's neuroscientist guest who talks about the brain chemistry behind love and rejection is loosely quoting anthropologist Helen Fisher and her fascinating 2008 TED Talk "The Brain in Love." Sometimes something is simply said too perfectly to rephrase.

A debt of gratitude to retired Cincinnati Police detective Jim Day for walking me through various missing persons scenarios and sharing his experience with domestic violence perpetrators and victims (as well as to Cris Freese for putting us in touch). And to Cincinnati's top-notch OB/GYN John Sullivan, MD, for his insights into how doctors' personal conflicts do and don't impact their practice—and for reading with pleasure everyone from Harlan Coben to Jane Austen to, well, me.

My understanding of the financials and fates of insurance policies I owe to my expert husband, Scott Strawser, who is always concerned with doing the right thing and does indeed believe in "following the money." There's no one I'd rather comingle my assets with.

With all of the above, any liberties taken were for the sake of the story, and any perceived mistakes are mine alone.

Acknowledgments

This book would not exist without the love and support of my husband, who amazes me every day with his unflinching enthusiasm, good humor, and seemingly endless well of patience. I'm beyond lucky to be his teammate. Our children inspire me constantly with their smart, funny, compassionate outlooks, and I am grateful for their sweet reminders of what's important in this world and of how we can so easily strive to be better, to do better. For them, I would do anything.

Endless gratitude to my agent, Barbara Poelle, who represents me so well that she has even been known to sell *me* on my abilities. My editor, Holly Ingraham, without question made this book better for her insights, and has again shown me what a thrill it can be to share a vision for a project. My publicist, Katie Bassel, is equal parts tireless and fabulous, and somehow can even make a long to-do list seem like fun. Jennie Conway, Nancy Sheppard, Jordan Hanley, Jennifer Enderlin, and the rest of the St. Martin's Press team have been a dream.

Special thanks to my beta readers: Amy Fogelson, Lindsay Hiatt, Amy Price, and Megan Rader, who offered invaluable encouragement and feedback during my first official year in the pressure tank. Deep appreciation as well to the sources who so generously lent their expertise to my research (I've detailed them in the Author's

Note, so if by chance you skipped it, please turn back so they can get the credit they deserve!).

One of the greatest pleasures of this venture onto bookshelves has been the expansion of my writing tribe. Grateful hugs to Sharon Short and Kim Dinan, and five stars to the '17Scribes group (notably Orly Kön|ig, Crystal King, Jenni Walsh, Lisa Duffy, and Kathleen Barber). My *Writer's Digest* colleagues made for a humbling cheering section: Gratitude to Brian Klems, Tyler Moss, Claudean Wheeler, Taylor Sferra, and the rest of the crew.

To my parents, Michael and Holly Yerega, and to all of my family and friends who have shown their support for this new endeavor of mine in ways big and small, I can hardly express what your vote of confidence means to me. Thank you for making so many late nights feel so very worthwhile.